Mummy's Tomb

History Hunters Book 3

PHILIP MONNIN

Cover design by Caleb Porter
www.portergraphicdesign.com

ISBN-13: 978-0-9982907-2-0

History Hunter Series

Pirate's Curse

Nazi Loot

Mummy's Tomb

For a complete list of works by Philip Monnin,
please scan the QR code below.

TABLE OF CONTENTS

Author's Note

Thank you for purchasing *Mummy's Tomb!*

I hope you enjoy reading it as much as I enjoyed writing it.

You are an important part of my reading community, and I'd be grateful if you would take a moment when finished and leave a short review on Amazon for *Mummy's Tomb*. Your review will help me in many ways and help others to discover this exciting Series.

SCAN CODE TO LEAVE A REVIEW

PROLOGUE

October 12, 1329 BC

The guard had been set with deadly intent. No living thing was to get within 200 cubits of the place. No man. No animal. So said the King. So it was done. Curious eyes were turned away in pain. Anyone who protested the arrangement was sent to meet their forefathers by the edge of an Egyptian sword.

▲   ▲   ▲

The small, solemn procession made its way silently through the limestone gateway and across the smooth stone slabs of the hallway floor. A colonnaded entryway marked the opening of the chamber containing the tomb. To the side of the opening the King stood, a hint of sadness hardening his young face. The light was dim, the mood somber. Each priest leading the procession bowed reverently before the King, then turned into the opening. Incense burners swayed to softly chanted prayers. Heavy, fragrant smoke curled upward into the darkness of the moonless night. All manner of funerary items paraded silently across the floor, carefully borne by the servants of the High Priest. It was the wealth of a nation given to one man for his use in the next life.

The King had arranged for every piece to be moved from its original resting place. He noted that the long trip up the Nile had not damaged anything. He knew each of the items was necessary for a successful continuation of the journey through the Field of Reeds in the next life. He, like all who had gone before him, understood that disturbing a tomb was sacrilegious. Yet, he knew in this case it could not be helped.

Finally, the gilded coffin passed by the King before disappearing into the chamber. He looked upon it with pity. *Such a great man! A free spirit! A brilliant mind!* As he pondered these things, he couldn't stop the knowing smile that was spreading across his face. He hoped no one would see it between the wavering lights of the passing torches. *And so brave. To take on all the gods...and even the priests.* He shook his head slightly to clear the thoughts from his mind. As the last priest passed him, the King, too, turned into the chamber and entered beneath the ever-watchful stone eyes of Amun.

Deep within the earth, the priests performed the required ceremonies as the King observed from a chair by the entrance to the room. Colorful depictions from the life of the deceased looked down from the walls of the new tomb. Each shouted out in silence his great, but misguided, deeds. Verbose prayers echoed off the limestone ceiling as the gods were beseeched to accept the remains of the once great Pharaoh into their favor. Carefully, each item was set in its proper place within the rooms of the tomb.

When the final gilded shrine was erected, the High Priest signaled it was time to leave the dead Pharaoh alone to contend with the gods the best he could. At a nod from the King, the servants were led into a small antechamber where they were quickly executed. The room was then sealed, and the significance of the secret ceremony was buried forever.

The King stood silently in the cool night air as the heavy stone slab slid into place with a grinding rumble, sealing the shaft to the tomb. Again the smile crossed his face. *The irony of it all…his final resting place directly under the eyes of the very god he tried to eliminate. It is my wish that this will be enough to make the ultimate amends to those he has offended.*

The High Priest came and bowed before him and said, "Oh King, may you live forever! What is my King's pleasure for the ten priests who stand before you after sealing the tomb? While it is sure that they know of tonight's proceedings, each has taken a pledge of silence that is to follow him to the grave. Shall they be allowed to live, or shall they pass into the next life tonight?"

The King looked out across the ten who stood nervously before him. On his word alone they would live or die. His mind went back to the man who rested 10 cubits below his feet. The King remembered how the man had lived, full of passion and full of *life*. He knew this man would let them live. He waved his scepter and said, "Enough of death."

With that, the King turned and left, following the unseen path across the floor. As the staccato sound of his walking stick faded into the cool desert night, the ten priests began to relax.

The High Priest turned in their direction. His stern gaze met theirs, bringing back the seriousness of their enterprise. "The great and powerful King—may he live forever—has granted to you your lives. I trust each of you will greatly esteem this gift and speak no words on what you have seen here tonight. For if you do, know that the gods will bring it to my ears, and on that day, *you will surely die!* Let the memory of the Heretic be buried in the same manner as he was buried here tonight…never more to see the light of day!"

A priest toward the back of the group tugged nervously on his tunic in the muted light. His life would end this very night if anyone saw the distinctly tattooed mark of the Sun Disk he carried on the inside of his forearm. He knew the High Priest well. He knew how the man clung to his regained power. And he knew how fanatically he had busied himself ridding the land of the followers of Aten!

CHAPTER 1

It shouldn't have been so difficult. After all, it was a calm, sunny day. What could possibly go wrong?

"Jay!" An exasperated Alyssa called to her schoolmate. "Do you think we have enough time to do this before the tour bus leaves for the airport?"

"No worries, Alyssa," came the reply. "I know what I'm doing."

"Yes, don't worry, Alyssa. Jay knows what he's doing, alright," added Conrad, the third of the group of friends. "He's an expert at getting into trouble."

"Ha, ha. Very funny," replied an undaunted Jay as he approached the owner of a small felucca by the main dock. A tourist brochure peeked from his back pocket, as if trying to break free from its khaki prison. "This will make your day. I promise!"

Fourteen-year-old Alyssa Garret glanced at her prep school friend Conrad Kingston and shrugged her shoulders. "When Jay gets something in his head, there is no stopping him."

Alyssa, the youngest among her friends at school, lived with her mom in Miami. Her friends regarded her peacemaking tendencies and sensitive manner more than an adequate offset to her age.

"When Jay gets something in his head, that's all there is in his head!" replied her sixteen-year-old friend wryly. "We knew the risks of coming on this trip with him before we left the States. We'll just have to manage to survive his antics for the duration."

Conrad's dry sense of humor was appreciated among his friends. Although he lived on an old English estate north of London, he was very down to earth, sparingly using a practiced 'high-born' attitude toward his American friends. The 'duration' that he referred to was a 10-day field study trip the three friends were taking as part of their class on ancient archeology at Barrington Academy outside of Washington, DC.

"At least we meet up with Geoffrey tomorrow at Luxor," sighed Alyssa. "He's had *some* success keeping Jay under wraps."

The 'Geoffrey' she spoke of was Geoffrey Barnsworth, a world-renowned antiquities expert and dealer. He was a frequent companion of their group of school friends, sharing a common love of history and mystery. A British expat living in America, Geoffrey's expertise was a welcome addition to their adventures as a group, known among themselves as the *History Hunters*.

The friends laughed and started down the short path to the water's edge in response to Jay's frantic waving. Below them, the cool blue waters of Lake Nasser beckoned, a welcome relief to the dry sandstone monuments behind them.

"Maybe this will turn out okay after all?" Alyssa said wishfully.

Before Conrad could reply, Jay shouted, "We're all set! A one hour boat trip and then back to the tour!"

As the pair approached the small traditional Egyptian sailboat, Jay added enthusiastically, "Meet Achmed el kibeer, the Chief. He owns the boat and will take us out for a ride." Jay completed the introductions. "I have also arranged for a little surprise," he added with his trademark grin.

As they settled onto the cushioned benches of the ancient wooden craft, the Chief pushed back from the shore, dropped the heavy center keel plate into its slot, and took his place at the tiller. Gripping a rope, he expertly managed the single sail and coaxed the boat into deeper water.

"Now, what were you saying about a *surprise*?" asked Conrad suspiciously.

Sixteen year-old Jay Wray was known among his schoolmates for living life to the fullest. The youngest of three siblings whose father was a successful R&B music producer in Los Angeles, Jay had a fully developed free spirit. His friends knew from experience that many times his penchant for adventure meant Jay getting himself entangled in his own schemes without any thought given to potential consequences.

"After the long flights and our first dusty temple tour, I thought a little relaxing diversion was just what we needed."

"Great." Conrad pursued. "So, just what do you have in mind, oh tour guide extraordinaire?"

"Gators."

"Gators? As in crocodiles?" asked Alyssa.

"Yes. The Nile kind. I hear they get really huge. The Chief says he can show us a few just down the shore."

At the mention of his name, Achmed glanced at his passengers. "I will show you. You will see, maybe."

"Super!" remarked Conrad as he looked at Alyssa. "Just what we need. Large reptiles around a small boat in a big lake on foreign soil. What's there to worry about?"

▲ ▲ ▲

The boat skimmed easily across the smooth waters of the lake. The small mud brick structures along the shoreline marked their slow progress. Here and there, cattle grazed lazily on the fertile river grass, paying no attention to the passing craft.

While Jay and Conrad scanned the shallows for crocodiles, Alyssa studied the quiet man who steered their vessel. He was of diminutive statue, about 50 years of age. His bare feet were braced against the side of the boat. He was dressed in a mud stained galabeya, the long male dress worn by many Egyptian men. There was something in his deeply tanned features that made Alyssa shiver. It lingered vaguely in her mind as something sinister, but she couldn't exactly define it. The man sensed her eyes upon him and cast a dark look her way. She quickly joined the boys in their search for scaled creatures.

▲ ▲ ▲

Achmed dropped the sail as the boat approached a thick tangle of roots and aquatic plants in a shallow cove on the lake. "Here," was his only comment as he pulled a wooden stopper from a water jar and took a drink.

Jay peered expectantly over the side of the boat, sure he would soon spot his prize lurking in the muddy water below. Alyssa and Conrad scanned the water on the other side of the boat.

Suddenly, their silent vigil was interrupted by a shout from Jay who was leaning over the side and pointing excitedly, "There's one! What a man-eater! He is HUGE!"

Conrad and Alyssa converged on Jay's side of the boat. The sudden weight shift tipped the vessel enough to spill Jay over the side and into the muddy water.

"Man overboard!" Conrad shouted. "Jay!"

"Watch out for the gator! He's right next to you!" Alyssa screamed as she pointed to the dark form in the water by the boat. "Hurry! Get out! He's going to eat you!"

Jay began yelling and thrashing around in the water. Through his splashes, he could see the object of his terror in the water next to him. He became even more frantic in his attempt to escape its jaws!

Achmed pushed Conrad aside and reached a wiry arm over the side. He grasped Jay's outstretched hand and pulled him upward. Jay stood in response to the man's iron grasp, surprised that the dark water only came to his chest. Conrad reached over the side and helped pull the scrambling boy into the boat.

As Jay struggled to catch his breath in the bottom of the boat, the man pointed to the water and uttered one word, "Log." He then sat in his place at the back of the felucca, a look of disdain on his face.

"Log? You spazzed out over a log, Jay? In four feet of water?" Conrad shook his head incredulously as he sat heavily on the cushions. "Ohhhhhh boy, what have I gotten myself into?" he asked as he ran his fingers through his sandy colored hair in exasperation.

Alyssa struggled to control an escaping laugh. "Jay, you acted like that log was a giant croc going to eat you." The giggle erupted. "I didn't know it was the *Wooden Creature from the Shallow Lagoon*!"

At this remark, Conrad joined in her laughter. "So much for the *relaxing* part of this excursion, but it has been a diversion! I really can't say it made my day, though."

A dripping Jay flashed his bright smile as his heart rate slowed. "I am glad you both approve. There will be no extra charge for the entertainment. And, you'll be happy to note, I didn't lose these." He held up his phone and earbuds from where he'd placed them on the bench before going overboard. Turning to Achmed he added, "Thanks for the hand, Chief. And for saving me from the killer log."

The dark man's voice broke through the friends' laughter, "No crocodiles today. We go back now." Without further comment, the man raised the sail and steered the boat back toward the Abu Simbel Temple complex.

Jay shrugged good-naturedly and stretched out in the sun, hoping his clothes would dry before they got back to the dock.

As the boat plied down the lake, Alyssa couldn't get the vision out of her head of the arm reaching into the water to pull Jay out—the arm with the strange tattoo of a disk that looked like the sun...a sun with several rays extending from it...rays with small hands attached to their ends. She cast a furtive glance towards the rear of the boat. *I will be so glad to get away from this creepy man and his creepy tattoo!*

▲　▲　▲

Last call for Flight 229 to Luxor. Last call for Flight 229 leaving for Luxor. If you are a ticketed passenger, please proceed to the gate.

"There it is!" Jay huffed, pointing to the gate. "Hey! Here we are! Hold the plane!"

The three schoolmates ran to the ticket counter and breathlessly held out their tickets and passports to the gate attendant. The man studied their documents and then looked at the still damp Jay with the slightly discolored clothes. The boy smiled innocently as he took his documents and headed down the ramp. Two minutes later, they were buckled into their adjoining seats, ready for takeoff.

"Did you see Rayes the tour operator looking at us when we boarded?" asked Alyssa. "I hope murder is illegal here because he may try it when we land."

"We'll use Jay as a human shield when we get off the plane," smirked Conrad. "A small sacrifice to keep us from harm."

Jay stopped scrolling through his tunes and responded, "Don't worry about Rayes, I'll explain and smooth everything over. Besides, I bet it's not the first time he lost a few tourists in the desert."

"I can only image how stressed out he was when we didn't show up at the bus. Likely ruined his day," Conrad stated sympathetically.

"I hope we didn't get him into trouble," Alyssa said as she turned in her seat to look back at him. "He still doesn't look too happy."

"I think I'll take a nap in preparation for my human shield gig," Jay said as he pulled the window shade down and closed his eyes. "Save my snack for me, will you? I'll eat it before we land."

▲ ▲ ▲

"Ahh, my wayward friends," Rayes said with false warmth as he greeted the trio inside the terminal. "I am glad you thought it proper to return to Luxor with the rest of us."

"Sorry, Rayes," Jay began, "you see, we had this little problem wh—"

"I am sorry for your problems," the guide continued coldly, "but Egypt is a more dangerous place today than it once was before the uprising. One never knows what trouble awaits just around the corner!"

The friends glanced at each other. They could not begin to appreciate the truth of the man's words. But soon, they would experience it...personally.

CHAPTER 2

"There he is," Alyssa said to Conrad and Jay, nodding in the direction of the hostess at the front of the restaurant.

The boys turned to see Geoffrey wave off the offer of assistance and begin making his way through the labyrinth of tables on the patio.

"Hello, my young friends. So good to see you again!"

Geoffrey exchanged greetings with Conrad and Alyssa, and the secret handshake with Jay before sitting down in the empty chair.

"So, how was your first full day in Egypt?" he asked the group. When he saw them glancing at each other, he asked with a mischievous glimmer in his eyes, "Have a bit of unscheduled excitement yesterday that I should know about? Perhaps come across a mummy, a missing tomb, or something of the sort?"

Jay answered for the group, his eyes full of mischief, "No mummies. Just a large wet piece of lumber."

Geoffrey's puzzled look turned to one of amusement as the friends told the tale of their adventurous boat ride.

"One would think that a masterpiece such as the Abu Simbel Temples would be enough of an adventure to satisfy even the most experienced world traveler," Geoffrey stated with a grin. "Yet, my young archeologists went in search of even greater sources of excitement. My, my. It makes a person wonder what it will take to hold their attention for the remainder of their trip." He raised his brows slightly, surveying the group of friends.

"Gee, Mr. B, we didn't exactly go looking for adventure," Jay explained. "It kind of found us by itself."

"I think it was more a case of it being attracted to the *adventure magnet*, Jay Wray, wouldn't you agree, Miss Garret?" Conrad asked.

"Indeed, Mr. Kingston," Alyssa replied. "Attracted like a positron to an electron."

"Well, that certainly explains everything," laughed Geoffrey. "Still, what would it take to top the adventure of the day, and," he paused, looking at Jay, "keep Mr. Adventure interested and engaged for another week in Egypt?"

The friends looked expectantly at Geoffrey, who merely added, "Shall we order dinner and perhaps discuss some ideas I have to make this trip much more than another field trip to some historic destination?"

▲ ▲ ▲

Geoffrey handed his menu to the waiter. The friends leaned in with anticipation of an adventure only he could conjure.

"Are you aware of the latest drama unfolding right next to us in the Valley of the Kings?"

The schoolmates looked at him quizzically before Conrad ventured a guess. "Our archeology teacher mentioned that there was some new activity related to King Tut and Nefertiti. She did not get into specifics, but she was pretty excited."

"Yeah, I remember that!" added Jay. "She said something about more treasure and things being hidden somewhere. I only remember the part about treasure, though," he added with a grin.

"Jay Wray!" exclaimed Alyssa. "You have treasure on the brain!"

"I do have quite a bit of experience with treasure, you know," Jay replied, referring to the earlier adventures of the History Hunters.

"Well," continued Geoffrey, "I have quite a tale to relate to you...one with a strong local flavor. In fact, it is one of the greatest mysteries of ancient Egypt." He looked around the table for effect before continuing, "It's a tale of mystery, intrigue, lost tombs, fabulous treasures, and missing mummies!"

"Did you say *mummies*, Mr. B?" Jay asked nervously. "Like the kind who walk around and show up when you least expect them? I'm a little less excited about all of this than before." His trademark zest for life temporarily disappeared from his eyes at the thought.

"The only mummy I ever saw walking around was *you* the last time you had a bad dream at school and woke up all tangled in your sheets," laughed Conrad.

"Quite right," Geoffrey said reassuringly. "The mummies I speak of don't walk. They do, however, play a large part in the great mystery I referred to."

After the waiter brought their food, Geoffrey continued, "Does anyone know the name, *Akhenaten*?"

His question was returned with blank stares between bites of food.

"Many people don't. Yet he and his wife are at the very center of this mystery." He took a drink of water before continuing. "Akhenaten was an 18th Dynasty pharaoh—"

"That was part of the New Kingdom period, wasn't it Geoffrey?" Conrad asked.

"Correct," answered Geoffrey. "I see someone was paying attention in class." He gave a knowing smile at Jay.

"I was just about to say the same thing," Jay said defensively, his dark curls flopping as he suddenly sat up straight. "We had a test on that three weeks ago. I aced it, by the way."

"I am sure you did, Jay," Geoffrey said, his smile deepening. "Anyway, Akhenaten was married to another important person in this tale..."

This time, Alyssa interrupted, "Nefertiti?"

"Well done, Alyssa. I see 'm in the midst of ancient Egyptian scholars," Geoffrey said admiringly. "So, we have identified two players in this mystery, Akhenaten and Nefertiti. It is my contention that neither of their mummies has surfaced, so to speak. However, there have been tantalizing clues associated with both of them. It has been theorized that there are hidden compartments behind the walls of King Tut's burial chamber, the KV62 tomb."

"Excuse me, Geoffrey, but what does the KV stand for?" asked Alyssa. She pushed a strand of blonde hair behind her ear, her eyes focused in concentration.

"Kings Valley...Valley of the Kings," he answered before continuing. "They have conducted a study of the chamber using ground penetrating radar and have detected some structural anomalies. These give credence to the theory that perhaps our queen, Nefertiti, lies peacefully in wait behind the walls."

"I remember now," Conrad interjected. "That was what our teacher was so excited about."

"I share her excitement," said Geoffrey as he finished his meal. "There have been no major finds since Howard Carter discovered Tut's tomb in the 1920's. The world is ripe with excitement for something new from Egypt, which leads us to the next piece of the puzzle. In 1989, Victor Loret discovered a tomb in the Valley of the Kings known as KV35. Does anyone know what was in this tomb?"

"Dead people?" Jay offered, smiling from behind his glass.

Geoffrey laughed. "Yes, dead people. In fact, many dead people."

Jay sat back in his chair with flair, his bright smile lighting his face.

Geoffrey continued, "There were no fewer than 13 mummies found in the tomb!"

"Sounds a little crowded to me, Mr. B!" exclaimed Jay with a chuckle.

"Very crowded. Some of the greatest pharaohs from antiquity were interred there."

"Why would they put so many in one tomb?" asked Alyssa.

"It was due to two long-standing problems," Geoffrey answered, "flooding and tomb robbers."

"So they were relocated to that tomb later on to keep them safe," surmised Conrad.

"Precisely. But even though the names of the mummies involved are a virtual *Who's Who* of antiquity, the real stars of the find were two mummies found lying helter-skelter on a pile of rubble...both women, and both unknown."

"Oh!" exclaimed Alyssa. "How exciting!"

"Indeed," replied Geoffrey. "At the time of their discovery, Loret named them The Elder Lady and the Younger Lady, because he did not know who they were. Since then, we have come to know that The Elder Lady is, in fact, Queen Tiye, the Great Royal Wife of the pharaoh Amenhotep III. Subsequent DNA testing has also determined that The Younger Lady, whoever she might be, is the mother of King Tut!"

"The plot thickens, Mr. B!" said Jay excitedly.

Geoffrey smiled. "But that is not all, my young friends...Amenhotep III and Queen Tiye are also the parents of the pharaoh Amenhotep IV."

The schoolmates did not recognize who this was.

"This is the same man as Akhenaten."

"This sounds rather more complicated a mystery than we first thought," Conrad stated. "How does Amenhotep IV become Akhenaten, and what does this all mean as far as the mystery is concerned?"

"That, my young archeologists, is precisely what I intend to show you firsthand this coming week," answered Geoffrey. "I have taken the liberty of contacting your school and offering my services to conduct your field study trip personally. They were kind enough to accept my offer. We begin on the morrow."

"Sweet, Mr. B!" Jay exclaimed as he stood and exchanged the secret handshake with Geoffrey once again. After sitting down, he added, "Now, how about we order some dessert?"

CHAPTER 3

The small man adjusted his spectacles and flipped the switch, flooding the table in bright light. Before him lay a bundled object, the worthless, rough burlap in stark contrast to the priceless artifact it concealed. The man's hands trembled slightly as he reached down and carefully began to unwrap the prize. He had handled hundreds of such objects during his tenure at the Egyptian Museum in Cairo. Even so, he fought the urge to recoil as he considered the origin of the piece and all it represented. Such was his respect for his heritage. But now, he had a different master who drove his actions. No longer was his motive pure love for wonders of the past. It was now mixed with greed...and a deep, abiding fear of the one who now directed the trajectory of his life.

Suddenly, there it was! He could feel the cool sweat on his forehead and the sticky sweat on his hands under the gloves. He held a small piece of the glory of Egypt past, part of his heritage. A mumbled *'Magnificent!'* was all that escaped his lips.

The robed man across the table from him was less impressed. But that was understandable. He was not driven by even a modicum of love for what lay before him. He was motivated by a dark purpose in a place where the ends justified any means.

The robed man spoke, "So, Zamir, what do you think? Will our clients find this piece as fascinating as you?"

For no definable reason, the bespectacled man cringed slightly in fear at the question. *Could the other sense his love for the artifact? Could he sense his love for what it represented? Could he sense his love for his country?* The cool sweat turned into small rivulets on his temples. Such thoughts would put him in danger of a quick end to his life.

"I...I believe it will be more than satisfactory to them," the small man managed to say. "As you can see, it is perfect."

The robed man studied Zamir coldly with eyes that ripped gaping holes into the depths of the small man's soul. He was pleased with the terror he saw on the now profusely sweating antiquities expert. He reached for the piece, taking it from trembling hands. He gave it a cursory examination and handed it back.

"Very well. Prepare it for shipment as we discussed. I will send one of our couriers for it tonight." He reached into a small shoulder satchel and handed the cowed man a folded piece of paper. "Prepare these instructions for the man who comes."

Zamir grabbed at the sheet, but his terrified hand would not function. As the paper fluttered to the table, the robed man threatened, "Fool! Be careful how you handle these instructions. Any missteps will have dire consequences!"

Zamir quickly retrieved the paper and placed it with the artifact. "Forgive me. I will be careful. I assure you."

"Mistakes will not be tolerated, *I assure you*," the man threatened. With a flourish of his robes, he turned and left.

It was not until the door closed behind the trailing bodyguards that the small man dared breathe. He reached into his pocket for a handkerchief and quickly wiped the sweat from his face.

How did my life come to this? I am a simple professor of archeology with a family to feed and few options in this new Egypt. I am not a thief...or worse.

His narrow shoulders sank at the thought. Slowly, he proceeded with his work.

▲ ▲ ▲

"Man, Mr. B, I didn't know archeologists started working while it was still dark," a slightly disheveled Jay stated wearily. "It seems like I didn't get any sleep last night."

Conrad snorted, "I can assure you that sleep deprivation is not an issue. You were out cold five minutes after you went to bed...and you didn't stop snoring until I pulled the covers off you this morning and let the cool desert breeze wake the dead."

Geoffrey smiled. "How are you doing Alyssa?"

"A little sleepy, but I brought my pillow along for the train ride," she said with a grin. "By the time we arrive in Asyut, I will be ready to go."

"Ready to go into the restroom to get ready to go, you mean," a teasing Jay added good-naturedly.

His remark was met with a *whack* from the pillow.

"Even in the desert, we lady archeologists must look our best." Alyssa shook her head with an exaggerated eye roll.

"Alright, class," Geoffrey interrupted. "Shall we be on our way?"

Geoffrey led the group out the front doors of the hotel toward a waiting taxi. Even at this early hour, the sounds and smells of the surrounding city of Luxor stirred on the air.

Their destination lay some six hours northwest along the Nile in the heart of the desert plateaus—Tell el-Amarna, known simply as Amarna, the city of Akhenaten. The train wound along the fertile strip of green that followed the great river northward. Everywhere, the scenes of an agricultural existence passed by the air-conditioned rail car. Boats of every sort could be seen navigating up and down the greenish brown waters of the Nile.

As they were nearing the end of the railway portion of their trip, Geoffrey prepared them for the day ahead. "Last night I spoke to you about the pharaoh Amenhotep IV, better known as Akhenaten. Today, we shall see the remains of a great city he built during the middle of his reign...Amarna."

"Why did he change his name, Geoffrey?" asked Conrad.

"That, my friends, is a fascinating tail." Geoffrey looked at the curious faces around him. "To tell that story, one must first go back to an earlier time."

Shifting to a more comfortable position in his seat, he continued, "As you know, the ancient Egyptians worshipped a virtual plethora of gods. Over time, as each pharaonic dynasty came and went, additional gods were added. By the time of Thebes, which you know as Luxor, there existed a triad of gods at the center of Egyptian worship—Amun, Mut, and Khonsu. Amun was the sun god father, Mut was the mother goddess, and Khonsu was their son, the moon god. Now, there were still a multitude of other gods to be worshipped, but these were the main three. And all worship revolved, as it were, around Amun, the sun god."

The schoolmates nodded their understanding.

"Shortly after Akhenaten—Amenhotep IV at that time— became pharaoh, he had a vision that upset the proverbial apple cart. Based on this vision, he decided there was really only one god worthy of worship, the sun disk god Aten. Now, you must understand that this was a radical concept rife with difficulties. First of all, the quality of Egyptian life ebbed and flowed based on what was perceived as the pleasure or displeasure of the gods. So, it was of utmost importance that none of them be offended. Secondly, the common people were used to worshipping multiple gods based on their family traditions and the word of the local priests, and they were most comfortable doing so. And last of all, there existed a very powerful priesthood who had everything to lose and not much to gain if their religious system was discarded."

"Sounds like Akhenaten was a real radical," commented Jay.

"Precisely. In fact, his new system of religion earned him the moniker, *The Heretic King.*"

The friends looked at each other.

"Akhenaten was wise enough to know that he could not beat the priests at their game on their home turf of Thebes, for this was the center of all religious activity at the time."

"You mean at the Karnak and Luxor temples?" asked Alyssa.

"Yes. Akhenaten had a vision of a new city, one where Aten could be worshipped, and one free of the old vestiges of other gods and their associated priestly traditions."

"So, Amarna," concluded Conrad.

"Amarna. And that, my young archeologists, is our destination today."

▲   ▲   ▲

Jay surveyed the dusty area before them as their taxi departed. "Where's the city?"

"What is left of it is spread out before you," Geoffrey answered with a wave of his arm.

"Not very impressive for a former capital of Egypt," added Conrad.

"On the contrary," Geoffrey countered. "Even in its ruined state, it is an astounding site."

The friends cast questioning sideways glances at each other. Jay, the most optimistic of the three, raised his eyebrows and nodded his head in an attempt to see what Geoffrey meant.

With a smile, Geoffrey continued, "An archeologist must be able to see what is unseen and imagine what once was. All you see before you is a vast, dusty plain containing the outline of foundations marked in the red dirt. I challenge you to see a magnificent city stretching seven miles along the Nile and reaching over a mile from the river toward the cliffs. Imagine, if you will, the main central quarter or city proper with a palace, temple, boat docks, and more that covered an area two miles by one half mile."

Jay squinted in the sunlight, surveying the unseen city. "I think I see what you mean, Mr. B," he said with the knowing air of a scholar, causing Alyssa to silently laugh. "And how long did it take him to build this city?"

"Approximately four years."

"Wow! All of this from a desert in four years?" Jay asked, dropping his scholarly tone.

"He was the pharaoh, you know," quipped Conrad, throwing Jay an equally intellectual look.

"He was much more than pharaoh," Geoffrey interjected. "To the Egyptian way of thinking, as Pharaoh, he was *god*!"

"In that capacity, I bet he could get things done." Jay exchanged a fist bump with a reluctant Conrad.

"He had at his disposal all the riches and resources of Egypt," Geoffrey continued. "And this was the key to his success in this unprecedented venture."

"So what happened to the city?" asked Alyssa. "The ruins we've studied in school have huge structural remains." She looked around. "There is nothing like that here."

Geoffrey answered, "Because of the rapid pace of development, there wasn't time to cut the massive limestone blocks necessary for lasting monuments. Instead, most structures were made from mud bricks whitewashed with a type of limestone plaster or paint. At most, the temple and the palace were faced with locally quarried stone. But in the end, it could not stand the test of time."

"That's too bad," said Conrad. "A lot of effort with not much to show for it."

Geoffrey smiled. "And *that* is precisely the rest of the story. You see, when Akhenaten died, his vision died with him. The momentum of the old ways remained hostile to him even after death. It was only a handful of years before Nefertiti, and even Tut, left the city. Later on, Amarna was intentionally destroyed as subsequent pharaohs sought to erase the existence of the dead Heretic King and gain favor with the traditional gods."

"What happened to Akhenaten?" Alyssa asked. "Where is he buried?"

"Yeah," added Jay, unable to contain his enthusiastic curiosity, "if the city was abandoned even by his queen, did he stay here or was he moved, too?"

"Excellent questions," Geoffrey said as he walked over to a local taxi stand. "And that leads us to our final destination here today...Akhenaten's tomb."

▲ ▲ ▲

"Hellooo!" Jay shouted down the long corridor.

"Jay! Be quiet!" Alyssa admonished.

"Just wanted to see if there was an echo," Jay said in his own defense.

"The only echo around here is inside your hollow head," commented an aggravated Conrad. "Let's be civil, shall we, and not act like boorish tourists."

"Okay, okay! Civilized!" Jay answered, raising his hands in a gesture of surrender.

"Besides," continued Conrad, "who did you expect to answer? Some mummy?"

A look of fear crossed Jay's face. "I didn't think of that. Do you think it's safe to go down there, Geoffrey?"

The older man smiled, "Perfectly. Besides, it has been my experience that it would take more than a shout to wake the dead, a fact confirmed by Conrad concerning you each morning!"

The group laughed as a relieved Jay added, "I just wanted to make sure. I'm not in the mood to run into some old guy wrapped in Band-Aids who's upset because we interrupted his beauty sleep." Jay glanced around him, still slightly ill at ease.

The group followed Geoffrey down the long, descending shaft. Deeper and deeper they went until they came to a large chamber.

"Here is Akhenaten's original tomb," informed Geoffrey. "As you can see, he is not here."

"There is not much of anything here," Jay observed. "Even the walls seem to have been scraped clean."

"Yes. The eradication effort was systematically conducted, even here in his tomb," agreed Geoffrey. After they had looked around some, he added, "Come with me. I will show you a room that still has a few carvings visible on the walls."

Geoffrey led them out of the burial chamber and up the shaft a short distance to another room set off to the side. "Here is Meketaten's burial chamber. She was the daughter of Akhenaten and Nefertiti."

As Geoffrey relayed the history of her death to the others, Alyssa walked over to the wall to get a closer look at the faint carved relief images. Geoffrey noticed that she seemed frozen in front of the images. He joined her and asked, "Are you all right, Alyssa?"

A pale Alyssa pointed to the wall. "That round disk with the hands...I've seen that before...Yesterday."

"You saw it yesterday? Where, Alyssa?" a concerned Geoffrey asked the obviously upset girl.

"It was tattooed on the arm of the Chief."

"The Chief? Who is that?" asked a puzzled Geoffrey.

"He was the boat captain who took us for a ride on Lake Nasser," Jay answered for Alyssa. "His name was Achmed, but he is called by *the Chief* by everyone."

CHAPTER 4

The friends sat down at a table in the refreshment tent by the tomb entrance.

"That image is the sun disk god Aten—Akhenaten's one true god," Geoffrey said to the group as they huddled around the photo of the wall relief on Conrad's phone. "The image is very distinct from the images of other Egyptian gods for two reasons. First, Aten was not depicted in the image of any created being, as was commonplace with the other Egyptian deities. And secondly, there are those curious hands reaching down on the ends of the sun disk's rays."

"I think they're creepy," Alyssa interjected as she clutched a cold bottle of water. "And why would anyone have that thing tattooed on their arm?"

"It is strange," agreed Geoffrey, "though tattoos are common these days."

"Look at those hands at the end of the rays! It's downright bizarre!" Jay stated emphatically. "Even weird!"

"From the mouth of an expert on the subject of weirdness," ribbed Conrad.

Jay let the comment slide, knowing his friend just wanted to start an intellectual banter of quick wit. "Sounds like we have another mystery on our hands, Mr. B."

"Indeed it does," Geoffrey said thoughtfully.

"It's almost like a cult symbol," added Jay.

"A cult of one?" asked Conrad critically.

"I was just saying." Jay's voice grew thoughtful, "After all, it is the symbol of a religion."

"Yeah, a 3,000 year old religion!" Conrad said with a laugh. "That's a bit of a stretch, don't you think?"

"Still," mused Geoffrey, "it is an interesting theory, Jay—one which I will pursue with my colleagues when we return to Luxor."

Jay smiled at Geoffrey's words. "Great minds think alike, right Mr. B?"

Conrad had prepared another comment salvo when Geoffrey interrupted, "In all the excitement, I think we forgot to address the one glaring question from our excursion today." When no one responded, he continued, "Where is Akhenaten?"

"Great question, Mr. B!" exclaimed Jay excitedly. "He's definitely not in his tomb. So where is he?"

Geoffrey surveyed the group and said, "That is part of the mystery we discussed yesterday. And tomorrow, we shall travel to the Valley of the Kings in search of the answer." He looked at his watch. "Right now, I suggest we get going or we will miss our train back to Luxor."

▲ ▲ ▲

By the time the group arrived at the train station in Luxor, it was early evening. The boys decided to walk back to the hotel, while Geoffrey and Alyssa took a taxi.

"What a long day on the train," Jay yawned as he stretched. "I was getting a little antsy being cooped up for so long."

A comment flashed in Conrad's mind, but he decided to let it pass. "Me too. That last hour was rough."

"This is just what the doctor ordered," said Jay as he lengthened his stride. "A nice walk in the night air. Now all I need is something to eat."

"Why don't we find the Luxor marketplace?" suggested Conrad. "I heard one of the chaps at the hotel telling a guest about it last night. They supposedly have everything a tourist could want—food, souvenirs, noise, photo ops..."

"What more could we ask for? Sounds good to me. Do you know how to get there?"

"No. I guess we could ask one of the locals. They seem like a friendly lot," answered Conrad.

Jay stopped and sniffed the air. "No need to ask. It's this way." He set off with a single dance move, following the smell of food cooking in the open air.

Conrad shook his head at Jay's never failing *joie de vivre* and followed him close behind.

▲　▲　▲

The marketplace was a hive of activity. Tourists mixed freely with locals. Western dress was interspersed with long garments and head coverings in an easy, peaceful coexistence. A cooling desert breeze completed the pleasant ambiance.

"Hey Conrad! Over here!"

The boy's attention was drawn to a food vendor cooking meat kabobs over a charcoal fire. Jay was excitedly pointing to the fire while the vendor explained the options and haggled over the price. Conrad quickly joined Jay who was exchanging some coins for two sticks of meat.

"How did you disappear so quickly, Jay? One second, we were looking in that shop, and the next second you are half a block away negotiating our next meal. Remember what Rayes told us about being careful around here?"

"Rayes was just mad at us. Nothing could happen *here*." Jay swept his arm with careless gallantry, pointing to the crowded avenue.

"Still," Conrad cautioned, "we should stick together."

"Sure thing," Jay said absentmindedly between mouthfuls of food before becoming interested in a vendor hawking replicas of ancient Egyptian artifacts.

The boys stood to one side of the booth, examining the different wares that were displayed. They thought it odd that they were not immediately beset upon by the vendor trying to convince them he had the best products in Egypt. Instead, they noticed the street vendor talking quietly to another man dressed in the traditional galabeya garment. After a minute, the vendor handed the man a folded piece of paper. The man opened it and nodded. The vendor then reached furtively under the table skirt and produced a bundle wrapped in linen. As the other man reached out to take it, the sleeve of his garment snagged, exposing a round tattoo on his forearm. The man quickly pulled the material back into place and looked across the table to see Jay and Conrad staring directly at him. The man's face pinched into a menacing glare as he turned and headed up the street in the direction of the older local marketplace.

"Did you see that?" Jay hissed under his breath to Conrad. "It's the same tattoo Alyssa saw on The Chief's arm!"

Conrad pulled Jay inside the spice store behind the vendor's table. "I saw it! But I don't like it! Did you see the look that guy gave us when he saw us watching him?"

"Yeah, he looked like he wanted to damage our goods," said Jay with a strange hint of excitement. "And did you see that ugly scar down the side of his head from above his ear to his jaw?"

Conrad nodded and commented dryly, "He looked like he was still mad about that!"

"I think we should follow him," Jay whispered as he peered from the shop doorway.

"Are you crazy? That guy is nothing but trouble."

"Yeah, but he is up to something. Did you see the exchange? Looked like he is smuggling something to me!"

"Even more reason to go back to the hotel!"

"Come on. Let's follow him," Jay urged as he took a step out of the shop. "There are too many people around for anything bad to happen."

Conrad's protest was cut short as Jay left him behind. Shaking his head, he stepped out and followed Jay down the street.

Jay, I'm going to kill you...if we don't get killed ourselves!

CHAPTER 5

Jay followed the mysterious man at a discreet distance up the broad marketplace thoroughfare. Conrad kept pace a few steps behind. Jay used the stalls of the various street vendors for cover as he slowly stalked his adversary. The man with the scar did not seem in a hurry. He appeared to be another of the locals out for an evening stroll.

The crowded tourist section of the market gradually gave way to a narrow dirt street. The colorful dress of the tourists was replaced by the ubiquitous galabeyas of the indigenous population. Loud vendors hawking their wares to uninitiated tourists surrendered to relaxing proprietors smoking hookahs and engaging in small talk with their neighbors. And then there were the donkeys. Everywhere the donkeys. And where there were no donkeys, there remained copious evidence that the animals had once been there.

Jay found it difficult to shadow the man safely. But as chance would have it, the man didn't suspect he was being followed and did not take precautions against the possibility. When they moved deeper into the darkening streets of Luxor, Jay and Conrad felt the eyes of the population following their every move. Still, they managed to keep their quarry in sight about a block ahead of them.

The boys probably could have tracked him down to the end if it had not been for a moment of inattention on Jay's part. Conrad saw it coming, but couldn't cry out because the man with the scar would have surely turned and discovered them. Jay did not see the little old woman exiting the shop laden with two bags of vegetables until a collision was unavoidable.

Jay managed to catch the woman and keep her from falling, but the contents of the bags flew in every direction.

"Oops!"

Jay scrambled to pick up the scattered produce as the old woman began wailing in Arabic. Everyone within two blocks heard the commotion, including the man with the mysterious package. When he saw he was being followed, he uttered something in Arabic and dashed down a squalid alleyway toward the river.

Conrad rescued Jay from the woman and shouted, "Sorry, everyone, but we must be going!" He then dragged Jay back in the direction of the tourist market.

When Jay recovered his composure, he shook loose from Conrad's grip. "What are you doing?" he protested. "Scarface is getting away!"

"Let him get away!" Conrad said determinedly. "We need to get out of here before it's too late!"

"No way! I'm going after him," Jay insisted, his eyes bright with excitement. "He cut down that alley up there. If we take this one, we can get back on his trail."

"You're crazy!" exclaimed Conrad, a little louder this time. "I'm not interested in dying a lonely death in some back street of Luxor! We need to go back to the hotel, and we need to do it NOW!"

But Jay was already gone.

Conrad paused for only a few seconds. Then he followed his friend into the darkness.

"Where are you guys?" an exasperated Alyssa asked out loud. She let the phone ring one more time before hanging up in frustration. *Knowing Jay, he probably didn't think about getting a phone SIM card for Egypt before we left from the States. I can't believe Conrad forgot, though. That wouldn't be like him at all.*

The time was now 10 pm and the boys should have been back at the hotel. Alyssa hesitated another minute and then hit the speed dial for Geoffrey.

A tired voice answered on the fourth ring, "Hello, Alyssa. How are you this evening?"

"Not well, I'm afraid," she answered, fighting the rising panic in her voice. "Jay and Conrad are not back yet. They promised to meet me at the pool thirty minutes ago, but didn't show. I'm getting a little worried."

Geoffrey was fully awake. "If this wasn't a foreign country, I would say it wasn't out of the ordinary for young men their age. However..." His voice trailed off in thought. "Tell you what, I'll meet you at the front desk in 5 minutes and we can sort this out. Okay?"

"Yes, Geoffrey. That will be fine."

A few minutes later, Geoffrey explained the situation to the hotel's night manager.

"I think we should give them a little more time, Mr. Barnsworth," she stated matter-of-factly. "I know the marketplace closes around 10 pm. Perhaps they took a wrong street back from there and are delayed. It is reasonably safe in this vicinity, so everything should be all right."

"Thank you," said an unconvinced Geoffrey. "Perhaps we should give them a little more time."

"If it would make you feel better, sir, I can have one of our security people take a walk around some of the streets near here. Perhaps the young men have lost their sense of direction."

"I would appreciate that greatly," answered Geoffrey. "We will take a seat by the entrance door and wait."

Geoffrey walked over to the leather chairs with Alyssa. "At least they are together. I can't imagine they could get into any serious trouble if they remain so."

"This is *Jay* we are talking about, Geoffrey," said Alyssa knowingly. "He needs no assistance from Conrad to get into trouble."

▲ ▲ ▲

"I can't believe it!" Jay whispered excitedly. "Three blocks over, one block up, and BINGO, there's our man!"

"I can't believe we are chasing him through the dark streets of a totally foreign city...in the dead of night, no less!" Conrad whispered back. "This is insane!"

"Insane or not, I want to know where Scarface is going." Jay edged along the dimly lit street and peered around the corner. He motioned for Conrad to follow as he said, "He's moving toward the Luxor Temple."

▲ ▲ ▲

The man watched the wall of the temple complex from the shadows across the street. He saw the security guard round the corner to the front of the complex. Stealthily, he dashed toward the temple grounds and pressed his body against the structure, willing himself into the shadows. After a moment, he gave three brief whistles like a bird. From the other side of the wall, his call was answered in a like fashion. A rope suddenly appeared over the rampart. The man slipped his foot into the loop at the bottom and was quickly pulled to the top. He dropped the package to unseen waiting hands and then disappeared down the other side.

Jay and Conrad watched all of this from the same shadows the man had used minutes before on the opposite side of the street.

"What do you think we should do?" Jay whispered, his eyes fixed to the temple wall.

"Run through the front gate and shout for the man to come out of hiding and turn the package over to us so we can go back to the hotel and get some sleep," stated Conrad sarcastically.

"I don't think that would work," Jay answered, his one-track mind in overdrive. "Besides, who could sleep after all this excitement? Let's run over to the wall. You can boost me up and I can take a look from the top."

"No way!"

"Okay. Let's go!"

Jay dashed across the road and hugged the mud brick wall. He waved frantically for Conrad to follow. His friend hesitated before following. Soon, Jay was crouching on top of the wall.

"Pssst! Conrad! Grab the end of my belt and come on up!" Jay called softly from above.

"Forget it Jay! Get down here before the guard comes back!" Conrad looked around nervously.

"Conrad!" Jay whispered louder. "I hear the crackle of the guard's radio. He's coming back! Hurry, get up here!"

Jay pulled his friend up the wall. "Great view from up here, don't you think?"

"I think this view is much better than what we will see next," Conrad answered as he peered down into the temple complex.

"What do you think we'll see next?"

"The inside of an Egyptian prison!"

"I'm sorry, Mr. Barnsworth, but our security guard saw no signs of the missing young men."

"Shall we ring up the police?" asked Geoffrey.

The manager replied, "I think that would be best. They handle this sort of thing quite often. I'm sure your companions just lost their way and are quite safe."

Geoffrey glanced over at Alyssa. Neither of them shared her optimism.

Geoffrey asked the woman, "Can you help me by phoning them, uh, miss..."

"Please call me Dimah," the woman answered, light wrinkles appearing softly around her eyes as she smiled. "It would be my pleasure."

Dimah dialed the number and began a conversation with the police, adjusting the already perfect bun in her dark hair with a single, prim gesture. Geoffrey had the impression that very little escaped the attention of this woman.

"They want to know their names and ages," she said, holding the phone away.

Geoffrey gave the details to her and she relayed them on.

"The police said not to worry. They will alert the patrols to begin a search."

"Thank you, Dimah," Geoffrey said appreciatively. "We'll go have a seat by the front door."

Dimah's dark eyes followed them. As soon as they were seated, Dimah silently slipped into the back office and made a call.

"There he is!"

"Where?"

"Back there. By the columns."

The boys crept silently through the shadowed ruins of the temple, using the scattered structures as cover. The man had been joined by two others and was walking toward the back of the temple. All three melted between the columns and vanished.

Jay and Conrad ran the remaining distance to the colonnade and hid behind one of the thick bases.

"Look!" Jay pointed. "They're going into that room at the back."

"Let's wait and see what happens," suggested Conrad.

To his surprise, Jay agreed.

Five minutes later, the man emerged alone, still carrying the package. He looked around briefly and then started for the opposite side of the complex, toward the river. When the other two men did not appear, the boys shadowed the lone figure's progress over the iron fence barrier and across the now empty boulevard beyond the temple. The man walked parallel to the road for 100 yards before turning into a heavily wooded lot.

"Okay, Sherlock," said Conrad softly, "now what?"

In response, Jay plunged into the woods as quietly as he could manage. Conrad followed close behind so he would not lose Jay in the dark thicket. The boys emerged on the other side atop a muddy embankment overlooking the Nile. They were just in time to see the man being pulled aboard a speedboat. The boat backed quickly away from the shore and then sped off into the darkness. Conrad and Jay watched helplessly as the red light from the cabin slowly faded into the watery vastness of the river.

CHAPTER 6

"Thank you. Good night." Dimah hung up the phone and walked over to Geoffrey and Alyssa.

"Well, Mr. Barnsworth," she said with a smile that didn't quite reach her eyes, "the police have informed me that they have located the young men. The *prisoners* will be arriving shortly via police escort."

"Thank heavens!" exclaimed Geoffrey, relieved that the ordeal was almost at an end. "Did the police say where they found them?"

"Yes. They were actually quite lost," she replied. "They were picked up along the highway that runs between the river and the Luxor temple. I'm not sure how they could have become so disoricntcd to end up way over there."

Geoffrey looked at Alyssa.

"Jay!" they said in unison.

Dimah raised an eyebrow. *Jay,* she thought.

▲ ▲ ▲

Alyssa sat on the edge of the bed as Geoffrey finished his interrogation. Conrad and Jay waited in silence for the sentence to be passed. The older man stopped pacing and turned to face the boys.

"That was quite a tale of adventure, and while I can understand your," he looked squarely at Jay, "*enthusiasm*, I do not believe it warranted the risks that were taken."

Jay was about to speak when Geoffrey held up his hand and continued, "Fortunately, the police assumed you were merely lost and did not ask more questions. It could have become quite involved, and messy, if they had known the truth."

"I told Jay we would end up in prison," Conrad slipped in before Geoffrey could continue.

"Prison would have been a preferable alternative to what might have happened," Geoffrey said with great seriousness. "We do not know who these people are, nor do we know what they are involved in. But dark alleys and secret meetings do not bode well for living a long and healthy life!"

"Or trespassing," Alyssa added, referring to the temple invasion.

"Or trespassing," Geoffrey agreed. He sat heavily in a chair and rubbed his tired face.

As Geoffrey was winding down, Alyssa was just getting started. "I tried to call you both—several times—but there was no answer."

"I didn't get a...Ohh-kay, yes I did," said Conrad as he pulled his phone from his pocket. "Sorry, I guess in all of the excitement, I didn't notice it vibrating."

"And what is your excuse, Jay?" Alyssa pursued. "Did you remember to get a SIM card for your phone so it would even work over here?"

Jay squirmed a little and answered, "Uh, it kind of slipped my mind."

"That makes your running around in the dark even more foolish!" the girl exclaimed in frustration. "Ahhhrrr! Two incidents in two days! I'm going to be crazy by the time this trip is over!"

Jay opened his mouth to give a teasing response, but thought better of it and sat back in his chair.

Geoffrey rejoined the conversation in a gentler tone, "When I returned to my room this evening, I placed a call to a colleague of mine and inquired about this sun disk tattoo business. He became rather agitated and dismissed it out of hand as nothing of consequence. I was a bit surprised at his response, as I have dealt with him on and off for years. Perhaps all of the upheaval in his country has left him somewhat more sensitive to any suggestion of nefarious activity."

Jay spoke up, "One thing we know for sure, there is some of that nefarious activity going on around here, and we tripped right over it."

"That has become obvious," Geoffrey stated. "I am hesitant to get the police involved in what so far has been circumstantial in nature. I believe I will contact another friend of mine to see if he can provide any insight. In the meantime, I suggest we change our plans for tomorrow and visit the Luxor Temple Complex instead of the Valley of the Kings, since it is fresh on our minds."

Jay smiled at the idea. "Great idea, Mr. B! We can stake the place out and maybe discover what those guys were doing in that small room at the back!"

"Wrong, Mr. Private Investigator!" Conrad countered. "Maybe we can just act like normal tourists and chill out for awhile."

Chilling out would have been a good idea.

▲ ▲ ▲

The man was livid. Not only had his quiet evening been interrupted by the call, but the report of such carelessness within his operation had left him without words. He could—and would—deal with the internal problem. The question was what to do with the external problem. He couldn't easily make it go away. Disappearing foreigners made a lot of noise in security circles. There was no easy solution. He pondered his options. Slowly, his scowl turned into a smile. *Yes*, he decided, *I will get more involved with my friends from America!*

▲ ▲ ▲

Abu al-Hasan was a stern man. Tall and imposing, he exuded a no-nonsense power. Those who dealt with him could never quite plumb the source of his unspoken forcefulness. Some thought it came from years of service in the highest levels of government. Others perceived a more evil origin. Perhaps it was both.

He entered the hotel restaurant with another man who scanned the room before taking up a position by the door. After an almost imperceptible pause, Abu walked toward Geoffrey and the group of young people seated at the table.

"Hello, Abu. It is good to see you again," Geoffrey greeted the man. "I was surprised to receive your call this morning requesting a meeting."

"I considered that perhaps my response to your telephone inquiry last night would be perceived as being rude by such a distinguished colleague as yourself," Abu replied.

"How long has it been? Three years?" Geoffrey asked the tall, thickly built man.

"Nearly four," the man responded precisely, standing stiff and straight as one who is accustomed to being constantly watchful. "It was soon after the last *adjustment* in our government, as I recall."

"I remember now. I was visiting a client here. Thank you again for assisting me with the necessary paperwork for exporting the purchased item. I'm certain I would not have been able to untangle the bureaucratic nightmare I found myself in without your personal intervention."

"Yes, well, sometimes it takes a certain *method* to get the necessary result in my country." The man paused before adding, "So, Geoffrey, who are your young friends?"

Geoffrey introduced each of the schoolmates and explained the purpose for their visit to Egypt.

The man greeted them as a group without shaking their outstretched hands. Ruffling his robes with a flourish, he sat down in the seat offered by Geoffrey.

"I trust that your time here will be informative and enlightening," he said to them as a group before adding a veiled warning. "Please, for your own sakes of course, stay focused on your objective here and do not stray from it. Things are not as they once were. There are forces at work behind the scenes that will not accommodate interferences of any type. With the loss of so much tourism, some of my people have turned to other means of supporting themselves."

"Yes," nodded Geoffrey with understanding. "I have noticed an increase in security since my last visit to your country. I have also heard there has been a continuing problem of antiquities thefts since the governmental changes."

"It is an age-old problem in Egypt, is it not?" the man asked rhetorically. "The difference being that it now is not the disjointed work of locals taking advantage of the odd opportunity to put some money into their empty pockets. It has grown into the business of very organized and determined groups. That is why I have suggested discretion in your activities here."

"You mean groups like the Mafia?" asked Jay impulsively.

Abu stared across the table before answering, "Perhaps it is not so much the Mafia, as you say, but groups who see the sale of our heritage as a means of financing their particular causes in this changing world."

"I think I know what you mean. Last night we—Ow!" Jay exclaimed as Conrad elbowed him.

Abu eyed the boys suspiciously.

"I think what Jay was referring to," Geoffrey hastily interjected, "was this business of the strange tattoo I asked you about last night."

"I see," said Abu thoughtfully. "I believe you are referring to the ancient cult of Aten, the sun disk god."

At the man's use of the word 'cult', Jay shot Conrad an I-told-you-so look.

"Yes," Geoffrey answered. "We have seen men wearing this tattoo twice in two days. It is such a distinctive mark. We were wondering if it had any significance."

"Yeah, like in smuggling or—Ow!" Conrad again silenced Jay.

Abu's face darkened. He stared at the boys for a few seconds before continuing, "There have been reports that this cult has gained popularity over the past few years. I am not surprised you have seen this mark being worn by others."

"Well, I'm sure it is nothing," Geoffrey said to mollify the man.

The man offered no further comment, but changed the subject, "So, how long will you be guests in our country?"

Alyssa spoke for the first time, "We will be here for another week, Mr. al-Hassan. Then we go back to school."

"I trust you will have much new knowledge to apply to your studies," Abu said politely. "There is no substitute for experience. It makes the theory more relevant."

Alyssa smiled at the man. "I know. I will never think Egyptian history is boring ever again!"

"Uh, well, yes." The man stifled a smile as he turned to Geoffrey. "I apologize for the short visit, but I must be on my way. I will be in Cairo for the next few days. However, we must visit together again before you go."

Abu al-Hasan stood abruptly and shook hands with Geoffrey. He bowed to the others and quietly walked away. The man by the door escorted him out to a waiting car. As the car sped away, Conrad and Jay couldn't help thinking there was much the man had *not* said during his visit.

CHAPTER 7

Jay joined the others in the lobby of the hotel, head bobbing to a tune only he could hear.

"I thought you said I spent too much time getting ready," teased Alyssa. "We have been waiting 20 minutes for you!"

"Hey! Being unassumingly casual takes a little prep time," the boy replied as he adjusted his pith helmet and slipped on his shades.

"Yes. Tacky khaki *is* time consuming," Conrad smirked.

"Funny, funny. At least I am prepared for today."

"And what exactly does that mean?" Conrad asked.

"You'll see," smiled Jay as he patted the small backpack he carried and headed for the door.

▲ ▲ ▲

"This place is fantastic!" exclaimed Jay, looking up at the large, red granite obelisk that marked the entryway into the Luxor Temple.

"Yes, it does look quite different when one views it legally...and in broad daylight," jabbed Conrad.

"This walled structure with the statues is known as the Ramesses Pylon," explained Geoffrey. "It was added to the original temple by Ramesses II, as was the large courtyard just inside. As we go further into the temple, you will see that these two sections are at a curious angle to the original temple works." Geoffrey turned around and pointed in the opposite direction. "But it lines up perfectly with the Avenue of the Sphinxes which leads to the Karnak Temple in the distance."

The older man led the schoolmates back toward the Pylon and stood at the base of the large seated statue. "This is Ramesses II himself. He reigned longer than most of the pharaohs, so you will see many of his building projects across Egypt. But that is another story for another time."

"This looks familiar," puzzled Alyssa. She raised a hand to shield her eyes from the bright sunlight to get a better look at the statue.

Conrad replied, "It should. He also built the Abu Simbel Temple."

"Home base of The Chief," Jay added.

"And the man-eating log," giggled Alyssa.

Geoffrey led the friends deeper into the temple complex.

"Wow! This place is gargantuan!" marveled Jay.

"It is amazing how much smaller things look at night, isn't it?" asked Conrad innocently.

"Geoffrey, what is that building up there?" Jay was pointing to the structure perched high on the tops of the columns in the Ramesses Courtyard.

Geoffrey smiled. "That is the Mosque of Abu el-Haggag."

"Is that reserved for really tall people?" Jay asked.

"No, Jay," chuckled Geoffrey. "Over the centuries this entire complex was slowly filled with sand and rubble. By the time that mosque was built in the 13th century, the rubble pile reached to the tops of the columns. So that is where they built the mosque, using the columns as a foundation."

"Amazing!" said Conrad. "When did they clean all of the sand and rubble out?"

"Sometime during the 19th century," answered Geoffrey. "They left the mosque intact up there. It is still in use today."

They walked to the back of the courtyard.

Geoffrey continued, "Here begins the original temple complex built by Amenhotep III, Akhenaten's father and King Tut's grandfather. These two rows of columns are known famously as the Colonnade."

Jay pointed at the wall to their left. "That was our point of entry over the wall last night. We followed Scarface right along these columns here. There is another gigantic courtyard through there. Come on. I'll show you!"

The group followed Jay into a large column-lined courtyard.

"This is the Sun Court. It was dedicated to Amun, the sun god. As magnificent as this structure is, something very unique with respect to this archeological site happened here."

"Yeah. Scarface and his friends came through here last night," Jay stated.

"I was talking about a cache of statues that were found in a pit under this very floor," said Geoffrey. "You see, other than that time, there has been no excavating on this site."

"You know what that means," Conrad opined for Jay's benefit. "There could be all kinds of treasures right beneath our feet."

This statement derailed Jay's one-track mind from finding Scarface and his friends to finding hidden riches.

"Treasure? Right below our feet?" Jay began thinking of the possibilities.

"Now Jay, don't start tapping on everything like you were doing in Germany when you were searching for hidden Nazi loot," warned Alyssa, thinking back to the stories Kim and Preston—the other two History Hunters—had told her.

"It worked there, didn't it?" Jay asked in his own defense.

"While it is possible there are things buried below us," Geoffrey said, "it is unlikely. This was a worship temple, not a tomb. You'll have to save your tapping for tomorrow when we visit the Valley of the Kings, Jay."

This put Jay back on his original quest.

"The bad guys went back through there," said Jay, pointing to the halls beyond the courtyard. "There is some kind of a room all the way in the back. We didn't go in, but they did."

"That room is likely the statue room, or what is known as the holy of holies," said Geoffrey. "You see, this entire complex was used for ceremonies surrounding the Royal Ka, or, as it is also known, the Cult of the King. They believed that the pharaoh was the incarnation of the dynastic god, Horus. That is why the pharaoh had such broad powers. He was the high priest for the nation."

Geoffrey led them back to a series of nooks and rooms.

"Once a year, when the Nile River overflowed its banks, there would be a festival that lasted for several days called the Opet Festival. The Theban triad of gods—"

"Amun, Mut, and Khonsu?" asked Conrad.

"Yes," continued Geoffrey. "These three would be carried from the Karnak Temple, down the long Avenue of the Sphinxes, and into this temple. The priests and the pharaoh would conduct all the required rituals, in effect, renewing the god-status of the king for another year. That is what these rooms are for."

By now, they stood outside the stone structure that Jay was so anxious to look into.

"This is it!" Jay exclaimed. "Conrad and I saw the three men go in, but only one man came out—Scarface—with the package."

Geoffrey led them into the chamber. It was empty except for a flat granite block on the floor.

"Hey!" Jay said a little too loudly. "There's nothing in here but that stone on the floor and some electric lights up on the walls!"

"There's not even another way out," added Conrad as he looked around the enclosed chamber. "That is odd. Jay and I saw all of them go in and only the man with the package come back out."

"His friends could have just stayed in here until after he left with the package, and then came out. You wouldn't have seen them if that's what they did," offered Alyssa. "They didn't really *have* to go anywhere."

This statement seemed to take the wind out of Jay's enthusiasm. He sat down on the stone block to ponder the possibilities.

"The block you are sitting on, Jay, once held a large statue of Amun. This was his shrine. Only the priests and the pharaoh were allowed in here." Geoffrey continued, "This entire end of the temple is built on a mound of earth. The ancients believed this was the original place of creation."

Jay jumped up, electrified. "Gee, Mr. B! That gives me the willies! Let's get out of here."

During the entire visit to the temple, a well-dressed man in expensive robes had followed the group. Though he stayed back enough of a distance not to arouse their suspicions, he managed to hear some of what Geoffrey had been relaying about the temple. As they started back toward the front of the structure, he approached them.

"Excuse me," the man said. "Are you Geoffrey Barnsworth?"

A surprised Geoffrey answered, "Yes, I am. Do I know you?"

The man cracked an almost authentic smile and held out his hand. "My name is Jafar Kazim. I am the Director of the Temple Complexes here in Luxor."

Behind him, two well-built men in dark glasses suddenly materialized. Their tailored suits couldn't hide the bulges caused by the weapons they concealed.

CHAPTER 8

"Please forgive me," Geoffrey said, "but I don't remember meeting you."

"No, it is I who must ask your forgiveness for intruding upon your privacy," the man said. "We met about five years ago when you gave a lecture in Cairo. I am sure that you meet many people after your talks, and that it is difficult to remember them all."

"Yes, this is true," replied Geoffrey. "I remember the conference, but that is about all, I'm afraid."

"It is no matter," the man continued unabated, "for I remember you. When I saw you here today, I thought I recognized you. I trailed behind you to make sure. When I heard you speak with such eloquence on the things of our history, I knew it must be you."

He saw Geoffrey and his young friends glancing past him toward his bodyguards.

"Unfortunately, a requirement of my position. You see, I am responsible for all antiquity sites here in Luxor. I make it a point to walk the sites on a frequent basis to ascertain the level of their maintenance, the number of tourists, and even to inspect our security measures. Since the attack a few years ago, I have been assigned a security detail who travel with me everywhere." His forced smile waned. "I sometimes long for the old days when young boys harassing tourists for baksheesh—tips—was my biggest challenge."

"It is a pleasure to meet you, Jafar." Geoffrey motioned toward the schoolmates. "These are my young charges for the week—Jay, Conrad, and Alyssa."

The friends exchanged greetings with Jafar.

"Such an esteemed group," Jafar said smoothly. "May I ask what brings all of you to our ancient city?"

Geoffrey described the purpose of their trip and gave Jafar a general idea of their plans.

"It is truly wonderful to have you here. Believe this when I tell you. I would be honored if I could show you around the Karnak Temple before you leave next week," the man offered. "That is, of course, if your schedule permits."

Geoffrey looked at the schoolmates and then answered for them all, "We would be honored to share your hospitality."

"Splendid," Jafar beamed. "Here is my card with my direct number. Please do call me. I look forward to being at your service."

With that, the man bowed and started toward his waiting guards. Suddenly, he spun back around. "I do not wish to alarm you in any way, of course, but a word of caution is in order. The recent changes in our country have given rise to an element of the population that is, how do I say it...of a more sinister nature. Yes, that is it. Please be careful where you go and with whom you associate. We would not want to see you put in any danger while you are guests here."

He bowed again. "I will wait to hear from you. Good day."

As the man passed from view between the columns, Jay exclaimed, "Man! Two warnings in one day! Three if you add Geoffrey's lecture last night," he added with a grin.

"Delivered by two rather interesting people," Conrad interjected.

"Each with bodyguards," Alyssa chipped in.

"Indeed," said Geoffrey thoughtfully. "It makes one take pause as we plan the rest of our time here in Egypt."

"By the way, Geoffrey, we know what Mr. Kazim does for a living. What about Mr. al-Hasan?" asked Conrad. "I don't recall either he or you mentioning it."

"Abu works for the Ministry of the Interior," Geoffrey answered as he once again started toward the front of the temple complex. "I am not exactly sure of his role in the new government, however."

"Mr. B, I want to check out one more thing back in that room," said Jay. "You guys go ahead to the Pylon. I will meet you there in 5 minutes."

"Jay!" said Alyssa suspiciously. "You aren't going to run off after somebody and get in trouble again, are you?"

Jay held up both palms. "No trouble. No trouble at all. It will only take a minute." With that, he turned and trotted toward the far end of the temple.

It would be trouble...and soon enough.

▲ ▲ ▲

The man with the scar sat quietly under a palm tree along the shore of the great lake. The wrapped package rested on the grass between his feet. He fought the fatigue that swept over him like waves from the passing boats. A light breeze blew from the north, bringing the sounds of big boats, motor vehicles, and excited tourists with it. He absentmindedly glanced in the direction of the sounds. The large seated statues of Ramesses glowed orange in the mid-morning sun.

It had taken him 8 hours to reach Aswan by boat and another 2 hours to get here by bus. He rarely slept when he was making a delivery, and it was beginning to take its toll on him. Soon, his ride would arrive to take him down Lake Nasser and across the border into Sudan. This portion of the trip would be uneventful, giving him the chance for a couple hours of sleep. Then it would be another 6 hours on two different trains before the handoff would be made at the designated spot in Port Sudan. By noon tomorrow, he would be back in Luxor

He pulled the sheet of paper from the folds in his robe. He reviewed the instructions once again, his mind quickly deciphering the symbols on the page. Every delivery was slightly different—different routes, different transport, and different drop points. This kept the smuggling operation safe from detection. Each time, he was just an Egyptian worker carrying a package home to his wife. Putting the paper back in its place, he stared blankly at the bundle below.

"Marhaban!"

The greeting jolted him from the fog of fatigue. He looked up quickly to see the felucca gliding a few meters from the shore. The man in the back expertly spilled the wind from the sail and the boat gently coasted to a stop on the muddy bank. The man with the scar climbed onto a small stump and stepped into the boat, his momentum separating the boat from the shore. He handed the package to the man in the back who stowed it away in a secret compartment. He then settled on the cushions and laid down to rest as the sail was once again hoisted. He felt the tug of wind on the boat and his mind relaxed. He knew there would be nothing to worry about until they landed once more. The Chief would handle everything. He always did.

▲ ▲ ▲

The friends lounged on a low bench in the shade of the Pylon wall. Alyssa looked at the time on her phone.

"Fifteen minutes," she announced. "We should have gone with Jay to make sure he stayed out of trouble."

"I doubt that would have helped," commented Conrad. "All of us would have ended up in an Egyptian prison. At least this way, we can visit *him* there."

Alyssa giggled. "You know, Geoffrey, you have some pretty peculiar friends around here."

"Very peculiar," added Conrad. "I was just thinking about our visits with both of them today. I can't shake the feeling they had something specific on their minds—something they *weren't* telling us."

"Or maybe something they were hiding," Alyssa mused, completing the thought.

"I was thinking precisely the same thing," answered Geoffrey as he fanned himself with his pith helmet. "I am planning to ring up another friend of mine and see if he could shed some light on Abu and Jafar."

Conrad glanced over at Alyssa and then to Geoffrey. "Another one? I don't know, Geoffrey. Two seemed an adequate amount of strangeness for one trip to me."

Geoffrey stopped fanning as he spoke. "The man I have in mind is well connected in this part of the world. He has always been a wealth of information. We have been acquaintances—friends really—for several years. I'm sure he would know both of the others and could help us decipher their intentions."

At that moment, Jay jogged up to them. "I'm back!"

"So you are," Conrad stated as he made a show of looking around. "What? No police?"

"None were needed," Jay replied. "Sorry, though. It took me a little longer than I expected."

"To do what?" demanded Alyssa.

"Oh, just a little experiment," Jay answered evasively, realizing he had already said too much.

"A what?" Alyssa asked incredulously.

"Hey. We're on a school trip. Experiments are allowed. I'll let you know the result," Jay sputtered.

Before Alyssa could continue her interrogation, Geoffrey came to Jay's rescue. "I think we should get out of this sun and get a bite to eat. Hunger and heat is a bad combination that leads to irritability. Is everyone ready?"

Unanimous assent sent them on their way.

Geoffrey led them down a small side street on the way to their hotel. "Dimah, the nice lady at the hotel, recommended a restaurant that is popular with the tourists near the marketplace. I thought we would try some of the local fare, if everyone agrees."

"Food of any sort would be welcome after a long morning of exploring, Mr. B," Jay said sincerely.

▲　▲　▲

They sat at a table toward the front of the restaurant. The doors that served as the front wall had been pushed to each side, opening the room to the street outside. Overhead, an ancient fan wobbled as it cycled on its endless journey. People ambled unhurriedly along, while all manner of motorbikes, donkeys, and carriages slowly rolled by. Across the narrow street, a similar restaurant plied its trade.

"I like this place!" said Alyssa. "It has so much character!"

"It has character, all right," Conrad agreed. "And he is sitting at the table with us!"

"Since I know you couldn't possibly be referring to Geoffrey, *I'll* take that as a compliment," said Jay with a smile. "You say so many nice things about me, Conrad. I'm beginning to think you really do like me."

Conrad and Alyssa exchanged amused looks.

A teenaged girl dressed in a gray abaya and royal blue hijab appeared at the table with the traditional greeting, "Assalamu alaykum."

The group politely returned her greeting.

"My name is Malika. Welcome. Are you ready to order?"

When the friends nodded, she began with Alyssa. "And what would you like?"

"The roasted lamb sounds delicious," Alyssa replied.

"That is one of my favorites," affirmed Malika. "It is made with a garlic herb sauce and comes with hummus and fried bread."

"That sounds great for me, too!" exclaimed a hungry Jay.

Geoffrey and Conrad agreed and ordered the same dish.

Malika took the menus and disappeared into the back kitchen.

"She seems like a nice girl," said Alyssa.

"Hey, maybe she could show us some of the local customs while we're here," Jay suggested. "That would be a good diversion from discovering gold and being chased by mummies."

Everyone laughed at Jay's comment, but in the end, it was a bad idea.

CHAPTER 9

The cool water of the swimming pool was a great antidote to the late afternoon sun. The friends soaked in the water and then lounged lazily in the shade. A small breeze stirred the palm fronds lazily above them, the clear blue sky their backdrop.

"This homework is killing me," Jay joked light-heartedly. "We had better not mention this back at school. Kim and Preston are probably cramming for a test as we speak." Jay referred to their other two fellow History Hunters.

"Yes, they are probably bundled away in coats and hats while we enjoy life at the oasis," Conrad added.

"We'll be back in the 'classroom' soon enough," Alyssa reminded them. "Geoffrey is planning on a full day in the desert tomorrow."

"Valley of the Kings, here we come!" shouted Jay as he ran and did a cannonball into the water.

"What time are we meeting Malika tonight?" Conrad inquired, doing his best to ignore Jay's antics.

"She said she would be finished at the restaurant at 7:30," Alyssa answered. "We are to meet her there and then she will show us around the marketplace."

Conrad glanced at Jay who was floating on his back and spurting water in the air like a whale. "It will be nice to actually *see* the marketplace this time, instead of playing *James Bond.*"

"I agree," Alyssa continued. "I asked Geoffrey to remind Jay to behave himself before we left the hotel tonight."

"Hopefully, he will also provide some handcuffs," Conrad added wryly.

▲ ▲ ▲

"There's Geoffrey," Alyssa said pointing to a chair in the corner of the hotel lobby.

The three schoolmates walked over to where the older man sat, quietly reading the day's newspaper.

As he saw them approaching, Geoffrey folded the paper and removed his reading glasses. "Off to the marketplace?"

The friends nodded in unison.

"It should be a pleasant and informative time for you. Malika was kind to offer. Give her my regards."

As the young people turned toward the door, Geoffrey added, "Make sure you stay with your new friend and do not pursue any additional adventure. We have had enough missing persons and police for one trip." He smiled, shook the paper out, and resumed his reading.

Conrad elbowed Jay at the comment. "Hear that?"

Jay responded too quickly, "I heard it, I heard it." His mind was already occupied with thoughts of all the possibilities their outing might bring.

▲ ▲ ▲

Geoffrey laid aside the newspaper when his phone began buzzing in his pocket.

"Hello, Geoffrey here...Oh, hi ZZ. Thank you for getting back to me so quickly...Yes, we are in Luxor...It is a beautiful place...Yes, the meetings with the two men were peculiar. Any insight you could provide would be greatly appreciated...Really? That would be splendid...Are you sure you have time? Great. I look forward to seeing you tomorrow...Cheers!"

Geoffrey smiled as he put his phone down on the table beside him. Now maybe he would get some answers to the questions he had. The antiquities business was never dull. Nor was it ever predictable.

He failed to see Dimah quietly arranging magazines on a table behind him. The look on her face revealed more than she intended.

▲ ▲ ▲

Malika was waiting out front when the three arrived.

"I finished early," she said, her white teeth flashing against her dark face. "Why don't we begin at the place where the local market transitions to the tourist area? That way, you will have an easy walk back to the hotel when we are finished."

As the friends agreed, she added, "Besides, it will give you a quick look at how we live day to day here in Luxor. The local market is quite different from what you would normally see as a tourist."

"Conrad and I got a little flavor of that last night," Jay said, the play-by-play memory running through his mind. "It is quite different!"

Malika did not seem surprised by Jay's comment. She merely smiled and said, "It's settled then. This way please."

As they began making their way to the marketplace, Conrad couldn't help noticing how busy the restaurant was that evening. *That's odd. I wonder how Malika managed to get off work so early.*

▲ ▲ ▲

The man stared out the window at the growing darkness of the city. Now that contact had been made with the Americans, he felt more in control. For him, it was all about control—control of his organization, control of his clients, control of the situations that arose, and now control of the intruders. Yes, control was the key to success. His world was a fragile place. One slip and things would be set in motion...*things he could not control.*

He pulled his phone from the folds of his robes and moved away from the window. With a single touch of the screen, he placed the call.

"Good evening Mr. Chin. I was calling to inquire about your satisfaction with the piece...Delightful, I am glad you are pleased...Yes, the same bank account...Really? Very interesting...Yes, I do have additional pieces immediately available...Of course, it would be my pleasure to make a selection for you...I will phone you once arrangements are made on my end. We can then finalize the delivery details...Yes, you will have them this week, within a few days if you like...I understand. Yes, it will make for very efficient packaging with the other piece...Very good. I will speak to you soon...Goodbye."

The man ended the call.

An unexpected bonus. Nothing like a satisfied customer to increase one's business. And he did not even ask the price.

An evil glint flashed in his eyes. He would remain in control no matter the cost. The feeling of power was too addicting to allow any disturbances to his plans.

He pressed the button to make another call. He could hear the ringing as he once again stared out the window.

"Hello, Zamir. It is I. I need you to begin preparations on three more pieces. Let us send the three golden statues we *liberated* from the Malawi Museum...Yes, those are the ones. I will send the courier for them tomorrow afternoon about 4 pm. Prepare the instructions with the same route and transportation means...Do not worry about the risk! That is my concern! Yours is only to prepare the pieces, nothing more!"

The man took a breath to calm himself. "I will provide the drop-off information and contact in the morning so you can complete the instructions...No, I do not need to see the pieces before you package them. I am *sure* you will do an adequate job so your children will have a prosperous future. Good night."

He ended the call.

Zamir is beginning to fancy himself a professional smuggler. He even worries that we are using the same transportation arrangements twice in one week!

He smiled to himself. The point was well taken, but he had everything under control. There was little to worry about.

▲ ▲ ▲

Malika led them to the transition point from the local market to the tourist market. Now that there was no urgency of danger, the boys could see the details of the stark transition— dingy, faded facades gave way to neatly-painted storefronts, the narrow dirt road suddenly became a paved street, sparse bare bulbs were replaced by bright lights, carts drawn by donkeys and motorbikes belching blue smoke were displaced by sight-seeing carriages.

Conrad watched Jay closely. He could see the wheels turning in his friend's head. Malika saw the distracted look on Jay's face too.

"Is everything okay, Jay?" she asked. "You seem preoccupied."

"I was just thinking of our visit here last night, that's all," Jay answered.

"Were you able to walk through the local marketplace at all?" the girl asked, her expression one of practiced innocence.

Conrad injected himself into the conversation. "We went in for a block or two, then we came back this way." *Right before we went that way!* he thought to himself, glancing down the dark alley snaking off to the side.

When neither boy offered a further explanation, Malika said, "Let us go to more comfortable surroundings," and led them into the tourist section.

The visit to the marketplace that night was a pleasurable one for the friends. Malika pointed out details that the average tourist would miss. She graciously answered their questions as they walked. Alyssa and her were like two old friends within an hour, chatting gaily as they explored the contents of shop after shop.

Everything was going smoothly until they came to the place where Conrad and Jay had encountered the man with the scar and the tattoo. Then, the peacefulness began to unravel.

"Hey!" Jay remarked. "Where's the booth that was here last night?" He exchanged a glance with Conrad as he pointed to the empty spot in front of the spice shop. "It was right here!"

Malika's eyes narrowed with curiosity. "What booth?"

Then it all spilled out.

"Last night Conrad and I stopped at a booth right here! It had some realistic-looking artifacts on a big table. The vendor was talking to another man. He handed him a paper...Man! I forgot to tell Geoffrey about that!"

"What are you talking about, Jay?" Alyssa asked.

"The paper! The vendor handed Scarface a piece of paper. It looked like it had some hieroglyphs printed on it. I am sure that is important somehow, but I totally forgot about it until now."

"What happened next?" Malika asked so quickly that Conrad stared at her, wondering why she was so interested.

"The vendor reached under the table and pulled out a package, some object wrapped in linen or something. The guy who took it had a long scar down the side of his face. When he took the package, I saw that Aten-thing tattoo on his arm!"

Malika's eyes flashed briefly.

"That is when we followed him down to the local's marketplace," added Conrad, hoping to avoid a complete disclosure of the rest of the night's activities.

He shot Jay a look. For once, Jay paid attention and understood its meaning.

"Yeah, we followed him for a bit and then we turned back," Jay finished.

Malika listened silently. There seemed to be more that the two boys were not saying, but she did not press them further. Still, her mind had logged away Jay's account of the night before, word for word.

CHAPTER 10

As the three friends entered the hotel lobby, they found Geoffrey standing at the front desk talking to Dimah. When they approached the desk, the woman nodded in their direction and said to Geoffrey with a smile, "It looks like we will not be needing the police tonight."

Geoffrey turned and addressed his young charges, "I thought I would wait up for your return tonight." He looked directly at Jay as he added, "Just to make sure *all* of you returned safely. Dimah was kind enough to keep me company. We had a lovely chat about the present state of Egypt and her fabled antiquities. As it turns out, Dimah is quite an expert. She graduated from the American University in Cairo with a Masters Degree in Egyptology and Coptology."

"Coptology?" remarked Jay. "What does police work have to do with Egyptology?"

Dimah smiled. "I never thought of it like that. Egyptology is a lot like police work. We are always using clues to solve the mysteries of the past. But the word *coptology* is the study of the ethnic and religious background of the people who live in this part of the world. My studies concentrated on the historical Egyptian lifestyle that predated any of the modern religions. If you have heard the modern term *Pharaonism*, it is similar."

"That sounds like the study of pharaohs or something," Alyssa offered.

"Pharaonism is actually a way of looking at things where one identifies with the ways of the pharaohs," Dimah explained. "It is a form of nationalism, and even religious practice, where the nation and religion involved are those of ancient Egypt."

"What I found fascinating about all of this is that it may explain the Aten tattoos we have been seeing," Geoffrey added. "Dimah seems to think this is a very real possibility."

"Yes," Dimah agreed, "there have been studies conducted that indicate the ancient religions of Egypt have been kept alive over the centuries, although somewhat secretly. It is very possible that there is still the practice of a cult religion associated with the Heretic King, Akhenaten—the cult of Aten."

Jay looked knowingly at Conrad. "Cult of one, huh?"

Conrad just shook his head.

"Oh by the way, Mr. B," Jay added excitedly, "I forgot to tell you something important about last night! Right before the vendor handed Scarface that wrapped package, he gave him a sheet of paper. When Scarface looked at it, I saw it had those hieroglyph scribbles on it."

"Hieroglyphs?" asked Dimah, her eyes alert. "I am not sure that is possible."

"I'm pretty sure," answered Jay confidently. "It was full of the same type of marks you see all over the place around here."

"That is interesting, but doubtful," Dimah said. "The practice of communicating this way has not been in use for over 1,500 years. There are very few people in the world who can read and write in hieroglyphs. I know. I happen to be one of them."

Noticing the confused look on her face about the rest of Jay's remark, Geoffrey filled the woman in on the details of the night before.

"I see," she said. "I must say that this sounds like serious business. Perhaps you should focus on your field study work while you are here. It would be much safer."

The group of friends dispersed to go to their rooms for the evening. Dimah turned and went to the back office to make a covert phone call.

▲   ▲   ▲

The man sat down in his desk chair, considering what he had just learned during the brief phone conversation.

So, the intruders know more than we initially suspected. They have seen the exchange in the marketplace. They have seen the sacred mark and have associated it with this activity. And they have noted our means of communication.

He narrowed his eyes as he mentally processed the implications of this new information.

Certainly, there are ramifications which must now be considered...There are precautions that must be implemented...There are contingencies which must be formulated.

He stood once again and walked to the window, looking out over the now darkening city.

Our ancient ways have been preserved for thousands of years. Even the power of later pharaohs could not snuff it out. Now we are on the verge of regaining what was lost so many years ago...our ways of life made alive through the absolute power of a ruler...the means of preserving our nation made possible through our worship of the one god, Aten.

His eyes gleamed with the dream of what he was trying to bring to fruition.

This heritage, which has been kept alive by the faithful for many generations, passing from father to son, must be given back to the people. The small flame must be allowed to grow into a conflagration, one that will consume the falseness that has settled onto our land. Our position in the world must once again be preeminent.

He stood quietly for a moment pondering the gravity of it all. As another thought passed through his mind, he smiled at its irony.

The very heritage we seek to regain must be financed by selling pieces of this same heritage to others who could never understand.

He forced his mind back to the present.

I must keep a close watch on the intruders. I must ascertain their intentions. I must keep control.

He turned with a look of determined satisfaction on his face. He had ways to maintain control...ways that the intruders would find *most* unpleasant!

▲　▲　▲

Conrad was not sure what it was that awakened him that night. It fluttered on the edge of his subconscious mind a long time, causing him to toss and turn. When it forced itself to the surface, he found himself awake and staring at the ceiling. He listened to the quietness of the night. All seemed in order. After all, there was not a sound to be heard in the room other than the ubiquitous hum of the air conditioning unit. He rolled over, intent on returning to the land of sleep. Suddenly, he sat bolt upright in his bed!

"Jay!" he called in the dark. "Are you awake?"

There was no answer and no snoring. He fumbled with the light on the nightstand, groping until he found the switch. The stabbing brightness temporarily blinded him. Yet, he already knew the answer. Jay was gone!

Jay dropped down from the wall and crouched in the shadows. All was quiet in the temple courtyard. He stealthily crept across the open space until he was safely hidden among the great columns. There was no need of a light source, for the temple was lit in its too-perfect manner—the ancient stones carefully accented by modern electric flood lamps.

He quickly made his way across the well-worn stones that paved the Sun Court. Now, he could relax a little. There were plenty of columns and stone structures to mask his activities from the watchful eyes of patrolling guards. Onward he pushed, ever deeper into the ancient temple. Only one thing was on his mind...

What would the result of his experiment yield?

▲ ▲ ▲

"Come in."

Conrad entered Geoffrey's room. The older man's expression was a mixture of fatigue and concern.

"You're quite sure he is not on the premises?"

"When I saw his empty bed, I checked the bathroom and then ran down the hall to the vending machines. I peeked in the lobby, but no Jay. I even went out to the pool, just to make sure."

"Did he say anything tonight that would indicate where he might have gone?"

"No. He actually behaved quite well...for Jay."

Geoffrey rubbed his eyes. "Did you check with Alyssa? Perhaps she knows where he is."

"No, I didn't want to wake her."

"Yes, I suppose that would have caused her unnecessary concern."

Geoffrey paced the floor as he considered what to do. "I wonder if Dimah has seen him?"

"I thought of that, too. But if we ask her, she will want to call the police again. I figured the best thing to do was to awaken you."

"Very wise, but I'm afraid that if Jay does not return soon, we will have no alternative but to get the police involved...again."

"Maybe we should have them lock him up until we are ready to return to the States." Conrad's tone was just a little too serious.

▲　▲　▲

Jay entered the chamber and looked up. It was still there, hidden beside one of the many floodlights positioned in the stone recesses at the top of the wall. He smiled. Perhaps his experiment would work after all. He checked outside the doorway for any sign of approaching guards.

All clear. Now to business!

He carefully placed his foot into a small niche in the wall and balanced against the bricks on either side of the structure's corner. Once he was steady, he reached up and grabbed the device while pushing away from the wall. He landed with a grunt.

Pretty graceful, if I do say so myself.

He hastened back to the entrance for a final check for guards. He peered around the corner and listened.

The coast is clear. Now, let's see what we have.

Jay stepped back into the chamber and quickly cycled through the photos captured by the motion detector on the tiny camera. He scowled to himself.

Man! Nothing but guards checking the empty room! I thought for sure I would get a shot of Scarface and his friends!

A disappointed Jay immediately decided to continue with his experiment. He deleted the photos and reset the timer so it could only be activated after the temple complex was closed for the night. Carefully, he repeated his balancing act on the wall and placed the device back in its hiding place. Before he jumped down, he adjusted the angle of the stand for a clear view of the room.

Satisfied, he leapt to the floor and made his way out through the complex. As he dropped down the other side of the outer wall, he congratulated himself on another successful mission into enemy territory.

The two men who observed him leave congratulated themselves as well. Both had bosses who would be pleased with their observations.

CHAPTER 11

By the time Jay got back to the hotel, the sky had gained the almost imperceptible light that marked the beginning of another day. He slipped in the side door of the hotel and began his ascent to the fifth floor using the fire escape stairwell. He quietly unlocked the door and tiptoed into his room.

I hope I don't wake Conrad. He would have some choice words to say about my returning to the scene of the crime. Besides, I still have time for an hour of beauty rest before we have to meet downstairs.

As he shuffled to his bed, he could barely see in the dim light of the clock display on the nightstand. But what he saw was enough. Conrad was gone! He was busted!

At this revelation, Jay sat heavily on his bed and took a breath, "This is not what I need right now! Conrad and Alyssa already think I'm crazy. And Mr. B...he is not going to be a happy camper. Not at all!"

Jay resigned himself to the inevitable. He left the room and headed down the hall to Geoffrey's room.

▲ ▲ ▲

"I guess we had better call down to Dimah and have her phone the police," Geoffrey said tiredly. "The streets of

Luxor are no place to be wandering around in the middle of the night."

"And with Jay," Conrad added, "there's no guarantee he's even in Luxor!"

Geoffrey raised his eyebrows and was about to say something when there was a furtive knocking at the door.

Conrad opened the door to see Jay standing sheepishly in the hallway.

"I didn't know you guys were having a party or I would have come down sooner," Jay said, attempting to defuse the situation.

"In!" was all that Conrad said before closing the door a little too loudly.

"Jay..." an exasperated Geoffrey started.

Jay took the offensive. "Sorry, Mr. B. You know that experiment I mentioned yesterday? Well, I needed to check on it so I—"

"You didn't!" Geoffrey exclaimed.

"He did!" Conrad ran both hands through his hair in frustration.

"Jay, trespassing is an offense that *will* land you in a lot of trouble, not only here, but back home as well. Your parents would not be pleased to have to gain your release from an Egyptian jail. And I am personally responsible for your safety and well-being, to your parents and to your school." Geoffrey sat down on a chair. "I just don't understand why you persist in such things. Don't you understand how serious this is?"

Jay hung his head and exhaled, "Yeah, you're right. I shouldn't have gone over there tonight. It was a huge mistake."

"And just what was so important that you risked going to jail over it?" asked Conrad.

"Well," began Jay, "yesterday morning I was thinking about what we had seen the night before—how Scarface and his two friends went into that holy chamber place and how only Scarface came out. I just knew there was something going on that we couldn't see. So, I went over to the electronics store across the street and bought a small spy camera. You know, the kind that uses a motion detector to take pictures when you're not there? Anyway, while you walked up to the Pylon at the temple yesterday, I went back and installed the camera in the chamber."

Conrad and Geoffrey looked at each other in disbelief.

Jay continued, "My theory was that I could catch what those guys were doing in the room at night with the camera."

"And how did it work out?" asked an angry Conrad.

"I went back early this morning—about 4 am, I think—to check on the camera," Jay explained.

"And did you get any photos of the men turning into sacred scarab beetles and climbing up the walls?" asked Conrad sarcastically.

"Not exactly," Jay responded.

"What did you see, Jay?" Geoffrey asked.

"So far, all I got are some photos of guards checking the room at night," Jay answered.

"So far? So far, Jay?" Conrad said loudly. "So you are planning on going back? Is that what I'm hearing?"

"Well, I thought—" Jay began.

"Jay, no!" Geoffrey said forcefully. "You must not go back! You have been fortunate—twice, no less—that you have not been detected. There shall not be a third. Is this clear?"

"Yes," Jay said dejectedly. "But I just know something big is going on. I can feel it. Besides, as you said, nobody saw me."

▲ ▲ ▲

"So you only saw him running across the grounds and climbing over the wall?" the man asked his informant.

"Yes. It appeared he was coming from the Sun Court. What else he did in the temple, I do not know."

"Did you check for any signs of disturbance?" the man continued.

"I did. There were no signs of anything. I do not know what the young man was doing in the temple so late at night."

The man replied, "Very well."

"Perhaps he was just curious and wanted to look around when no one was there?" the informant stated hopefully.

"We do not have a place for curious people. What we do is hidden in the open so those who do not know to look will not see it. Curious people, on the other hand, could cause us great difficulties."

"What do you wish me to do?"

"Keep your eyes open for the intruders."

The man ended the call.

This is peculiar. I wonder what the young trespasser was looking for? Is it possible he suspects something? But how? We are always so careful. I will have to look into this further.

He looked at his watch.

Mr. Chin is an early riser. I will see where we will make the drop tomorrow.

He dialed the number. On the fourth ring, Chin answered.

"Hello, Mr. Chin. I wanted to inform you that we would be able to make your delivery tomorrow after business hours...The statue in front of the bank? Yes, I know it...Very well then, the courier will meet you there...Yes, I will have the bank wire you a deposit request...I am glad

you are pleased. Give my regards to your clients...
Goodbye."

He immediately dialed Zamir.

"Good morning...Yes, it is early, but such efforts pay our bills. How are you progressing with the packages? You cannot be late...Excellent. Now, the drop off address is Osman Digna Street. The Bank of Sudan. He will be met under the statue...Yes, this is correct. Finish the instructions paper and have everything ready by 4 pm today...By the way, Zamir, how is your family?"

The man smiled as he listened to the flustered professor on the other end of the line. He could almost feel the moisture from the man's palms coming through the phone. He ended the call. *Such fear is a good thing. It keeps everyone in line.*

He glanced at the calendar on his phone. *Only one more loose end to take care of today.*

▲ ▲ ▲

The group waited outside the hotel while the bellman hailed a taxi. As they loaded into the back of the small van, Geoffrey told the driver, "Valley of the Kings, please."

The man nodded, started the meter, and merged into the growing morning traffic.

"Today," Geoffrey began, "we will be visiting the KV55 tomb. As you remember, this tomb is known as the Amarna Cache because of what was discovered there. When Edward Ayrton entered the tomb, he found a puzzling assortment of seemingly unrelated items. A gilded wooden burial shrine for Queen Tiye—Akhenaten's mother. Jewelry belonging to Amenhotep III and his daughter. Calcite canopic burial jars originally belonging to Kiya, who was Akhenaten's secondary wife. Clay pharaonic seals for Amenhotep III and Tut. Even four so-called magical bricks from Akhenaten's tomb. And, of course, we had the mummy who was later identified as being the son of Amenhotep III and the father of Tut."

"Why 'Amarna Cache', Geoffrey?" asked Alyssa.

"For two reasons," answered Geoffrey. "First, it is obvious that the KV55 tomb was meant for someone else. It was unfinished and unpainted, both pointing to a hasty repurposing, as it were. Secondly, and even more obvious, all of the objects were somehow related to Akhenaten in Amarna, and appeared to have been moved from there sometime after his death. It is thought that since Queen Tiye had outlived her husband Amenhotep III, that Akhenaten brought her to live in Amarna, and subsequently buried her there."

"Sounds like a great mystery," stated Conrad.

"The real mystery is the identity of the KV55 mummy," Geoffrey stated. "He has the markings of having been a pharaoh who was hastily put in someone else's wood coffin and relocated. The canopic jars were modified, pointing to reuse. The convenient evidence suggested the mummy was Akhenaten, based on the four bricks, two of which bore his name. Even the initial DNA testing pointed to Akhenaten. It indicated the mummy was the son of Amenhotep III and Queen Tiye, and the father of Tut. But there are reported issues with the interpretations of the test, especially when the DNA of Tut's two mummified stillborn daughters is taken into account."

"It sounds like you have partially solved the mystery, Geoffrey," said Conrad.

"Well, I do believe that the KV55 mummy is really Smenkhkare, Akhenaten's brother," admitted Geoffrey. "But this just deepens the mystery. Where is the mummy of the Heretic King?"

CHAPTER 12

The taxi crossed the bridge over the Nile and continued to travel north along the river. After about 10 minutes, the van turned westward once again.

"Here we are," noted Geoffrey. "We are entering the Valley of the Kings."

His words hung like electrified air among the friends. They were entering the fabled necropolis of the Kings of Egypt!

"Why did the pharaohs and queens choose to be buried here?" asked Jay. "Back in the day, this would have been a pretty big journey. They needed to swim across the Nile and then tote everything up over the hills and down into the valley. Seems like a lot of extra work to me."

"Excellent question," Geoffrey answered. "There is great significance to this location. In ancient times, this necropolis, or burial ground area, was known as Western Thebes. It is near the religious center of worship at the temples in Luxor, which was known as Eastern Thebes."

He stopped to see if everyone was listening before he continued. "The Egyptians were keen on the idea of an afterlife—a place they called the 'Field of Reeds'. They believed that when they died, they had to travel all night through the underworld to get to this Field of Reeds.

Furthermore, they thought the sun entered the underworld on the west side of the Nile. And they believed it would escort the dead through this underworld to the afterlife. As you will see shortly, the Valley of the Kings was the perfect place for burial as the sun seems to set in the very cliffs behind the valley."

After the taxi stopped and Geoffrey paid the fare, he continued his explanation. "Another reason this was a perfect place for the tombs is that it could be easily guarded. The only way in is through these narrow channels in the cliffs."

"I would have fired the guards," said Jay, looking around. "They didn't do such a great job of guarding the tombs. Most of them have been stripped clean."

Geoffrey chuckled at the young man's observation. "This is true, Jay. However, you must remember that the current pharaoh was only concerned with the tombs of his family. As dynasties came and went, so did their diligence over the tombs of the past."

"Maybe there are still a few for us to find," Jay said optimistically. "I wouldn't mind finding Akhenaten's tomb and getting a share in his treasure."

"Here we go again," Conrad groaned. "You probably won't stay out of prison long enough to find anything!"

"Okay, you guys," interjected Alyssa. "Let's get back to reality."

The group began the long decent to the valley floor. All around them, they could see dark openings scarring the gray-brown earth. The cliffs of the valley surrounded them on every side, silently testifying to the solemn end of the valley's inhabitants.

"Many people think the Valley of the Kings is just a single valley," stated Geoffrey as he continued teaching, "but this is not the case. There are actually two wadis, or ravines—the main eastern branch where we are, and the larger western branch just over those cliffs there." He pointed to their left as they walked. "Most of the tombs we know of are here in the eastern portion. We know of only a few pharaohs buried in the western wadi."

"Could there be more to find in the western branch?" asked Alyssa.

"Likely," answered the older man. "There could also be additional tombs right under your feet."

Suddenly, Jay's eyes held the familiar glimmer of unbounded possibilities. He began paying close attention to where he was walking.

Geoffrey continued, "For instance, King Tut's tomb remained hidden for centuries because it was covered with the rubble of other tombs that had been built above it." He looked about wistfully. "This valley has not yet given up all of her secrets."

Alyssa asked another question, "How many tombs have they discovered so far?"

"Sixty-three," Geoffrey answered. "But with Jay here, who knows, perhaps we will find another?"

"Don't encourage him," Conrad groaned. "He might decide to take a midnight run out here next."

As they made their way to the bottom of the long path, they did not see the man following them. A man in robes!

▲　▲　▲

The ancient fax machine began to ring. The man walked over to the back room of the mud brick hut where it sat on an equally old table. The machine connected to the sender with a series of noises that reminded the man of the braying of his broken-down donkey. He smiled at the thought. He snatched the single sheet from the whirring machine and studied the strange marks on the paper.

Another shipment. I am to meet the courier at the palm tree grove along the shore and transport him across the border to Sudan.

His mood improved with this news. He liked this kind of work on the big lake better than fishing.

▲   ▲   ▲

Geoffrey showed his special pass to the security guard. The guard studied it closely, comparing the photo with Geoffrey's face. Satisfied, he said, "Follow me, please," and led the group to the entrance of KV55. He produced a series of keys on a large ring and sorted through them until he found the correct one. He inserted the key and the lock surrendered. He pulled open the gate and led them to a steel door. The key ring routine was repeated. The guard pulled the door open, revealing a long, dark passageway. Stuffy air, the odor a curious combination of earth and old, hit their faces as they stood at the entrance. The guard stepped in and switched on the lights, illuminating the recesses beyond.

"Please be careful not to disturb anything," he said politely. "I will await your return to the land of the living." He turned away, grinning at his own cleverness.

Jay raised an eyebrow at his remark. "Land of the living? Where are we going? The land of the dead?"

"I guess we will know when we see who is down there," teased Conrad, sensing Jay's unease. "Perhaps Akhenaten will meet us and give us a personal tour."

"Conrad! Stop!" Alyssa frowned. "You're weirding me out."

"Alright, class," interrupted Geoffrey. "Shall we?" He gestured for the others to lead.

"After you, Mr. B," Jay invited a little nervously.

Geoffrey turned and led the group down into the tomb.

None of them noticed that their robed follower had stopped and was standing across the central pathway, waiting for their return.

▲ ▲ ▲

All along the lengthy corridor were signs of water damage and general disrepair.

"As you can see," said Geoffrey, "this tomb was never finished. It became a convenient storage place for the shipment from Amarna."

"Kind of like a 'mummy's warehouse'," quipped Jay.

"Yes, but the real mummy's warehouse, as you call it, is KV35, which we will be visiting tomorrow," Geoffrey answered.

As they walked deeper down the shaft, Geoffrey continued. "This tomb was in poor condition when it was discovered. Not only was there debris everywhere down the entry shaft, but the burial room showed signs of cave-ins."

He led them into the burial chamber. "You will note that there is nothing on the walls, just a whitish plaster. Over here, you can see where large chunks of the ceiling have fallen in, mostly due to water seepage from above. There had been so much water over the centuries that all of the wooden items in the tomb had rotted."

"Wow, Mr. B, this is a dingy and creepy place to bury a great pharaoh," observed Jay.

"Yeah," agreed Alyssa. "Why would they do that?"

"Convenience?" Conrad raised his brows.

"Yes," answered Geoffrey. "This was likely meant as only a temporary stopover for the mummy, with a more formal place to be prepared later. Then, it looks as though it was forgotten."

"That is amazing!" exclaimed Jay. "How could you forget a pharaoh's mummy?"

"I have a theory," offered Geoffrey modestly. "I believe that King Tut brought each of his family members back from their tombs in Amarna to be buried properly here. In the midst of this, he died unexpectedly and some of this work was left undone. Subsequent pharaohs pitched in a little in an effort to protect the mummies from being desecrated, but in the end, it seems that the effort failed."

"That is quite a theory, Mr. B," Jay said amazedly. "Maybe Tut was able to get Akhenaten and Nefertiti buried before he died."

"That would explain why they've never been found." Conrad ran a pensive hand over the plastered wall.

Alyssa had been quiet during most of the discussion. Now, she asked a question. "Geoffrey, why was Tut so determined to bring those people, I mean, mummies back from Amarna?"

"Tut grew up there and lived there, most likely until he became pharaoh, and perhaps for a short time afterward," said Geoffrey. "So he knew them all. They were his family."

"That makes sense," Alyssa said with a look of understanding.

"But I think it was more than that," Geoffrey added. "Tut saw the political fallout caused by the actions of the Heretic King. He probably realized that continuing the worship of Aten was not possible and would lead to his ruin. I suspect that Nefertiti preceded him as pharaoh and was the one who began the move back to traditional worship. The mysterious Smenkhkare was likely also involved."

"So, Tut wanted to save the family name?" pondered Alyssa.

"More than that," Geoffrey stated solemnly, "I think Tut wanted to save those who had been entombed at Amarna from the sure desecration that was to come."

The group emerged from the tomb into the bright sunlight. They were engrossed with watching the guard lock the tomb and escort them a short distance up the pathway. They did not see the man in the robes who studied them from across the path. He, however, saw them.

CHAPTER 13

"Are you serious?" Jay exclaimed. "That is *very* cool, Mr. B. You must have really good friends here in Egypt."

The other two schoolmates shared Jay's enthusiasm over Geoffrey's announcement that they would be allowed to enter Tut's tomb. It had not occurred to them that this was even possible. Since the opening of the replica tomb, few had been allowed to see the original.

"What is an archeological field trip without a visit to the tomb of the famous boy-king?" asked the beaming antiquities dealer. "I have a long association with many in the archeological community here. I merely made a few inquiries, and here we are."

The security guard enjoined them once again, "Please do not touch anything or take photographs. This is one of the most famous archeological treasures of Egypt. It must be preserved at any cost."

He opened the heavy steel doors for them. "I will await you—"

"We know," Jay said to the man, interrupting him. "You will await our return to the land of the living."

The guard turned with a laugh, delighted that the boy had remembered his words from before.

The robed man watched all of this with amused detachment.

Geoffrey Barnsworth must have some powerful friends.

▲ ▲ ▲

"Oh, Geoffrey, this is fantastic!" Alyssa was beside herself. "I've seen photos but being here gives me goose bumps! It's SO amazing how some paint on the walls can make such a difference compared to the other tomb."

"Yes, we only saw the first step in decorating a tomb in KV55—the white plaster on the wall," said Geoffrey. "This tomb started the same way, but they followed through with detailed drawings on the walls, then the precise bas-relief carvings, and finally painting the entire scene in the six basic colors of Egypt."

"It is spectacular!" agreed an equally excited Conrad. "I have seen displays at the British Museum, but they cannot compare to the real thing. Just think, three-thousand years ago this was a fresh paint job!"

"I am glad you approve," laughed Geoffrey. "What do you think about it, Jay? You seem a bit quiet."

"It's great, Mr. B," Jay agreed. "I was just thinking about how much more spectacular Akhenaten's tomb would be."

"You were just thinking about how much treasure Akhenaten's tomb would hold," barbed Conrad.

"Well," Jay said seriously, "as a major pharaoh, his tomb would be larger."

"Unless it was robbed," Conrad noted.

"Even Tut's tomb was broken into," Geoffrey informed them. "Twice, actually. But it was discovered and resealed both times. No one knows how much the looters made off with. Even so, this was the most intact tomb ever found."

"It was probably the mummy's curse that kept this place safe," Conrad said, trying to get Jay going.

"What curse are you talking about, Conrad?" Jay asked seriously. "You know how I feel about curses."

"It is an old wives' tale without substance," Geoffrey soothed. "For many years, people believed it. It made a good storyline for some 1950's B-grade horror movies, but that was about it."

"So it wasn't true?" Jay asked, glancing at Conrad with suspicion.

"No. Statistically the number of deaths of people involved with this tomb was no higher than the norm," Geoffrey assured. "Each one just received more press, and that spun the perception of there being a real curse completely out of control."

"Whew! I'm glad to hear that, Mr. B!" a relieved Jay exclaimed. "Curses can ruin your day!"

"Before, you were wondering about Nefertiti's whereabouts," Geoffrey said, changing the subject. "It is thought that she is right over there, behind those walls." He pointed to the two ornately painted walls making up the back of the burial chamber.

"Is that where they used the ground-penetrating radar?" asked Alyssa.

Geoffrey nodded. "Yes it is. The results seem to indicate there are additional chambers behind those walls."

Conrad jumped in, "I saw that TV special. It is pretty convincing."

"It has been discovered," the older man continued, "that there was some repurposing of items here for Tut as well. For instance, the golden burial mask he is so famous for seems to have been made for a woman. The beard was added later, and the ears changed out. Also the original cartouche, or name tag, has been modified from some else's name to his."

Geoffrey stared at the walls in question and continued, "That would also explain why the young king was somewhat crammed in the front rooms of this tomb after he died. His own tomb, KV 23, was not yet completed and they were required to bury him within the prescribed period of time. It would be poetic justice for Tut to be buried here in Nefertiti's tomb if he had indeed moved her from Amarna." Geoffrey smiled as he continued, "It would also be an archeologist's dream to find her. In any case, we will know soon enough if she is here."

"I want to know where Akhenaten is buried," a determined Jay stated. "I don't think they will let us dig in here for Nefertiti. Our only chance of finding anyone is to find him."

Conrad commented, "Us and a million others who are looking."

Jay didn't hear Conrad. His mind was slowly putting together some very odd-looking pieces of a puzzle.

▲ ▲ ▲

"How did you like the tomb, young man?" the guard asked Jay when the group came back to the surface. "It is something that most will never experience."

"I thought it was a super place to visit," Jay answered, "but I like it up here in—"

"The land of the living," they both said in unison.

The guard chuckled and locked the entrance behind them.

"I tell you," he said as he checked the lock a final time, "it was not always so easy to laugh about what I said." The guard grew serious. "My family has guarded these tombs for four generations. My great-grandfather used to tell tales about the land of the dead below in these tombs. Tales of noises, strange lights, incense, and chanting. It gave me a scare as a young boy." He smiled and shrugged his shoulders. "But here I am."

"Have you ever witnessed anything like that?" a skeptical Conrad asked.

"Only once," the man answered solemnly. "It was about 15 years ago. I was working the night shift alone. Part of my job was to walk around and check the tombs."

"I don't think I'd like that job!" Jay said emphatically, his curls dancing as he shook his head. "I would have the willies all the time."

"I don't know what it is that you call 'the willies', but I can tell you that many nights I was afraid. But I had a young family to support and a tradition to uphold, so I did it," the guard continued soberly. "Anyway, I came to what is called KV5—the largest of the tombs in the valley. I heard what I could only describe as a ghostly chant that echoed out of the main chamber from below. I ran very fast all the way out of the valley."

"What was it?" a puzzled Jay asked.

"I do not know," the man answered. "The next day my father and I came to investigate. We searched the tomb, but found nothing except an odd smell...like incense. Anyway, that was the only time."

Jay looked wide-eyed at Conrad who only shrugged.

"I hope you enjoy your stay in my country," the guard said as they thanked him for his assistance. "There is much to see and much to discover."

The group began their ascent up the winding drive leading from the tombs.

"Geoffrey Barnsworth," a voice called from behind them.

They turned to face a distinguished-looking man dressed in robes.

CHAPTER 14

"ZZ! How are you?" Geoffrey stepped toward the man and shook his hand.

"I am well, my friend," the man answered. "It has been too long since we have pondered the great mysteries of ancient Egypt together."

The three schoolmates stood with astonished looks on their faces. The man speaking with Geoffrey was of local descent. He wore the traditional clothes of a well-to-do Egyptian man with flowing robes of expensive fabrics. He wore them with an aura of power and purpose. His dark hair was flecked with grey and closely cropped, as was his beard. His face was accented by a pleasant smile, flashing easily as he spoke. He carried himself with the confident air of a man well acquainted with the twists and turns of life. In all, he struck the schoolmates as the type of man Geoffrey would call his friend.

Geoffrey pulled himself from the pleasantries to make introductions. "ZZ, these are my three young archeologists-in-training—Alyssa, Conrad, and Jay."

The man bowed graciously. "Zaid Zakiya at your service. It is a great pleasure to meet the friends of my most distinguished colleague. And, as Geoffrey has already indicated, you may refer to me as ZZ."

The friends exchanged greetings with the smiling man. His mannerisms were pleasant and sincere, a welcome change from the meetings of the previous day.

"So, ZZ, what brings you out here?" asked Geoffrey. "I thought we were to meet you at the hotel this afternoon."

"Yes, well, my schedule changed, and as I was eager to see my good friend, I made inquiries at the hotel. I discovered that you had left earlier for the Valley of the Kings. Since I knew your penchant for dark and dusty tombs, Geoffrey, I decided to take the chance of catching you out here. Besides, it is not every day that I get to see a legend such as you practicing his craft."

Geoffrey chuckled. "While I do not consider myself to be a legend, I do appreciate the compliment. And, I am glad that you could join us out here today among the real legends."

"I see you have explored KV55 and KV62. You are undoubtedly interested in the family heritage of the famous King Tut."

The friends looked at each other in amazement at the man's ability to ascertain the truth behind their visit today.

Seeing their reaction, Geoffrey jumped in, "ZZ is an expert in ancient Egyptian history. His father was a well-known archeologist with the Egyptian Museum in Cairo. ZZ learned firsthand at his side."

"Yes," ZZ added, thinking fondly of the memories. "My father was very good at what he did. He truly loved our Egyptian heritage and all it had contributed to the world. He wanted our people to understand its significance. He was involved in many site restorations, including the move of the Abu Simbel Temple Complex to its present location when the Aswan High Dam was constructed. He, too, was interested in sorting out the lineage of Tut. I am sure that you have seen by now that this is no simple task."

The schoolmates nodded.

"It is confusing with all of the mummies and missing people," Jay added. "But I think we're catching on. Now all we need to do is find Akhenaten, and then we can go home with an 'A' on our field trip grade card."

ZZ laughed heartily at Jay's comment. "I see that Geoffrey has infused you with both his knowledge *and* his zeal for such tasks. I only wish it were that easy. This is a mystery that has puzzled the sharpest minds in archeology for over a century." Not wishing to dampen their enthusiasm, he added, "But with Geoffrey and yourselves involved, it is not far from the realm of possibility."

The three friends beamed at the compliment.

The man turned to his friend. "You see, I have followed the exploits of you and your young friends since we last spoke. Pirate treasure in America and Nazi gold in Germany...Not bad, for a mere antiquities dealer and his young cohorts, eh? So why not a missing mummy in Egypt? I take it you believe it is possible to find the tomb of one of our missing pharaohs...Nefertiti or Akhenaten, perhaps?"

Now it was Geoffrey's turn to be astonished. "Why, yes. Yes I do...Yes *we* do. But how did you guess?"

ZZ smiled. "You forget, my good friend, that I, too, am enamored with such things. It is a love born from the many hours I spent with my father as he dug and probed the sands of Egypt. I have often thought of the thrills such discoveries would bring. To hold the articles of our great past civilization and to contemplate their significance..."

After a few seconds of silence, the man shook himself back to the present. "Please forgive me. These are very strong feelings. This is undoubtedly why Geoffrey and I have become such close friends over the years. We share the same bond with the past."

"So, are you an archeologist, Mr. Zakiya?" asked Alyssa.

"Please, ZZ."

"Oh, sorry...ZZ," she said shyly. "Did you follow in your father's footsteps?"

"The answer to that is *yes* and *no*," the man answered. "Yes, because I have dabbled in the study and practice of my father's vocation—his contribution to our nation, really. And no, because I realized early on that there are other, more significant ways to impact the future of Egypt."

"ZZ owns an import/export business in Cairo," Geoffrey explained.

"It is really just a shipping company," said ZZ humbly. "I have been honored to see it grow and become significant."

"Significant is the key word," added Geoffrey with a smile. "It is the second largest shipping company in Egypt, and ZZ is well known throughout North Africa."

"Shall we leave the pharaohs to the mysteries of Egypt and have some lunch?" ZZ asked. "I have my car waiting above, and it would be my pleasure to treat you to some authentic Egyptian food in one of the best restaurants in Luxor."

"That sounds great, ZZ!" Jay said excitedly. "Walking in the footsteps of the pharaohs gives me an appetite!"

The group chuckled in agreement with Jay's sentiments as they made their way up the final grade out of the valley.

"Would you mind terribly if we stopped at the hotel first so we could freshen up," Geoffrey asked his old friend. "It has been a rather hot day in the valley. I'm afraid that my friends and I have not yet acclimated to your weather."

Conrad commented from the back of the group, "Thank you, Geoffrey! I think my roommate could use a shower!"

"Hey, watch it," said Jay good-naturedly. "I will have you know I'm wearing the best in antiperspirant technology in addition to the latest in super-wicking fabric."

"Better report a technological failure," was the quick reply from Conrad. "You stink."

"Boys, boys!" Alyssa interrupted. "That is not proper conversation in front of a lady."

"Or our guest," added Geoffrey, arching his eyebrows for emphasis.

"It's okay, Geoffrey," laughed ZZ. "I remember being their age once. It is not a problem to stop by your hotel first."

ZZ's car was really a large, black SUV with darkly tinted windows. Two burly men wearing sunglasses opened the doors and efficiently prepared to depart. Their expensive suits worn over black silk crew neck shirts advertised loudly that they were bodyguards. So did their discreetly concealed weapons.

CHAPTER 15

"Mr. Barnsworth!" the man at the front desk hailed as Geoffrey entered the lobby with the others. "You have a message."

"Oh. Thank you," Geoffrey replied as he walked over and took the slip of paper from the man. He put on his reading glasses and read the note. "Oh, dear. This does not bode well for us."

"What is it, Geoffrey?" Alyssa asked for the group.

Geoffrey replied, "Some bad news, I'm afraid. It seems one of the guards at the temple saw a young man bearing a striking resemblance to Jay on the Luxor Temple wall early this morning. Our friend, Jafar Kazim, the Director of Temple Complexes would like me to phone him about this report."

"Oops."

Conrad looked at Jay. "So much for not being seen."

"Well, I didn't see anybody," Jay answered defensively.

Geoffrey walked to the chairs in the corner of the lobby to make the call. Sitting down, he pulled the Director's card from his wallet. After a long breath to calm his heart, he dialed the private number on the card. On the third ring, Jafar answered.

"Hello, Jafar? This is Geoffrey Barnsworth returning your call."

▲ ▲ ▲

In a few minutes, Geoffrey ended the call and sat contemplating the conversation.

"What did he say?" asked Jay nervously, thoughts of prison cells dancing in his head.

"Probably that he is having you deported for trespassing on a sacred Egyptian temple site," commented Conrad.

Geoffrey slipped his phone into his pocket. "He wanted to confirm that it was you who had been seen...I told him that he was correct, that you had indeed been on the wall."

"I'm dead!" Jay despaired, plopping down in the chair next to Geoffrey. "They are going to put me in jail! I'll never see the light of day until I'm an old man!"

Geoffrey's mouth twitched as he stifled a small smile and continued. "Jafar said he was initially very surprised that someone such as yourself would think to do such a thing. Then, he told me something quite surprising. He said he had thought it over, carefully considering all sides of the matter. In the end, he said he could see how someone your age might become so overawed by such a magnificent historical site to want to climb the wall and view it for yourself at night."

"That's all?" asked Conrad incredulously.

"Sounds like maybe he did the same thing many years ago himself," concluded Alyssa. "And he has a guilty conscience."

"Perhaps," Geoffrey considered. "In any case, evidently the guard did not see any of Jay's other shenanigans. Only him atop the wall."

"Whew!" Jay exclaimed. "That was too close for comfort! I can tell you one thing for sure, Mr. B, my trespassing days are *o-ver*!"

"I believe that Jafar anticipated they would be," said Geoffrey. "He told me to ask you not to persist in such things, and he reiterated that the site was very important and must be protected from harm."

"On the whole, I'd say you were lucky, Jay," stated Conrad. "I don't think I'd cross Mr. Kazim on this by messing up again while we're in town. As it is, he is likely upset with you."

"I should have thought so myself," said Geoffrey, "except Jafar once again asked us to come as his guests to the Karnak Temple before we depart Egypt."

"I guess that's a good sign," Jay said. "He could have invited everyone but me for the tour."

"Yes, well, ZZ is waiting for us outside with the engine running," Geoffrey reminded them. "So, let us endeavor to be down here in 15 minutes or less."

As the elevator opened on the fifth floor, everyone scurried off to their rooms.

▲ ▲ ▲

"Tell me, Geoffrey," said ZZ after they had ordered their food, "What was the purpose of Abu al-Hasan's visit?"

"I phoned him to ask him about a strange tattoo we had seen twice in two days," said Geoffrey as he stirred some cream into his tea. "It looks to be the same symbol as one finds on many of the bas-reliefs dealing with Akhenaten—the sun disk god with the rays ending in hands."

"Aten," ZZ said matter-of-factly.

"Yes, Aten," Geoffrey confirmed.

"I saw it first when we hired a boat on Lake Nasser," Alyssa chimed in. "Jay wanted to go out and look for Nile crocodiles." She glanced in Jay's direction. "The captain of the boat—"

"The Chief," Jay interrupted.

"Yes, *the Chief*," Alyssa affirmed. "He had the tattoo on the inside of his forearm. I'll never forget it."

"And then Conrad and I saw the same tattoo on the arm of another guy in the Luxor marketplace," Jay added. "We—"

Conrad interrupted this time, "We were looking at some really realistic artifacts and another man at the booth had the same tattoo on the inside of his forearm."

"That is interesting," said ZZ as he rubbed his beard thoughtfully. He turned to Geoffrey and asked, "And what did Abu say about it?"

"He said he was not surprised, as there had been a growing interest in what he called the Aten cult," Geoffrey answered. "He downplayed it as insignificant."

"Yes," Jay posited, "it was like there was a whole lot more about this Aten cult tattoo thing than he was telling us."

"Do you know Abu?" Geoffrey asked his friend. "I am no more than an acquaintance of his. I first met him about ten years ago at a conference. I then saw him again about four years ago when he helped me clean up some paperwork issues for a client. I know he works somewhere in the Ministry of the Interior. Beyond this, I do not know him. As Jay said, something seemed odd about what he said and what he did not say."

"I know Abu and I know of him," ZZ stated as he sipped a cup of hot tea. "Yes, he is in the Interior Ministry. He deals with security issues, especially the pervasive smuggling problem that has plagued my country for millennia."

"Smuggling? Hey, I—ouch!" Jay covered his ribs from further attacks.

ZZ looked over at the boys but did not say anything.

"Uh, what Jay was going to say," smoothed Geoffrey, "is we guessed the tattoo might have been associated with smuggling in some fashion or other. An outlandish idea, I know, but it seemed somehow correct."

"As I was about to say," ZZ continued with a hint of irritation, "Abu has his enemies. There have been persistent rumors of him playing on both sides of the fence."

"You mean he polices smuggling *and* he participates in it?" asked Conrad.

"That is the rumor, yes," ZZ answered.

"Hmm," Geoffrey said thoughtfully, "that might explain his warning."

"His warning?" ZZ looked quizzically at his friend.

"Yes. Abu warned us to mind our own business, or we could find ourselves in trouble. He said that Egypt was not the same as it once was, and that there are people dedicated to smuggling...Dangerous people, I would presume."

"What he said about smuggling is true," ZZ said in a serious tone. "But to warn you when you hadn't done anything pertaining to *not minding* your business, that is odd."

"Do you think the tattoo is tied to smuggling?" Jay asked, his mind focusing like a laser beam on the idea.

"Jay!" Alyssa said shaking her head, "Please stop talking about smuggling. You are imagining things."

"Perhaps," ZZ said purposefully. "I have heard of the religion of Aten having a resurgence among my people. It is possible that someone has hijacked the symbol with evil intent."

"And Abu?" Geoffrey asked. "What is your advice?"

"I would be careful around the man," ZZ said sincerely. "Especially since he has given you this warning."

The courier entered the office precisely at four in the afternoon. Zamir was performing a final inspection of his packaging effort. He smiled slightly, inwardly pleased at his handiwork. The package looked like something a workman would be carrying, exactly as it should. No one would suspect the priceless relics of Egypt contained within the windings. He looked one final time at the sheet of paper, interpreting the hieroglyphs to make sure the instructions were clear and accurate. When he was confident all was in order, he handed the sheet to the man. Once the paper was secured in the man's galabeya, Zamir handed him the package. The man turned and was gone.

My family is well and will continue to be. But the day is coming when I will turn the tables and end this time of being a hostage of fear.

CHAPTER 16

The waiter began to deliver food as the hungry diners looked on.

"First, we will enjoy two very common dishes—Dukka, which is a dip made from herbs, nuts, and spices," ZZ informed, "and Ful Medames, which consists of a lava bean paste mixed with oil, garlic, and lemon juice."

He passed the plate of Egyptian baladi bread. "Tear off pieces of this bread and dip it into the dishes."

"This is good!" exclaimed Jay as he sampled both.

"This dish," said ZZ as he pointed to the Ful Medames, "dates back to the time of the pharaohs...the Twelfth Dynasty. It means 'buried', which is how the dish was first made—by burying the pot in hot ashes and cooking it."

"I really like this," Alyssa said pointing to the other dish.

"Dukka is delicious. Each family has its own secret recipe that is passed down for generations," said ZZ. "My mother made the absolute best. But this is good, as well."

Next, the waiter brought out individual bowls of Kushari and set them before each person.

"This looks like pasta," observed Conrad as he sampled the dish. "But it sure doesn't taste like spaghetti."

"Kushari is arguably the Egyptian national dish," ZZ said with a smile. "The interesting part of it, though, is that it is a British contribution from over a century ago. We have improved upon it by adding rice, caramelized onions, and chickpeas to the pasta and tomato sauce."

"Wonderful," Jay said with his mouth full.

Once the dishes were collected, the waiter delivered a large platter of fragrant meat pies and set it in the center of the table.

ZZ continued, "This is Hawawshi. As you can see, it is a meat pie. However, as you taste it you will notice it is specially seasoned and prepared. This was one of my father's favorite foods. While we ate mainly vegetables, when we had meat, many times it was this dish."

"This is remarkable," Geoffrey commented. "So simple, yet so elegant on the palette."

The meal they enjoyed together was filled with banter accented by frequent bouts of laughter as ZZ told stories of his life growing up in Egypt. Even Jay commented that his exploits were minor compared to some of ZZ's.

"And here we have a traditional dessert," announced ZZ as the waiter rolled the dessert cart to the table. "It is called Konafah."

"It looks like little pie slices," observed Jay as he prepared to attack the dessert item on his plate.

"It is actually a pastry made from cooked noodles wrapped around a center of whipped cream. Here, they serve it with pomegranate syrup drizzled on top." ZZ smiled as he watched Jay. "Does it meet your approval?"

"Yes!" was all Jay could say between bites.

As the waiter brought out fresh hot tea, Jay sat back in his seat contentedly, sipping on his steaming cup. "That sure beats what they serve us in the cafeteria at school! It will be hard to go back."

"I never noticed your disdain for any food set before you," Conrad commented. "Usually, we have to stand back to avoid personal harm." Jay's love of a good meal was well known among his friends.

"I have to keep up my energy," Jay said in a serious tone. "One never knows what might be coming just around the corner."

The truth of Jay's words would soon be borne out.

▲   ▲   ▲

"Why don't we take a walk down to the river," ZZ suggested as they left the restaurant. "It has cooled off and the company is most pleasant."

"I would like that," Alyssa answered. "I've only seen the Nile through the window of a train or car and not up close."

"Then you are in for a treat," her host said with a smile. "There is a walkway along the river where you can observe its workings all you like."

The group made their way the few blocks to the river, discreetly shadowed by the two bodyguards. A concrete walkway overlooked the river. Benches were scattered along its length, perfectly positioned in the shade of trees.

"The Nile River has always been the center of Egyptian life," ZZ informed the group. "It winds its way northward from Sudan to a large delta before dumping into the Mediterranean Ocean. The fertile ground on either side of the river is the line of demarcation between the large expanses of desert to the east and west. If it were not for this river, there really would be no Egypt."

Everyone sat in contemplative silence, watching the various vessels ply up and down the river. Jay nudged Conrad as a speedboat roared by close to the shore. Conrad shook his head 'no' to discourage any remarks by his friend of their encounter with a similar boat.

"We know about Aten and Amun, the sun deities. Did the ancient Egyptians have any Nile River gods?" asked Alyssa.

"They did," answered ZZ. "His name was Hapi. He was associated with fertility and water. As you know, the people relied on the river for survival. They were acutely aware of the annual cycles of the river, such as the floods. Of course, they had the deposit of silt during the flood season that provided the rich soil for crops. But they also had an elaborate system of irrigation canals to water the crops as they grew. We do not get much rain."

"I was wondering about that," said Jay. "A once-a-year watering would not be enough under this hot sun."

"This is true," said ZZ. "Water was the main provision of the river. But there were others as well that most people do not think of."

"Right now, I'm not thinking of any others," Jay admitted.

ZZ laughed. "What about transportation? The river has always made it possible to move building materials from their source to where they were needed. Limestone, for instance, came from quarries that could be many miles from the building projects the pharaohs were conducting. Even the straw to make bricks had to be moved to the building sites, along with water. The Nile made this possible."

"I never really appreciated that before," said Conrad. "Overland routes through the desert would have been difficult."

"There were some routes through the desert," ZZ said, "but the river was the superhighway of the day."

"Speaking of superhighways, what about the speedbo— Ow!" said Jay as Conrad applied the elbow.

ZZ looked over at Jay and Conrad, a light frown crossing his face. "I'm sorry, Jay. I didn't hear what you were trying to say."

"Oh, it was nothing," Jay said evasively. "Just one of those stray thoughts."

"Yes," said ZZ with a knowing look, "you seem to have these *stray thoughts* regularly."

"That's for sure," Alyssa added with a smile. "Too often."

"I can think of another important item related to the Nile," Geoffrey said as he steered the conversation back to the subject.

The three schoolmates looked at their friend expectantly.

"Papyrus," Geoffrey stated. "Egyptian paper."

"Yeah," said Jay as he moved out of the range of Conrad's elbow. "That is what they wrote their hieroglyphs on. And we know all about them, don't we?"

ZZ raised his eyebrow at Jay's last remark.

"What Jay is saying, ZZ," explained Geoffrey, "is we have theorized that any smuggling group could evade electronic surveillance by using sheets of paper containing hieroglyphs to communicate."

"That's right," Jay added. "And nobody could read them if the messages were intercepted."

"That is an interesting idea," ZZ agreed. "Perhaps we will read about just such a thing in a mystery book sometime. But for now, it is not practical. It takes years of study to understand the hieroglyph language. Surely you know this, Geoffrey?"

"Yes, I suppose you are right," Geoffrey said reluctantly. "Still, it was an interesting theory."

ZZ pulled his phone from a pocket within his robes so he could check the time. "I am sorry to say our pleasant visit must come to an end for now. I have a business meeting this evening in Luxor. Shall we go back to my vehicle so I may drop you at your hotel?"

As they walked back from the river, Jay had another stray thought. *I need to find a way to check my camera in the morning.*

Chapter 17

The SUV wound its way through the late afternoon Luxor traffic. When it pulled up in front of the hotel, Geoffrey and his young friends unloaded. The schoolmates said their goodbyes to ZZ, ready for a dip in the cool waters of the pool. Geoffrey lingered awhile with his friend.

"Thank you, ZZ," Geoffrey said to the man still seated in the vehicle. "It was great to see you again."

"Likewise, my friend," the man said jovially. "I will be in Luxor for two more days. Perhaps we could all meet again before I leave for Cairo at the end of the week."

"I would enjoy that immensely," Geoffrey smiled in response to this information.

As he turned to go into the hotel, a sudden thought crossed Geoffrey's mind. "ZZ!" he called out, tapping in the vehicle's window glass.

As the dark pane glided down, Geoffrey leaned into the interior. "I forgot to talk to you about our new friend, Jafar Kazim, the Director of Temple Complexes here in Luxor. He approached me while I was conducting a tour of the Luxor Temple for my budding archeologists. He seemed to know much about me, saying he had met me years ago at a conference. I don't recall the man."

"I know of him," ZZ simply said. "What is your concern?"

"I don't know exactly," Geoffrey said thoughtfully. "But there was something false in his friendliness, if you know what I mean."

ZZ smiled at his friend's perception.

Geoffrey continued, "He went out of his way to ingratiate himself, even to the point of inviting us for a personal tour of the Karnak Temple. Yet, I felt as though he was testing us somehow, or looking for information."

"Geoffrey, I suggest you be careful around this man as well," ZZ said. "He has...a *reputation*. He is not to be trusted. Where he is found, duplicity is not far away."

"Like Abu, he also gave us a warning or, as I perceived it, a veiled threat," Geoffrey added. "I felt as though he very much wanted us to be away from Luxor."

"This is interesting." The man absent-mindedly scratched his beard in thought. "Perhaps I need to probe into Jafar's current activities more deeply. He is politically minded. I have the impression he cares little about the sites he is responsible for or the antiquities of this country, but only for his position."

"He has been persistent in his invitation. Do you think we should accept his offer of a tour?" Geoffrey asked, clearly uncomfortable with the man.

"I see no harm in this, my friend," ZZ said with a smile. "You and your young friends will find the temple fascinating. Just be aware that Jafar is a man who is not worthy of your confidence."

"Alright, then. Cheers." Geoffrey waved as the window slid shut and the vehicle disappeared into the traffic.

It sounds like we have two men who could be involved with Jay's smuggling ring.

Conrad and Jay lounged by the pool after Alyssa had gone back to her room. They idly watched some younger children splashing and shouting gleefully in the shallow end of the pool.

"I like ZZ," Jay said as he stretched in the waning sunlight. "He and Geoffrey are clearly good friends."

"Yes, it is amazing how many friends Geoffrey has scattered about the world," Conrad agreed.

"You mean like Jafar, who Mr. B didn't even know was his friend? I don't know about you, but I think that man is as fake as a two-dollar bill."

"Those are still in circulation in the States, you know," Conrad stated.

"What?"

"Two-dollar bills."

"You know what I mean." Jay laced his fingers behind his head. "There was all that business about danger and staying out of trouble. It was like he already knew we had been looking around the night before."

At this, Conrad sat up. "You think so?"

"I don't know what to think. It's just strange that's all."

"Why would he let you off the hook then?" asked Conrad, referring to Jafar's phone call about Jay being seen on the wall. "He had the perfect opportunity to solve his problem."

"I have been wondering over that one, myself." He stretched again. "It doesn't make sense unless..." Jay sat up and faced Conrad. "Unless he is not sure what we know and do not know!"

Conrad saw where Jay was going. "Right! He is keeping us close so he can see how big a threat we are to his smuggling operation."

Jay smiled. "What did you say? *Smuggling operation?* I thought you said it was all a coincidence? Now it's an operation? How perceptive of you."

"Well, I have new information I didn't have before."

"What kind of information?" Jay probed.

"That there is an Aten cult around here, for one," Conrad admitted.

"Just like I thought."

"Yes."

"And for number two?" Jay pressed.

"And number two, we have attracted a lot of attention in a short couple of days."

They had attracted a lot of attention...including from the man who was slowly pushing the broom by the edge of the pool!

"Did you hear anything?" the man asked.

"Only that they talked about a smuggling operation," the voice on the other end said quietly.

"Did they know they were being watched?"

"I saw no sign of this."

"Very well. Shadow the two young men. Call me immediately if you see anything else I would want to know."

The man ended the call.

Now this will become a little more intriguing.

Jay lay on the bed staring up at the ceiling while Conrad checked his email. They had a free evening. Geoffrey had some business calls to make. Alyssa had already left with Malika to explore the remaining shops in the marketplace. The only question left was what they would do to occupy themselves.

"What did Geoffrey have to say when he phoned?" Jay asked as he considered their options for the evening.

"He said to make sure you stayed out of trouble," Conrad answered a bit too readily. "He initially liked my idea about locking you in the bathroom, but he was afraid you would figure out a way to escape through the exhaust fan."

"Ha, ha...I already told him that my trespassing days were over. I don't need new accommodations at the local *Criminal Inn*...Still..."

Conrad closed his laptop and turned to face Jay. "Still what?"

"Still, I would like to check that camera somehow after tonight to see if anything showed up."

Conrad leaned over the bed and looked Jay in the eye. "As long as you can figure out a way to check it during business hours, that is fine. But *no way* are you going to check it tonight! No way!"

"Like I said, no trespassing for me." Jay thought for a minute and then sat up suddenly on the edge of his bed. "Hey! Maybe we should take a walk down by the river and see if that speedboat is lurking around."

"Really?" Conrad asked incredulously. "Do you remember how many boats we saw out on the river this afternoon? I do—too many!"

"It was just an idea," Jay said as he flopped back on the bed. "Somehow we need to get a closer look at the smugglers' boat. If we could just swim out and get on board, we could find out what they were smuggling."

"Where do you get such ideas?" Conrad said, shaking his head in disbelief as he sat down on the chair.

"I saw it in a movie once," Jay explained. "You see, there was this man who—"

Jay's story was cut short by Conrad's ringing phone.

"Hello, Alyssa. What's up?" Conrad asked.

The boy turned wide-eyed toward Jay. "You're kidding! Okay. Stay where you are. We'll be there in ten minutes!"

Jay sat up. "What did she say?"

"It looks like the booth that sells the artifact reproductions is back in business!"

CHAPTER 18

"There they are!" Jay pointed to where Alyssa and Malika stood just inside a pottery shop.

Conrad pulled Jay to a stop. "Okay, here's the plan," he said, trying to catch his breath after their run from the hotel. "We walk over there and join them one at a time. Got it?"

"Got it."

"No sudden moves, and do not stare at the vendor. We don't want him to notice us. We want him to conduct business as normal. Got it?"

"Act like normal business without sudden staring." With a grandiose flourish Jay pulled out a pair of shiny sunglasses and put his earbuds in his ears. "How's this for incognito?"

Conrad did a double take at his excited friend and said in exasperation, "You have got to be kidding me…"

Jay's innocent look was almost believable.

Conrad shook his head. "We're wasting time, Hollywood. Lose the costume. I'll walk over first. Wait for my signal and then join us."

Conrad pushed Jay back behind a vegetable stand before his friend could protest and slowly walked toward the girls.

Along the way, he stopped to examine some leather goods and even had a short haggle with the proprietor. He cast a furtive glance toward the smuggler's booth and then walked straight for the girls.

"Conrad!" Alyssa gasped. "Am I glad you guys are here! Malika and I were just wandering through the remainder of the shops from last night when I looked up and there it was! I knew it was the booth you and Jay were looking for as soon as I saw it."

"Hi, Malika," Conrad said quickly before answering his schoolmate. "Yes, Alyssa, that's the booth. Has anyone matching the description of Jay's Scarface been by yet?"

"No. Only tourists so far."

"That's good." He turned to Malika. "Can you talk to the shop owner and ask her if it is okay if we rest here awhile? I don't want to have her shoo us out of here at the wrong moment."

Malika hesitated, her eyes darting furtively between the two friends before she slowly walked to the rear of the shop and spoke with the owner. Conrad and Alyssa could hear the rapidity of her speech. When it went up in pitch, Conrad glanced at Alyssa, mouthing 'uh-oh'. Alyssa listened for a moment and just shrugged. A minute later, Malika was back. She self-consciously straightened her hijab.

Her voice was a bit clipped when she told them, "She says it's fine. Just don't block other customers out."

Conrad's blue eyes studied the girl a moment longer. He then turned to motion for Jay to come and join them in the shop. All thoughts of Malika's strange behavior left him as he surveyed the street. Jay was nowhere to be seen!

▲ ▲ ▲

As Jay watched Conrad work his way to the girls in the pottery shop, an idea formed in his mind. He slid his sunglasses back into his pocket and stowed his earbuds away.

Costume…now that *is an idea.*

Forgetting what his friend had told him, he started back toward a shop he and Conrad had run past on their way into the marketplace. Finding it, he went inside. Fifteen minutes later, a young man vaguely resembling Jay emerged from the shop. He wore a gray two-piece Serwal Kamis—a loose-fitting shirt that extended to his thighs and loose drawstring pants. On his head sat a blue turban that kept his hair neatly tucked inside. Leather sandals and a shoulder pouch completed his outfit.

The disguised boy quickly made his way back up the marketplace street. As soon as he could see the man's booth, he nonchalantly strolled across the street into a tobacco shop and pretended to inspect the many products on display. When the shopkeeper approached him, he turned and walked over to the vegetable stand where he could watch both the pottery shop and his quarry half a block away. When he saw Conrad looking for him, he waved furtively, but his friend did not recognize him.

This is a sweet disguise. Even Conrad doesn't recognize me.

This thought emboldened Jay even more. He decided he could get closer to the booth without being recognized by the vendor. With this in mind, Jay started zigzagging his way toward the booth the same way he had watched Conrad do it.

I feel like a private detective. Jay Wray, Private Eye!

When he came to the spice shop directly behind the replica booth, he stopped and acted as though he was inspecting the wares.

"Oh no!" whispered Alyssa. "I think I just found Jay!" She pointed to the Egyptian man standing in front of the spice shop.

Conrad resisted the urge to run down the street and drag his friend back to the hotel. "I have a bad feeling this is not going to work out so well."

"Conrad!" hissed Alyssa. "Is that the man you guys were looking for, the one just down from the booth?"

Conrad saw the man with the scar walking slowly toward the replica booth. When the vendor saw the man coming toward him, he looked carefully up and down the street. Seeing nothing suspicious, he reached under the table and pulled a backpack-sized package of wrapped linen and handed it to the man.

Jay was alternately watching the transaction and trying to fend off the persistent shop owner. The owner mistook him for a local and was trying to converse with him in Arabic. The more Jay ignored the man, the louder he became. The replica vendor had just handed a folded piece of paper to the scarred man when the shop owner began a loud harangue and chased Jay out of his shop.

Jay's eyes locked momentarily with Scarface as the shop owner gave Jay a rough shove, sending him crashing into the table and spilling the replicas on the ground. The booth vendor started ranting at Jay as well. As Jay was trying to extricate himself from the growing mess, he saw Scarface running up the street toward the local market.

Conrad told the girls to stay where they were and ran to Jay's assistance.

"Sorry! So sorry!" He yelled at the gathering crowd as he pulled Jay away from the destroyed booth.

"Let's get out of here!" he said to Jay. "These people seem to have forgotten what customer service is about." Jogging, he pulled Jay along behind him until they were out of the marketplace.

"Whew!" Jay said. "That could have been ugly. Thanks for saving me."

"It was ugly," Conrad answered as his breathing slowed. "I'm not EVEN going to ask you what you are doing in those clothes. Let's get back to the hotel."

Jay held out his arms, his charm in full motion, "Nice thinking, hmm?"

Conrad glanced around Jay and started walking toward the hotel.

"No. Wait, Conrad." Jay's voice was serious again. "We need to find Scarface and see what he is up to."

"He is a thousand miles away by now. No way we can catch him."

"He will probably go to the temple again. We could go there and catch up to him," a focused Jay said without much thought of the consequences. When he saw the look on Conrad's face, he added, "Right. Not a good idea."

The two walked for another block before Jay snapped his fingers and stopped. "Wait. I have a better plan." He looked into the suspicious eyes of Conrad and continued, "We can go down to the river and see if the speedboat shows up. We know where to find it from the last time...and, besides, it's not illegal."

After a bit of convincing, Conrad agreed to Jay's plan.

Happy to get his own way, Jay teased, "I don't know, though, we may need to get you one of these disguises. Your version of 'business as normal' may get us discovered." Jay pointed to Conrad's western style of clothing.

His friend just gave him a warning look.

"Here, I'll let you borrow my shades. I think they would totally complete your look." Jay's supposed generosity fell on deaf ears as Conrad forged ahead toward their destination.

"Hey! Wait up!"

The man with the scar peered out from the darkness by the trash bin. For thirty minutes he had run down alleyways and side streets, frequently backtracking until he was sure that no one was following him. In his hands he held the package. In his pocket were the instructions he had not yet read. He steadied his breathing, relieved that he had not been caught. The scar on his head reminded him of how important it was to be reliable in this business. He had no intentions of failing to make the delivery. His mind replayed the scene in the marketplace. He had almost not recognized his foe. But he had seen his eyes, and the eyes never lied. This was the second time the young American had interfered. There would not be another. His boss would see to that.

Cautiously, he resumed his journey, walking as casually as his frayed nerves would allow. Up ahead, the backlit visage of the temple loomed.

▲ ▲ ▲

Jay emerged from the wooded area and stared out across the dark river. Conrad joined him at the edge and looked up and down the bank.

"Over there," Conrad whispered. "See that fallen tree by the riverbank?" He waited for Jay to find the place he pointed to in the dark.

"I see it."

"I think we should hide down there. That way, we can see the woods up here and also be close enough to see the boat."

Jay nodded in the dark. "Okay, let's go."

They slowly worked their way down the uneven bank leading to the river. Conrad dared not use the flashlight on his phone out of fear that the speedboat was laying in wait just off shore. More than once, one of them stumbled and fell, bringing their descent to a halt while they made sure they were not detected.

After Jay's third time tripping on his billowy pants, Conrad's mask of seriousness dropped. "How's that 'sweet disguise' working out for you now, Hollywood?" He grinned in the dark.

Jay decided it was a good idea to keep his temporary vision of becoming a Private Investigator to himself. He hiked up his pants with the exaggerated dignity of silence and kept moving.

Five minutes later they were hidden in the brush of the fallen tree.

"What are we going to do if Scarface shows up," asked Conrad in the dark.

The form next to him replied, "I would like to get close to the boat if possible. Maybe we can get a registration number or name from it."

"That can be your assignment," Conrad remarked. "I'd better text Alyssa to tell her we're trying to find Scarface and not to worry."

"Tell her we are NOT at the temple."

"Good idea." Conrad whispered through a smile that Jay could not see.

"And tell her not to text back," Jay said softly. "It wouldn't be good for your phone to light up at the wrong time." Jay was back in PI mode. His eyes searched their surroundings as the thrill of the hunt moved into full swing in his mind.

"Another good idea." Conrad shielded the light from his phone the best he could from any prying eyes. He didn't want to attract trouble in such a remote place.

▲　▲　▲

The low throb of an engine reached the shore where the boys were hidden. They strained their eyes in the darkness to see if it was coming their way. Ever so slowly, the sound came closer and closer. A dark shape without lights could be seen approaching them on the water. It was a speedboat edging toward the shore, its bow pointed upriver, fighting the flow of the mighty watercourse. About fifteen feet from shore, the captain cut the power back and allowed the water's current to nudge the nose toward the shore. When it was roughly perpendicular, he gunned the engines slightly, pushing the boat onto the grassy bank.

The shadowy outline of a smallish man jumped from the bow and tied the boat to a tree. He walked silently downstream for thirty yards and then turned upstream toward the boys' hiding place. He stopped not ten feet from them and listened. Even though both boys held their breath, they were sure the man could hear the hammering of their hearts.

CHAPTER 19

Alyssa's phone vibrated as they walked back to the hotel.

"It's a text message from Conrad," she said as she unlocked her phone. "He says they are trying to find that Scarface man...and not to worry."

"Where are they?" Malika asked, her tone intentionally casual.

"I don't know. He didn't say. Just that they are *not* at the temple."

Malika looked at her new friend. "I hope they are okay."

"Me too," said an anxious Alyssa. "Here's another text. It says not to text them back. Hmmm. That seems odd."

Malika just smiled. Conrad and Jay were very clever.

When they came to the hotel lobby, Malika said, "I must go home now. Perhaps I will see you tomorrow."

Alyssa hugged her. "Thank you for showing me around. I'm sorry you got mixed up in all of this."

As Malika walked away her young face grew dim. She thought to herself, *I was already mixed up in this.*

After rounding the corner, the girl stopped and pulled a phone from her handbag. She knew what could happen if she failed. Her report was short and precise, just as he wanted it.

▲ ▲ ▲

The man paced back and forth across the room. His mind turned this new information over and over again, mixing it with what he already knew. This was his way—to think and process and think some more. For this reason, he had risen to a place where so many had not. They lacked discipline. This, he felt, was because they were not committed. He was committed...and very diligent.

The young intruders have put some of the puzzle together. I will now have to make one booth disappear while another appears. I must also reassign Taavi to new duties where he will not be noticed as Scarface. Since he has made it to the temple, they will never locate him. The plan can be executed tonight as it was designed. In the future, however, I will need to rethink some of our procedures.

The man was calm and cool despite the disruption the young visitors had caused him. He stopped and stared out into the dark city.

Barnsworth is not a problem, nor is the girl. The young men, though, are dangerous. Perhaps an accident will help them decide it is time to go home.

He smiled. Accidents were his specialty.

▲ ▲ ▲

The small man from the boat seemed to sense something. He stood motionless in the night, like a dog sniffing the wind. He intently scanned the terrain around him. Conrad and Jay did not move. They willed themselves to melt into the foliage of the fallen tree. Still, their adversary persisted in his watch. When the man's phone chirped, both boys nearly launched into the air. Jay clutched at his chest, feeling his pounding heart. Conrad put a warning grip on Jay's arm. The man calmly answered his phone, speaking in low tones. After the call ended, his eyes carefully swept the area one last time before he climbed aboard the boat and disappeared into the cabin.

Jay was the first to whisper, "I thought we were goners. That guy almost has X-ray vision or something. I swear I could feel him seeing right through me."

Conrad answered softly, his eyes focused where the man had vanished from sight, "Maybe it's time to rethink getting closer to that boat." His expression had turned skeptical.

But by the time he turned to face Jay, the boy was already up and moving toward the vessel.

Conrad groaned in dismay.

▲ ▲ ▲

"Hello Alyssa," Dimah greeted cheerfully. Her keen gaze noted that Alyssa was alone. "Where are the others?" The woman softened her question with a smile.

Alyssa leaned her elbows on the counter. "Geoffrey was making some business calls tonight. And the boys are not back from the marketplace, yet."

"The marketplace?" Dimah asked with surprise. "Returned to the scene of the crime, did they?" She glanced at the clock and continued, "That place should be winding down by now."

"Yes, hopefully they will be back soon," Alyssa answered. "You know boys that age, they probably took the long way back to burn off some energy."

"Perhaps you are right," Dimah said, her tone laced with doubt. "Did you have a nice time? I believe I saw you with that local girl, Malika?"

A look of surprise crossed Alyssa's face. "You know Malika?"

"Yes, I have seen her around here before," Dimah answered nonchalantly. "What did you girls do?"

"Oh, you know...girl stuff," Alyssa said, starting to feel interrogated. "There were some shops we didn't get to see last night. So, tonight we walked around and explored those."

"What was your favorite?" Dimah asked, another smile inviting Alyssa to relax.

Without thinking the girl answered, "The clothing stores." A smile crept across her face and escaped as a giggle.

"What is so funny?"

"Oh, nothing," Alyssa said, still giggling. "You see such interesting people in places like that. I was just thinking of one of them."

"Yes, well, I often wonder how the locals see the tourists who come through here. I suspect they consider many of them to be rather interesting as well."

"I'm sure you're right, Dimah. Some of us are *very* interesting." She stifled a yawn. "I think I'm going to go up to my room. We have a big day tomorrow. Goodnight."

"Goodnight," the lady said and went back to her work.

As the elevator doors closed behind Alyssa, she said to herself, "I hope Jay and Conrad don't find Scarface or any other trouble tonight."

▲　▲　▲

Jay quickly closed the gap between the tree and the speedboat. He knew there was no place to hide. If the man suddenly reappeared, he was in big trouble. Smugglers carried guns. He was pretty sure of that.

He was surprised at how the ambient light made it possible to see the details of the boat. It had a faded red hull that had seen better days. Unfortunately, there were no numbers on the bow. Jay made a quick decision. As quietly as possible he stepped into the water and made his way toward the stern. He had expected the water to be cold, but it was pleasantly warm. The depth of the river increased quickly, which was probably why the smugglers had chosen this place to land. Jay soon found himself treading water to stay afloat. When he reached the rear of the boat, he could see a registration number, but couldn't read it in the darkness. On a whim, he allowed the current to carry him around the stern where the name of the boat should be. He strained his eyes to see the words, but whatever had once been there had been painted over.

That is when he felt it more than heard it. Footsteps in the boat caused the boat to shift slightly in the water. He let the flow of water push him farther across the back. He reached up and grabbed a loose mooring rope, using it to keep himself from floating down the shore. He glanced up the bank to see what was happening. The blue-white glow of a cell phone blinked out at the edge of the trees. Scarface was coming!

The boat lurched again, signaling that someone had jumped onto the beach. Jay inched toward the front of the boat, keeping low in the water. He could see the smallish man loosening the rope that held the boat to the shore. He could also see Scarface making his way down the steep bank toward the boat. The angle he took would bring him right by Conrad's hiding place. Jay's mind started racing. Conrad could be in danger!

No one ever figured out why Jay did it. He didn't really know himself.

When Scarface reached the fallen tree, Jay popped out of the shallow water and yelled at the top of his voice, "You are surrounded! Nobody move!"

CHAPTER 20

The small man with the rope whirled around and gazed open-mouthed at the apparition that was emerging from the river. The sight was so unexpected he was frozen in place. Jay tried to rush out of the water, but the combination of mud and the weight of his wet disguise turned his surge into a slow motion struggle.

Scarface watched the scene below him wide-eyed in disbelief. His mind was still keyed up from the incident in the marketplace. Now, the primal fight or flight instinct warred within him. He hesitated in indecision.

At that very moment of hesitation, Conrad reacted in a way that surprised even him. He yelled just as loudly as Jay had seconds before, "Drop the package!"

Scarface took an involuntary step backwards up the bank. The *flight* part of his instinct was beginning to win the war for his actions. He fell backward over an exposed root and involuntarily reached out to break his fall. The package tumbled from his grasp and rolled several feet down the bank. He eyed it for only a split second before continuing his escape. Conrad shot out of his concealment in the brush. He charged toward the package. Grabbing it, he turned to face the terrified man to whom it had recently belonged.

Scarface struggled backward, using his hands and heels to claw for some traction in the loose soil. He rolled over and tried to get his feet under him. Conrad yelled again for him to stop. This spurred the man on more desperately than before.

The short man on the rope had turned to face the commotion on the riverbank above him. In the faint light, he could see his partner trying to get away from the other man who had yelled. The sound of sloshing water behind him brought him back to the threat by the boat. He turned just in time to take the full force of Jay's tackle in the chest. The man dropped like a sack of bricks as Jay's head hit him in the jaw. Jay looked up from the ground to see how his friend was doing.

By this time, Scarface was beginning to scramble up the bank. In his haste, he tripped and fell. His head hit an exposed rock, momentarily dazing him. Conrad left the package and clambered up the bank after him. Scarface heard the sounds of his approaching pursuer. He rolled over on his back and desperately kicked both feet at the onrushing boy. The force of the blow stopped Conrad's forward motion. He dropped to his knees. Scarface flung himself at the boy. They both rolled down the embankment to where Jay was climbing up. Jay tripped over the hem of his soaked pants, his arms flailing around him. He landed on top of the other two, his elbow inadvertently smashing into Scarface's left eye, and the struggle ceased.

Both boys sat there panting for a moment.

Jay rubbed the lump on the top of his head. The throbbing mass pinpointed the exact spot of his earlier impact with the small man's jaw. He shook his head, glancing at their unconscious adversary, inwardly hoping the guy was okay. "Looks like I'm in one piece. How about you?"

"Just a bit of a scrum, that's all," said Conrad as he brushed some dirt from his hair. "I'd say we're quite better off than those two."

Both boys sat silently as they considered what they had just done. Later, they would look back on it and say it was mostly an adrenalin-induced reaction to imminent danger. Right now, it just seemed like a bad dream playing out in slow motion.

It was about to get worse.

Alyssa checked her phone for the tenth time in five minutes.

"Come on, you guys!" she said in the frustration of her growing fear. "Call or text or *something!*"

She waited another five minutes before finally deciding. She knew she had to take the chance of ruining whatever her friends were doing. She needed to know what was going on. Her trembling finger pressed the call button. She paced back and forth while the ringing on the other end began.

"No, no, NO!" she cried as the call went to voicemail.

Now, what am I going to do? Wake Geoffrey again? I can't believe this is happening!

She sat down nervously on the edge of her bed. *I'll try one more time. Maybe they were busy.*

They were definitely busy.

"That will be quite enough!" the British voice behind them called out. "Do not move! *You* are surrounded!"

Jay and Conrad jerked their heads around to see a large man standing on the bank below. In his hands was an AK-47 pointed directly at them. They both could see the man by the rope stirring back to consciousness. They looked at each other in disbelief. *Where had this new guy come from?*

As if he could read their minds, the man said, "It seems you did not take into account there could be more than one of us on the boat." He sneered menacingly, "I think you will find this to be a most unfortunate oversight."

He turned his head slightly and said something in Arabic to the smaller man on the ground. As he did, Jay started to position himself for a quick getaway. The man caught the motion out of the corner of his eye. He swung his full attention back to the boys. "I would NOT recommend any gallant attempts at escape. I am quite effective with this, especially at close range." He waved the gun barrel at them for emphasis. Jay sat back down dejectedly.

The man continued, "Your plan, if that is really what it can be called, was doomed to fail from the first. We are not amateurs here, as you have assumed."

The man by the rope rose sullenly to his feet. He rubbed his jaw gingerly and glared at Jay. He wanted a chance to show the boy what it was like to tangle with him on even terms. But the man with the gun spoke again and motioned for him to attend to Scarface. He slowly climbed up the rise to where his comrade lay. He roused the man and helped him to his feet.

Scarface soon appeared behind the prisoners, glaring at both boys. Roughly he nudged Conrad with his burly arm, knocking him off balance, then trudged down to where the package lay. Turning toward the boat, Scarface climbed aboard with the package under his arm and vanished below.

Jay whispered, "Are you okay?"

Conrad panted through clenched teeth, "I think we made them mad."

Jay grinned in spite of the situation. "We held our own pretty good until the big guy with the popgun showed up."

Conrad rubbed one of his bruises. "Let's stay cool for a bit and see how things play out."

"I don't think we have much choice," Jay said ruefully.

Meanwhile, the small man had scrambled down the bank and was speaking quietly to the man with the gun. The large man grunted and motioned toward the mooring rope with his head. The man bowed slightly and once again took up his station on the rope.

In a few moments, Scarface reappeared with some rope and duct tape. He jumped down on the bank with a grin made even more evil by his blackened left eye. The man with the gun nodded toward them and said, "We are going to help both of you to remain cooperative until it is decided what will be done with you. Please do not resist Taavi as he secures your arms and mouths."

Soon the two friends were trussed up, gagged, and awaiting their fate.

Scarface handed the captain Conrad's phone. The Brit pressed the power button and saw two alerts. "It seems someone is worried about you."

He dropped the phone in the dirt and smashed it once with the rifle butt. He then threw the remains into the murky waters of the river.

"You will not be needing that where you are going."

CHAPTER 21

The man hesitated for a moment at the news from the boat captain. This was an unexpected turn of events. In fact, it had caught him by complete surprise. Few things ever did. He paced slowly as he thought, the phone still at his ear. He knew the weight of the decision and he carefully pondered the consequences of each possible course of action. In the end, he was left with few options. *This must be contained. This must be controlled.*

"Yes, I am still here," he answered the inquiry concerning his silence. "We stay with the original plan. The delivery must be made. Now, we will have two more packages to be delivered. Take them with you to Aswan. Put them in the truck with the false bottom and deliver them to the Chief. He will know what to do."

After the captain acknowledged his instructions, the man added, "Tell the Chief to wait for my orders on their disposition. He can house them in the special room under his animal shed until he returns from his transport duties." He paused and then said, "One more thing...Make sure both cargoes arrive in good shape. I hold you responsible for this—personally."

The man ended the call. He sat quietly in the dark room thinking through all that needed to be done in order to keep his business viable. As he mentally checked off each item, he felt once again in control. That is how he liked it.

▲　▲　▲

The large man put his phone back in his pocket. He now had explicit orders. It was also clear what would happen if he failed. He shuddered slightly at the thought. He had seen it before when others failed their assignments. For men in his position, it only happened once. He did not want to share the same unpleasant fate.

Turning, he walked the short distance to where the two boys sat under the watchful good eye of Scarface. He spoke matter-of-factly to the prisoners, "It seems that your lives have some value after all. I have been instructed to take you on a little trip with us. I assure you, if it were up to me, it would be a short voyage." He smiled coldly. "But it is not up to me. So this is what is going to happen. You will be taken on board. You will be secured below. And, my young stowaways, you will behave yourselves. Do you both understand what I am telling you?"

He waited for both of them to nod before he turned his attention to the other two smugglers. He then made it perfectly clear to them that they must not abuse their passengers in any way. He threatened that he would not stand for it, and his boss would not tolerate it. The two men understood his intent. Neither would cross the boss. A great fear of him was something they all shared in common.

Conrad and Jay were lifted onto the boat and led below. Red lights, designed to enhance night vision on the river, illuminated the worn interior. Diesel fumes mixed with the smell of sweat and mildew in the stuffy confines. Scarface pointed to the berth and commanded, "Sit!" He produced another rope and bound them to a beam that ran overhead. He gave them enough slack to either lie down or sit upright, no more. Any chance of escape faded from the boys' minds as they stressed the bonds on their arms and wrists. The ropes did not stretch, and the knots were secure.

The captain came below to inspect the security of the prisoners. "Once we are underway, I will have the tape removed from your mouths and the ropes from your arms. As long as you are quiet and well behaved, they will remain off. I will see to it that you have some water and perhaps even some food." He turned and left.

The schoolmates could feel the boat being pushed from the shore and boarded. The engines cranked for a few seconds before they caught and roared to life. The boat backed slowly away from the bank and into the current. The sound of small waves slapping against the hull was muted as the boat idled into the middle of the river. A minute later, the engines were gunned to life and the boat leaped forward. The gentle staccato of water against the hull gave way to a rush, accented by loud bumps as the bow cut through the wakes of other vessels in the night.

As promised, Scarface returned to remove their gags and the ropes that pinned their arms to their sides. He left only the bonds that held their wrists behind their backs. He roughly pushed a cup of cool water into each of their mouths for a brief drink, spilling half of it on them. He left without a further word.

"Service with a snarl," Conrad muttered as he tried to get comfortable on the smelly mattress.

"He does need to work on his bedside manner," Jay agreed.

As the boat speed increased, Conrad said, "I hope the captain has good night vision. I don't see how he can drive so fast without any lights or radar."

After a few minutes, Jay asked, "I wonder where they're taking us?"

"I'll be happy as long as we keep moving," Conrad said stoically. "I don't fancy a swim in the river with these ropes on."

Both of them shuddered at the last comment.

▲ ▲ ▲

Alyssa couldn't delay any longer. She had tried to phone Conrad again, but there was no answer. She had to phone Geoffrey.

After five rings, he answered, "Hello, Alyssa. Trouble with Conrad and Jay again?"

The girl told Geoffrey the details of their adventures in the marketplace and how the boys had gone off to find Scarface.

"Conrad's text said not to text him back, but I tried calling him twice. Both calls went straight to voicemail. Now it's midnight and he still didn't answer when I called again...Geoffrey, I'm worried!"

"I see," said Geoffrey as he became fully awake. "Let me think about what we should do...will you be all right?"

"Now that you know what is going on, I will be," the girl answered honestly. "Oh, one more thing!"

"What is that?" Geoffrey asked.

"Conrad's text said that they were *not* at the temple."

"That is quite peculiar. Why would they specifically want us to know that they were not at the temple?" Geoffrey pondered. "Well, in any case I will phone you once I have a plan of attack."

Geoffrey lay looking up at the ceiling as he wrestled with what to do. A plan formed in his mind. ZZ!

▲ ▲ ▲

"ZZ, this is Geoffrey...Yes, it is late. And I'm very sorry to be calling you at this hour, but I need your help. Conrad and Jay have gone missing...Yes, I'm afraid it is quite serious. I believe it is somehow connected to a smuggling ring the boys believe they ran across a few days ago...Yes, smuggling...I know it sounds preposterous, but I believe they were correct in their conclusion...Yes, those types can be a rough crowd...No, I don't know if Abu or Jafar are behind it...That is what I wanted to talk to you about. Should we get the police involved or not? I am not acquainted with how the wheels of law enforcement turn here. I was hoping to have the benefit of your experience...Yes, I believe that would be fine...Okay, I will have the hotel staff put on some coffee and I will meet you in the lobby in 30 minutes. Thank you, ZZ. Goodbye."

Geoffrey ended the call with a sigh. "Conrad and Jay, I love a mystery as much as you do, but it is not wise to go off half-cocked on such a dangerous enterprise as this appears to be."

The older man quickly dressed. He phoned Alyssa to let her know what was going on. He overcame her insistence to come down to the lobby by explaining she would need her sleep for the events of the following morning. He then walked down the hall to the elevator. As he waited for the car to come up, he entertained a hope that the boys would come bursting through the lobby doors at any minute. As he stepped into the elevator and descended to the quiet lobby, he knew this would not be the case.

CHAPTER 22

The droning of the boat engines overcame fear and adrenaline. The captives soon dozed off. Most of the smaller boats were off the river at night, so the water was smooth. The large boats were few. When they approached the speedboat, the captain would slow the engine and glide over their sharp wakes. This was the pattern throughout the nighttime hours. Scarface came to bring the boys more water and a meat pie, but he found them asleep. He did not rouse them, thinking they were safer prisoners in this state than if awake and plotting an escape.

An hour before dawn, the boat slowed and entered a marina to take on fuel. When the engine was cut, an eerie silence invaded the berth where Conrad and Jay lay. Conrad was the first to stir. As soon as he was conscious, the fingers of panic and despair began gripping his heart once again. He strained to hear what was happening outside their musty prison. He could hear the faint hiss of fuel entering the tanks in the center of the boat. Here and there he caught a word before the rest of the sentence was snatched away by the cool night breeze. He thought to yell out, but figured the negative consequences would far outweigh any possible advantage gained. Plus, it was likely the smugglers used facilities frequented by those of similar vocations. Stopped ears and blind eyes would be of little help to them.

Jay stirred beside Conrad. "Wh-where are we?" he whispered as he fought the cobwebs clogging his head.

"I don't know. I think we stopped for fuel."

"Any idea what time it is?"

"No, I dozed off like you. It's probably been hours, though. I doubt any smuggler worth his salt would begin his adventures with less than a full tank of fuel."

The boys felt the boat roll slightly and heard footsteps above them.

"It looks like it's time to leave," Conrad observed. "I think we should try to sleep so we will be alert in the morning."

"Sounds good to me, I'm really tired."

The sound of the engine turning over was followed by the throaty hum of the exhaust. Sleep came shortly after the boat resumed its journey to the unknown.

▲   ▲   ▲

"Geoffrey!" ZZ greeted. "How are you holding up, my friend?"

"Better since you are here to share this most trying burden. Please, come and have some coffee. Dimah, the night manager, just brewed it."

The two men sat down at the table to begin plotting the way forward.

"So, Conrad and Jay believed they had found a smuggling ring," ZZ began methodically. "Why did they think this?"

Geoffrey told him about their initial encounter with the man with the package who had the Aten disk tattoo. He recounted their subsequent chase into the Luxor Temple that ended at the Nile River. ZZ listened attentively, asking questions here and there for clarification.

"Tonight, they evidently witnessed the same handoff routine in the marketplace—and the same cast of characters. However, after they left on foot, the only communication was a text from Conrad to Alyssa."

"I assume there has been an attempt to contact them since then?" ZZ asked, mentally checking steps off his list.

"Yes, Alyssa phoned them several times before she awakened me with the news." Geoffrey sagged a little in his chair as he recalled the conversation with her.

"Do we have any idea where they could have gone?" ZZ continued.

"Only a guess based on a strange phrase in the text to Alyssa."

ZZ leaned in. "And what was this strange phrase?"

"The text said specifically that they were *not* at the temple. It might have been Jay's way of assuring her that, while they were getting into trouble, they were not getting into *that* kind of trouble. But I think it also is a clue for us."

"A clue?"

"Yes," Geoffrey continued. "Assuming, of course, that the setup was the same as the first night, and knowing we can rule out the temple, I believe it leads us to the river."

"At the site of the first boat pickup?" ZZ asked following Geoffrey's logic.

"Precisely."

"That is plausible," ZZ said rubbing his beard. "Do we know where on the river they observed this boat pickup? The Nile is a large waterway."

Geoffrey answered, "The first night, they were picked up by the police along the highway that runs between the river and the temple. I assume the spot is somewhere near there."

"Since we have a couple of attempted calls, we should be able to track down the cell towers involved when the call was received. We can then triangulate the approximate location of the phone at the time."

"How do we do that?" Geoffrey asked with a puzzled look on his face.

"I have good contacts at the regional phone company. I can call them as soon as *normal* people get up." He smiled at Geoffrey.

Geoffrey chuckled in spite of the situation. "Normal. Well, yes, I wouldn't know anything about that." He continued, "This would at least tell us where to look. The next question is, do we get the police involved?"

"I was initially thinking we should. But now I think maybe we should check out the pickup spot first to see if anything turns up. The police will use brute force to solve the case. Smuggling and kidnapping call for a little finesse. I have adequate contacts, we just need a clue to put us on the trail."

Dimah came over to refill their cups. Geoffrey introduced the woman to ZZ.

"Do you think you can find those two young men?" Dimah asked ZZ, her gaze surveying him. "What Geoffrey has described is dangerous. The times have made many desperate. How will you find them? The police?"

"I have the utmost faith in ZZ's abilities," Geoffrey told her reassuringly. "He believes getting the police involved at this time would be a mistake. I believe he is most qualified to help at this point."

"I share your concern about getting the police involved," Dimah continued, her intense gaze turning to Geoffrey. "It is possible they might do something and accidentally force the hand of the kidnappers. We do not want such people to do anything rash."

"We are in agreement, then, to give ZZ the first crack at it." Geoffrey smiled grimly at his friend.

Dimah watched the bearded man with worry in her eyes.

The first light of the dawn started to transform the clear eastern sky. Before long, the morning light found its way into the bowels of the boat.

Conrad nudged Jay. "Looks like we are traveling south. I saw some sunlight off the port side of the boat."

"Port side? Which one is that?" Jay asked the landlubber question.

"Left. Left is port and right is—"

The boat's engine slowed and the vessel lost its plane on the water. As it settled deeper, the boat edged slowly forward. The door to the berth opened, revealing the large hulk of the captain.

"A bloody good morning to you, my passengers. Have a delightful evening, did we?" His British accent was not as smooth or posh as Geoffrey's.

"The room service could use a little improvement," Conrad commented.

The captain let out a hearty laugh. "Right! That is a good one. I will tell Taavi of your displeasure with his abilities as a porter. Now, down to business. We are near the end of the first leg of your journey. You will be transferred to a waiting vehicle—a truck. I am going to untie you and allow you a restroom break before we step over to the truck. I warn you right now, any trouble will be your last. Do we have an understanding?"

The boys looked at each other and then the captain. "Agreed."

"All right, then," the man said. "Taavi! Come and untie our guests, let them visit the restroom one at a time. And feed them something...with some water. I don't want it said that I run an inhospitable ship!"

The scarred man did as he was told, but the glare from his puffy eye betrayed his true desires toward the captives.

After a quick bite, the boys were brought topside. At first, they could not see because of the blinding brightness of the morning sun. Once their eyes adjusted, though, they saw they had tied up along a remote stretch of the shore about a mile from the Aswan Low Dam!

"Okay, gents! Let's move along now!" The captain nudged them onto the shore. They were quickly ushered through a thin tree line to a box truck.

"In you go!" he said gruffly as the small man kept lookout.

The floor of the truck contained an open compartment just large enough for them to squeeze into and lay down. A couple of burlap sacks had been thrown in for padding. The prisoners crawled into the cramped compartment and stretched out with their heads toward the front.

The captain placed the wrapped package at their feet on a thick padding of straw.

"I will let you guard this on the journey." He laughed loudly at his version of a joke.

Scarface picked up the floor section and prepared to close them in.

The big Brit leaned over one final time and said, "My part of the journey is finished. I leave you in the good hands of Taavi and Nebi. They will deliver you to your destination. Cheers!"

The last thing the boys saw before being sealed in darkness was the smirking visage of Scarface. He quickly bolted the floor panel in place and roughly closed the rear door of the vehicle.

They were a long way from Luxor. How could anyone possibly find them?

CHAPTER 23

Geoffrey sat at the table with Alyssa and ZZ. They had just finished a breakfast that none of them felt like eating. Geoffrey had told Alyssa about their early morning discussions. She was eager to begin the search for her friends. ZZ was on the phone with his contact at the telephone company. He had been on hold for ten minutes, and sat patiently sipping the last of his coffee.

"Yes," he said, setting the cup down and motioning to the others. "Very good…No, that is all for now. Goodbye."

Geoffrey and Alyssa looked at the man expectantly.

"The location where two calls were received is less than half a kilometer south of the temple. We can safely assume it was by the river and conduct our search there." He hesitated a few seconds and added, "There was no indication that a third call was received. We unfortunately must also assume that the phone was destroyed before the final call was made."

ZZ looked at Geoffrey and gave a slight shake of his head as a warning to make no further comment in front of Alyssa. Geoffrey nodded. He understood the ramifications of what his friend had just said.

ZZ motioned for the bodyguard stationed at the entrance to the restaurant. The burly man approached the table and bent down to hear the instructions. He nodded and left through the door.

"I put my vehicle at your disposal," he said graciously. "Shall we go and see what we can find of our two young friends?"

▲　▲　▲

The truck bounced on roads rampant with potholes. Each time the rear wheels found one, the truck bed jarred loudly. The boys braced themselves the best they could. If it were not for the cramped conditions, they would have been thrown around mercilessly. The ride was bone crushing as it was. The meager padding of burlap offered little protection from the severe jostling.

Almost as soon as it began, the pitted surface gave way to the smoothness of a modern concrete road. At first, the boys were wary that it was just a passing condition and that they would soon resume their rough ride. As the miles stretched out beneath them, it became obvious that they could relax.

"Man," Jay exclaimed above the road noise, "I feel like a scrambled egg!"

"You feel like you need to go on a diet," complained Conrad. "Every time we hit a bump on your side, you flew up and crushed me against my side."

"I'm sorry you're so delicate," Jay replied as he adjusted the lump of burlap under his head.

All around them they could hear the sound of other vehicles rushing by on the road.

"We must be on a highway," Conrad surmised. "I wish I could see out of this box."

"Yeah," Jay agreed. "Now I know what a mummy feels like."

The truck maintained a steady speed as it drove toward its destination. The boys pushed and pried at the floorboards above, but they were fastened solidly in place. By craning their necks, they could see small pinholes of light down by their feet. As they felt around the interior of the box, they found holes leading to what felt like rubber hoses. Fresh air entered the box through them as they traveled.

"Very clever," Conrad said as he studied the system. "The holes by our feet draw air out which forces new air through the tubes. I wonder what happens when the truck stops."

"I don't want to know," Jay replied uneasily as he thought about experiencing a slow asphyxiation. "But I do want to know what they are smuggling."

Jay felt the package down by his feet. He began to move it around, maneuvering it slowly forward. He was able to work it until it rested on his shins. Because of the tightness in the box, he couldn't quite reach it with his hands to pull it forward.

"Conrad, give me a hand or foot or something. I have the package on my shins but can't quite reach it. I need to get it up over my knees."

"I'll see what I can do," Conrad replied as he struggled to turn over on his side away from Jay. "I might be able to bump it with my heel."

"Ow!" Jay's leg flinched a little too readily, colliding with the low ceiling of their enclosure. He bit back a frustrated cry.

"Sorry. I didn't think that felt like the package."

Slowly the boys inched the bundle up beyond Jay's knees where he could grasp the linen.

"Got it!" Jay exclaimed.

He wiggled and pulled the package forward until it rested on his abdomen. He felt around on the linen to see if there was a way to rip it open. He couldn't find any.

"This thing is really wrapped tight!" he exclaimed as he

gave one final tug. "It seems like it weighs about twenty pounds...and I can definitely feel three different objects inside."

"Are they objects or bags of drugs?" asked Conrad, trying to determine just what the smugglers were trafficking in.

"Objects...the first one feels like some kind of a figurine or statue or something. The second feels like it is the same kind of thing. I can't really feel anything distinctive about the third, except it is long and skinny."

"They could be real ancient Egyptian artifacts," Conrad offered. "Those would be worth the effort of smuggling!"

Ancient Egyptian artifacts. Jay's brain toyed with this piece of the puzzle.

"Whatever they are, we had better put them back," Conrad cautioned. "The less our hosts think we know, the better."

Five minutes later, the linen bundle was back in the straw at their feet. The truck rolled on.

▲ ▲ ▲

The bodyguard pushed his way through the dense undergrowth leading to the river. ZZ and Alyssa followed him. Geoffrey brought up the rear of the makeshift caravan. Even in the shade of the towering trees, it was hot. After a few minutes, the man burst through the foliage and into the sunlight. The others followed.

Below them lay a steep slope that led down to the river. There was nothing visible to the left or right beyond this small clearing.

"This may be it," ZZ said. "You can see that the shore is fairly cleared of brush. A perfect place for a landing."

"Yes," agreed Geoffrey. "Seclusion and solitude. Two things a smuggler would value."

"What are we waiting for?" asked Alyssa impatiently as she pushed past the men. "Let's go down and see what we can find."

"Right," said Geoffrey. "Be careful. The bank is steep."

The group slowly made its way down the embankment, using a zigzagging pattern to safely make the descent.

"There are signs that someone has been here recently," ZZ observed, pointing to footprints in the soft earth.

"It rather looks like there was a struggle over here," Geoffrey said as he stooped to examine some particularly disturbed dirt.

When they reached the riverbank, ZZ examined the ground by the water's edge. "Here is where the boat came ashore. You can see the impression made by the bow in the river grass."

"And there are footprints leading into or out of the water on both sides of the indentation," Geoffrey observed.

"It definitely looks like the place. The question is now one of determining the identity of the boat and the direction it took." ZZ scanned the river as he considered the magnitude of this task.

As the men were discussing the possibilities, Alyssa had wandered off toward a fallen tree. What they had discovered at this place made her very worried about her friends. If Conrad's phone had been destroyed, as ZZ seemed to think it was, there would be no way for the boys to contact them...or for them to track the boys' location. They needed to find a clue—anything—or it would be impossible to find them!

Her eyes combed the ground for a sign. She, too, could see clear signs of a struggle. She stepped over the trunk of the fallen tree. Footprints! Two sets! *Jay and Conrad must have hidden here!*

Something else caught her eye. It was a folded piece of paper! It lay trapped in the brush by the tree. She rushed over and grabbed it. She let out a gasp as she unfolded the slightly rumpled sheet. *Hieroglyphs!*

CHAPTER 24

"Geoffrey! ZZ! I've found something!" Alyssa shouted, waving the piece of paper.

The men clamored up the bank to where she stood.

"Good show, Alyssa!" Geoffrey exclaimed as the girl handed him the sheet. "This is just the thing we needed. Perhaps it will give us a clue as to where Conrad and Jay are."

"Yes," agreed ZZ. "Where did you find it?"

The girl excitedly responded, "It was caught in the brush right there." She pointed at the tangled greenery.

Geoffrey studied the sheet for a moment and then handed it to his friend. "What do you make of this, ZZ? It is a message in hieroglyphs. Can you read it?"

"I can only make out a few of them," ZZ responded. "Not enough to make any sense of things."

"How did it get here?" Alyssa asked.

"I would guess one of the perpetrators accidentally dropped it," Geoffrey deduced. "Perhaps in the struggle."

"Yes," ZZ agreed. "You can see it has been stepped on." He pointed to the dirt stains and the crumpled appearance of the sheet. "The wind could have blown it over to where you found it."

"How will we find out what it says," the girl asked. "Not everyone can read hieroglyphs."

"Precisely. That is likely why the smugglers used this form of communication." Geoffrey looked at his friend. "A perfect way to stay off the grid so there would be no electronic trail."

ZZ's face was serious. He nodded. "And it would look like gibberish to anyone who happened across one of them."

"So how will we find out what it says?" Alyssa persisted. "None of us can read it."

"Dimah," Geoffrey answered. "She said she knew how to read them."

A man watched silently from the tree line above. The place where he lay was hidden from the watchful eyes of the bodyguard. He slowly wriggled back into the underbrush and made a quiet phone call. The three below had found a paper that had aroused their attention. This must be reported.

The truck slowed and turned off the main road. The pace was slower now, but the road remained smooth. Outside the box, the boys could hear what sounded like trucks or busses lumbering along with deep, throaty growls. From the road noise, they could tell they had turned onto a two-lane road. The truck slowed even more but kept a steady pace. From the frequent sounds of vehicles rushing by, Conrad concluded they were behind a slower moving vehicle and could not pass.

The airflow through the box diminished with the speed of the truck. The fresh air became tainted with the distinct smell of diesel exhaust. Jay pushed his face in front of the air intake hole and breathed deeply. He did not like the implications this turn of events brought.

▲ ▲ ▲

Back at the hotel, the group approached the front desk clerk, who greeted them. "Good morning, Mr. Barnsworth. How may I help you this fine day?"

"It is important that we speak to Dimah," Geoffrey answered, trying to keep the tension from coming through his voice. "We do not have her personal number and we're hoping you could ring her up for us."

The man hesitated a moment before speaking, "Of course you know that Dimah works during the evening hours? She is likely sleeping right now at her home."

"I realize this is an extraordinary request," Geoffrey explained, "but we must speak to her as soon as possible."

"This is quite out of the ordinary," the man answered. "One moment please while I locate the general manager."

The man disappeared into the suite of offices behind the desk. In a moment, he emerged. "Mr. Hasini has stepped out of the office. Please have a seat in the lobby while I try to locate him."

The disappointed group turned away from the man and walked across the lobby to some chairs by the front door.

"This is not good," Alyssa said dejectedly.

"Yes. Every moment is crucial at this juncture," Geoffrey agreed.

After about 10 minutes, a tall, thin, impeccably dressed man approached them with a smile.

"I am Ali Hasini. I understand that you wish to contact Dimah?"

"Yes," Geoffrey answered as he stood. "It is a matter of utmost importance."

"I am afraid that this will not be possible," the man answered stiffly. "We do not disturb our employees when they are off duty. It is hotel policy."

Geoffrey was about to protest when ZZ stood and began speaking with the man in Arabic. After a minute of what at times was a heated conversation, the general manager nervously adjusted his glasses and said, "I understand the seriousness of the situation. I will contact Dimah at once and ask her to join you here."

"What did you say to him ZZ?" asked an amazed Alyssa. "He sure decided to become cooperative."

ZZ answered nonchalantly, "I merely reminded Mr. Hasini of two things—that you were guests in his hotel and the owner of this chain of hotels was a very close friend of mine."

Geoffrey and Alyssa smiled and sat down to wait for Dimah.

ZZ made several phone calls as Geoffrey studied the page of hieroglyphs.

"The Egyptians developed this highly detailed writing form over a period of one thousand years," the older man explained to Alyssa. "Several scholars studied them, but could never quite crack the code, so to speak. The markings on the various monuments, statues, and tomb walls spoke volumes. We just could not hear what they were saying, though we could see that it was something spectacular. There exist some simplified translations of symbols to alphabet letters, but these do not suffice for anything as elaborate as this." He waved the paper.

"Dimah will be able to help," Alyssa said confidently. "She is a very smart lady."

"She is, indeed," Geoffrey agreed.

Alyssa sat quietly for a minute, deep in thought.

"You look like you are puzzling over some deep mystery," Geoffrey observed. "Care to share?"

"I was just thinking of something you said," the girl replied. "If that sheet contains a complex message, how could the commonplace smuggler understand what it said? Wouldn't they have to spend much time studying hieroglyphs at a university or somewhere in order to be able to read the message?"

Geoffrey laid the sheet he was studying down on the coffee table in front of them. "I don't know, Alyssa, but that is an astute observation—one I did not consider before now."

"Maybe Dimah can help us with that as well," the girl replied as she settled back to wait.

No more than 30 minutes later, the woman walked through the lobby entrance and directly toward the group. Her professional attire was highly starched and looked fresh. Not a hair was out of place. Dimah's eyes were alert as she gave them a preliminary glance. All three stood to greet her.

"I came as soon as I could," she said apologetically. "The morning traffic was a bit heavy."

"There is no need to apologize," Geoffrey quickly said as he offered her a seat beside them. "It is we who should ask your forgiveness for disturbing your sleep after a long night of work."

Dimah sat down. "I take it you have found something related to the disappearance of your two young friends?"

"Yes," Geoffrey replied. He handed her the sheet containing the hieroglyphs. "We found this at the place where they were evidently abducted. Can you decipher it?"

A look of surprise briefly crossed her face as she saw that the offered sheet of paper contained hieroglyphs. She sat back in her chair to compose herself and to study the markings. After a couple of minutes, she said, "It seems to be written in kind of a code. There are complex sections that are more like headers or subjects. These are followed by a very simple alphabetized phrase."

Geoffrey looked at Alyssa. "That would explain how a person uneducated in such matters could understand the basic intents of the instructions."

"Yes," the woman confirmed. "It would be relatively simple to teach someone the alphabet and where the phrases began and ended."

"What does it say?" Alyssa asked impatiently.

"It says that the package is to be taken by boat to Aswan. It is then to be driven by truck to pick up location 'C'. It is to cross the border via boat on Lake Nasser and unloaded at Wadi Halfa in Sudan. It is then to travel by train to Port Sudan where it will be delivered." She stopped for a moment to explain, "I cannot clearly see the street location. It is badly smudged with dirt. But it looks like an Osman something Street or road, if that makes sense. And it is to be at a statue. I cannot see more than this."

Alyssa looked excitedly at Geoffrey. *Would they be able to find Conrad and Jay, and catch the smuggling ring in the act?*

▲ ▲ ▲

The Chief heard his fax machine begin its familiar routine. As the paper was ejected, he picked up the first sheet and read the hieroglyph message.

Ah, what is this? An unexpected fax from Zamir. The drop point has been compromised and a new one initiated...and I will be entertaining two guests who will arrive this morning.

He crumpled the note and threw it on the table as the second sheet finished printing.

And here are the new instructions.

He carefully folded the paper. He would give it to Taavi when he arrived. The Chief hurried out to prepare the special room below the stable.

Chapter 25

The stable was little more than a lean-to built into a hill on the back of the lot. The rear two walls of the shelter were made of mud bricks, and at one time had been plastered over and painted white. Years of neglect had seen most of the plaster flake off and mix with the straw and animal droppings on the floor. The remaining two sides on the front were open with rough wood fencing completing the square shape. In between the fences was a latched gate. The roof consisted of hand-hewn poles supporting several crosspieces of similar construction. Palm branches had been bundled and placed on this framework to provide shelter, mostly from the sun. Once, the building had been used for a herd of sheep and goats the man had raised. Now, since The Chief had taken up his new career, it was used only by a broken-down donkey, some scraggly chickens, and a wide variety of rodents. The structure was partially shaded by a trio of palm trees that had decided to make the fertile dirt around it their home.

A hinged, wooden door had been set into the floor at the back corner of the mud brick walls. It rotated up on heavy hinges and was fastened in place with a wooden peg in a clasp. When not in use, it was covered with straw and virtually invisible. The trap door led down a short flight of rickety stairs into a stone-lined cellar. There was an old bench along one wall and some shelves along the other. There were no windows in the room, just a ventilation pipe that led to the roof. The room was dry and cool and smelled of mold and old straw. It was used at times to store merchandise. Now it was to be put to a different use.

The Chief ambled toward the stable. He opened the gate, causing the chickens to scramble out of the way. The donkey idly looked at the man, its forlorn stare a mirror of its physical condition. The Chief often wondered why he kept the beast. Maybe it reminded him of his simple life in the past, before the day his wife and son were killed during a petty robbery of his humble abode. Eight years had gone by, but the memory still shook him. That was the day he decided to live for himself and to gain what he could any way he could. Besides, the animal didn't eat much and only required a bucket of water every other day or so. He patted the donkey and walked to the back corner.

The man kicked and scraped the straw from over the door. He removed the pin from the clasp and pulled the door upward. The hinges squealed their protest at his disturbance. The motion pulled the musty air upward to meet the man. He paid no attention as he descended the squeaking steps to the floor below. He looked around. He noted that there was no place to tie his guests.

No matter. They will not go far with the door locked from above.

Anything that could be used as a weapon he took above. An armload of straw was tossed down the hole, and an old bucket for their personal use was carried down. He would only need to give them some food and water before he left. The man looked around one more time and slowly climbed the steps, leaving the trap door open to circulate some air. He patted the donkey one more time, and walked toward the river to prepare his boat for the journey ahead.

▲ ▲ ▲

"Here we go again!" shouted Jay as the first pothole announced that the side road they had turned down was unpaved. He braced himself and hoped this leg of the journey would be very short.

"Just stay on your side of the prison!" Conrad shouted back as he tried to find a way to avoid the painful jolts of the vehicle.

The truck traveled at a moderate speed down the road. Still, it was too fast for the occupants in the back. By the time the vehicle slowed to turn, they were bruised and sweating from the exertion.

The truck rolled to a stop. The boys could hear the cab doors open and then slam shut. They expected to be freed from the box any moment, but no one came for them. They waited in the dark silence.

"I wonder what's going on?" Jay asked as they waited. "I can't wait to get out of this tomb."

"I don't like your choice of words," Conrad replied, "but I feel the same way."

"What should we do when we get out? Should we make a run for it?" Jay's mind whirled with the possibility of liberty.

"I don't think I could run more than 50 yards even if we could get away," Conrad answered. "We have been mummies in this tomb for hours."

"Yeah, you're right," Jay agreed. "I probably couldn't run even that far. I am stiff and cramped and tired and bruised and—"

"And jabbering too much," Conrad interrupted. "Let's listen and see if we can hear anything *out there*!"

The boys strained their ears, but there was no sound except the sighing wind in the palm fronds and the occasional bird chirp. Suddenly, in the distance they heard the distinct sound of a blaring foghorn.

"I've heard that before on this trip," Jay said, racking his brain for the answer.

"Me too...but where?"

"Ship!" Jay shouted too loudly in the enclosed compartment. "That's the sound of those big cruise ship horns! You know, the ones we saw the first day on the lake."

Conrad tensed with excitement. "That's right! We must be somewhere close to the lake! We've been heading south the entire time!"

"Man!" Jay lamented. "We're a long way from Luxor. It's going to take some major detective work for them to figure out where we are."

▲　▲　▲

"I have just phoned my associate down in Sudan," ZZ said as he ended the call. "He will give the police in Port Sudan an anonymous tip about the smuggling drop somewhere along Osman Digna Street at a location by a statue. Perhaps the police can take care of that loose end for us. Now," he continued, "I suggest we travel down to Aswan and see what we can sort out. I have my plane waiting at the airport to take us there."

"I don't know what to say, ZZ," Geoffrey said with gratitude. "Your generosity is humbling, and we are indebted to you."

"Oh, ZZ," said Alyssa, "you're the best!" She gave the robed man a heartfelt hug. "We would have been in big trouble without you."

"Yes, well, it is not enough for my old friend...or my new ones," he said embarrassedly. "Dimah, you are also welcome to join us in the search, if you desire of course."

The woman hesitated a moment, weighing the options in front of her before declining. "I had better stay here and—how do you Americans say it—hold the fort. You may need something in Luxor, so here is where I can be of greater help. I will give you my cell number. Please call me if you find out anything or need anything...even during the day."

The others chuckled at the reference to her sleeping time and thanked her for her help. She headed out the door for some much needed rest.

"I think we had better pack a small overnight bag," suggested Geoffrey. "We do not know what we will find and how long it will take."

"That is a great idea, my friend," said ZZ. "I will go and do the same. I will return in 30 minutes."

An hour later, the group was in the air, winging toward Aswan.

▲ ▲ ▲

Nebi and Taavi exchanged greetings with The Chief down at his boat. The man had checked everything out and made the vessel ready for the trip. Fresh water and provisions were already loaded and secured. It would be the next morning before he would return from his excursion.

He handed Taavi the sheet of paper he had taken from his fax machine. The scarred man read the message quickly and put it in his robe. It was then he discovered the original instructions were gone! The sheet had fallen out somewhere. The man went white with fear. He knew mistakes were not tolerated. He weakly told the Chief about the missing instructions. The other man shrugged and assured him that they would get to Wadi Halfa without further incident. This did little to allay his fear of punishment.

Nebi told The Chief about the two prisoners he was to keep. The man motioned them up the bank toward the truck.

"I hear someone coming!" Jay hissed in the dark. "I hope they let us out of here."

"They'll have to come back sometime to get the package," Conrad said. "I should think they would let us out at the same time."

Their conversation was interrupted by the sound of the roll-up door being raised in the back of the vehicle. They felt the worn suspension springs give as someone climbed onto the truck bed. The sound of a ratchet wrench announced their imminent freedom from the box. Suddenly, a bright light pierced the darkness, blinding both Jay and Conrad. They felt rough hands pulling them out of their prison and standing them upright.

Both boys swayed unsteadily as their eyes became accustomed to the light. The first thing they saw shocked them! *It was the Chief!*

CHAPTER 26

The plane touched down just over two hours after it left Luxor. The flight had been uneventful. After a delicious snack once airborne, each of the passengers had stared out the window at the shapeless desert landscape below. Within an hour, each of them had dozed off and remained asleep for the better part of the trip. Now they were landed, refreshed, and ready to go. The question was, *go where?*

The plane taxied its way across the labyrinth of runways toward the hangar. ZZ was on the phone the entire time, speaking in low emphatic tones. When he ended the final call, he was smiling broadly.

"My associate here in Aswan has informed me that a farmer believes he has seen our lost young men."

"Where?" asked Geoffrey, almost afraid to believe such good news.

"North of the Low Dam, along the river," ZZ responded. "We will go at once and speak directly to this man. Perhaps we are back on the trail once again, yes?"

"How did your associate find this out so quickly?"

ZZ smiled. "I have many associates, observant men all of them. They are adept at getting things done for me when I ask."

"Did he say anything else?" asked Alyssa.

"Only that the farmer saw two young men being escorted into a box truck. We will go and personally verify this information."

The plane came to a halt at the hangar, and the engines slowly spooled down. The copilot came back to the main cabin and opened the door, extending the ramp. ZZ's bodyguard climbed down the steps and made sure the plane and the tarmac were secure. The passengers descended the steps and were ushered into a waiting SUV, identical to the one in Luxor. Luggage was quickly placed in the back of the vehicle. After the guard climbed in the front seat, the driver sped through the airport gate. Alyssa marveled at the precision of it all.

▲   ▲   ▲

The Chief was just as surprised to see Jay and Conrad as they were to see him.

"So, we meet again, my young crocodile hunters," the swarthy man said with a laugh. "This time it looks like it is you who have been hunted."

With that, the man turned and jumped from the truck. Rough shoves from behind sent Conrad and Jay in the same direction. This time it was Nebi who held an AK-47 to deter any ideas of resistance or escape.

The boys followed the Chief across a grassy field behind a mud brick hut. They could see the glimmering waters of Lake Nasser through breaks in the trees that lined the shore. A boat tied to a stump rode gently in the water. Jay nudged Conrad and motioned with a jerk of his head toward the vessel. It was the same one they had ridden in only a few days before—a few days that now seemed like a lifetime.

Just ahead, up a short rise, an animal stable came into view. The Chief led the way with a deliberate pace. The chickens were outside the enclosure and ran to one side as they passed. The man opened the gate and went inside, followed by the boys and smugglers. The donkey moved out of the way, clearly afraid of so much commotion in his normally peaceful life.

At the back of the structure, the Chief stopped by the open trap door and motioned toward the dark hole in the floor. "Go! Down there!"

Jay was the first to disappear into the darkness, followed by Conrad. They gingerly descended the rickety steps and stood at the bottom of the stairs as The Chief came down.

The man spoke roughly, "This will be your new home until I get back tomorrow. Then we will see what it is I am to do with you!" He grinned as a thought came to his mind. "Perhaps you would like to see the crocodiles again, yes? You would provide them with a very good meal!" His laugh sent shudders down the spines of both boys.

The Chief started up the steps and called back over his shoulder. "I will be right back with some refreshments for you. Then, I will give you some privacy." Again his laugh echoed in the chamber.

After the man was gone, the boys stared at the single exit from their makeshift jail cell.

"Do you suppose..." Jay said hopefully.

Nebi peered down at them from above, the rifle cradled in his arm.

"I do not," answered Conrad. "Not in a million years."

The boys looked around the dingy cellar. It dawned on them they would soon be shut up in the darkness once again.

"Man!" Jay said with agitation, "I don't like the life of a mushroom. I need light."

"Well, it looks like we will not be getting much of that down here," Conrad said matter-of-factly. "I suggest we get ourselves oriented and organized."

Jay watched as Conrad paced off the floor in both directions.

"Five paces by four," Conrad said. "Now, let's take a look at this shelving." The boy pulled and pried at the wood, testing each shelf down the wall.

"What do you think this is for," asked Jay, holding up the old bucket.

"One guess," Conrad said, giving Jay a look.

"Really?" Jay said as he dropped the bucket and wiped his hands on his Kamis trousers. "Great."

"You had better put that thing where we can find it later," Conrad said with a hint of humor. "We will not be wanting to send out a search party to find it in the dark when the time comes."

"Wonderful."

"I think we should put that straw over here by the bench," Conrad directed. "That will be our bed tonight."

"Fantastic."

Conrad stepped over to the stairs and surveyed their handiwork. "Just like the Ritz," he quipped.

"Marvelous."

A shadow extinguished the square shaft of light from above. The squeaking top step announced the Chief's return. The man slowly descended into their prison cell. In one hand he held a pitcher. In the other, something wrapped in a towel.

"Dinner is served. It is the house specialty."

The man handed the pitcher of water to Conrad and the towel to Jay. Conrad set the pitcher on the top shelf while Jay unwrapped the towel, revealing a plate holding four meat pies.

"I made them myself. My dead wife's recipe." He smiled at the memory of her cooking skills before continuing, "This is all you will have until tomorrow, so guard it well."

He saw Jay look questioningly at Conrad.

"The mice and rats would love to eat them before you do." He laughed heartily at the look on Jay's face. "What, the mighty crocodile hunter is afraid of some tiny rats?" Again the boom of his mirth filled the musty chamber.

"You have food, water, and, of course, the bucket. I think it is all you need."

He started up the steps and then stopped. Leaning over the railing he said, "Do not waste your time trying to escape. No one will hear your cries, and the door above is locked. Have pleasant dreams."

He creaked up the stairway. Once above, he hesitated for a moment before he let the trap door slam shut, plunging the boys into darkness. A rattling noise on the door indicated it was being locked.

"Great."

▲ ▲ ▲

The farmer was a spry old man. His skin was as sunbaked and weathered as the land he worked. Deep furrows on his brown face spoke silently of the years and adventures of his life. He chattered with excited terms in his native language. His arms were a flurry of gesticulations as he described what he had seen earlier that morning.

"That's odd," said ZZ when the man had answered a question. "He is quite adamant that there was one foreign boy and one local boy."

Alyssa giggled. "That local boy was Jay. He disguised himself in the marketplace so he could get close to the smugglers."

"I see," ZZ said as he completed his questioning.

He thanked the old farmer and gave him a reward for his information.

Turning to the others, ZZ said, "The man told me a boat landed here—a red boat—and unloaded the two young men.

They were escorted to a box truck and placed in the back. The boat captain departed back downriver toward Luxor and the truck departed south toward Lake Nasser. He said this took place this morning, so we are about four hours behind them."

"At least they are still in good health," Geoffrey said with relief. "I was not so sure after I saw the signs of struggle on the riverbank."

"So," said Alyssa, "they traveled south in a box truck. How do we know where they went or where they now are?"

Her question hung in the air between them.

CHAPTER 27

Nebi pushed the boat from the shore and turned to walk up the gentle embankment to the truck. He had to drive back to a marina north of the dam. From there, he would catch a ride to Luxor on one of the many boats that plied the river. He was tired and still angry at how Jay had bested him the night before.

Behind him on the lake, the Chief raised the sail and steered the little craft about a kilometer out into the open water. Here, he would look like any other fisherman and not be scrutinized by the patrol boats. Attention of any kind was a bad thing for smugglers. They needed to look like the rest of the faces in the crowd.

Scarface had calmed some and sat sullenly on the front of the boat, feeling the puffiness of his now black eye. His anger toward the two boys was secondary to his dread of possible punishment for dropping the instructions the night before. Mistakes in this game could be deadly. He did not want to find out firsthand. Before long, the weariness of sleep deprivation and the dying adrenaline rush combined with the serenity of being on the water. He lay back on the cushions and was soon asleep.

The Chief watched the water zip by as he trimmed the sail for maximum speed. It was a good day for sailing. The waters were calm and the breeze steady. His thoughts turned to his two prisoners. He wondered at their fate and of his hand in it. He had seen men die before. That was part of this dangerous game they all played. But these young men...his son would have been their age by now. He shook these thoughts from his mind and sailed on.

▲ ▲ ▲

Jay sat on the bench in the darkness. Conrad sat next to him, the water pitcher and the plate separating them. Each had finished a meat pie and both were trying to decide what to do with the second one.

"The Chief wasn't kidding," Jay said as he leaned back against the wall. "That is some family recipe. I think those were better than the ones we had with ZZ at the restaurant."

"I agree," said Conrad with a satisfied sigh. "They were large, too. I don't believe I could eat another right now."

"I could."

"Well don't. This is all we get until tomorrow," Conrad chided.

"Do you think there are rats down here?" Jay asked uneasily. "I don't like those critters."

"I doubt it," Conrad said thoughtfully. "Probably some mice, but that's about all."

"You seem sure about that," Jay stated, somewhat relieved.

"I am. Usually there are rat snakes in these kinds of buildings. They eat most of them."

"Seriously?" asked Jay, his uneasiness growing once again.

"Totally," Conrad replied. "It's common knowledge."

"Great. This keeps getting better all the time."

"Try to keep your mind occupied," his friend said. "I'll guard the meat pies from any nibbling rodents."

"I think I want to get out of here. How did the shelves look? Any possibilities?"

Conrad answered, "The second shelf from the bottom is loose, but I don't think it's heavy enough to batter through the trap door. It looked pretty sturdy."

"I may give it a try anyway, just for something to keep my mind occupied."

"Knock yourself out."

Jay felt his way along the wall until he came to the shelves. He reached down to the shelf in question and gave it a pull. It moved. He found the loose place and started to work it back and forth. With each pull, the board moved more and more. *One more pull ought to do it.*

Jay pulled with all his might. The board came loose and so did Jay. His momentum took him across the room where he smacked into the far wall. The board fell to the floor and the boy with it.

"Are you okay, Jay?" Conrad asked anxiously. "When I said to knock yourself out, I didn't expect you to take me literally."

"I'm fine. Just fine," Jay grunted. He crawled on the floor feeling for the board.

"Watch out for the bucket."

"Super."

Conrad heard the board hit the stairs and then the wall.

"Is everything all right?"

"Just a few control problems," Jay answered. "But I'm making good progress."

He slowly made his way to the top of the stairs. He felt around the trap door and bumped it a couple of times with his hand. It moved slightly on the side where the clasp was located.

"I think I've found a weakness," Jay said to Conrad. "There's a little give on one side. Maybe if we knock it with the board, it will come free. How about a hand?"

"Be right up."

The boys took the board and began banging on the door from below. The door withstood blow after blow with little improvement in the gap.

"Let's stop for a minute," Jay said. "I'm getting tired."

"Me too. I don't think the board is heavy enough."

"It sure got heavy toward the end," Jay remarked.

"You know what I am talking about. We need something with more mass."

"The bench?"

"The bench," Conrad confirmed.

"Okay, just don't knock the meat pies on the floor."

▲ ▲ ▲

The black SUV sped toward Aswan.

"What should we do next, ZZ?" Geoffrey asked.

"I am hopeful that my associates will once again put us on the trail of our young friends. I should get a call at any time."

"Where are we going?" Alyssa asked.

"I thought we would wait by the High Dam. There is a beautiful overlook where we can get some refreshments," the man answered. "As Geoffrey knows, the dam is a massive structure."

"Yes," Geoffrey added. "You have just seen the Low Dam. Even though it was raised several times, the Nile floods could still top it. So they built the High Dam during the 1960s. As you will soon see, it is very large."

Ten minutes later, the dam came into view.

"That is amazing!" exclaimed Alyssa.

"It is even larger when you are on top of it," said Geoffrey as he remembered his first time on the dam.

"It must have been a great thing for the Egyptian people if it stopped the flooding," the girl said thoughtfully.

"Yes and no," ZZ said. "Yes, it did stop the flooding. No, because it caused problems by limiting the silt that flowed downriver and fertilized the shores of the Nile."

"And," added Geoffrey, "because it raised the water level behind the dam and flooded a lot of land, they had to relocate thousands of people, as well as about twenty monuments and sites."

"I remember that Abu Simbel was one of the sites moved," Alyssa said. "They talked about it when we took the tour."

"Yes," ZZ agreed, "it was the most famous site moved, mainly because it was well publicized."

The SUV wound its way along the approach road to the overlook area.

As they parked, ZZ said, "Why don't you two go and look around? I am going to wait here until I get a call."

▲ ▲ ▲

The boys slowly carried the bench up the stairway. Jay took the lead and positioned the end of the bench where it would do maximum damage to the door.

"Okay," Jay said, "on three. One...Two...Three!"

The bench hit the door with a crash that echoed through the cellar room like thunder.

"Again. One...Two...Three!"

Over and over they hammered at the trap door, slowly loosening the clasp on the top.

"Let's rest for a minute," Jay said as he tried to catch his breath. "I think we are getting close."

They carried the bench back down to the foot of the stairs. Jay sat down while Conrad made his way over to the shelves and found the water pitcher. He joined Jay and each took a drink.

"We sure made a lot of noise," Conrad said as they rested. "It's a good thing our host and his friends are gone."

"I bet that old donkey upstairs is wondering what is going on in his nice quiet home," Jay laughed.

The donkey wasn't the only one wondering what was going on.

CHAPTER 28

On the way to the truck, a thought crossed Nebi's mind. At first, he dismissed it outright. He did this mainly out of fear—not of the thought, but of his superiors. If they ever heard of him acting on this thought, his life would be in danger. As he sullenly trudged toward the truck, the thought kept nagging at him, prodding him to act. He actually stopped once by the hut, thinking...considering. He had shaken it off and was now at the vehicle. He propped the rifle against the bumper of the truck and climbed up to shut the rear roller door. It came down with the sound of a passing train. He jumped off the truck and latched the door. He snatched up the rifle. The weapon felt cold and calming in his hand. In that instant, he knew what he *should* do, but decided to act on the impulse fluttering through his mind.

Even before he reached the stable, he could hear the sound. It was a deep, hollow *thump* mixed with a metallic rattle. The sound was methodical, like the ticking of a clock. Bang...Bang...Bang. He opened the gate and entered the structure. The donkey was agitated. He ran past the man to freedom. The man paid no attention to the fleeing beast. He was focused on the trap door latch that jumped to the rhythm. Bang...Bang...Bang.

The prisoners below were trying to escape!

Nebi considered the possibilities. He smiled at the notion of the two being shot while escaping. It was a thought born of revenge wanting to be fully satisfied. He gripped the rifle in anticipation. His musing was fleeting, however. His superiors might not see it the same way as he did. That could put his life in danger.

Another thought, almost as satisfying, crossed his mind.

Yes, I will show them who is now in control. And they will grovel before me and beg for their lives.

▲　▲　▲

Geoffrey tapped on the window. As it opened, he asked, "Any word from your associates?"

"I have given the description of the truck as told by the farmer to all of them. As you can imagine, there are many such vehicles in a city this large. We know from the message that the contraband will be transported down the lake. This will likely be by felucca, as this would not arouse the attention of a patrol boat. I am certain they would not cross over this dam with the truck so they could avoid the checkpoint inspection. It is likely they are south of the city somewhere in the direction of Abu Simbel. My associates in that area are conducting a search. I am confident they will soon bring a report we can act upon. In the meantime, I would like to join you for some refreshments at the overlook cafe."

ZZ closed the window. His bodyguard stepped out of the passenger seat and opened the door for his boss. Together they walked across the parking lot with Geoffrey and Alyssa.

▲　▲　▲

Nebi paused. The pounding from below had stopped. He listened for a minute before he walked over and started scraping the straw from the door.

"Do you hear that?" Conrad said quietly. "Someone is coming!"

Jay whispered something to Conrad.

Conrad was about to respond when Jay went into action as the pin was pulled from the hasp in the door.

Slowly, the trap door swung up and away with a squeal of the hinges. Compared to the total darkness of a moment ago, the chamber was flooded with light from above. A shadow crossed over the hole in the floor. It was Nebi!

The man looked intently down into the cellar below. He could see Conrad sitting on the bench at the foot of the stairs. Jay was nowhere to be seen.

"Where is your friend?" Nebi demanded.

Conrad cast a quick glance in Jay's direction. "He is over at the bucket."

"Tell him to come back to the light where I can see him."

"Jay, our friend wants you," Conrad said loudly.

"I heard him," Jay replied just as loudly. "I will be there in a minute."

A bareheaded Jay emerged from the shadows. He furtively kicked something under the bench as he noisily sat down. "Here I am."

Nebi crept down the steps, the AK-47 pointed at them menacingly. As he descended, he said, "Now the tables are turned. It is you who are surprised and at my mercy! I think it is unfortunate that you were shot while trying to escape!"

A shocked look crossed the boy's faces. This spurred Nebi on as he continued to climb down the steps.

"Won't it look a little suspicious to your boss if we are found dead down here?" Conrad asked trying to buy them some time.

Nebi laughed ruefully, "I will drag your carcasses upstairs and make it look as it should."

As the man talked, Jay was focused on the step directly below him.

One more step...Come on, just one more step...One—

As the man's foot began to fall on the next step, Jay suddenly reached down at his feet and pulled. The strip of cloth leapt off the step, catching the man's ankle. Nebi pitched forward, eyes wide in surprise. The rifle barked, spitting lead into the wall above their heads. Nebi fell forward with a loud crash.

Conrad kicked the rifle away while Jay jumped on the man's back. Nebi fought like a wildcat, kicking and punching. But the combined force of Conrad and Jay subdued him.

Jay pulled the cloth strip that had been his trip wire free from the stairs and hogtied the man securely. For good measure, he stuffed the towel from the food plate into Nebi's mouth.

As the boys sat down, Jay said, "I knew that turban would come in handy!"

Conrad just shook his head, inwardly thankful for his friend's disguise.

After a minute, Jay stood up. "I think we should get out of here."

"What do we do with him?" Conrad asked.

"Leave him. We can send the police back later."

Nebi glared at the boys with pure hatred.

The boys left the man and his rifle and quickly climbed the steps. At the top, Conrad started to close the trap door.

"Wait a minute," Jay said. "I'll be right back."

He descended into the cellar while an amazed Conrad looked on. In less than a minute, Jay's grinning face appeared from below.

"Here, hold this," he said as he handed Conrad the plate with two meat pies and then climbed out of the hole. "No need for these to go to waste!"

Conrad let the door slam shut and inserted the wooden peg in the clasp. "One down and two to go!"

Jay looked at him quizzically.

"We are the two. Let's go!" Conrad yelled with a smile.

The boys hustled out the stable and across the lot. Jay slowed at the hut, wanting to look inside.

"What are you doing?" demanded Conrad, slowing as well. "We need to get out of here!"

"This will only take a minute."

"Nothing ever takes a minute with you!"

Jay opened the door and walked into the smuggler's hut. The interior was stark—mud brick construction with one main room and two sleeping rooms. Wooden posts and beams supported a tin roof. The furniture was sparse and ancient. A table and four chairs occupied a place by a simple kitchen. A stool, another chair, and some cabinets completed the decor. Electric wires were strung where needed. Simple bare bulbs provided light.

Jay walked to the back to peek in the other rooms. The main bedroom had a bed and a dresser. The bed was unmade, its coverings bunched and in disorder. As he was taking it all in, he heard Conrad call from the other room in the back.

"You had better come in here!"

Jay walked into the last room. It was small by any standard and nondescript...except for what Conrad had found!

"Why in the world would The Chief have a fax machine?" Jay asked. "He's not running a business center here."

"That's what I was wondering...until I found this!" Conrad held a crumpled piece of paper.

Jay took the paper and suddenly everything became clear. It contained a series of hieroglyphs!

"So this is how they communicate without risking detection!" Jay exclaimed in wonder. "They send faxes containing hieroglyphs, and the smugglers know what the next delivery job will be."

"Maybe the police will be able to trace the sender of these faxes," Conrad mused. "But right now, we need to get out of here before someone traces us."

The boys ran out of the hut and over to the truck.

Conrad flung the driver side door open, but Jay stepped past him. "I'll drive, if you don't mind."

"I do mind."

Jay paid no attention and glanced at the ignition. "Bingo! The keys are here!"

He turned the key and the truck engine came to life.

"Are you coming with me or not?" he asked Conrad who was still standing by the door.

Jay put the truck in gear while Conrad ran around the front of the vehicle and climbed in the passenger side door.

"Have a pie!" Jay said as he handed the plate to Conrad and gunned the engine.

The truck turned north on the road and headed for freedom. The meat pies were gone before they reached the paved road leading to Abu Simbel.

▲ ▲ ▲

Up ahead the boys could see the looming temple complex built into the side of an artificial mountain. Fresh air blew through the open windows of the truck, lifting already high spirits. A black car started to pass the truck on the left. As it came even with the truck, the passenger side window rolled down and a man brandishing a gun motioned for them to pull over.

"Man!" Jay cried. "That guy has a gun! He wants me to pull over!" He glanced at Conrad. "What should I do?"

"Pull over!"

"What?"

"Pull over!" Conrad repeated. "He has a gun and you do not!"

Jay let out a cry of exasperation and eased the truck to the side of the road and stopped in a cloud of dust. The car pulled in front of them to block their escape. The boys sat nervously as the passenger with the pistol jumped out and walked toward the truck.

"Now what?" Jay exclaimed as he pounded on the steering wheel.

CHAPTER 29

ZZ's phone rang. He answered it as his friends looked on. "Yes? Very good...Really? That is news I am glad to hear...Yes, detain the truck until we get there."

He ended the call and said, "My associates have found a truck resembling the description from the farmer. It was heading north toward Abu Simbel. It has been observed that there was a local driving the vehicle with a foreigner as a passenger." He smiled. "I wonder who they could be?"

"Jay and Conrad!" shouted Alyssa. "You've found them!" She rushed over and hugged the man.

"Well...actually my associates have found them," the embarrassed man said as he attempted to escape the girl's grasp. "I merely reported the fact. They have been stopped and detained until we arrive."

"That is great, ZZ!" Geoffrey said with relief.

The man bowed slightly as he gestured toward the SUV. "Shall we go?"

While they pulled onto the highway heading south from the dam, ZZ made several more phone calls, his soft Arabic voice calmly issuing orders.

Alyssa was amazed at how controlled the man was in the midst of all the excitement. *No wonder he is successful at everything he does.*

▲　▲　▲

"Whew!" Jay wiped the sweat from his forehead. "I thought we were toast...again!"

He and Conrad leaned against the front of the truck waiting for their friends to pick them up.

"So did I," Conrad agreed. "I couldn't figure out how they had managed to find us so fast after we escaped. It didn't make sense."

"I never got that far," Jay admitted. "All I saw was the gun. All I could think about was the gun!"

The boys laughed easily about being pulled over by ZZ's men now that it was over.

"I can't wait to see everybody," Jay said. "There were times I was not so sure that would ever happen."

"I know what you mean," his friend said. "It didn't look good for us."

"It's a good thing that Nebi guy wanted to get even with us," Jay laughed. "That made it easy to get out."

"It didn't seem so easy when the lead was flying," Conrad reminded him. "I would have preferred to just bust out with the bench."

"And miss all the excitement? I will—"

Jay never finished his sentence. He saw the black SUV approach and cross over to their side of the road. The back door burst open and Geoffrey spilled out, followed by Alyssa.

Alyssa ran over and hugged them both, tears streaming down her cheeks. "I never thought I would see you guys again!"

"We would never let that happen," Jay said. "Who else could keep you guessing about what we were going to do next?"

"You mean who would keep her guessing about what trouble you were going to cause next!" Geoffrey exclaimed as he shook the boys' hands and hugged them both. "Are you both okay? You don't look any worse for the wear. And, Jay, you look passably authentic in that garb."

"Good to see you too, Mr. B." Jay laughed.

"Yes," quipped Conrad, "now, someone else can take over keeping him out of trouble for awhile."

Geoffrey and Alyssa launched into a thousand questions about their abduction, captivity, and escape. The interrogation was only interrupted by ZZ who had been conversing with his men and now joined the group.

"I see that the young men are in good health," the man said pleasantly. "There were times this past day when we were not so sure this would be the case."

"Thanks for helping us out, ZZ," Jay said gratefully.

"Yes," added Conrad. "We really appreciate all you have done."

"It was my pleasure," the man replied as if this was a normal everyday occurrence for him. "I am glad you are safe." Then he added in a serious tone, "Perhaps you can now stay focused on the purpose of your trip and out of trouble?"

The man allowed the questions to start flowing again before he interrupted once more. "I would like to see the place where you were kept. You can ride with me. My associates will take care of the truck with the police."

Everyone, including the driver got out of the SUV. The bodyguard stood surveying the property, alert for any signs of trouble. The staccato slamming of vehicle doors was the only sound they heard. As a group, they started walking across the grounds toward the hut. There was no sign of the boat through the breaks in the tree line by the shore. All seemed quiet.

The bodyguard cautiously moved toward the hut with pistol drawn. The driver, who had likewise drawn his pistol, backed him up. It was obvious to the group of friends that this was not the first time they had done this. After the hut was cleared, both men emerged and posted themselves at the two front corners, awaiting instructions.

"Why don't we go up to the stable first?" suggested Jay. "We can show you the cellar, and you can bring Nebi the smuggler out."

ZZ agreed and nodded to his men to proceed up the slow rise to the structure. The group trailed the guards at a safe distance. In front of the stable, the donkey was grazing on the green grass, peacefully unaware of another invasion of his domain. The guards shooed him out of the way and entered the stable. The driver came back to the gate to give the 'all clear' sign, and the friends proceeded up the hill. When they entered, they saw the bodyguard standing by the open trap door.

ZZ conferred quietly with the man and then turned around. "You say you left the man in the cellar and the door was locked?"

"Yes," said Jay, sensing something was wrong. "We hogtied him with my turban and left him at the bottom of the stairs with the gun."

"The door was open and the man and his gun gone when my associates here arrived. There is no apparent sign of the door being forced from below."

Jay and Conrad looked at each other in shock.

"That's impossible!" Conrad exclaimed. "There is no way he could have escaped!"

The boys rushed down the steps into the cellar. Everything was as they had left it, but the man was clearly gone. The cloth strip of the turban was laying in pieces at the foot of the stairs. Jay gathered them up, noting that a sharp instrument had been used to cut through the material. They trudged back above ground, a look of confusion on their faces.

"I don't understand what could have happened," said Jay dejectedly as he held out the handful of cloth for inspection. "This is what is left of the turban we used to tie him with."

"It looks like some of the man's friends came back and rescued him," said Geoffrey. "But it doesn't matter. The important thing is that you are safe."

ZZ agreed, "Yes, this is most important. The other man is a matter for the police."

Jay brightened up as another thought occurred to him. "Hey, we want to show you what we found in The Chief's hut!"

The boy led the group down the hill to the hut. Jay entered first, followed by the others. The guards remained outside.

"This is the main room. As you can see, nothing out of the ordinary," Jay intoned, acting as the tour director. "If you come this way, I'll show you the two back rooms."

Jay led them past the bedroom and entered the small room at the back of the hut.

"Right over here in the corner," he began as he breezed into the room, "there is a—"

The boy stopped mid-sentence. The fax machine and the crumpled hieroglyph note were gone. Even the phone line had been removed. There was no sign they had ever been there!

Jay was furious. "I can't believe they cleaned this place out! After all the work we did to discover the smugglers den!"

"Work? Discover?" Conrad asked incredulously. "We didn't work, we were brought here under threat of death. We didn't discover anything but what it was like to have another chance at life!"

"Okay, okay. Wrong words. But just the same, we were outmaneuvered by the bad guys when we were so close to busting them," Jay said, still a little wound up.

"As Geoffrey said," Alyssa soothed her friend, "all that matters is you're safe. The rest is something for the police to deal with."

They loaded into the SUV for the ride back to the airport. Jay sat silently in the back. Even while Conrad relayed the details of their brief but exciting time as prisoners, Jay was uncharacteristically quiet.

This makes my head hurt. I was so sure we had busted this case wide open.

They hadn't yet, but they would have another chance sooner than they thought!

Chapter 30

It was evening before they arrived back at the hotel. ZZ dropped his passengers off and bid them farewell. Four very tired friends trudged into the lobby.

Dimah greeted them as they entered, "It is good to see you safe. It sounds like you had a close call with what could have been a very bad ending."

"We are glad to be back," answered Jay. "This has not been the best 24 hours of my life, that's for sure!"

Dimah turned to Geoffrey and said, "Thank you for phoning me and letting me know how everything turned out."

"I thought it was the least I could do," Geoffrey replied. "Especially after all of your assistance."

The lady smiled at Jay. "There is only one thing that is not clear to me. Did you find out what they have been smuggling?"

Jay looked at Conrad in dismay and shook his head.

"I can't believe we forgot to tell you!" the boy exclaimed. "We know what they are smuggling...at least we have an idea."

Everyone turned their attention to Jay.

"When we were trapped in the truck, in that secret compartment, the smuggled package had been stored down at our feet. There was little room to move around in that tight box, but we managed to work the bundle up so we could see what it was. It was wrapped tightly in linen. We couldn't tear it, but we could probe around a little."

Conrad nodded, but didn't add anything to the narrative.

Jay continued, "There were three items wrapped individually and then bundled together. I'm pretty sure that all three were some type of figurines, each probably about eight to ten inches in length. I could feel the outline of two of them. I couldn't tell exactly what the third one was because the padding was too thick, but it seemed long and kind of cylindrical."

Everyone stared wide-eyed at the news. All wondered why they had not asked this question before.

"So, you didn't you see any of them?" clarified Dimah.

"They were wrapped really well, so all I could do was feel through the linen."

"Antiquities?" Geoffrey asked Dimah.

The woman did not reply, letting the question hang in the air.

"That's what we think," Conrad interjected. "They were— are—smuggling ancient Egyptian artifacts."

"Yeah," Jay added. "We made sure they were not bundles of drugs or anything like that."

"It had to be something valuable," Conrad completed his thought. "That is why we're sure it is antiquities they are smuggling."

"This has huge ramifications for my country," said Dimah. "And you are both lucky to be alive today. The people who do such things look at life as a cheap commodity."

In the absence of immediate excitement and impending danger, the seriousness behind her words finally settled in on all of them. It *was* a miracle they were still alive!

"I need a shower and some sleep," said Jay with obvious fatigue. "I want to forget about this day. Just wash it off and forget about it."

Everyone agreed. They said their 'good nights' to Dimah and headed for their rooms. Everyone was eager to get some rest.

Everyone except Dimah, that is. She was just getting started.

▲　▲　▲

Jay came out of the bathroom, escorted by clouds of steam from his long, hot shower. Conrad lay quietly on his bed staring at the ceiling. His thoughts were so intent and serious that he didn't even comment as the steam floated above him in thin wisps.

"How do you think they found out?"

Jay finished toweling his hair and bounced down on his bed. "About what?"

"Nebi being a prisoner and us escaping?"

Jay threw his balled-up towel in the direction of the bathroom door and missed.

"That, Conrad, is the question of the day." Jay looked at his friend who continued to stare at the ceiling. "We were gone, what, forty-five minutes? An hour max?"

Conrad rubbed his face with both hands. "About," he said with a yawn.

"They had to work pretty fast," Jay said, thinking out loud. "Get there, get Nebi out, take down the smuggling communications center, and get clean away before we could get back. I don't understand it." He lay back on his bed and pulled the covers over him.

Conrad thought a minute and then continued, "It's almost like someone was tipped off. It's not like they were watching the place. Otherwise, they wouldn't have let us escape."

The only reply was the sound of Jay's gentle snoring. Conrad reached over and clicked the light off.

It smells like we have a spy in our midst...but who?

▲ ▲ ▲

The Sudanese police inspector ended the call from his chief detective. He exhaled in frustration. They had found only two places on Osman Digna Street that had a statue. One was a small park, the other the Bank of Sudan. He had placed his men at both locations. Neither had been the drop-off place for the smuggled goods. That left only three possibilities as far as his tired mind could conceive: The call had been a hoax, the caller had been wrong, or the smugglers had been tipped off about the stakeout.

He slipped into his suit jacket and headed for the door of his office. He turned off the light and locked the door before heading down the quiet hallway. While he was intent on stopping the smuggling of antiquities out of Sudan, he could only do so much. As it was, valuable resources had been used on an anonymous tip. He knew, though, he would do it again—a thousand times he would do it again—until the madness stopped.

He greeted the officer at the night desk and stepped out into the cooling night air. Perhaps the next time, he would be successful. Perhaps he would discover who was doing the smuggling and who was creating the demand. Now it was time to go home to his cold dinner.

▲ ▲ ▲

The man sat quietly in his office. It had been an eventful day, an almost disastrous day. Yet, he had managed to eliminate the evidence and avoid detection. *And,* he had successfully delivered the goods.

A new smuggling way station could be set up. That was an easy thing. A new dummy corporation could be assigned as the owner of the land and buildings. The Chief could be relocated to the other side of the lake and become a simple goat herder for a while until things settled down. His boat would never be found at the bottom of the lake...nor would its final passenger, Nebi.

He put aside such thoughts and dialed the number. It was answered on the second ring.

"Good evening, Mr. Chin. I am checking on your satisfaction with the merchandise that was delivered this evening...Very good. I am pleased that you appreciate my selection...Yes, I am sorry for the sudden change of the drop-off point. We are cautious to protect both of our investments in this endeavor...Yes, we must take ever greater precautions in this rapidly changing world...It was a pleasure doing business with you as well...Good night to you."

His phone went dark.

Tomorrow we will see if the intruders have had enough excitement to satisfy them for one trip. If they do not make arrangements to leave tomorrow, I will have to...induce them by way of a group accident.

CHAPTER 31

"How did everyone sleep last night?" Geoffrey asked the group of less than perky school friends as they joined him for a late breakfast.

"It was a long couple of days, Mr. B," said Jay as he reached for a glass of orange juice. "I think I could have slept another couple of hours. It seems like I had a restless night or something."

"I can tell you it was the *or something*," Conrad said. "You were in such a deep sleep that even a couple of pops from my pillow didn't wake you. And then there was the snoring. I was surprised there was any paint on the walls this morning, sonic scrubbing and all."

Geoffrey stifled a smile. He knew Jay's ability to sleep deeply and wake slowly. "How on earth did you get the mummy down here this morning?" he asked Conrad.

"I reminded him that if he missed the late breakfast, he would be waiting a couple of hours before he could graze again. That did it straightaway," Conrad replied.

"And how about you, Alyssa?" Geoffrey inquired. "Did Jay keep you awake from down the hall?"

"I slept fine," the girl answered. "I could have used a little more. For some reason, I thought this would be a *relaxing* trip."

The man nodded his understanding. "I anticipated you all would be worn out today, so I changed our itinerary a bit. I phoned Jafar Kazim this morning and accepted his invitation to tour the Karnak Temple Complex with him today. It should be informative...and low key."

"Low *key* is for *me*, Mr. *B*," quipped Jay with a smile.

"Yes, it sounds great," Conrad agreed. "It will give Jay a chance to check out the walls of that temple to see if *they* are scalable at night."

"You guys!" laughed Alyssa. Her expression turned prim as she looked at Jay. "I think Jay has given up trespassing, right?"

"I have, Alyssa. Thank you very much," the boy replied as he drizzled syrup on his waffle. "I think I will let Conrad take the lead on the next temple invasion."

"No thank you. I think I would like to be a plain old boring tourist for a day," Conrad said between bites of eggs. "You know. Look at the sites and marvel at their 3,000 year old appearance. Snap a few photos. Listen to Jafar. All that."

"Yes, well, I don't think our tour today will be boring. But I understand what you are saying," said Geoffrey. "Jafar told me that we will have access to areas of the complex that are off limits to most people."

"Right up Jay's alley," commented Conrad. "*No* means *go* for him."

"That was really nice of Jafar," Alyssa remarked. "He didn't have to go through all of this trouble if he didn't want to. We might find out he is a really nice man."

"Well, I don't think we have a reason to expect otherwise," Geoffrey said graciously. "I am sure he is a busy man given all of his responsibilities. It was kind of him to show us around."

"I didn't get warm fuzzies from him the last time we met, but he did cut me some slack when I umm..." Jay stopped

Conrad finished the sentence for him, "When you trespassed illegally on state property...in a foreign country."

"What I was trying to say," Jay continued, "is that I am willing to give him the benefit of the doubt and assume he is a nice man, too."

Everyone ate in silence for a few minutes, simply enjoying the pleasant peacefulness of the nearly empty dining room.

"You have already seen the Luxor Temple," Geoffrey said as the plates were cleared and he sipped his tea. "The Karnak Temple is separate, but related. Both were constructed to serve the interests of the Theban Triad of gods."

"Amun, Mut, and Khonsu," Alyssa said from memory.

"Well done, Alyssa," Geoffrey praised. "I am glad at least one of you is learning something new this trip."

"And they both share in the Opet Festival celebration," a smiling Conrad added. "I picked up a few things so far."

"And there is the Avenue of the Sphinxes," Jay added. "That is another way they are connected...literally."

"Right...By the by, I received a phone call from Abu al-Hasan this morning," Geoffrey said, changing the subject.

"The Interior Ministry guy?" Jay asked.

"One and the same," Geoffrey answered. "It seems he would urgently like to meet with us to discuss your little, uh, excursion up the river." Geoffrey looked at Jay and Conrad.

"How did he find out about that?" asked Jay suspiciously. "I mean, all of that only happened yesterday."

"He didn't say. Quite frankly, it caught me a little off guard," Geoffrey admitted. "Anyway, we will be meeting with him late this afternoon or early evening, once we are finished at the Karnak Temple."

"Another interrogation!" Jay complained. "I wonder when they will end?"

"Probably the minute *you* leave Egypt," sniped Conrad, a mischievous look in his blue eyes. "That's the last possibility of us having any of your shenanigans to answer for."

"Look," Jay offered, "we only have four days left over here. I would like to be Joe Tourist the rest of the time. Mr. B has some more interesting stuff to show us...and I still want to find Akhenaten."

Alyssa and Conrad exchanged amused looks, neither convinced by Jay's words.

▲　▲　▲

"Geoffrey! So good to see you again!" the overly friendly man exclaimed. "And you have all of your young archeologists with you! Excellent!"

"Thank you for inviting us, Jafar," Geoffrey answered, shaking the man's outstretched hand. "We are looking forward to an informative and relaxing day with you here at the temple."

The three friends echoed Geoffrey's sentiments appreciatively.

Jafar eyed them as a man who knew more than he should. "Yes. I understand a relaxing day would be a welcome change from your recent excitement." He looked directly at the boys as he spoke.

"Uh, yes," Geoffrey hesitated. "How did you know about our...adventure?"

The robed man shrugged. "It is part of my job to know what is going on when it comes to stolen antiquities."

The group of friends could only look at each other in shock, as the man continued, "Do not be alarmed. It is a matter of routine, I assure you. I have many eyes here in the city and out into the Necropolis across the river. This is, after all, the tomb robbing capital of the world."

"Not such a great tourist slogan," Conrad whispered to Jay with raised eyebrows.

The man continued, "You young men are very fortunate to have escaped with your lives. Smugglers are a dangerous crowd. They are ruthless. And, I promise you this, they will seek revenge."

Jay shuddered at this last statement. "Revenge? For what?"

"For interfering with their operation. For disrupting their plans. For forcing a curtailing of their activities. For putting them at risk with the authorities...Need I continue?"

"Uh, no. I guess that about covers everything," Jay said sheepishly.

"But Jafar," Geoffrey protested, "surely this gang could see that Jay and Conrad merely stumbled upon them by accident?"

"I do not think they make such distinctions," the man said severely. "At least that has been my experience with them these past thirty years."

Seeing the nervous looks on the faces of his guests, Jafar returned to his jovial personality. "I am sorry. I can see I have upset you. My only wish is that you would not experience an unfortunate outcome to your visit in our beautiful land. I merely want to express that you are not in casual danger here. If this gang, as you call them, would like retribution, they surely know where to find you." He gazed at them for a few seconds before he continued, his face covered with a plastic smile, "But let us put this unpleasantness behind us, shall we? I have a marvelous behind-the-scenes tour arranged for you. I hope it will be the highlight of your trip!"

Jafar turned and bowed graciously. "Please follow me. And please ask whatever questions you have, especially you, my curious young archeologists."

Jafar led the way through the huge Pylon wall into the temple complex. Geoffrey walked on one side of the man and Alyssa on the other. Jay and Conrad followed a few steps behind.

As the man was answering a question from Alyssa, Jay whispered, "He sure is a bundle of encouragement. That's twice now he's tried to scare us off."

Conrad whispered in reply, "He had some good points, though. We really did get in the middle of the smugglers' operation. I'm sure they are not the least bit happy with us right now. We could be in danger. I didn't think of this before."

"I know what you mean. I thought after yesterday afternoon, the mess was behind us." Jay cast a furtive glance back at the two watchful bodyguards who were following the group at a respectful distance. "At least we have our own security detail while we are here with Jafar."

"Somehow, I don't feel any safer," Conrad said quietly. "I couldn't get a thought out of my head last night while I *wasn't* sleeping."

"What thought was that?"

"That there is a leak in the information flow somewhere."

"A spy?" Jay hissed.

"Yes, a spy."

"It's funny you should mention it," Jay said quietly as he leaned toward Conrad. "I was thinking the exact same thing all the way back from the Chief's house yesterday."

CHAPTER 32

"There are actually four different sections in our temple," Jafar informed his captive audience as they strolled down the main avenue leading deeper into the complex.

"I didn't realize that until Geoffrey mentioned it this morning," Alyssa said to the smiling man.

"Geoffrey is a learned man," Jafar complimented. "Most people see only this main section that we are currently in and think the rest of the complex consists of nothing but off-limits ruins. But that is not the case. There are actually active digs and restorations going on in the other areas."

"Have they made any remarkable discoveries?" Conrad asked.

"They have found countless artifacts," Jafar answered. "That is why the other temples and structures are not for the public. As you can imagine, securing such a huge area is difficult. If these were opened to everyone, it would be impossible to control the flow of our Egyptian heritage into the wrong hands."

"Smugglers?" Jay asked.

"And worse." The man frowned. "So, we try to keep track of all who are admitted into the restricted areas. Yet, things still happen."

Jay's interest was growing. "Have they found any tombs here?"

The man stopped abruptly. His eyes drilled into Jay. "Tombs?"

"You know. Like missing pharaohs or queens?"

"Jay is interested in the possibilities raised about Nefertiti being buried in Tut's tomb," Geoffrey explained. "He thinks there are others who could be found here."

"I can assure you that there are no tombs on the temple grounds," Jafar said, his plastic smile in full bloom. "You see, the pharaohs knew their only chance to walk through the Field of Reeds—"

"In the afterlife," interrupted Alyssa.

"Yes, my astute young archeologist, in the afterlife," Jafar confirmed with a polite nod. He then continued the thought, "His only chance in the afterlife was to be buried on the west side of the Nile. They were adamant about this fact. Hence, the Valleys of the Kings and Queens."

"Do you think Akhenaten is buried over there somewhere?" Jay asked innocently.

"Akhenaten? Why do you ask this?" Jafar said, looking darkly at Jay.

"Well, I know he is still missing, and I thought maybe we could get a clue to his tomb when we looked around here today."

"My young friend, I can assure you that Akhenaten has already been found." The smile was full blast now. "He was the mummy in KV55."

"Geoffrey doesn't think so."

Jafar turned to Geoffrey and asked, "Is this true?"

Geoffrey cleared his throat. "I do not subscribe to the theory that such a pharaoh would have had a son like Tut and there be no record of it anywhere. Besides," Geoffrey continued, "I do not believe the DNA evidence would bear this out as even a possibility under closer scrutiny."

Jafar's face seemed to grow a shade darker. "I see. Well, we should discuss this over some strong Egyptian coffee sometime. I would like to know what a distinguished man such as yourself thinks on this subject."

Jafar turned to continue the tour. The group followed his lead.

"As I was saying, this is the main public section of the complex. It is known as the Precinct of Amun-Ra. There is also the Precinct of Mut, the wife of Amun, the Precinct of Montu, the war god, and even the Temple of Amenhotep IV, before he became Akhenaten."

At this, Jay's ears perked up. "He has a temple here?"

"Had. When he died, much of what he had done as Akhenaten was destroyed—erased by the priests who were hungry for power and by pharaohs who were afraid to oppose them," the man said with a note of bitterness. "I'm afraid his temple here was not spared. There is little left."

He motioned everyone toward the huge structures in front of them. "Come, I will show you the main temple, and then we will see the others."

▲   ▲   ▲

"This place is huge!" Conrad exclaimed as he marveled at the seemingly endless rows of massive columns.

"Magnificent!" Geoffrey said with appreciation.

"This part of the complex has that effect on most visitors," Jafar said with evident satisfaction. "This is the Great Hypostyle Hall," he said with a grand sweep of his arm. "It is the second largest religious structure in the world. In American terms, it is over 50,000 square feet in size. There are 134 columns." He pointed upward. "Some of those cross beams or lentils on top weigh 70 tons each!"

The friends looked around in wonder at the site.

"How did they get those beams up there?" Alyssa asked.

"There are several theories, but few answers," the man said. "We don't know with certainty."

"The Egyptians were great architects and builders," Geoffrey added. "We cannot duplicate most of their feats, even with modern technology."

"They had time on their side," Jafar commented. "This entire complex is one mile wide by two miles long. It has additions dating from the Middle Kingdom to the time of Alexander the Great. Thirty pharaohs contributed to the structures you see around you. Archeologists have identified no less than 433 gardens within the complex. Its scale is almost incomprehensible."

"Amazing," Jay said, clearly in awe of the place.

"As I recall, Jafar, much of the work was done by the New Kingdom pharaohs of the 18th Dynasty," Geoffrey stated. "The same as the Luxor Temple."

"That is correct, my friend," the smiling man said. "And later by Ramesses II. But it was during the 18th Dynasty that Thebes was established firmly as the religious center of Egypt."

"With the exception of Akhenaten."

"Yes, this is true," Jafar affirmed. "But after his death, it was quickly moved from Amarna back to here. I think it all rather tragic."

"Why is that?" Geoffrey asked.

"Most of what Akhenaten accomplished in his life was wiped out in a few short years. Even Tut moved quickly back to the old ways."

The man turned and led them past security through a small steel gate. Beyond were remnants of foundations, piles of rubble, and a few carved stones peeking out from the scruffy Egyptian grass.

"This is all that remains of Akhenaten's temple," the man said quietly. "It was destroyed and the materials used for other building projects."

The group surveyed the desolate sight before them. Each could not help but feel sadness over what had become of the Heretic King.

"Let us go on to more pleasant areas," Jafar said. "The Precinct of Mut is up ahead to the south."

The group stopped in the middle of a vast field of ruins as Jafar continued, "These are the remains of the temple. While in a ruined state, you can see it was not utterly destroyed and carted off."

They walked through the temple and came to a terrace.

"Down there is the Sacred Crescent Lake. It is famous the world over," Jafar intoned.

"This place is gigantic!" Jay exclaimed as he looked out over the expanse.

"There is yet one more place to show you...the Temple of Montu. It is nearly a half-mile walk to the north side of the main temple. Is this too far in this warm sun?" Jafar asked.

A chorus of "no's" was the response.

"Very well," the man said. "Let us walk this way then."

"Everything looks so small on the map, but when you get out here, it is actually large," said Alyssa.

"Thirty pharaohs vying for the favor of the gods added up to a lot of building over the centuries," Jafar explained. "Even this sandstone was quarried over 100 miles from here and floated down the Nile on barges."

"A tremendous undertaking," Geoffrey agreed.

"The people believed the pharaoh was the embodiment of god. Whatever pharaoh wanted was done," Jafar stated. "Everything."

After looking through the ruins of Montu's temple and the Gateway of Ptolemy III, the group passed back through a gated portal into the main complex. They inspected the large toppled obelisk of Hatshepsut and the remains of her building projects before moving toward the exit avenue.

"Well, my friends," Jafar said, "that concludes my tour. I hope you found it enjoyable."

Geoffrey responded for the group. "This was gracious of you. A marvelous day, indeed."

The man smiled, obviously pleased with the effect his tour had had on the group.

"Oh, Geoffrey," Jafar said, "could I have a final word with you?"

He and Geoffrey walked a short distance from the others.

"Please take what I said earlier seriously. I apologize for being so adamant, but I don't think you realize the danger you and our young friends are in." Jafar looked intently at Geoffrey before continuing. "I think you should consider leaving Egypt tomorrow and taking these young people out of harm's way."

"Tomorrow? Do you think—"

"I do not think. I know!"

CHAPTER 33

The four friends strolled along the Avenue of the Sphinxes toward the Luxor Temple. They planned to stop at the restaurant where Malika worked for a bite to eat before meeting Abu at their hotel. The late afternoon sun was warm and the breeze blowing off the Nile fresh. The emotional fatigue of earlier in the day was slowly being replaced by a general physical weariness. They decided to take a break on some benches in the shade of two palm trees.

"*That* was an amazing experience," Alyssa said excitedly. "When you see all of it like we did, it is definitely overwhelming."

"Agreed," said Geoffrey. "One of the things I love about the various monuments of Egypt is that each one evokes a different emotional response. Some exude grandeur, making you feel small and insignificant in the larger scheme of things. Some are simple and elegant, inviting you into their secrets. Some are expansive and almost overwhelming to the senses."

"Speaking of overwhelming," Jay commented, "I thought Jafar's warning was a little bit over the top."

"So did I," agreed Conrad. "That is the second time we have met the man and the second time he has warned us about danger."

"I had never thought about what he said, though," Alyssa stated. "I just believed all the smuggling business was behind us. Now, I don't know for sure."

"I, too, have been mulling over his warning," Geoffrey admitted. "He was adamant about it, and would know about such things from his line of business. I think we should consider what he said. Perhaps we should cut our trip short and head back to the States. I would never forgive myself if something happened to any one of you."

Jay was astonished. "Head back? I don't know about that, Mr. B. We haven't found any missing mummies."

"Or their treasure," Conrad added with a smile.

"Right. Or their treasure," Jay agreed. "Besides, I can't believe the smugglers would do anything else to draw attention to themselves...especially causing an international incident by messing with us!"

Conrad was going to make a comment about Jay being a one-man international incident when Geoffrey continued, "Still, I think we should consider his warning as being valid and remain cautiously alert. We can talk about it more tonight after our meeting with Abu."

They all agreed that Geoffrey's suggestion was the best course of action and put the warnings about danger out of their minds.

"I'm hungry," Jay stated. "Let's go do some international consumption at the restaurant."

Everybody laughed and resumed their trek once again.

Behind them, a dark man dressed like a tourist walked out from between two sphinxes and resumed following them. His beady eyes missed no detail as they observed everything from behind the dark glasses the man wore.

Across the avenue, a professionally dressed woman observed the man following the friends. She began to shadow them all.

▲ ▲ ▲

"This is more like it!" Jay exclaimed as he settled comfortably into his seat at the restaurant. "A cool glass of tea. Some fresh bread and dip. A soft chair. Just what I needed."

"I'm a little tired myself," Alyssa admitted. "I'm glad we don't have much else to do today. I think all the excitement is catching up to me."

"You haven't seen excitement yet," Conrad commented wryly. "Wait until Jay's food order comes out. Then you'll see excitement!"

"I didn't notice you were fasting," Jay replied in defense. "I have to keep up my strength. You never know when the situation will call for more action. It's best to be fortified and ready!"

"Oh! Here comes Malika from the kitchen," Alyssa interrupted, waving to her friend.

Malika approached the table, a look of relief apparent on her face. "I am so glad you are unharmed," she said with emotion to Jay and Conrad. "When you disappeared, I feared the worse."

Jay cast a strange glance at Conrad.

"How did you know we had disappeared?" Jay asked. "It was late at night and only Alyssa and Geoffrey knew about it."

The girl's face reddened. "Oh," she stammered, "I, um, I guess I heard the rumor among the locals here. Anyway," she said, changing the subject, "I am glad everything is now fine. I am working in the kitchen today. I just wanted to come out and say hello."

The girl turned without another word and walked back to the kitchen.

"That was a bit strange, don't you think?" Conrad said. "Something is going on around here. Information leaks out like sieve."

"Quite," Geoffrey said thoughtfully. He stared at the doorway to the kitchen. "There seems to be something Malika is not saying."

"She was obviously relieved to see the boys," Alyssa stated in agreement. "I just can't believe she would be mixed up in all of this."

"I don't know who is doing what anymore," Jay said. "I do smell a big mystery here, though. It makes me even less thrilled about leaving this place before we get to the bottom of it."

"Maybe Geoffrey is right," Alyssa said as she looked at her friends at the table. "Maybe we should be more cautious and aware of any potential danger."

All of them became quiet as their lunch was served and they chewed on both their food and their thoughts.

The dark tourist man listened to every word from the next table as he unobtrusively sipped his coffee and pretended to watch the people passing by on the street.

The lady watched them all from the outdoor cafe across the narrow street.

▲　▲　▲

When they arrived back at the hotel, Abu al-Hasan was sitting quietly in a chair by the door. His bodyguard was standing by the entrance, his vigilance a well-practiced habit of training.

The man stood as they entered and waited for them to come to him.

"Hello, Abu," Geoffrey said as he shook the man's hand. "How are you?"

"I am fine," he answered. "I came here to see how you were doing."

He bid them all to sit down around the coffee table and then continued, "I have heard things...disturbing things." He looked gravely at them.

Geoffrey answered, "Well, yes. You see—"

Abu held up his hand for Geoffrey to stop. "I know all about what has happened."

Seeing the surprised looks on their faces, he continued, "It is my business to know such things. You may not understand this, but I am in charge of security within the Interior Ministry. My jurisdiction includes—very specifically—antiquities...*stolen* antiquities. As you know, we have quite a history of such things in this country. Many would like to obtain pieces of our heritage...Buyers for the pleasure of owning a piece of the magnificent past...Thieves, for more dark and evil purposes."

He waited for the last statement to sink in. "I have at my disposal numerous resources for monitoring such activities. But I have fewer resources for combating them. My associates in this endeavor include the common local Egyptian on the street as well as the brightest professionals in the security world."

Abu stood and began to pace back and forth in front of them. "What you have encountered is the smuggling of antiquities."

When Jay nudged Conrad, the man said, "I see that you have surmised this very same fact."

He continued to pace back and forth, his hands behind him, buried deep within the folds of his robe. "Both the Egyptian secret police and the Sudanese police forces are involved with the effort to curtail the pilfering and sale of such items. Even with the information gathered from your activities, the smugglers are no closer to being discovered. We know only what their method of communication has been and where one of their routes lay. To them, this is only a disruption and not the end of their activities."

"We have received warnings from Jafar Kazim," Geoffrey offered. "He says we are in imminent danger and should leave the country immediately."

"And what do you say, Geoffrey?"

"I am not sure what to think of all of this. Do you believe we are in danger?"

Abu stopped his pacing and looked directly at them. "Yes, I believe you are in danger. That is why I have come to see you. Jafar is no fool. He has been involved with antiquities for years. It is thought that he walks on both sides of the line."

This time Conrad nudged Jay.

"You concur," Abu said. "Let me ask you, did Jafar show genuine concern for you, or was it just pretense for his own wishes that you were out of his way?"

The friends sat uncomfortably with these thoughts.

The man continued, "Even your friend, Zaid Zakiya, is not above suspicion. As you have no doubt seen, he is a man not to be trifled with. He is well connected and well financed. Both of these are essential to a successful smuggling business."

"Are you saying ZZ is involved in this smuggling activity?" Geoffrey asked in disbelief. "He was so helpful in finding Jay and Conrad."

"Did you not find it even slightly suspicious the ease at which he made progress from having no information of their whereabouts to stopping the young men as they were driving a truck...one of hundreds of such trucks in that vicinity?"

The friends looked at each other in wonder at these new possibilities.

"My point is simply this: you are in grave danger. Not only have you disrupted a multi-million dollar smuggling operation, you do not even know who the enemy is."

He sat on the front of his chair and leaned toward the group. His eyes flashed a certain power as he added, "For all you know, I am the head of the smuggling ring!"

Abu adjusted his robes and sat back in the chair. Nobody spoke.

After a moment, Jay broke the silence. "Do you think this is somehow related to the Aten cult? You know, the guys with the sun disk tattoo?"

"If it is, the added element of religious fanaticism makes your presence here even more dangerous. I think it is time you wrapped up your school trip and went back to America. As I told you the last time we were together, *there is no substitute for experience...it makes the theory more relevant.* You have experienced the reality of smuggling. It is no longer a theoretical game."

The man stood to leave. "I have other business here in Luxor I must attend to. Thank you for your time."

Abu motioned to his bodyguard who moved swiftly to open the lobby door. As he was about to exit, he turned to face them one last time. "You have cheated death once, my young friends. Do not be foolish enough to think there will be a second time."

CHAPTER 34

"That ended well," Conrad said as he sat with the others after Abu had left.

"Man! Two threats in one day!" Jay exclaimed.

"They both were just warning us," Alyssa said, trying to be helpful. "Maybe they are sincere in their concerns for us."

"You see them as warnings. They feel like threats to me." Jay shook his head. "So much for a peaceful day."

Geoffrey sat in quiet contemplation as the friends talked. Suddenly he spoke, "It's hard to believe that ZZ could actually be mixed up in this. I have known him for a long time. But what Abu said about the ease with which ZZ located you both causes me to pause, I must admit."

"I find this all confusing. Who is friend and who is foe?" Alyssa questioned. "I can't tell anymore."

"Even Malika was suspicious today," Jay added.

"And Dimah," Alyssa said softly, remembered the woman's many questions.

"The easiest thing would be for us to leave in the morning, as has been suggested by Jafar and Abu alike," Geoffrey mused. "It would not be my first choice, but perhaps..."

"How about we give this one more day?" Jay asked the group. "If we see anything dangerous, we leave. If not, we forge on until the end of the week, looking for Akhenaten."

At that moment, Dimah walked over to the group.

"Hello, everyone," she said pleasantly. "Did you have an enjoyable day?"

"Yes and no," Conrad answered without offering an explanation.

Dimah looked puzzled.

"What Conrad is trying to say is that we had an incredible tour of the entire Karnak Temple Complex," Geoffrey explained, "but we had two disturbing conversations. I'm afraid these have put us in a quandary."

"Yes, I saw you with Abu al-Hasan," Dimah replied.

"You know him, then?" Geoffrey asked.

Dimah hesitated before she answered. "He is a well-known man who has survived the many changes in our country. I am sorry to say he is both admired and despised by others who have had dealings with the Interior Ministry."

"He knew all about our kidnapping adventure...even the fact that the smugglers are moving contraband artifacts out of the country," Conrad added.

"That is undoubtedly why he is involved," the woman replied. "This is his specialty—artifact smuggling. He is quite good at it...almost like he can think as a smuggler would. Who was the other conversation with?"

"Jafar," Geoffrey answered. "He felt it necessary to warn us of danger both before and after his private tour of the complex."

"I see," Dimah nodded.

"The trouble is that both men—and even ZZ—have been implicated in turn by the others as we have spoken with them these last few days," Geoffrey explained. "Now, we don't know who we can trust in this matter." He shook his head. "Both Abu and Jafar have told us in no uncertain terms that we should leave before harm can come to us from the smuggling gang."

Dimah looked from face to face. "And what are you going to do?"

Geoffrey was silent for a moment. The others sat quietly as he thought through the options. Finally, he answered resolutely, "We are going to remain in Egypt for now. Tomorrow, we will visit the KV35 and KV5 tombs in the Valley of the Kings."

▲ ▲ ▲

Geoffrey ended the call and placed the phone on the nightstand. He stood and walked into the bathroom. He studied the man staring back at him in the mirror. The man looked tired. And worried. He splashed some warm water on his face and dried it with a towel. He then walked back into the room and sat wearily on the chair. He replayed the phone conversations in his head.

ZZ had echoed the concerns of Jafar and Abu. He, too, believed there to be danger lurking as long as they remained in the country. The smugglers, he had said, were clearly willing to do what was necessary to stay in business. This made them dangerous. Additionally, as a group, Geoffrey and his friends had disrupted the smugglers' operation, causing untold expenses and delays. For this offense, there would be no forgiveness. ZZ was persistent in this belief above all others. He updated Geoffrey that the smuggler's hut, the phone line, and the truck were all registered to a fake company that did not exist. ZZ also told him that nothing had come of the stake outs in Sudan, so the gang was still intact, at large, and dangerous. In the end, ZZ had suggested that a curtailing of the study trip and a flight back to America was the wisest decision.

The calls to Jafar and Abu were less cordial but with the same result. Both men reiterated the danger of remaining in Egypt, and implicated each other and ZZ as being involved in the smuggling.

His mind wandered to Malika. Had Alyssa befriended her, or vice versa? How could she have known of the boys' disappearance?

And then there was Dimah. The woman had been helpful during their stay in Luxor. Was it genuine? Or was she working with one of the others?

Geoffrey ran a hand through his hair as he sat there. He hoped he had made the right decision to remain in Egypt—especially now that everyone knew his plan to stay another day and visit the Valley of the Kings.

Wearily, he crossed the room to his bed and turned out the light. Maybe a good night's sleep would make things seem more obvious in the morning.

▲ ▲ ▲

The man sat outside on the rooftop patio that overlooked the city. The cool breeze was slowly dissipating the pungent odors from the city streets below. One by one, the stars appeared overhead in the deepening darkness of the night sky. It was his favorite time to think. So peaceful. And quiet.

So, the intruders have decided to ignore my warnings and remain in Egypt. I do not understand such stubbornness in the face of danger. It is Geoffrey who is most determined. The others will do as he decides.

He drew a deep breath of the night air and slowly exhaled.

I do understand how to arrange accidents. I believe it is now time.

▲ ▲ ▲

Jay and Conrad were out by the pool. After swimming several laps, they had wrapped themselves in towels and sat talking on two deck chairs. Their only companion was a man slowly stacking the unused chairs midway down the pool deck.

"I'm glad we're staying," Jay said to the other boy. "I think something is going to bust loose in all this. I can just feel it."

"I know what you mean," Conrad replied. "I just hope we are not the thing that busts loose!"

"Who do you think is the smuggler?" Jay asked curiously.

"I don't know for sure. It could be any of the three musketeers. Each of them has the means. And we know what the motive is—money."

Jay was quiet for a moment. He suddenly said, "I think the key to this is that holy room in the Luxor Temple. Something is going on. We need to find out what it is."

Conrad was about to reply when a voice behind them said, "Excuse me sir. The pool is now closing for the evening. Are you finished with your chairs?"

CHAPTER 35

They stood at the top of the valley road looking down the grade that led to the tombs. It was mid-morning and the tourist busses were just beginning to arrive. A cool breeze stirred the clean desert air, the sun's heat not yet apparent. Shadows lingered on the slopes of the hills surrounding the final resting place of the pharaohs.

"Which tomb will we visit first?" Jay asked curiously. "The *Mummy Warehouse* or *Ramesses Hilton*?"

"I planned to visit KV35 first," answered Geoffrey, referring to Jay's *Mummy Warehouse*. "Later, we will visit KV5."

The group of four friends began the long descent into the Valley of the Kings.

"How many mummies did they find in this one tomb, Geoffrey?" asked Conrad.

"There were fourteen in all. The owner of the tomb was Amenhotep II, the great-grandfather of Akhenaten. His mummy was found in its original sarcophagus in the main burial chamber."

"How did all of the other mummies get into the tomb?" asked Conrad. "Did they walk in?"

"Not funny," Jay said with a shudder. "Especially when we will be down there visiting."

Geoffrey chuckled at Jay's irrational fear. "They were reburied by a 21st Dynasty High Priest named Pinedjem II. As we know it, he did this to keep them from tomb robbers."

Soon, they arrived at the valley floor and walked to the entrance of KV35. Geoffrey showed his pass to the guard who grunted and led them to the steel door guarding the entrance.

I do not like this guy, Jay thought as they followed the sullen man. *He has a hard face that tells the whole world to stay away from him.*

The guard unlocked the door and switched on the lights.

"Don't touch," was all the unfriendly man said as they stepped from the warm sunlight into the coolness of the tomb's entrance hall.

Once they were out of earshot, Jay commented, "That guy gives me the creeps. I don't know what happened to the guard from our last visit, but I want him back!"

"This one wasn't too friendly at that," Conrad agreed.

"Maybe he's having a bad day," Alyssa said in the man's defense.

"I think he's having a bad life," Jay commented as they walked deeper into the earth.

About 100 feet in, the tomb passageway came to a well room that was 30 feet deep. A wooden scaffold had been built across the chasm. But in the past, it had been intended as a deterrent to grave robbers.

Just beyond the well room, the tomb took a sharp left turn into a large pillared chamber. Another 50 feet of downward slope brought them to the brightly painted main burial hall. They walked down to the lower level of this pillared hall and found a decorated sarcophagus.

"This tomb was discovered by Victor Loret in 1898. This is where they found Amenhotep II," Geoffrey explained, pointing to the painted stone sarcophagus. "His mummy was in good shape and was intact in his original coffins."

The older man led the students to one of the burial chambers that branched off the main burial hall. "This was one of the chambers that held the other mummies. There were three found here, partially unwrapped by tomb robbers before they were relocated here without their coffins. Two of them we know as the Elder Lady and the Younger Lady. The other was a boy, who has not been identified with any certainty."

"Didn't you say before that the Younger Lady was the mother of King Tut?" asked Alyssa.

"Very good, Alyssa," Geoffrey said with delight. "She has been identified as such through DNA testing."

"And what about the Elder Lady?" asked Conrad.

"Queen Tiye," Jay answered for Geoffrey. "She was the mother of Akhenaten."

"And very good, Jay!" Geoffrey exclaimed.

"If you're going to discover the missing tomb of a pharaoh, you had better know the facts," Jay replied seriously.

Conrad shook his head in disbelief at Jay's comment.

Alyssa asked, "Where did they find the other mummies, Geoffrey?"

"Right this way," Geoffrey answered as he led them to another side chamber.

As he ducked inside the lighted chamber, he continued, "There were nine mummies in coffins arranged neatly in this room. They had never been disturbed by grave robbers, so they were easily identified by their markings, except for one unknown woman."

"That was like hitting the mummy jackpot!" Jay exclaimed as he tried to imagine the sight.

"Yes," Geoffrey agreed, "It was quite the find. And there was another unidentified mummy found in that chamber we passed after the well room. He was lying in a ceremonial boat instead of a coffin."

"Looks like he was a last minute addition," Jay remarked. "Just passing by, I suppose."

Geoffrey chuckled. "Another mystery of the mummy's tomb."

"How did they make the mummies?" asked Jay as he examined some of the paintings in the main burial hall. "These old guys sure lasted a long time after being buried."

"It is an exact science," Geoffrey replied. "When the person died, the body was taken to a specialist. This person offered different levels of mummification, based on the ability of one's family to pay."

"Paying was no problem for the pharaohs," Conrad noted.

"Yes," Geoffrey continued, "they had the best of mummification techniques. First the body was shaved and washed. The brain was removed and discarded. Then the vital organs were taken from the abdomen and chest cavity, dried in salt, and placed in decorative jars."

"Canopic jars?" Alyssa asked.

"Exactly." Geoffrey resumed, "There were four different jars. These would be buried with the body later. The heart was typically removed and embalmed and then later placed back within the chest cavity before the body was wrapped."

"That sounds odd," commented Conrad.

"They believed that the heart contained the personality of the person, so it was very important," Geoffrey explained. "The body cavity was filled with salts and aromatic substances and then the entire body was covered with a divine salt called natron. It remained this way for about forty days."

"Why the salt?" Jay asked.

Geoffrey replied, "To dry all fluids from the body. After this process was complete, they would wash the body and rub it with oil to soften the skin. The body cavity would be filled with linen rolls soaked in resin so it would hold its shape. They then wrapped the body in up to twenty layers of linen strips, each soaked in a gum resin. Many times, a long narrow board was incorporated into weavings on the back of the mummy for stiffness."

"So much for your walking mummy, Jay," Conrad remarked. "Rather difficult to get around with a board woven into your underwear."

"I'm feeling better already," Jay said with relief.

"Anyway," Geoffrey said to complete the explanation, "it took about fifteen days to wrap the mummy. The entire process took about seventy days."

"Why did they mummify the remains, Geoffrey?" asked Alyssa. "It seems like a lot of work."

"The ancient Egyptians believed that the body of the person needed to be preserved so it could be reunited with the soul after death. That is why even the poorest of peasants would pay to be mummified."

"Remarkable," Jay said.

"It was at that," Geoffrey agreed. "Now, I suggest we head back to the surface so I can show you something else that is remarkable." Even in the dim light of the burial chamber, Geoffrey's eyes twinkled in mischief.

"Land of the living, here we come!" shouted Jay as he led them on the long climb to the surface.

CHAPTER 36

The sun from the entrance silhouetted Jay as he emerged from the depths.

"Back in the land of the living," he said to the surly guard who sat on a low wall of stone awaiting their departure from the tomb.

The guard grunted and began to walk toward him as the others came into the light one by one.

Great sense of humor, Jay thought to himself. *I definitely don't like him.*

Geoffrey made his way to the wall and sat down. "That was quite a climb. I need to rest for a moment."

The others joined him and watched the guard as he shut off the lights to the tomb and turned the key in the lock of the protective steel door. The man locked the gate and positioned himself near the resting group, waiting for further instructions.

"Have some water," Alyssa offered her friends as she pulled several small bottles from her backpack.

Eager hands accepted the refreshment.

"I also brought some fruit and peanut butter," she said cheerfully.

"No. No eating here," the guard snapped. "Only drink."

Alyssa glanced at Geoffrey who nodded. She put the food back in her pack and silently sipped from her bottle.

After a few minutes, Geoffrey said, "The next tomb we will visit has nothing to do with Akhenaten's family or his missing mummy." Seeing the look of disappointment on Jay's face, he continued, "I thought that since we were here, though, you would want to see something of a tomb being excavated."

Jay's interest came back to life. "You mean like being dug out and new parts being discovered?" He looked at Conrad with a smile.

"Indiana Jones suddenly looks excited," Conrad said to the others. "Who knows what you will find down there, Jay? Perhaps someone famous."

"Maybe I will," he answered growing more animated as the thought sank in. "I can see the TV documentary now...*Mummy Unwrapped*, featuring Jay Wray, world-renowned archeologist and treasure seeker." He was about to add something about being a former Private Investigator but his ribs were too close to Conrad for him to risk it. He kept the thought to himself.

Geoffrey chuckled as Conrad and Alyssa shook their heads at Jay's antics. The guard just stared at the boy in silence.

Geoffrey continued, "KV5 is the most unusual tomb in the valley. As you will see, it began as a typical 18th Dynasty tomb, with perhaps two or three chambers. But what happened from there is nothing short of magnificent."

He smiled at the inquisitive looks on the faces of his young charges. "Shall we go and take a look?"

Geoffrey stood and walked over to the guard. He spoke briefly to the man and showed him some papers. The guard shuffled through them and thrust them back at Geoffrey. He stepped past the group and began walking down a path.

"Let's follow Mr. Sunshine, shall we?" Conrad said as he started down the path after the man.

Geoffrey talked as they walked. "You will see that this tomb is relatively near the surface. In fact, much of it is less than 15 feet under ground, as measured at the entrance. There is a lower section, though, that goes as deep as 45 feet, maybe deeper."

"So it has multiple levels?" Alyssa asked.

"Yes. But because of the lay of the land in the valley, KV6 is actually above a portion of it, and KV5, where we just were, runs very close to some of the rooms from the side."

The guard had opened the steel gate and walked down some steps to a steel door. He turned the key in the lock and opened the door, revealing a dark gaping hole in the earth.

"These things always look kind of creepy to me from above," Jay said as he watched the man disappear into the darkness.

"What? The world-renowned treasure hunter has the willies?" Conrad teased.

"No. I just like it better when the lights are on."

Conrad continued his needling, "By the way, Geoffrey, isn't this the tomb our last guard was telling us about? You know, the one where he heard the chanting and smelled the burning incense?"

Jay's eyes started bugging out of his head. "Are you serious? This is *that* tomb?"

"I believe it is the one he was talking about," Geoffrey said as he tried to recall the man's story. He looked at Jay, "But even if it is, they never found anything."

"And it was a long time ago," Alyssa added quickly, trying to allay Jay's growing apprehension.

"Maybe I should just wait up here while you guys check it out?" Jay offered weakly.

"You mean stay up here with our guard friend," Conrad asked.

Jay looked down the steps to see the frowning man glaring at him.

"Then again, maybe not."

"This is most likely the extent of the original tomb," Geoffrey said as they stood looking down a short flight of steps from the second chamber. And this is what was originally discovered back in 1825. It was probably filled with so much rubble that they thought this was all there was to the tomb. Even Howard Carter took a look around years before he discovered Tut. He was so unimpressed that he used this tomb as a dumping ground for rubble from his other digs."

"So when did they discover the rest of this tomb," asked Conrad as he stooped down to peer into the next chamber.

"It was not until the late 1980's that the tomb was examined in more detail as part of the Theban Mapping Project."

"Isn't that the program that measured and mapped all the known tombs?" Alyssa asked. "We studied some of the tomb layouts they had online before we came over."

"Correct. They began to clear the rubble out of the rooms just beyond where we are standing. They discovered that this tomb went on and on and on. By 1995, they had found over 70 additional rooms and vaults." Geoffrey started down the steps. "Come along. I'll show you."

At the bottom of the short stairway, a hall stretched off to the left and the right. Before them was a massive pillared hall.

"This is the largest chamber in the Valley of the Kings. From here, in every direction, run hallways with rooms on either side."

"Why so many?" Jay asked, still nervously looking around after Conrad's earlier revelation. "I mean, a pharaoh only needs a couple of rooms in his tomb."

Geoffrey led them past the pillars of the brightly painted hall and down a long central shaft-like hallway. He stopped at the first chamber on the left so the schoolmates could look inside. "Ramesses II built this tomb for his sons…and likely his daughters and other relations."

"How many sons did he have?" Jay asked incredulously.

"At least seventy."

"That would have made for some pillow fight," Conrad added with a smile as he nudged Jay.

"Indeed," Geoffrey answered. "The tomb was pillaged in antiquity, but they have found evidence that at least six of the royal sons were interred here. And there may have been up to twenty. It is difficult to tell."

Geoffrey turned and led them down the dimly lit hallway, further and further from the entrance. They walked past chamber after chamber on each side of the shaft that led deeper into the mountain. Some had been completely excavated. Others still held debris.

"How far does this go back," Jay asked, his nerves beginning to get the best of him.

"Just a little further," Geoffrey answered. "There is something else very unique about this place."

In less than a minute they arrived at the end of the long hallway.

"There it is," Geoffrey said quietly. "The statue of Osiris."

The friends stood quietly, each admiring the carved piece standing in a niche.

"There is nothing like this in any other tomb," Geoffrey said. "It is magnificent."

Jay was no longer looking at the statue. He had taken a few steps down another hallway that stretched to the left and to the right off the main one they had just traveled.

"How many chambers are in this place?" he asked as he gazed to the end.

"So far, they have found over 120," Geoffrey answered. "But they are still discovering more. They believe the tomb contains at least 150 chambers."

"Amazing," said Conrad. "I would—"

His sentence was interrupted that very second by a sound that even later they could each describe in detail. It started low and then built on the volume of many voices joined together.

A deep wailing chant rising from somewhere within the bowels of the tomb!

CHAPTER 37

The friends were frozen in place, the haunting melody sending chills of terror through their bones.

"Wh-what is that?" Jay stammered, as he looked at the others, desperate for an answer.

"I don't know," Geoffrey replied as he fought the growing sense of alarm that harassed his mind.

"It's coming from back toward the entrance," Conrad said as he involuntarily pointed down the long hall toward the pillared room.

Alyssa said nothing but moved closer to the others.

"We'd better get out of here!" Jay shouted in panic. "Maybe the mummies have been unleashed and are coming for us!"

They had taken only a dozen or so steps toward the entrance of the tomb when the lights flicked out, plunging them into complete darkness. The group stopped and immediately grabbed for each other.

"What's going on, Geoffrey?" Alyssa wailed in the blackness. "Why did the lights go out?"

Geoffrey's phone screen lit up, casting a bluish glow in the stone hallway.

"That's better," the man said. "At least we can get our bearings."

"I don't like this, Mr. B. That is the same sound the guard told us about hearing years ago. And this is the same tomb it came from!" Jay strained to see down the long shaft, looking for any signs of movement in their direction.

"Let's move toward the entrance," the man suggested. "I'm sure there is a logical explanation for all of this."

"Yeah, like some of Ramesses' sons have decided to get up and stretch their legs!" Jay said as he tried to keep his cool.

"Geoffrey, I'm scared!" Alyssa cried as she held onto his arm. "Please get me out of here!"

The group moved slowly down the hallway. Each time they came to the next set of rooms, they stopped and played the feeble light into them before moving on. Their trip down the passageway took them a full five minutes. The chanting continued growing louder as they approached the great pillared hall!

"Do you smell that?" Jay asked as they entered the large room. "It smells like one of those incense burners or something."

The friends stopped. The faint odor of pungent spices hung in the air.

"That guard told us that he and his dad smelled the same thing when they investigated this tomb years ago," Conrad recalled.

"He also said that they didn't find anything else," Geoffrey added, trying to keep everyone calm.

They crossed the great hall, cautiously looking into the darkness behind each row of pillars as they passed through. When they came to the hallway leading to the exit, the huddled group stopped.

"The chanting is coming from that direction," Jay said, pointing to the right.

"That is the section the archeologists are still exploring," Geoffrey stated.

"Maybe we should go and check it out," Conrad suggested. "Who knows what we may find?"

"That is *exactly* why we shouldn't go and check it out!" said Jay, his panic level rising again.

"I don't know," Geoffrey said. "Perhaps it would be best to get to the surface and let the authorities come down and see what is going on."

They all agreed and moved carefully toward the stone steps that led to the surface, pushed along by the chanting from behind.

▲　▲　▲

"It's locked!" Conrad's words echoed in the chamber.

"What?" Geoffrey exclaimed in disbelief.

He moved toward the heavy steel door leading to the surface. Handing Alyssa his phone so she could hold the light, he tried the door. It held fast.

"This is strange. The guard knew we were down here. Surely, he would not have locked us in." Geoffrey stepped back from the door, trying to make sense of it all.

"Maybe he thought we had already left?" Alyssa asked hopefully.

"Whenever there is a group in a tomb, the guard is required to remain at the entrance until everyone is out," the older man replied, debunking her theory.

"And we are definitely not out," Conrad said.

The chanting below them continued, muffled by the stone that separated them from its source. They stood quietly in the darkness, trying to decide what to do next.

Suddenly, there was the sound of a metallic click and light flooded the tomb. As their eyes adjusted to the sudden brightness, they saw a grinning Jay standing by the light switch.

"I thought we could use a little light on the subject," the boy said. "I don't like these places in the dark."

Geoffrey looked at his phone. "No signal."

"Me either," said Alyssa.

"There is too much rock and steel above us," Geoffrey said in explanation. "They have kept cell towers away from the valley on purpose to maintain its peacefulness."

"I'm not feeling too peaceful right now," Jay commented.

Conrad began pounding on the steel door and yelling for assistance.

"I don't think that will help," Geoffrey said. "The sound of your voice won't penetrate those doors. And even pounding on them with your hands isn't enough. The entrance is below the surface. We need a way to make a louder noise. Perhaps someone will hear."

"What about going down and getting a rock from below?" Conrad offered. "That should make enough noise."

"Yes, I think that is a good strategy," Geoffrey answered. "We should find something in the area they are still clearing."

"You mean the place where the chanting is coming from?" Jay asked in surprise. "No thank you, Mr. B. I would rather stay up here than tangle with some group of grumpy mummies!"

"We can leave you up here all alone to guard the door while we go down," Conrad said, knowing this would cause Jay to reconsider.

The boy hesitated for hardly a second before making a decision. "I think we should stick together on this one."

They stood at the beginning of the hallway that led into the newly discovered wing of the tomb. The chanted melody was clearly coming from its depths.

Jay looked nervously at his friends. "What do you think we should do?"

"I think we should go down there and find out what's going on," Conrad answered determinedly. "I, for one, have had enough of this nonsense."

"Geoffrey?" Alyssa asked.

"At this point, whoever it is or whatever it is seems content to remain below," the man answered. "They obviously know we are here and could come for us at any time. I agree with Conrad. We should find the source."

Conrad led the way down the corridor, stepping over the debris that had yet to be cleared out. The deeper they ventured, the louder the chanting became. They passed beneath a section of wooden beams that shored up the crumbling limestone above. A lone black wire snaked along the wall beside them, connecting the lights down the passageway.

"I think it's coming from that last chamber on the right!" Conrad said quietly to the group.

They stopped while Conrad inched forward. Slowly he positioned himself outside the doorway to the room. He glanced back nervously, took a deep breath, and then burst into the room with a loud shout!

A few seconds later, the chanting abruptly stopped. The sudden silence startled the friends in the hallway. Conrad emerged from the room carrying a small music player and two speakers.

"Here's what was chanting," he said as he held the device out for them to see. "It was a recording."

"Really?" said a disgusted Jay. "All that drama for a digital tune?"

Before anyone could respond, there was a loud sound of a heavy blow on wood behind them. They turned in time to see a shower of stone and dust filling the corridor. The cave-in tore at the black wire on the string of lights. There was a bright flash of an electric arc accompanied by a loud *pop!* And then total darkness!

CHAPTER 38

The sound of coughing filled the passageway. Even in the darkness, the rapidly expanding cloud of dust was felt as it hit them in the face. Their oxygen supply was replaced by dusty air. Geoffrey managed to get his phone turned on, lighting up the milky dimness. The illumination revealed more than tear streaked faces and red, irritated eyes. The hallway was blocked!

▲ ▲ ▲

Dimah greeted the front desk clerk as she prepared for her shift. "Anything special about today that I should know?"

The man answered, "Not much. But Mr. Barnsworth received an urgent message from a Mr. Abu al-Hasan. The man inquired if Mr. Barnsworth or his young associates were here. I told him they had left for the Valley of the Kings this morning and had not yet returned. He told me it was urgent that he should be contacted immediately upon their return." The man pointed toward the wooden cubbyholes behind the desk. "I put the message in Mr. Barnsworth's box."

Dimah wished the man a good evening and waited until he had disappeared through the front lobby door. She pulled her phone from her handbag and quickly dialed a number. When she heard the man's voice on the other end, she said, "Hello, Uncle."

▲ ▲ ▲

Conrad and Jay inspected the caved-in section. The dust had settled into a thin layer of white, fine particles down the hallway behind them. Each of them bore a coating of the same on their clothes and hair.

"It doesn't look good, Mr. B," Jay grunted as he moved a heavy piece of stone from the pile. "It's completely blocked."

Conrad agreed as he wiped his hands on his pants. "We'll have to dig our way out."

"Just be careful," Geoffrey warned. "The ceiling has obviously been weakened over the years by water seepage. It may come down on the lot of us if we are not careful."

The two boys went back to work on the wall of rubble. Geoffrey and Alyssa watched the progress of their toil, making suggestions and helping with the larger stones. Bit by bit, they dug into the pile of debris, depositing it in a half-empty chamber to the side.

"I wonder who left the mini boombox down here?" Jay grunted as the rock he was wrestling with came free and rolled down the pile. "Whoever it was wanted us to come this way so they could knock the beam down and trap us like rats."

"I'm afraid their plan worked perfectly," Conrad said as he dug.

"Yes, quite well," Geoffrey agreed. "We had been warned we were in danger. I never dreamed anything would happen out here. Otherwise, I would have taken the offered advice and cut our trip short."

"If we get out of here, maybe we should pack it in," Conrad stated. "Their message has been received loud and clear."

"*When* we get out of here, you mean," Alyssa corrected. "You are making great progress so far."

"I wonder how far this cave in goes on the other side?" Conrad asked as he sat down on the pile to rest.

"I was just thinking about that," Geoffrey answered. "I remember walking under the section of roof shoring timbers when we came down here. As I recall, it was only one section of about four feet."

"Let's hope so," said Jay as he sat down beside Conrad. "My two shovels are starting to get sore." He gingerly rubbed his hands together.

"Why don't you take a rest and eat something," Alyssa suggested. "I have that food the guard wouldn't let us eat before...and four more bottles of water."

The girl dug into her backpack and handed out her supplies to eager hands.

"How much battery is left on your phone?" Geoffrey asked her.

"I'm at sixty-five percent."

"I have forty-two percent," he answered their unasked question. "We will need to conserve the power. Is everyone set with their food and drink?"

Everyone was.

"Good. I will shut mine off while we eat."

Immediately, they were cast into that peculiar darkness that can only be experienced underground. The blackness was so deep and the silence so profound that it could be felt more than seen or heard.

"Now I know how the mummies feel," Jay said. "I personally prefer the light."

The friends ate in a silence that was only interrupted when one of them shifted uncomfortably on the pile of debris.

After about ten minutes, Jay stood to his feet in the darkness and said, "Time to get back to work."

The sound of movement filled the passageway, followed by the light of Geoffrey's phone.

"Can you see well enough if I just keep the main screen on and not the flashlight?" he asked. "If you run into anything puzzling, I will switch to the flashlight so you can see."

The feeble light proved to be insufficient for the task and Geoffrey had to use the more powerful flashlight. The boys labored on, alternately digging and moving stones. After forty-five minutes, Geoffrey's light gave out. The phone battery was dead. Alyssa's phone came to life and the digging continued with renewed urgency. They had only about an hour and then they would be consumed by the darkness without a remedy.

▲　▲　▲

"Hey!" Jay shouted from the top of the pile. "The pile gave way a little! I think we're almost through!"

"Be careful," cautioned Geoffrey from below. "There may be more cave-ins once you clear some space."

Conrad scrambled up the debris to where Jay was quickly pulling stones out and letting them roll to the floor. Both worked feverishly. A small gap appeared in the pile. They could see through to the other side!

Another twenty minutes of digging had cleared a space large enough to crawl through. Except for one minor cascade of material from the ceiling, it looked like it would hold long enough for them to escape.

Conrad made his way over the top of the pile to the other side. He pulled some loose material from the hole and stuck his head back through.

"Tomb tours begin in one minute," he said to the relieved group below. "Please queue up for your turn through the tunnel."

Jay first helped Alyssa up the pile while Geoffrey held the light from below. Conrad grabbed her arms and pulled her through to the other side. Once she was safely at the bottom of the pile, Jay turned and said, "Your turn, Mr. B."

"I really think I should be the last one out," Geoffrey replied.

"No way, Mr. B," the boy replied. "This is my tunnel and I will be right behind you!"

Geoffrey slowly climbed the loose pile of rubble and handed the phone to Conrad through the hole.

"Are you sure?" he asked Jay.

"Positive. I think it will make a great ending to my TV documentary, don't you? Make sure you get me on video when I climb out, Conrad."

Ten minutes later, they were back at the steel door.

"Do you want the honors, Indiana Jones?" Conrad asked a very dusty Jay.

"Yes I do," he replied.

Jay lifted the rock and began to pound on the steel doors. The sound reverberated past them and down into the tomb like thunder.

It was a very nervous security guard who, after five minutes of indecision, fumbled with the keys in the locked door. A vision of a man waiting on the other side of the steel portal filled his terror torn mind...an old man wrapped in linen strips!

The guard flung the door open and leapt back in fright. His face showed relief when four dusty strangers walked out into the light of the late afternoon sun.

The friends explained to the surprised guard what had happened. The man kept answering that he didn't know the surly guard, and there was no such man fitting his description. He had not seen anyone leave the chambers below. But that was not particularly assuring because he had been stationed at another tomb about fifty yards away. It was only by chance he had heard them pounding on the door.

"Well, Mr. B, that was a memorable tomb after all," said Jay as they began their climb out of the valley. "I didn't think it was possible for a relaxing visit to be so exciting!"

"Too exciting for me," Alyssa said with a giggle. "I will sure have some interesting things to include in my report when we get back to school!"

"Perhaps it would be best to omit some of the gory details," Geoffrey suggested. "Otherwise, this might be the last field study trip the administration will approve."

"You have a point, Geoffrey," the girl replied. "They wouldn't believe it anyway."

▲ ▲ ▲

"What happened to you?" asked a shocked Dimah when they arrived at the hotel. "You look like you have been traveling for weeks across the desert!"

"It's a long story," Geoffrey said as he asked for his key.

Dimah handed him the key and the message from Abu.

"What's this?" Geoffrey asked as he read the note.

"The day clerk took the message. He said it was urgent," the woman answered.

Geoffrey motioned for the others to wait as he walked to the house phone and dialed the number. He had a brief conversation and then hung up.

"What's wrong, Mr. B?" Jay asked. "You look like you just saw a mummy."

The man stared at the floor and answered slowly, "It's ZZ. I'm afraid he has been arrested."

"Arrested?" Conrad said in surprise. "For what?"

"Smuggling."

CHAPTER 39

Geoffrey relayed the details from his call with Abu. "He said he knew ZZ and I were close friends, so he wanted to tell me first-hand."

"I can't believe it! ZZ is the nicest person ever!" Alyssa frowned in concentration.

"So, how is Mr. Al-Hasan involved with this?" Conrad asked.

"He's in charge of security at the Interior Ministry," Geoffrey answered. "Smuggling countermeasures are a major focus of his department's activities."

"Did this have anything to do with our getting kidnapped?" Jay asked.

"Abu told me that they have had ZZ under surveillance for several months. He was suspected of smuggling, but was so clever in his methods, it took this long to close the net on his operation. Abu said it was the ease with which ZZ had located you and Conrad that helped them put the missing pieces into place."

"Wow. Sorry Mr. B. I kind of feel responsible for ZZ's arrest."

"Nonsense," Geoffrey replied to the boy. "If this is true, it was just a matter of time before he was found out. It is in no way your fault." The older man shook his head in sad disbelief. "I have known ZZ for many years. He has always been helpful...and a true friend, really."

Dimah had been listening with interest. "He seemed like such a nice man," she echoed Alyssa's sentiment as she tried to ease Geoffrey's sorrow. "It is a shame this had to happen while you were here."

Geoffrey sighed, his mind still refusing to believe his friend was involved. "Well, I think it would be good if we said our goodnights and went upstairs. It has been a *very* long day. Oh...please feel free to make use of room service tonight if you would like. I have lost my appetite."

As the man turned toward the elevator, Jay asked, "Are we going back to the States tomorrow?"

Geoffrey stopped and thought for a minute before he responded. "I do not think so. If ZZ was the smuggler, we are now out of danger...plus, I would like to see if I could find out where ZZ is being held and visit him, if possible."

"Goodnight, Mr. B. See you in the morning."

Geoffrey waved without looking back and vanished into the elevator.

"Poor Geoffrey," Alyssa said quietly. "He looked crushed at the news."

"And poor ZZ," Conrad added. "He is going to see the inside of an Egyptian prison a lot longer than Jay would have for trespassing in an old temple."

Conrad headed toward the elevator with Alyssa. "Let's go."

Jay followed them like a man in a dream. What Conrad had said set his mind spinning. *Trespassing in an old temple! My camera! How could I have forgotten about it?*

The boys feasted on cheeseburgers and fries in their room. They had the window open and the coolness of the desert night was slowly invading.

"Man, this really hits the spot!" Jay said with satisfaction. "All of this tomb raiding business generates an appetite!"

"You generate an appetite even when you're asleep!"

"Hey, a man has to eat, you know."

"You have that perfected, I assure you," Conrad answered as he sipped his soda.

"What do you think about all this stuff with ZZ?" Jay asked as he dunked two fries into the ketchup. "It's kind of weird he would have been working against himself by having us kidnapped and then rescuing us later."

"He didn't have us kidnapped. We managed that on our own."

"True. But still, why would he save us? He could have done us in and went on about his business without risking being discovered?" Jay persisted.

"Maybe out of friendship for Geoffrey. I don't know." Conrad pushed his plate away and sat back in his chair. He looked at Jay across the table and said, "What I do know is that Abu doesn't strike me as someone who would just arrest him for the fun of it."

"Unless *he* is the smuggler and he's trying to throw everyone off his trail by pinning it on ZZ."

Conrad looked at Jay. There were times his friend amazed him with his insight.

"You gonna eat those fries, Conrad?"

Whump! Whump!

"I said it's time to get up, sleepyhead!"

Jay looked blurrily at the figure standing over him with arm raised, ready for another blow. "Okay! Okay! I'm up!"

"Just because you're out hunting for pharaoh mummies, you don't have to act like them."

A puzzled look crossed Jay's face.

Seeing it, Conrad explained, "By sleeping like the dead! Gee whiz, Jay. Your brain is slow in the morning! You need a hot shower! Get up!"

Jay staggered from his bed and into the bathroom. Conrad heard the shower curtain slide open on its hooks and the water begin running.

Now maybe we can get downstairs at least in time for lunch.

Fifteen minutes later, they met Alyssa in the hotel restaurant.

"I had a fabulous sleep," the girl yawned as she brushed a strand of her blond hair behind her ear. "How about you guys?"

"I slept—"

"Like the dead," Conrad interrupted Jay.

"And I would *still* be asleep if it wasn't for Paul Bunyan here, chopping on me with his pillow," Jay said peevishly.

Alyssa giggled at the mental image of Conrad's 'alarm clock' waking Jay.

"It took that," Conrad answered unapologetically. "Besides, if I wouldn't have whacked you until you got up, you would have missed *two* meals today!"

"I see your point," Jay said with a grin. "That would have been tragic."

"Speaking of tragic," Alyssa said, "I saw Geoffrey right before you guys came down. He found out where they are keeping ZZ and went to see if the police would allow him see his friend."

"ZZ's being held here in town?" Conrad asked.

"That's what Geoffrey said. I guess his smuggling operation was based here in Luxor."

"Good spot for it," Jay said. "Lots of old Egyptian artifacts to pilfer and smuggle away."

The friends sat in silence for a moment.

"What do you guys want to do today?" Alyssa asked. "It sounds like we have the day to ourselves. I don't know how long Geoffrey will be at the police station."

"I wouldn't mind chilling out by the pool for a couple of hours," Conrad said. "I've had enough excitement for one trip."

"I was thinking the same thing," Alyssa stated. "I'm still kind of tired. Besides, we don't really have anything else to do. And next week, it's back to cold and classes."

"Ugh," Conrad moaned, "don't remind me. I'm not ready for that yet!"

Jay had been quiet during the exchange.

"How about you, Jay?" Alyssa asked. "Does a quiet afternoon at the pool suit you?"

"Well," Jay began, "I guess a couple of hours wouldn't hurt anything. But I still have some unfinished business I want to take care of."

"What kind of unfinished business?" Alyssa asked suspiciously. "Nothing dangerous, I hope!"

"I was just thinking," Jay began, "I—"

Conrad interrupted, "Whenever you are *just thinking*, somebody ends up in trouble!"

Alyssa nodded in agreement, "We've had enough trouble to last us a long while."

"As I was saying," Jay said with a hint of irritation, "a couple of things still need to get wrapped up before we leave."

"Such as?" Conrad asked.

"Such as finding out where Akhenaten's tomb and mummy are."

"That's a tall order," Conrad stated.

"You never know. I have this feeling we are close."

"And what else?" Conrad persisted.

"I want to know about that room in the back of the Luxor Temple."

Conrad leaned toward his friend. "What are you talking about?"

"Even with ZZ in jail, we don't know what was going on in that room the night that Scarface first met the boat on the river. Three men went in, one man came out. And why would he even go in there? Why not go straight to the river and get on the boat?" Jay looked at his friends. "I just want to know what is going on there, that's all."

"Jay!" Alyssa exclaimed in frustration. "You can't go back and start trespassing in the temple again. You'll get put in jail for sure the next time!"

"I wasn't going to trespass."

"What then?" Conrad demanded.

"My camera. I just want to get it and see if anything has been captured on it at night. I don't need to trespass. I just need to get into the room like any other tourist, climb up in the corner, and grab it off the stone ledge."

"And how will you make sure you won't get caught doing all of this?" Conrad asked as he crossed his arms and sat back in his chair.

"That's where you both come in."

CHAPTER 40

Throughout their lunch, the friends discussed Jay's plan to visit the holy room at the temple. Alyssa was definitely against going. Conrad was making Jay justify why it was worth the risk.

"I'm still not sold on why we should help you with your wild idea about getting the camera," Conrad said. "We should let it go and enjoy the rest of our trip."

"Not knowing for sure would be torture," Jay explained. "It will only take a minute for me to climb up and get the camera off the ledge. All we have to do is wait until nobody is around. One minute. That's all."

Conrad looked across the table at Alyssa. She didn't look convinced.

"Let's say we agree to go with you," Conrad posited. "When would you want to do this?"

"Today."

"When today?"

Jay smiled as he saw that his persistence was beginning to pay off. "Late in the afternoon. Right before the temple closes. That way, few people will be around. The tour busses will be gone. We can make the grab and get out of there."

"And what happens if there *are* people around?" Alyssa asked. "Then what is your plan?"

"We will leave it for the next day. Simple," Jay said as he flashed his million-dollar smile. "No risk. No danger. I promise."

Conrad looked at the girl. "What do you think?"

"I think we're crazy...but, okay."

"Yes!" Jay said loud enough for the people at the next table to look over.

"Jay Wray, I'm only agreeing to this because you will be impossible to be around until you can get this crazy idea out of your head that something is going on at the temple," Alyssa added.

"Don't worry," Jay assured her. "With a plan as simple as this, what could possibly go wrong?"

Conrad and Alyssa exchanged looks.

▲　▲　▲

The three schoolmates lounged around at the pool. Despite the light breeze, the sun's heat beat down from a cloudless sky. Only the cool water and the shade of the palm trees made being outside this time of day bearable.

"Something has been bothering me about the business in the tomb yesterday," Jay said as they soaked in the clear water of the pool. "If ZZ was already arrested or about to be, who was messing with us down there?"

"I doubt if ZZ himself would have been the one in the tomb, even if he was running around free," Conrad answered. "He would have had one of his henchmen do the dirty work for him."

"And he would have planned it way before we actually got there," Alyssa added. "Even the fake guard would have had to get in position before we arrived."

"I guess you're right," Jay said. "But whoever it was, they went to a lot of trouble to set it up and make it happen."

"I think they were trying to scare us into going back to the States," Conrad said. "They wanted us out of the way."

"And they wanted what we knew to go with us," Alyssa said thoughtfully. "Then, things could settle back down to normal."

"I see that," Jay continued. "But what about the other people who knew what was going on?"

"Like who?" Conrad asked.

"Like Dimah. She has been involved with this whole deal. She would have been a risk once we left. And what about Malika? She saw the handoff in the marketplace. She's another loose end."

Conrad was once again amazed. "Good points, Sherlock. But what do they mean?"

"They mean, my dear Watson, that getting us out of here would not solve the problem for the nasty blokes," Jay answered in his best British accent.

"Blimey!" Conrad retorted with just as much accent. "That calls the whole bloody lot of them into question, now doesn't it?"

"That is exactly what I was thinking," Jay said. "Whose side is everyone on?"

▲　▲　▲

Geoffrey sat patiently in the lobby of the local police station. He watched the comings and goings of the officers and the locals as a normal police day unfolded before him. He tried to relax, but inside, the confusion concerning his friend gnawed at him. He stared at the floor trying to make sense of everything that had happened during the last few days.

"Mr. Barnsworth," The desk sergeant called, "the Captain will see you now."

"Thank you," Geoffrey answered appreciatively as he rose and walked to the desk.

"This way, sir. Right through these doors."

Geoffrey followed the man down the spotless white hallway to the last door on the left. After knocking and ushering Geoffrey into the room, the police officer left, closing the door behind him.

"Geoffrey Barnsworth, it is a pleasure to meet you," the tall officer said as he rounded his desk to shake Geoffrey's hand.

"Do we know each other?" Geoffrey asked in surprise of the man's greeting.

"Not personally, no," the man answered. "But I am familiar with you and your work. Your reputation precedes you."

"Well, thank you."

"Please sit down," the Captain invited. "I understand you have inquired about Zaid Zakiya."

"Yes, he is my friend," Geoffrey responded. "I was hoping I might be able to see him."

"I'm sorry. That will not be possible."

"I understand this is a bit unorthodox, but I—"

"I'm sorry, Mr. Barnsworth, but I have my orders...all the way from the top. You see, Abu al-Hasan, the head of security with the Interior Ministry, has forbidden any visitors. In fact, he is personally questioning the prisoner right now."

"I see," Geoffrey said. "It's just that I believe there has been some kind of mistake. I don't think ZZ would have done such a thing."

The tall man stood. "I can assure you, Mr. Barnsworth, that Mr. al-Hasan has made no mistake. His methods are very precise."

The man walked Geoffrey back down the hall to the front desk.

"I will tell Mr. al-Hasan you were here. Please, enjoy the rest of your stay in our country."

Geoffrey stood outside the police station for a few minutes before hailing a taxi. Things did not look good for his friend.

▲ ▲ ▲

"Are we ready?" Jay asked his two friends as they assembled in the hotel lobby.

"Do you think we should tell Geoffrey?" asked Alyssa.

"No," Jay responded. "Mr. B has enough on his plate. We'll be back before he even knows we're gone."

Alyssa looked at Conrad nervously and then followed Jay out the front lobby doors. As they exited, they nearly collided with Dimah who was just coming in for her shift.

"Hello," the lady said pleasantly. "You seem to be in a hurry someplace."

"Yes," Jay responded furtively. "We are going to visit the Luxor Temple one last time before we head back to school."

The woman stopped and studied them intently.

"Legally," Jay assured her. "As tourists."

"Does Geoffrey know?"

"No. He went to visit ZZ," Jay answered as he turned to go. "We'll be back before him."

Dimah watched them go. Her intuition told her they were up to something.

Jay hurried the group on their way, intent on putting some distance between them and Dimah's potential interrogation.

"Close call!" Jay said as they crossed the parking lot. He cast a quick glance back toward the hotel. "I thought she was going to keep asking questions and not let us go."

"Yes," agreed Conrad. "She seemed overly interested in what we were doing."

"Maybe she is just worried about us," Alyssa offered. "You know, after all that has gone on."

"Maybe," said Jay. "And maybe not."

"We better hurry," Conrad reminded his friends. "We don't want to be seen running about the place. That would definitely raise suspicions."

The friends quickened their pace for the short walk to the temple complex.

▲　▲　▲

The crowds of tourists had thinned by the time they passed the Pylon leading into the temple.

"So far, so good," Jay grinned. "I love it when a plan comes together. Everyone is either gone or preparing to leave."

The friends made their way to the rear of the complex. Here and there, they saw guards making their patrol rounds. The three did their best to act nonchalantly as they meandered through the various sections of the temple. Up ahead, they could see their destination. They huddled to hastily make their plans.

"Okay," said Jay, issuing orders like a general. "Alyssa, you will stay right here and keep watch. Just act like you're interested in something and keep taking photos of stuff. You know, like tourists do. Conrad, you'll stand just outside the room while I go inside. If someone is coming, just cough."

"Cough?"

"And loudly. That will be the signal."

Jay and Conrad walked over to the chamber. After casting a final look around, Jay entered while Conrad stood watch outside. Finding no one inside, Jay glanced up at the stone shelf. The camera was still there!

Perfect! Now all I need to do is climb up.

He had just started up the wall when he heard the sound of coughing outside the room. Jay hesitated for only a moment before deciding to try to get the camera down before anyone came in. He balanced himself and reached for the small device.

A voice behind him shouted, "Stop! What are you doing up there?"

CHAPTER 41

The three friends stood silently under the watchful eyes of two guards. One of the security cameras had broadcast their huddled meeting, raising the alarm. Conrad had been detained first, followed by Jay. Alyssa saw what was happening and came to help her friends. All three of them now awaited the arrival of Jafar...and their fate.

"Not looking good for the home team," Conrad whispered to Jay. "Now we know *what* could possibly go wrong."

"Ten seconds more and we would have been home free," Jay whispered back. "Ten seconds!"

"They took the camera?" Alyssa asked quietly.

"No, I have it."

"Did you get to look at it?" Conrad whispered.

"Not yet."

"Tremendous."

Jay motioned to one of guards. "Would it be possible to visit the restroom while we are waiting?"

The man looked uncertainly at the other guard who shrugged and motioned for him to go ahead.

Jay left with the guard as Conrad and Alyssa waited.

Five minutes later, Jay rejoined his friends. His face was lit up with excitement.

Conrad gave him a questioning look.

Jay just nodded.

▲ ▲ ▲

It took Jafar fifteen minutes to arrive. He breezed into the stone room and faced the friends.

"I am sorry for all of this," the man said with his plastic smile, "but we cannot be too careful after the incident at the Karnak Temple a few years ago."

He turned to speak quietly with the two guards in Arabic. He seemed to be questioning them. They nodded and pointed toward Jay. Jafar made a final comment and the guards left the room.

The friends looked at each other and began to relax. Perhaps Jafar was a decent man after all.

Jafar turned toward the schoolmates. "I have sent them to finish closing the temple for the evening. This is no longer any of their concern. Now I must ask you what you are doing here." He waited for their response, his smile never fading.

"Well," Jay began, "we wanted to come back one more time before we left to go back to school. This is such a nice temple, we—"

"What of the camera?"

"The camera?" Jay asked innocently.

"Yes, the true objective of your visit," Jafar said with less patience. "The one that holds photos that you examined in the restroom."

A shocked look crossed Jay's face. *This guy misses nothing!*

The man held out his hand.

The boy fished in his pocket and reluctantly pulled the tiny device out. Jafar snatched it out of his hand. He turned the camera on and began to scroll through the images.

"I see," he said. "This will prove to be more than a little unfortunate for you."

A quiet word brought his two bodyguards into the room.

"Do not try anything and do not cry out," the man threatened. "Either action will result in your death!"

The friends looked at each other in shock at the man's words.

He held the camera out in his hand. "As for this…"

Jay was reaching to take it back when the man let it fall to the stone floor. It clattered as it hit, tiny pieces of the plastic casing breaking off. Jafar stomped on it unceremoniously, destroying the evidence before Jay's horrified eyes.

"I do not think it will be needed any longer. You have seen too much. Now you must pay the price of intruders!"

The friends began to protest.

Jafar held up his hand to silence them. He walked to the back of the small room and pressed one of the ornate stone blocks in the wall. A slow rumbling sound of stone grinding on stone was heard. The statue base block began to move into the back wall, revealing a large dark opening.

Jafar motioned to one of the bodyguards. He disappeared through the floor, the sound of leather soles on stone the only evidence of his movement. A moment later, the opening lit up from the chambers below. The steady tramping of the man's feet announced his return. When he emerged, his gun was drawn.

"Now if you don't mind, I would like you to accompany me to your final resting place below!" This time the man's smile seemed genuine.

"Hello, Geoffrey," Dimah greeted. "How was your visit with ZZ?"

"Not much of a visit, I'm afraid. They wouldn't let me see him. I was told that Abu was questioning ZZ and was not permitting anyone else to speak to him...Uh, how did you know I went to see ZZ?"

"Jay told me earlier," she answered, a small smile on her face. "He and the others said they were going to visit the Luxor Temple one more time before they left the country."

"The temple! Surely not again?"

Dimah nodded. "That is what he said."

"I hope there is no further trouble."

Dimah glanced at the large clock on the wall behind the desk. "The temple is closing now. They should be back shortly."

"Do you mind if I wait here with you?"

"That would be no problem," she responded. "Would you like something to eat?"

▲ ▲ ▲

The friends accompanied one of the bodyguards through the opening in the floor and down the dimly lit sandstone steps. Jafar followed in turn, the second bodyguard bringing up the rear. The sight that greeted them at the bottom of the stone stairway stunned them. Light bulbs had replaced ancient torches on the walls, flooding the entire lower level in bright light. Pharaoh-like statues of a man—both standing and seated—lined the main hallway leading from the bottom of the steps. Brightly painted bas-reliefs adorned every wall with depictions of a life three thousand years in the past. Ornate columns and urns flanked the doorways of chambers to the left and right of the main hall. As they passed these, the friends could see carefully selected accoutrements arranged for easy access in the afterlife.

Jay nudged Conrad, his eyes bright despite their dire situation. It looked like they were in the pristine tomb of a pharaoh!

The lead guard stopped and turned to face the procession. Behind him, they could see a large pillared chamber. Vivid colors flashed from each surface, flooding the senses. In the center of the room stood an equally well-preserved sarcophagus. Above it, on the wall, was painted a scene of a pharaoh and his queen making an offering to the sun disk god, Aten.

"Akhenaten!" Jay said softly.

"Yes, Akhenaten," Jafar confirmed as he walked past the group and into the burial room. "To some, he was the Heretic King...but to us, he worshipped the true god of the Egyptians...Aten!"

The man turned quickly, his robes flowing around him. "Come, my young archeologists and see a sight like no other in Egypt," Jafar invited. "One that remains exactly as it was over three thousand years ago when the great pharaoh was placed here to rest eternally."

Jay walked around the sarcophagus, taking in every detail of the red granite container. He examined the walls, soaking in their magnificent colors. This was the tomb of a pharaoh as it was meant to be.

His wonderment was interrupted by Jafar's voice behind him. "Take it all in, my young intruder. It is the last thing you will see in your short life!"

Jay whirled around to face the evil man. "What are you going to do with us?" he demanded.

Jafar met his gaze and said, "Tonight, you will be offered to Aten as eternal servants for your favorite pharaoh, Akhenaten. Then, you and your friends will be sealed in a chamber with the rest of his slaves from so long ago."

"You can't do this," Conrad challenged. "It's murder!"

Jafar walked up to the young man. "I can *and* I will."

Jafar spoke to the two guards and walked back to the hallway leading from the burial chamber. He turned abruptly and faced the schoolmates.

"I must explain myself. You see, I am the high priest of Aten. I lead a growing number of worshippers of the authentic Egyptian god." He pulled up the sleeve of his robes to reveal a sun disk tattoo.

"You're one of them!" Jay exclaimed. "*You* are the smuggler!"

"And kidnapper!" Conrad added.

"Not ZZ," Alyssa finished.

Jafar silenced them again with a raised hand. "Mr. Zakiya—ZZ as you call him—is a smuggler. I deal in something more valuable than goods...I deal in ideals."

Seeing the puzzled looks on their faces, he continued, "I intend to restore the ancient worship of Aten to the Egyptian people. On the wings of this worship, we will once again rise to the eminence of a world power, as we once were so long ago. I trade small pieces of our history—artifacts—for money to finance what you would call terrorist activities. To me, they are merely tools to be used for the attainment of my goals."

"So you *are* a smuggler!" Jay insisted.

"No!" the man shouted. "I am a dealer in the future of my people. Nothing more. I do not waste my time moving goods and contraband items around, as your friend ZZ does."

He shuffled his robes and smiled. "I must leave you for a short while to prepare for our evening ritual. You may have free reign down here until I return. I'm sure you will display the respect that the contents of this tomb demand...as King Tut did when he brought his uncle back from Amarna to be buried here."

CHAPTER 42

"Where can they be?" Geoffrey said as he paced back and forth. "They should have been here by now."

"Do you have any idea where they have gone or what they have done?" Dimah asked.

"The only thing that I can think of is that Jay believed something strange was going on in the statue room at the back of the temple. Evidently, the first time he and Conrad followed the smuggler, the fellow went into that chamber with two others. Jay is quite adamant that only the man with the scar exited. The others simply vanished."

"Do you think they went to examine that room again?" Dimah asked, not fully aware of the situation.

"It is possible. Jay said he had set up a motion activated camera in the room, but I'm not sure if that was what he was after."

Dimah sat quietly for a moment. When Geoffrey walked out the front door to see if the young people were coming, she pulled out her phone and dialed.

"Hello, Uncle. I think we have a situation that needs to be addressed immediately."

Conrad, Jay, and Alyssa were left alone in the tomb. Jafar had departed with both of his bodyguards, sealing them in.

"So much for Jafar being on our side," Conrad commented. "He is really a whack job."

"Conrad, I'm afraid," Alyssa said, fighting back the tears. "What are we going to do?"

"I don't know, Alyssa," the boy responded, putting an arm around her shoulders. "Hopefully, someone will find us."

Jay came back after looking around the tomb. "This place is amazing! It's full of treasure and all kinds of things...all in perfect condition."

"A lot of good that will do us," Conrad replied. "What was on the camera, anyway? It sure made Jafar flip out."

"Photos of him and others dressed in white robes opening the secret doorway and entering and exiting the tomb," Jay replied. "There was even a photo of Scarface."

"No wonder he decided to nab us and bring us down here. We blew his cover."

"Did you notice how he dismissed the temple guard security detail?" Jay asked. "I don't think they know what is going on."

"Probably not. All this has been a well-kept secret for three thousand years. The fewer who know about it the better for him," Conrad said. "Hopefully, for our sakes, that secret will somehow come to an end tonight."

Jay sat quietly for a minute, something clearly on his mind.

Alyssa noticed and asked, "What, Jay? I can tell when the wheels are turning."

"I was replaying the photos in my mind. I just recalled one thing that is interesting."

"What?" asked Conrad.

"Whenever they came down here in white robes, the big slab up there stayed open."

"It probably was built only to be opened from above," Conrad said. "I doubt that Akhenaten would need a way to get out!"

The friends looked at each other. Maybe they had a chance after all. Someone might notice!

▲ ▲ ▲

After what seemed like an eternity of waiting, the schoolmates heard the familiar rumble of stone above them.

"Show time," Conrad said. "Be alert for any chance to escape."

Sandals appeared on the stairs and slowly morphed into humans as the men descended step by step. Each was dressed in elaborate floor length white robes with colorful trim. The first man carried an incense burner that he waved back and forth to the cadence of a growing chant.

The three friends looked at each other. *Incense and chanting!* Jafar was the one who tried to trap them in the tomb the day before! Not ZZ!

Each man in the processional quietly chanted the eerie melody in words that the schoolmates did not understand. Some carried different priestly artifacts, others ancient-looking scrolls of papyrus. The last to descend was Jafar. He wore a golden headdress with blue striping. The sides of the head covering draped down the front and back to his shoulders on both sides, in the style of a pharaoh. In one hand, he carried an ankh, the ancient symbol of life. In the other, he held a shiny, chrome-plated pistol, a more modern symbol of death.

Jay could sense more that see that Jafar's bodyguards were stationed above, guarding the exit. There was no way to escape.

Jafar motioned with the pistol for the three to join the procession directly in front of him. As a group, they marched slowly into the burial room. They positioned themselves around the sarcophagus, directly in front of the Aten painting on the wall. The priests began an elaborate ceremony of chanting. Clouds of incense rose to the ceiling, eventually swirling through the tomb's entrance out into the night air. After about fifteen minutes the ceremony stopped.

Jafar spoke. "Now my young intruders, you have been offered to Aten as servants for his pharaoh." He smiled broadly and said, "He has accepted the offering."

He motioned to an ornately decorated wall. "Behind this wall is the place where you will begin your service."

One of the priests pressed a round medallion in the center of the wall. It slowly began to open with a rumble of ancient stones and mechanisms. A peculiar smell of mold and spices came from the room, one the friends could not quite place.

Jafar motioned them into the room with the pistol. As they entered, the friends saw the source of the odor. Before them, stretched out in rows, were the skeletons of twelve men, still dressed in white robes. They looked at the gruesome site and then at each other.

"These were buried with the pharaoh by the decree of King Tut. They were to serve as Akhenaten's slaves in the next life."

Alyssa began to cry softly at the sight.

"But do not think too harshly of Tut," Jafar continued. "He was not utterly cruel. In his mercy, he spared all of the priests who had come down into this tomb to lay Akhenaten to rest. One of them was an ancient relative of mine. It is from him, throughout the many generations, that this secret has been passed, father to son. And with the secret of this tomb, the worship of Aten was also preserved."

Jafar stepped back from the room. "Now you will join these faithful servants."

The friends began to protest, but a shot over their heads from Jafar's gun silenced them.

"And now, I bid you farewell," he said with a bow.

"Not so fast, Jafar!" an authoritative voice shouted from behind him.

Jafar whirled around in surprise, the smile leaving his face. Before him stood Abu al-Hasan, surrounded by an Egyptian Special Forces Team.

"I suggest you drop your weapon, or it will be you who visits his forefathers tonight!"

Jafar was quickly unarmed and secured. The rest of the priestly procession were rounded up and handcuffed.

The three friends ran from the room and began firing questions at Abu. He merely pointed toward the entrance where a very relieved Geoffrey was rushing over. Dimah followed close behind, smiling broadly.

"Geoffrey!" The three shouted in unison. "We are *so* glad to see you!"

"Are you unharmed?" the shaking man asked in earnest. "Did he hurt you?"

"Just our pride, Mr. B," Jay answered for the group. "We almost had it—the camera—and then we were nabbed by the temple security guards. Before we knew it, we were down here with Akhenaten."

"What?" Geoffrey exclaimed in surprise.

"Akhenaten, Mr. B!" Jay confirmed. "Come on, I'll introduce you!"

CHAPTER 43

Jay told his version of what had happened that night under the methodical questioning of Abu al-Hasan. Geoffrey listened intently as the tale unfolded, asking questions of his own. Conrad and Alyssa added their commentary here and there to round out what Jay had said.

"Remarkable," Geoffrey said when Jay finished. "To think such things have been going on here for millennia without anyone finding out."

"I have been investigating this Aten cult for several years," Abu said. "I have spoken to several of the adherents, but they never could tell me who was behind it."

"Did they all have the tattoo?" Jay asked.

"Yes," the man answered. "It seems to be part of the ritual initiation into the group. It appears that Jafar recruited from the cult members to populate his smuggling ring. That is why you saw the mark on some of them."

"Was he smuggling Egyptian antiquities?" Conrad asked. "When we were kidnapped, Jay and I thought that was what the bundle contained."

"That is correct," Abu answered. "In the past, they pilfered tombs and temple grounds—for instance the ongoing digs at the Karnak Temple Complex. More recently,

Jafar has taken advantage of the unrest in our country to rob our museums of their treasures."

"Why was he doing this?" Alyssa asked. "He told us he wanted Egypt to regain its place of prominence in the world. His country seemed to be important to him. It doesn't make sense he would steal from it."

Abu considered her question for a moment before answering. "Jafar had delusions of a new world order. His vision was one where Egypt would return to both the religion of Akhenaten and his pharaonic version of government. In his mind, Jafar was to become the next pharaoh of Egypt!"

The friends looked at each other in amazement.

"This was what I was telling you about a few days ago," Dimah added. "The mixture of religion and nationalism…it would take a potent combination like that for the Egyptian people to accept such an extreme dictatorship."

And to think, I once suspected her of being one of the bad guys, Alyssa thought abashedly.

As if sensing the girl's thoughts, Dimah looked at her and smiled.

"I don't see how he could have brought that about," Geoffrey mused. "He would have to overthrow the government and manipulate millions of people in the process."

"Jafar was more than a smuggler," Abu said in explanation. "Much more. He was a terrorist. We suspect that he has been behind many incidents here, including the terror attack at the Karnak Temple in 2015—an attack on the very site where he was the acting Director."

"It is difficult for me to understand such a man," Geoffrey said, shaking his head. "It is almost beyond comprehension."

"Yes," Abu agreed. "But to men such as Jafar, it is a simple thing. The end always justifies the means. Whatever it takes to achieve their vision of reality is not only justified, it is to be expected."

▲ ▲ ▲

The temple was cordoned off and security forces put in place to protect the tomb. Jafar and his men were taken to the police station and subjected to intense questioning about their smuggling and terror activities. Abu had his lieutenant escort the friends and Dimah back to the hotel.

That night, none of the schoolmates slept peacefully. Too much had happened—from their brush with death to the images of the mummy's tomb. The visions replayed over and over in their heads, chasing sleep away.

Each of them eventually gave up and made their way down to the lobby in the morning. Geoffrey was already there, reading the local newspaper.

"Good morning," he greeted. "I hope you had better luck with sleep than I did."

"Not much," Conrad admitted. "Even Jay was up most of the night."

"I was just making plans for my TV documentary," Jay explained. "It's not every day that a mummy's tomb is discovered with the mummy still in it."

"Especially if the mummy is a pharaoh," Alyssa added with a giggle.

"I think you are a little late," Geoffrey said as he showed them the front page of the newspaper. "It has already been announced that a pristine tomb was discovered under the Luxor Temple. It even names us as helping infiltrate the group who wanted it to remain hidden."

"Cool, Mr. B!" Jay said excitedly. "I feel an 'A' coming on for my trip report!"

"I'm sure that can be arranged," Geoffrey laughed. "After all, I am officially your professor. All I will need is a detailed account of your trip...say three or four thousand words."

"How about an oral report, Mr. B?" Jay asked hopefully. "I can tell you all about it on the plane ride back to the States!"

"I will have to think about it," Geoffrey said with a chuckle. "I might agree to such an arrangement *if* you can stay out of trouble for the next two days."

"Good luck with that," Conrad said. "Trouble is his twin."

"It won't be a problem," Jay promised, ignoring Conrad. "I'm going to be too busy putting together my documentary."

"Speaking of that," Geoffrey said, "Abu has invited us to spend the next two days helping to catalogue the contents of Akhenaten's tomb. It is something that no one this century has had the opportunity to do. I think it will be a rather good end to our trip, don't you think?"

"That's for sure, Mr. B!" Jay exclaimed. "As Abu always says: *There is no substitute for experience. It makes the theory more relevant.*"

▲ ▲ ▲

The next two days were like a rushing dream. Unimaginable treasures were carefully photographed, mapped, tagged, and recorded. As the full extent of the Heretic King's treasure became known, the world once again made Egypt its focus.

Abu kept them informed of his investigation. He told them that a local professor named Zamir had been arrested, as had the street vendor and the man called The Chief. Taavi the Scarface and Nebi had disappeared. The red speedboat had been located and a search for its British captain was in progress. The girl, Malika, had been interrogated but not arrested. Jafar had forced her to spy on the schoolmates by threatening to close her parent's restaurant if she refused.

Jafar refused to talk, but Zamir volunteered to testify against him in exchange for immunity. The willing professor was able to supply valuable information on Jafar's terror network. Abu's men were busy raiding several local apartments and warehouses in an effort to round up the terrorists.

Abu also confirmed that ZZ had been operating a large and profitable smuggling operation in North Africa, but was not involved in the antiquities thefts. He dealt only in hard to get electronics and communications equipment.

The night before the group was scheduled to fly back to the States, Abu hosted a dinner in their honor. Many important dignitaries attended the affair as a show of thanks from the Egyptian people for their efforts.

As the speeches and the congratulations wound down, the group of friends had a chance to reflect on the unimaginable events of the past ten days. Dimah joined in their reminiscing.

"One thing I don't understand, Geoffrey," Jay said, "is how Abu managed to find us."

"That is quite simple. We knew you had gone to the temple and we guessed that you wanted to get the camera. So, when you didn't return at a reasonable hour, it was time to pull out the secret weapon."

"The secret weapon?" the boy questioned.

"Yes. Dimah," Geoffrey replied as he pointed to her.

"Abu is my uncle," she explained with a smile. "I keep him informed of things down here in Luxor."

"We were beginning to wonder about you," Jay admitted. "I'm glad you turned out to be on our side!"

"You are quite welcome," Dimah said as she raised her glass to toast them. "Here's to another successful mystery solved by the History Hunters!"

As they raised their glasses in celebration, they did not know how quickly they would be embroiled in a 150-year-old mystery deep in the South as they searched for *Confederate Gold!*

EPILOGUE

For over two centuries, the splendors of Ancient Egypt have gripped the imaginations of the western world with unparalleled fascination. What had become to the locals a common element of the past, partially buried in the sands of time, became a sensation as tales of wonders and treasures were brought back to Europe and America from the time of Napoleon forward. Pyramids of unimaginable proportions, puzzling hieroglyphs, limestone, sandstone, and mud brick structures, treasures of gold and precious jewels, and, of course, mummies—these were the wonders hidden in the shifting desert sands.

While much was uncovered and discovered, modern technology is only now unearthing the stories behind the wonders. Ground-penetrating radar, new methods of site mapping and preservation, and DNA testing are the new tools replacing manpower and shovels. And with every solved puzzle comes the thirst for more answers to the remaining questions.

One of the most fascinating eras of this great past civilization is the 18th Dynasty of the New Kingdom period, stretching from the 16th to the 11th centuries BC. Within its majestic history we find intrigue, controversy, upheaval, unspoiled treasures, a few missing persons, and many unanswered questions. Beyond the most famous character of this time period, King Tutankhamun (known popularly as King Tut), two enigmatic figures stand out from the rest. The historical notoriety of these two is surpassed only by the fact that their mummies and tombs have arguably gone missing for three millennia. They are the pharaoh, Akhenaten, and his primary queen, Nefertiti. Equally mysterious is Smenkhkare, who appears to have had a brief reign as pharaoh following the death of Nefertiti and before King Tut.

Five tombs and the facts shrouded in their dusty pasts figure prominently in the great mysteries of the 18th Dynasty. Three tombs have been unearthed in the Valley of the Kings, while two remain elusive to even the most determined sleuths.

KV62 (Tomb 62 in the Valley of the Kings) was discovered by Howard Carter in 1922 and is best known as King Tut's tomb. In it were found a sampling of the riches of Egypt, largely unspoiled by thieves.

KV35, discovered by Victor Loret in 1898, contained the re-interred mummies of several pharaohs. It also contained two mystery mummies dubbed *The Elder Lady* and *The Younger Lady*. The general consensus is that The Elder Lady is Queen Tiye, wife of Amenhotep III, mother of Akhenaten and Smenkhkare, and grandmother of Tut (via the mummy found in KV55). It is also thought that DNA evidence points to her as the mother of The Younger Lady, but this is not conclusive due to DNA confusion associated with the prevalent intermarriage within royal families. The Younger Lady's DNA indicates she is the mother of Tut. It also points to her being either a daughter of Amenhotep III and Tiye, or the daughter of Akhenaten and possibly Nefertiti.

KV55 is known as the *Amarna Cache*. Discovered by Edward Ayrton in 1907, it contains items that would have been brought from other tombs in Amarna. Of greatest interest and discussion is the mummy found in a borrowed sarcophagus. DNA testing has shown it to be the son of Amenhotep III and Queen Tiye, as well as the father of Tut. The suggestion that the mummy is Akhenaten has been much discussed and disputed—discussed because the Akhenaten mummy has never been found, and disputed because thorough DNA analysis of Tut and the mummies of his two unborn daughters does not allow it to be Akhenaten. It is therefore more likely that this mummy is Smenkhkare, Akhenaten's younger brother who married The Younger Lady.

The missing tombs are then those of Akhenaten and his queen, Nefertiti. The location of Akhenaten's tomb is the subject of this book. There is a belief that Nefertiti's tomb lies beyond doorways hidden behind the walls of Tut's tomb. Ground-penetrating radar studies seem to support this hypothesis, and its truth will soon be determined.

Akhenaten was born Amenhotep IV, the second son of Amenhotep III and his Great Royal Wife, Tiye. The reign of pharaoh Amenhotep IV is famous for three specific reasons. First, he upset the entire Egyptian religious structure by introducing what was basically monotheism (the worship of one god instead of the plurality of gods) embodied in the sun disk god, Aten. It was at this time that he changed his name to one that has come down to us from antiquity, Akhenaten. Secondly, he moved the base of worship from the temples at Thebes (now known as Luxor) to a new location along the Nile River named Amarna (Tel-Amarna today). With these two acts, he displaced the powerful priestly class, drawing their ire while making many enemies, and earned the title, *The Heretic King*. The third, and perhaps equally notable reason for his fame as a pharaoh is that he elevated the status of his Great Royal Wife, Nefertiti, to one of equality with him.

Akhenaten was buried initially in Amarna, in a tomb that can be visited today. Upon his death, the uproar over his one-god worship led to the gradual abandonment and destruction of the city, and a return to Thebes and its temples as the religious epicenter. There remains no trace of his mummy or funerary objects (the KV55 mummy and 'magical bricks' notwithstanding). These were likely moved to the Valley of the Kings and re-interred in an unknown tomb.

Nefertiti is considered one of the most beautiful queens of Egypt (her name attests to this fact and means 'the beautiful one has come'). A spectacular painted bust exists to give us a good idea of her visage, housed in the Neues Museum in Berlin, Germany. But Nefertiti was much more. While little is known of her genealogy, the records in stone show her greatest attribute—*power*. She appears to have been the co-regent of her husband, Akhenaten, reigning with him as pharaoh toward the end of his life. And it is likely she became the pharaoh Neferneferuaten upon his death. It has been suggested that as pharaoh, she began to undo the one-god teachings of her husband and tried to placate both the gods and the priests, an effort made permanent by King Tut after her death.

Smenkhkare could be known as 'the shadow pharaoh'. Little is known about him, but he likely played a significant role in the history of Egypt. Many believe that he was in fact Nefertiti, as they both had the same throne name Neferneferuaten. But their Epithets differed, as seen in their cartouches (their abbreviated hieroglyphic name tags). Evidence suggests he was Akhenaten's younger brother, and it is strongly suspected that he is the mummy of KV55, and hence, the father of King Tut.

King Tut was initially named Tutankh-*aten* in deference to the sun disk god Aten. He changed his name to Tutankh-*amun* as he restored the multi-god worship of the past, beginning with the primary sun god, Amun. Tut went on to re-establish Thebes as the religious center of the day, giving power back to the priests and restoring their festivals. He did much finishing work on the Luxor Temple built by his grandfather Amenhotep III. Though he worked to restore the multi-theism of the day, he was later disparaged as part of Akhenaten's heresy, and much of his work was altered. When he died unexpectedly, he was buried in a tomb more typical of a queen than a king.

The Luxor Temple is one of two main temples in the city of Luxor (Waset—*City of the Was (Scepters)*—in ancient Egypt, and Thebes later on). It was built primarily by Amenhotep III, with major additions by Ramesses II, and minor work by Tut and Alexander the Great. The temple is dedicated to the Cult of the King, and was associated with the annual rejuvenation of the pharaoh as god. This occurred during the Opet Festival celebrating the yearly inundation of the Nile River onto the fertile lowlands. The Royal Ka—the Theban triad of gods (Amun, the sun god father, Mut, the mother goddess, and Khonsu, the moon god son) were worshipped in the temple. The temple contained several magnificent structures culminating in the 'holy of holies' where the statue of Amun stood on a base block of limestone over a mound thought by the ancients to be the place of creation. This area has never been excavated.

The Karnak Temple Complex is the other main temple in Luxor. The complex is the second largest ancient religious site in the world. It is actually a series of temples that total the contribution of thirty pharaohs. It is most famous for its Great Hypostyle Hall, which contains a veritable forest of 134 columns and covers 50,000 square feet. It is connected to the Luxor Temple by both its purpose (the Theban triad of gods) and the Avenue of Sphinxes, which runs between the two temples.

Egyptian hieroglyphs adorn many of the structures and artifacts from Egyptian antiquity. Initially thought to hold secret meanings by way of a series of complex compound thoughts, scholars have discovered their very systematic and specific meanings. Using cross-referenced tools such as the Rosetta Stone found by Napoleon's men, the strange markings have slowly given up their secrets. Now, they can be read by experts with little effort. Outside of the experts, though, few can understand their meaning. While used effectively for communication over a period of 3,500 years, they have not been used since the third century AD.

The buried riches of the pharaohs have proven to be a magnet for thieves. Since antiquity, tombs have been plundered and desecrated for their precious contents. It seems that the Valley of the Kings, and its sister Valley of the Queens locations were chosen because of their limited access and ease of guarding the tombs. Nevertheless, countless antiquities have been stolen and priceless artifacts destroyed. Even in recent times, the urge to possess these treasures or to use them to finance criminal networks and terrorism have driven the continuation of thievery and plundering. Since 2011, beginning with the Egyptian governmental uprising, an estimated $3 to $6 billion worth of artifacts and treasures have been stolen. Most of them have not been recovered.

www.ingramcontent.com/pod-product-compliance
Lightning Source LLC
Chambersburg PA
CBHW071253170626
46809CB00001B/194

Cisco Bandits
A Gwynn Reznick Mystery

Inge-Lise Goss

Olivebranch Press

IN LOVING MEMORY OF MY MOTHER,

Metha K. Thomsen

.

ACKNOWLEDGMENTS

My gratitude goes out to the wonderful people I worked with while I was an auditor. The knowledge I acquired through them about the oil and gas industry laid the foundation for this novel. I am especially grateful to my husband, Peter Goss, for reading very rough drafts and always giving me encourage words to continue writing. I wish to extend a thank you to Nancy Buford, Ernest Walwyn, Jo Anne Plog and Debbie Prince, members of the Rainbow Writers Group, for the education I obtained through their critiques. I especially want to thank my outstanding editors—Christine A. Walsh, Nancy Buford, and Toni Michelle. Last, but not least, I want to give a special thanks to Michelle McCarty, author of *The Jewel Box*, for the help she provided in the last round of edits.

PROLOGUE

Arne Boden stepped out of his truck at an oil well site and heard leaves rustling. Gazing in that direction, he saw branches swaying and strained his eyes to get a better look. Ambient light from the stars allowed him a glimpse of a shadow moving through the trees. Could it be the sought-after cougar—the animal that had attacked and mauled two unarmed hikers? He climbed back into the driver's seat to retrieve one of his rifles hanging on the rack secured above the back window. The rifles were gone. He cursed to himself, believing Janice's son had borrowed them again to do a little target practicing without asking. Arne reached under the driver's seat to retrieve his pistol. Clenching his teeth, he came up empty handed and shouted, "That damn kid!"

He stared through the windshield at the broken oil well pump and knew he should have tackled the repair job during the daylight, but Janice wanted him to see her new bedroom set. Arne would never turn down an opportunity like that. He leaned back in his seat and scanned the area for any sign of the cougar. Nothing. The branches no longer moved. He perked up his ears and intensely listened for unusual sounds. An owl hooted. With the clanging of the broken oil pump vibrating through the air, he couldn't pick up any other noise. Arne opened the glove box, pulled out a flashlight and flipped the switch. No light appeared. "You've got to be kidding!" he blurted out. He fished through the compartment, searching for the new batteries. They were gone.

Arne started the engine and repositioned the truck so the beam from the headlights glowed on the well. Still concerned about the cougar, he cautiously eased out into the crisp night, shut the door and grabbed a piece of pipe lying in the truck bed. Suddenly, he heard the click of the doors locking and knew his keys were dangling from the ignition. His eyes roamed over the area as he tried to comprehend how that could've happened. Everything looked peaceful. No sign of anyone else around. He gripped the car handle in a useless attempt to open it. Arne stuck his hand in his pocket to retrieve his cell phone, then remembered it was on the charger in the cab.

He rummaged through the supplies in the truck bed, looking for a piece of wire to unlatch the lock. Snapping of twigs and rustling of leaves erupted behind him. Securing the pipe firmly in his hand, he spun around and saw three male silhouettes emerge from the dense foliage.

Arne jumped down from the truck bed. "What do you guys want?" He backed away as the figures took a step closer to him. The men's features came into focus and Arne sighed, recognizing them.

"What are you guys doing out here?" he asked, dropping the pipe into the truck bed.

"Rules," the leader said.

A cold chill swept over Arne. His eyes darted between the three stern-faced men. Glaring at them, he wondered why one member of the Brotherhood wasn't among them—his buddy, the guy who promised to watch his back if something went wrong. "Where's Turk?"

"He couldn't make it this evening," the leader said with a sneer. "Did you forget your pledge?"

"No." Arne's muscles tightened and a lump formed in his throat. "I only told one person. That's all!"

"When you agreed, you knew there were no exceptions." The man moved closer to Arne.

One of the other men stepped back into the foliage and dragged a canister labeled "Hydrogen Sulfide" out from behind a bush.

Arne's eyes fixed on it, beads of sweat lined his forehead and his hands became moist. A wave of terror shot through his body. "I won't tell anyone else," he stammered, gasping for air.

"We know you won't," the leader said, clasping onto Arne's arm.

Arne grabbed the man's wrist, jerked around and swung him against the truck's tailgate. A blow struck Arne between his shoulder blades, followed by a smack to the back of his neck, sending him buckling to the ground.

The leader staggered to his feet, jabbed a finger at Arne's face and his mouth curled into a sinister smile, taking a breath. "Consequences. You violated the rules, a breach of trust. You were aware of the cost," he said, while the other two men stretched out Arne's arms and pinned them against the coarse rocks and crusted soil as he squirmed, wiggled and flung his feet, striving to escape.

Veins stood out on Arne's neck. "You won't get away with this!" he yelled, fear gripping his features.

Ignoring the outcry, the leader headed to the dark foliage. His comrades knelt on Arne's shoulders, leaned on his extended arms with all their weight. When the leader returned with three safety masks, he distributed two to his associates and slipped on the third. Arne wiggled and screamed for help. The leader yanked the cylinder above Arne's head, secured the attached mask over Arne's face, glared at the man lying helpless on the ground and turned the valve. Within a few seconds, Arne's eyes rolled back into his head. He stopped squirming.

.

CHAPTER 1

The warm night wind blew through the trees and Gwynn Reznick's feet ached as she trudged along the side of a dark, narrow, isolated road wearing a pair of stilettos. Not her choice of footwear, but a requirement in her assigned investigation role as Gwynn Wagner, accountant for Prudell Energy Company. Her flashlight began to flicker and she pounded the side of it, bringing it back to life. A large boulder stood in her path and she decided to take advantage of it. She sank down on top of it, slipped off her heels, wiggled her toes and sat peacefully, watching the dried leaves falling from the maple and oak trees swirling through the air and landing on the pavement. She raised her head and gazed at the moon and stars, wondering what Ruben—her boss, boyfriend and mentor, was doing at that very moment.

Off in the distance she heard the sound of a diesel truck approaching and suspected it belonged to Dave Prudell, the guy who had been making passes at her since she started working for his family's company. She pressed her lips together and thought: *Dave's looking for me. Doesn't he understand I'm engaged!* Gwynn wasn't actually engaged, but that was part of her cover. After attempting to avoid Dave at Marty's, a bar in town that served as a post-work hangout place for Prudell employees, most of the evening, she didn't want another uninvited flirtation. She stepped into her shoes and ducked into the thick bushes behind the boulder.

Tires squealed as the vehicle maneuvered a sharp curve. Gwynn tapped her index finger on her lower lip, trying to figure out why Dave would travel that fast if he was searching for her along the side of the road. He had to have seen her car still parked in Marty's parking lot. Gwynn had assumed Dave was responsible for it not starting, so he could drive her home, just like he did last week when she mysteriously ended up with two flat tires. That evening she had given him the benefit of the doubt, thinking it could have occurred earlier from loose nails when she dodged construction debris scattered along the highway. *Two car mishaps—not a coincidence.* She shook her head, *Dave isn't the swiftest guy in town, but most of the single gals, even a few married ones, would have loved the attention of the good-looking cowboy.*

The clash of metal reverberated from the road. Gwynn dropped to her knees, peered around the boulder and saw two light-grey Chevy trucks barreling past—the second vehicle's bumper whacking into the back of the first.

Dust billowed and brakes screeched about five hundred feet ahead of Gwynn. Loud male voices rang out, but she couldn't decipher the words.

Staying hidden among the dense bushes and tall wild grasses, she crept closer with only the moon lighting her way. Hitting, smacking, the unmistakable sounds of men fighting, echoed through the trees as she stealthily moved forward.

"You bastard!" a man shouted with a deep, raspy voice. "You did nothing!"

"I couldn't!" another man said, gasping for air.

Gwynn reached the edge of the clearing with only a few tall, overgrown bushes separating her from the men. She hunkered down, peeked through a small opening between the brushes and caught a glimpse of cowboy boots. Suddenly, a shot rang out followed by a moan, then silence. Gwynn sank to the ground, felt the sheath on her calf to make sure her knife was still in easy reach. She pressed her lips together, angry with herself for not being armed with a pistol. It was attached under her driver's seat, undetectable to curious strangers or thieves. Gwynn stayed motionless, waiting for an opportunity to get a better look and listened to heavy footsteps on the graveled shoulder of the road.

A truck door slammed shut, an engine roared and the vehicle sped away, leaving a cloud of dirt and spreading rocks in its wake.

Gwynn inched out of the bushes and saw a man, face down, surrounded by a pool of blood. She raised her flashlight, flipped the switch, but no light appeared. She pounded it again. Nothing. It was as dead as the man lying at her feet.

In the dim nocturnal light, her eyes scanned the victim. Gwynn thought she knew who it was and wanted verification, but couldn't chance leaving fingerprints behind by moving the body with her bare hands. She darted into the trees and came back with two short branches. Holding them at different angles, she managed to turn the victim's head and found herself staring at Mike Drumlin, a Prudell employee, a guy who she played pool with earlier at Marty's.

His Silverado's door stood wide open. Gwynn suspected the assailant could be back soon, so she hurried to the vehicle to take a quick look inside. Documents were strewn on the floor. Leaning in with only her elbows touching the mat she picked up one sheet and used it to gather the papers. Hearing the sound of a diesel engine, she dropped the papers, except the one with her fingerprints on it and swiftly moved behind a cluster of overgrown bushes. She knelt down and stuffed the page into her purse. Wanting to identify the assailant, Gwynn broke off a few twigs to clear a small opening and looked through it. A minute later, a dark sedan zooms past without even slowing down, as it maneuvered around the protruding truck.

Gwynn headed to the Silverado again. A headlight beam from an approaching vehicle struck the nearby trees. She leapt behind a cedar tree, breaking off her stilettos heel in the process. She crouched, ran her fingers along the dirt searching for it, but came up empty handed.

"You take his feet. I'll grab his shoulders," the raspy-voiced man said.

"Get all that stuff out of there!" another man shouted with a nasal twang in his voice.

Peering around the tree, Gwynn saw several pairs of feet clad in cowboy boots. From her vantage point, everything above the men's knees was outside her line of sight. One voice seemed vaguely familiar, yet she couldn't pinpoint where she had heard it.

"He'll be right up to clean the area," the raspy-voiced man said.

Gwynn knew it was time to leave even without her heel. Staying low she prowled deeper into the foliage, remaining parallel with the road and feeling grateful the full moon helped illuminate her way. When she could no longer hear any voices, she moved to the pavement and awkwardly sprinted up the road, running on the balls of her feet in her damaged stilettos for quarter of a mile.

At the head of her driveway, she stopped to catch her breath. The sound of metal crashing, glass shattering and a horn beeping erupted from the woods behind her. Assuming the noise was caused by someone cleaning up the crime scene, she briefly glanced in that direction, then shuffled two hundred feet to the house. It was a modest 2-bedroom with white, wood siding that she had supposedly inherited from her Uncle Virgil Sorenson, who had passed away at the age of 84 without any heirs.

Gwynn flopped on the couch, yanked off her shoes and raised her feet to the cushions. Every breath she took burnt her lungs. Remembering the sheet in her purse, she fished it out and unfolded it. In the center of the page, printed in bold letters, was "Flow Line Layout." Under it the word "Adjustments" was handwritten. She noted in the bottom corner it stated: "Project #112." She speculated if it might have any significance to Drumlin's death. In case there was a connection, Gwynn decided she'd look through Prudell's project files on Monday.

Feeling hot and sweaty, she inhaled deeply, rose and strolled into the bathroom. She quickly showered, slipped on a robe and headed to the kitchen.

She pulled out the top drawer, set it on the floor and retrieved her N-phone, a non-traceable cell phone, tucked behind it. She stared at the device. It had never been used during the time she had been in Bloomfield, New Mexico. She shook her head *Two months—six weeks longer than I thought I'd be here and I still don't even know why I'm here.*

She pushed the on button and was both surprised and relieved when it lit up. She punched in the contact number and waited. It rang twice.

"Why are you using this phone?" Ruben snapped over the airwaves.

"Well hello to you, too," Gwynn replied, irritated.

"What's up?"

Gwynn filled him in on the events of the evening.

"You didn't recognize the voices?" Ruben asked.

"The one sounded familiar. It might have been the guy who played pool earlier with Dave at Marty's, but I'm not positive."

"Does he work for Prudell?"

"Yeah."

"When will you be around him again?"

"Monday. Ashton Prudell is having a meeting with all the employees to go over some changes he's planning to implement."

"Do you know what they are?"

"Haven't got a clue. I could be more helpful if I knew what I'm supposed to accomplish here."

"You're right on task—you became a Prudell Energy Company employee."

"That was easy with my impressive, doctored resume."

"It was your striking looks—high cheek bones, slender, curvy body, long legs and seductive hazel eyes," he said in a sensuous tone.

Gwynn's cheeks flushed. "Ashton checks out my boobs every time he walks through the door."

"Five days a week. I'd like that."

"You can, seven days a week."

"I wish I could. The job here is dragging on longer than I had anticipated."

"Any idea when you can come and at least visit me? Remember, you're supposed to be my fiancé!"

"Soon."

"You've been saying that for a month!" Gwynn hissed.

"One of these days, I'll surprise you. Sunday I'll call on your regular cell phone. We can talk like lovers—no mention of business."

"Haven't slipped up yet."

"In case you should encounter additional crime scenes, make sure you're carrying more than your knife," Ruben said with an edge to his voice.

"It was just because I didn't have my car."

"That's not an acceptable excuse."

"Okay, boss, got it."

"Talk to you Sunday," he said and disconnected.

"Thanks for letting me say goodbye," she said, turning off the phone.

Gwynn stuck it back into the hiding spot, pushed the drawer in place and put on a pot of water for tea as the image of the murdered man flashed through her mind. It wasn't the first dead body she had seen, nor would it be the last given her chosen profession. She wanted to relax, maybe catch a movie on television, before climbing into bed.

The pot whistled. At the same time, the doorbell buzzed.

.

CHAPTER 2

Gwynn charged into the bedroom, dropped her robe to the floor and swung a holster over her shoulder with the handle of the gun protruding. She put her robe back on, hiding the weapon and went to the door.

Pulling back the curtain covering the door window, she saw two police officers standing on the porch and a patrol car behind them. Gwynn latched the chain and cracked the door open.

"Sorry to bother you, Miss, this late at night, but we saw your lights on," the short, blond officer said.

"What can I help you with officers?"

"There was a truck rollover down the road, a half a mile."

Trying to remain calm, Gwynn's hand braced the rim of the door frame. "Was anyone injured?"

"Yes. One victim. We're here because the heel of a woman's shoe was discovered next to the crash. We're checking this area for a potential other victim who might have become disoriented and wandered away. Have you heard or seen anything unusual in the past hour?"

Ruben's words popped into Gwynn's head: *Never lie about clothing or shoes. They can be traced to the owner. If they are discovered someplace they shouldn't be, lie about how they got there.*

"The heel you found probably belongs to me," she said. "My car wouldn't start so I walked home. The shoulder of the road isn't meant for stilettos. I tripped. It snapped off and I wasn't able to find it. Do you by any chance have it on you? I'd like to get the shoe repaired."

The taller, brown-haired officer went to the patrol car.

"When was that?" the shorter officer asked.

"A little over an hour ago." Gwynn wanted to say earlier, but she had been seen at Marty's. Also, she wondered why he didn't ask where she had been walking from, since he was interested in the time.

"Shortly before the accident," he said, cocking his brows and tapping the handle of his gun, secured in a holster around his waist.

Gwynn sensed he was skeptical about her response. *Had I been seen on the road?*

The taller officer returned holding a plastic bag with a high heel inside. "Is this it?" he asked, raising it in front of her face.

"Let me get the shoes," Gwynn said. She closed the door and went to the bedroom. On the way back, she stopped in the bathroom and quickly wiped the dirt off the shoes. She eased the door slightly open with the chain still in place and handed them to the taller officer.

He compared the severed heel to the one on the undamaged shoe. "Thanks, Miss," he said, giving Gwynn the shoes and the heel. "It's good you weren't on the road when the accident happened—it scattered debris on both sides. You really should have asked a friend to drive you home or taken a cab," he said in a condescending tone. "It's too dangerous walking along roads in the dark—no one can easily spot you."

"Is there anything else?" Gwynn asked, anxious for them to be on their way.

"No. That takes care of it," the shorter officer said.

Gwynn closed and bolted the door. Instead of leaving the key sticking out of the dead bolt like she normally did, she removed it and laid it on the side table, out of reach from an arm entering through the door window. She wondered about the officers' visit. *Would they check around the area if they found just a heel at the accident?*

Over the weekend Gwynn cleaned the house, dealt with her car and hung around all day Sunday waiting for Ruben's call. Finally, at 9:30 p.m., the phone rang. She glanced at the caller ID and smiled to herself—it was him.

Picking up the phone, she blurted," I was just about ready to give up on you."

"Miss Wagner, this is Heidi Anderson from Mr. Madison's office. He asked me to give you a call to let you know he's been tied up in meetings and won't have an opportunity to call you. He wants me to pass on his regrets."

"He's having meetings on a Sunday," Gwynn said through gritted teeth.

"Yes. We've all been here all day trying to finish up a project," Heidi said, but Gwynn knew the voice belonged to Holly, one of Ruben's employees and she also knew that Holly would never use her real name or Ruben's over a line that wasn't secure.

"Will it be finished today?" Gwynn asked, hoping. She longed to be in Ruben's arms.

"Soon."

"Thanks for the call," Gwynn said and slammed down the receiver, thinking *if I hear 'soon' one more time I'm going to scream.*

CHAPTER 3

The morning light shone through the kitchen windows as Gwynn sat at the table sipping coffee. She felt irritated that Ruben hadn't filled her in on the investigation or even given her a hint as to why he needed an inside person at Prudell, though she suspected it was because he didn't want her snooping around until some of his other employees arrived. Then she mulled over their conversation the night of the crime. He gave no indication that the killing could have a bearing on the reason she was in New Mexico. Yet she couldn't shake the nagging feeling that it had to be somehow linked to the investigation.

Ruben's clients either didn't want the cops involved, or the police had failed to solve the crime. In most cases it was the former. Gwynn knew the police would never realize a crime had been committed Friday night since it had been covered up to appear to be a car accident. The victim worked for Prudell. *Could there be two isolated crimes associated with Prudell Energy Company?* She doubted it and decided to work under the premise that they were connected. First she'd try to figure out the identity of the assailant and his helpers. She suspected that the short, blond officer who came to her house that night was either involved or knew a participant.

Gwynn drove to the Prudell office building, isolated in the center of ten acres six miles south of town. At 8:25 a.m. she strolled into the structure. The receptionist, Marilyn, a stocky, middle-aged woman, with salt-and-pepper hair, was talking on the phone.

The front lobby held an espresso-colored leather couch flanked by two suede chairs and a curved wood counter that Marilyn sat behind. A large painting of the Prudell family—Ashton, Dave, Carol and their parents, hung above the couch.

On the other side of the room were two workspace cubicles with four foot walls separating them. Gwynn's desk and a row of file cabinets stood in one cubicle. The other one was smaller and used by the part-time employee, Debra, a college student. The wall behind the cubicles contained floor-to-ceiling glass panels that extended the entire length of building, giving everyone inside magnificent views of the hills and the natural beauty of the desert. Ashton Prudell's office and the conference room also abutted the glass wall.

The offices of Alex Hayes, the Chief Financial Officer, and Dave Prudell were on the other side of the building. They had large windows, but their views weren't as desirable. Between their offices and Ashton's was the break room.

The company also leased office space in the center of town that housed three employees—Charles Norr, the Marketing Director; Ralph Hunter, his assistant; and an engineer, Turk Carlsen. Field employees frequently stopped by that office. Gwynn had driven by the nondescript brick structure. Four other companies also occupied that building. Prudell was the only one that didn't have a name displayed on the marquee. Gwynn was familiar with the names of the employees because of payroll records.

Marilyn hung up. "Did you hear about the car crash Friday night?"

"I know there was a crash on my street, but that's all," Gwynn replied, though she knew about it firsthand and it had been plastered all over the news. Small towns don't have many deadly car crashes, especially those requiring the fire department to put out the flames.

"A guy was killed—Mike Drumlin. He worked for Prudell."

"Mike Drumlin? I played pool with him once."

"What a shame. Nice guy. He had only been with the company a couple of years. He came in occasionally and said hello on his way to Mr. Prudell's office. He's the second Prudell employee who's died from an accident in the past three months."

"Second? How did the other one die?"

Marilyn pressed her lips together and shook her head. "Tragic. At a well. A sour well. Hydrogen sulfide poisoning."

"Didn't he have a gas monitor?"

"It malfunctioned. Arne Boden. A real sweetheart. That was a sad day around here."

The phone rang. Marilyn snagged the receiver.

Two employees dead, Gwynn thought as she sat down at her desk and turned on her computer. Staring at the screen, she pondered if the other death was an accident.

Marilyn ended the call. "Did your guy make it to town this weekend?" she asked, straightening magazines on a side table.

"No. He had a project he had to finish."

"Well, you can tell him from me," she said with a flash of anger. "There are a lot of guys around here that would love to sweep a pretty gal like you off her feet if he keeps staying away. Are you sure you want that guy? You're not married and he's already ignoring you. Sweetie, it just isn't going to get better when you tie the knot."

"He promised he'd come soon," Gwynn replied, feeling awkward.

"That's what he told you last week," she said, swinging her head back and forth.

"Good morning, ladies," Ashton said, walking through the doorway. He was a medium-sized, forty-four year old man, graying at the temples, with a round face. He looked professional in his silver-rimmed glasses, dark blue slacks, light blue dress shirt and a red necktie.

Ashton made a detour over to Gwynn's desk and gazed over the wall. "How was your weekend, Gwynn?" he said, eyeing her chest.

"Relaxing," Gwynn said with a smile, looking at the top of his bent head. The blouse she wore gave him just a little peek of her cleavage—part of her Gwynn Wagner image.

"Mr. Prudell," Marilyn said, "a Mr. Shelton would like you to give him a call before the meeting."

"Raymond," Ashton said, turning around and moving toward the reception desk.

"Is there anyone else who can't make it to the meeting?" he asked Marilyn.

"No, there's just the two," Marilyn said and then he vanished down the hallway.

The entrance door flew open and Dave Prudell stepped over the threshold. "Helloooo, Gwynn," he said, making a beeline to her desk and ignoring Marilyn. "I looked for you at the ranch. You never showed."

The ranch was owned by Dave's parents, the elder Prudells. It was well equipped with horses and an Olympic swimming pool. Prudell employees had a standing invitation to visit every Saturday. Gwynn had been there four times since she started working for the company, but she had grown tired of fighting off Dave's attention. However, part of her assignment was to blend in so she couldn't completely avoid him.

"I stayed home because Ross planned on visiting over the weekend."

"Did he show?" he asked, raising a brow.

"No. Something came up."

"Again." Dave rubbed his chin as he scanned her face.

She gazed at him. *He's probably thinking I'm naïve to believe all my fiancé's excuses and allow him to ignore me for two months without getting mad about it. Little does he know.*

"That ring on your finger might not mean the same thing to him as it does to you."

"Speaking from experience?" Gwynn asked.

Without answering her question, Dave gave her a mischievous smile.

Loud chitchatting came from across the room as the workers stormed in. Prudell Energy Company had twenty-six employees—twenty-three were men. Nine lived and worked near Artesia, New Mexico. Marilyn had made motel reservations for them since the meeting was scheduled to last all day.

"Dave," a guy said loudly, standing by the couch.

Gwynn's head swung in that direction. *The voice!*

"Be there in a minute, Turk," Dave said, gesturing with his hand. He turned back to Gwynn. "How about a movie?"

"Remember," Gwynn replied, pointing to her engagement ring.

"Sure." Dave lightly shook his head and walked away.

Gwynn scrutinized Dave's appearance, thinking he didn't even slightly resemble his brother. Dave was thirty-two, tall and had broad-shoulders, well-formed muscles, brown hair and a close cut beard. He always wore jeans and looked like he had been busy herding cattle. She thought that was probably why he spent his weekends at the ranch so he could help take care of the livestock. He seemed out of place in an office environment.

Ashton stood at the head of the conference table with twenty-one employees crowded around it. Marilyn and Gwynn sat next to a side table full of refreshments—coffee, breakfast breads and sweet rolls. Debra, the part-time employee, couldn't make it to the meeting and Charles Norr, the Marketing Director, was out of town.

Ashton crossed his arms waiting for the workforce to simmer down and give him one-hundred percent of their attention.

"Before we begin, most of you have probably already heard about the car crash that took Mike Drumlin's life on Friday evening. He was a loyal employee and he will be missed. The office will be closed Thursday afternoon so those in Bloomfield can attend his funeral. Very sad, leaving two teenagers without a father." He paused and slowly moved his head, eyeing his employees.

It seemed strange to Gwynn that no one, except Marilyn, showed any sign of grief over the death of their coworker. Instead, most of them were just looking around, like Ashton had just announced the weather forecast. Marilyn, on the other hand, had shed a few tears.

Ashton cleared his throat. "You're probably wondering what this meeting is all about. Prior to the announcement appearing in the local newspaper, I wanted you all to know that Prudell Energy Company is expanding. Last week all the pieces fell into place and we acquired ownership of Johnson Brothers Trucking Company. Now we will be able to control our oil transportation costs on the wells not connected to a pipeline."

The employees clapped and cheered.

Ashton explained how the transfer of trucks and facilities would occur along with assigning everyone to help make the prior Johnson Brothers' employees feel welcome. He gave a rah-rah speech about team work.

At 10:30 he broke to give everyone an opportunity to stretch their legs. After break, he was only interested in meeting with the fieldworkers, excusing Hayes, Gwynn and Marilyn.

Gwynn went outside under the pretense she wanted fresh air, but what she wanted was to check for dented front bumpers. Light grey Chevy Silverado trucks were issued to all field employees and other employees who went out in the field often. Today, the parking lot was full of grey trucks. Based on Turk's voice, she surmised he was the assailant, but wanted verification.

Most of the vehicles were parked with their hoods facing the building. A group of the guys stood smoking outside near a rock garden close to the street. Gwynn casually strolled along the sidewalk surrounding the structure as her eyes scanned the trucks. She noticed a dent close to a front headlight and accidently dropped her purse to get a better look. Around the crushed metal she saw specks of reddish-orange paint, picked up her purse and sauntered further down the sidewalk. After clumsily allowing her purse to slip out of her hand two more times and discovering no confirming damage, she found herself next to the floor-to-ceiling windows by the conference room.

She glanced in and spotted several guys looking in her direction, including Dave. It appeared they weren't paying attention to Ashton. Gwynn moved to the other side of the trucks and walked toward the entrance. As she came around the corner, she saw it—a smashed in back bumper and a dent in the tailgate. Inching closer, she didn't see a speck of another color—only light grey. Gwynn noted the license plate number and hurried inside.

When she reached her cubicle, she attempted to start up her computer to check if the damaged truck was issued to Turk. A screen appeared: 'Temporarily Down for Maintenance.' Then she recalled Marilyn telling her the computer systems would be down and upgraded with additional security during the Monday meeting. She didn't want to wait for it to be up and running again so she opened the second drawer of a black file cabinet and pulled out several automobile expense folders. Thumbing through them as fast as she could, she stopped and eyed an invoice—the one she had been searching for. The vehicle had been assigned to Turk Carlsen, the guy with the familiar voice. She leaned back in her chair, feeling confused. She had assumed the assailant had driven the second car—not the first. *Interesting.*

After stuffing back the files, she headed to a small room just a little larger than a closet between Dave's and Hayes' offices. She carried a handful of invoices that needed to be checked against the information in the project files before payment, but in reality they had all been paid and she should have dropped them off in Marilyn's basket to be filed.

With the meeting still in session this was her opportunity to snoop around. She opened the file drawer labeled: "Projects 100-130" and lifted out the folder "Project #112: Cisco Unit Flow Line." She shuffled through it, occasionally stopping and reading some of the invoices. Putting it back into its slot, Gwynn squinted at the file cabinet as she wondered why there wasn't any mention about adjustments—all the work had been completed fifteen years earlier. She straightened her spine. Anger boiled inside her. *Ruben needs to tell me why I'm here—is this adjustment important?* Gwynn took a deep breath and planned to spend her time investigating Drumlin's death. At least until Ruben gave her something else to investigate.

Flicking off the light, she left the file room.

"Gwynn," Hayes said, waving his hand for her to come to his office. Alex Hayes had been hired by Ashton's father thirty years before. He was a bit under six feet, husky, with a round face, recessed hairline and wore thick glasses on his narrow nose.

She stepped into his doorway. "Yes."

"Do you have any project files at your desk?"

"Completing Well 26-10, do you need it?

 "No, not that one. On your way back, can you ask Marilyn if she has any workover files?"

"Sure." Gwynn turned and bumped into Dave. "Is the meeting over?"

"No. Ash just likes to listen to himself talk. Half the guys in the room are having a hard time staying awake." He took a step closer to Gwynn. "How about a beer after work?"

"Okay," she replied with a smile, knowing Turk was one of his buddies. She had observed them sitting next to each other at the meeting and chatting during breaks.

His eyes popped wide-open. "Six."

She nodded and headed to the lobby.

CHAPTER 4

At 6:10 p.m. Gwynn entered Marty's. Dave stood and raised his hand, motioning her to his table. A brief smile flickered across her lips when she noticed Turk and another guy were seated at the table.

An empty chair stood next to Dave's. She eased into it and sat quietly, while Dave and the guys chatted about sports. Her eyes darted around the room, searching for other Prudell employees. She saw Ashton in a corner booth with Janice, a forty-year-old, slender, bleach-blonde who dressed like she wanted more than a beer with her plunging necklines and extremely tight jeans that probably took her five minutes to zip up. Gwynn had seen Ashton before with Janice and wondered if they had anything going, but Marilyn claimed Ashton was a happily married man. If that was the case, you'd expect him to come in, drink a beer, play pool and then depart for a home cooked meal. When he's talking to Janice, he's not in a rush to leave.

Dave gestured for his buddies to get lost and turned his attention to Gwynn. He reached for her hand resting on the table. She immediately lowered it into her lap. "I was just checkin' if you still had that ring on your finger."

Gwynn raised her hand and looked at the one-carat diamond. "It hasn't gone anywhere since I talked to you this morning."

Disappointment showed on his face. "What type of brew can I get you?"

"Bud Light."

He motioned to the waitress and she hurried to the table.

"Look at you two, here together," Linda said with a big smile. She worked in the café next door and occasionally helped out in the bar. She had befriended Gwynn when she first came into town. Linda and Virgil, Gwynn Wagner's uncle, had been friends for over twenty years and Linda was surprised to learn he had a niece. Gwynn had explained she didn't know she had an Uncle Virgil until he passed away. Bad blood in the family had separated Virgil and his sister, Gwynn's mother. The two siblings hadn't spoken for over forty years. Due to Gwynn's absentee boyfriend, Linda had been after her to start seeing other guys.

Dave ordered. Linda beamed and sauntered away from the table.

Gwynn suspected Linda thought she had finally taken her advice about dating, but doubted Linda was happy about her going out with Dave. He had a reputation—love 'em and leave 'em. She turned toward the man with the reputation and asked, "Who were the guys you were talking to earlier?"

"They work for Prudell," he said with a confused expression.

"I know that. They were at the meeting. I just don't know their names."

"You never met?"

Gwynn shook her head.

Dave nodded toward the pool table. "The big guy that looks like a shaved gorilla is Turk Carlsen. The butt-ugly shorter guy is Brad Williams."

"What do they do for Prudell?"

"Turk's an engineer like me. Brad's a pumper. He works in the field. You interested in those guys?" he asked, narrowing his eyes.

"No, no. I just haven't been introduced to all of Prudell's employees. Working on the payroll, I know the names, but it would be nice to be able to match them up with a face."

"You need to go to the ranch more often. You'll get to know all of them."

"I didn't know you were an engineer."

"Licensed and everything."

Gwynn felt surprised, maybe Dave was smarter than she had given him credit for. That explained why he spent so much time in the downtown office where all the engineering drawings, charts and maps were produced.

After Dave downed his beer, he wanted to play pool. Even though Gwynn wasn't good at it, she agreed to one game, thinking it would give her a chance to observe Turk—who talked to him, and if he showed any indication that he was concerned about something. *He has buddies that know what he did.*

Dave led the way to the pool tables. They were all being used. He talked to Turk and Brad and they agreed to rotating players. Gwynn and Dave would play one game, the winner would go against Brad and then Turk would be the opponent in the following game since he believed he was the most skillful player. While Turk and Brad finished their current game, Dave went to the bar to get another beer.

Gwynn glanced around and spotted Ashton still in the corner booth with Janice. They were seated on opposite sides, but leaning over the table. It appeared their faces were only a few inches apart. Ashton caressed Janice's arm, scooted off the bench and headed toward the door. He stopped when he came face-to-face with a guy who had a goatee. Both men glared at each other for a minute without saying a word. Then, Ashton walked to the door. The man went to Janice's booth and scooted in next to her.

"How's it going?" Linda asked, carrying a tray of empty bottles and glasses.

Out of the corner of her eye, Gwynn saw Dave was only a few feet away. "I'll take a late lunch and fill you in tomorrow," she said, thinking it would give her an opportunity to acquire information and not give any.

Linda waitressed at the Town Café, an eatery frequented by Gwynn's co-workers, and she was Janice's sister. Over the past two months, Linda had told Gwynn tidbits of gossip about most of Prudell's employees. Gwynn had politely listened since her assignment was to blend in.

"Make it after two," Linda said.

Gwynn nodded as she saw Janice and the guy with the goatee heading toward the pool tables. When they were close, the guy briefly kissed Janice's lips and stepped away from her.

Dave put down his beer.

Janice walked up to him. "How you doing, babe?" she said, snagging his arm.

He put his hand over hers and forcibly removed her hold, his jaw clenched. "Just fine."

On prior visits to Marty's, Gwynn had been with the girls, either Linda or Debra, the part-time employee. She had played pool a few times with some of the guys. On Friday nights, when the place came alive with a performing band, she had danced with a couple, but Dave always butted in. She had observed his body language whenever Janice approached him and suspected they had some history that didn't end well.

Dave racked the balls. Gwynn broke, but didn't manage to get even one ball in a pocket. Then Dave started clearing the striped balls from the table, downing two with his first strike.

Gwynn's attention was immediately drawn away from the game when she caught a glimpse of the guy with the goatee talking to Turk. She moved to the other side of the table to get closer. The guy spoke, but his tone was too soft for Gwynn to hear what he said.

"It's all taken care of," Turk said to him. "Nothing to worry about."

The guy didn't look convinced. He went to the bar and stood next to Janice. Gwynn had seen him before at Marty's, but didn't have a name to go with the face and she didn't want to ask Dave for another name. *Keep a low profile*, Ruben's words rang through her mind.

After Gwynn lost the game, she picked up her purse to leave.

"How about a rematch later in the week?" Dave asked.

"Maybe."

CHAPTER 5

Gwynn stepped into the Town Café just before 3 p.m. the next day. It was a large, open eatery, yet it still had a cozy feeling with the colorful, flowered wallpaper hanging above the chair rails and cedar stained wood below it. A vase filled with fresh flowers sat in the center of each table. A counter lined with bar stools ran along the left wall. On the right wall a row of windows overlooked the town park across the street.

Linda brought an order out from the kitchen to one of the two occupied tables. Gwynn sat down, away from the other customers and looked out the window at the almost deserted park.

"Hi, sweetie," Linda said, putting down a glass of water in front of Gwynn. "I didn't think you were going to make it. Have you already eaten or do you want to order some lunch?"

"It's been a busy morning. I'm starving. How about a Rueben?" Gwynn smiled after she said it, thinking about the Ruben who invaded her dreams every night.

"You got it," Linda said, scribbling on her pad. "Anything to drink?"

"Just water."

"Be right back."

Five minutes later, Linda delivered Gwynn's order and eased down in the chair across from her, holding a cup of coffee. Linda's eyes dropped to Gwynn's hand. "You still engaged?"

Gwynn nodded with her mouth full.

"Seeing you with Dave last night, I thought you got rid of that guy."

Gwynn swallowed. "No. Only a beer with a co-worker. That's it."

"Honey, you've got to get that ring off your finger. It isn't doing ya any good around here."

Taking another bite, Gwynn gave her a crooked smiled as she

thought the ring had kept her safe from pawing hands.

Linda placed her cup on the table and said, "Janice thinks you're the reason Dave hasn't been coming around to her place."

"Dave and I have nothing going on. We're just friends. Last night I saw Janice with Ashton. It appeared she liked him, even if he's married."

"That's the problem—married men. My Phil never would've looked at another woman, but he was one of the good guys."

Linda was an average-sized woman in her late forties with a round pleasant face framed by dark brown hair. Her husband Phil passed away at the age of forty-one six years earlier from lung cancer.

"So Janice doesn't have anything going with Ashton?"

"They have plenty going, it just isn't going anywhere. Her main squeeze right now is Kevin Whitehead, a bad guy. He treats women like they were placed on earth to serve, nothing more."

Gwynn couldn't recall that name on the payroll. "Kevin? He's not a Prudell employee."

"No. He works at an oil company in Farmington, the same one that some of the guys worked for before they started at Prudell. Kevin met some of them at Marty's. He's been hanging around there ever since."

"Is he in his mid-forties, tall, slim, with a trimmed goatee?" Gwynn asked describing the guy she had seen with Janice the night before.

"That's him. Haven't seen any other goatees around Marty's."

Gwynn wondered why Ashton had stared at him. "Did he use to work for Prudell?"

Linda shook her head. "No. His only connection is the guys who used to work in Farmington. Who knows, maybe they'd still be there if Prudell hadn't acquired a couple of companies that were going under and doubled the workforce."

"When was that?"

"Two, three years ago."

Gwynn thought that was good information, but not particularly helpful in solving the crime and decided to get started on her list of questions. "Did you know the guy killed in the car crash, Mike Drumlin?"

"A little. He'd come in and sit at the counter, read the newspaper and drink coffee. A grumpy sort of fella. The guys would say hi to him. He'd just nod at them, except for Turk and Brad. When they came in, he'd stroll over to their table."

"Marilyn mentioned that another employee died a few months ago, Arne something?"

"Arne Boden. A great guy! Just as nice as could be. He helped Janice out whenever she needed a handyman to fix something. He had the hots for her; even asked her to marry him. Arne bought her a gorgeous ring and left it with her so she could think it over. But Janice doesn't stay with the good guys. She likes the bad ones, or the ones that are hard to get. I keep telling her she's getting too old to play the field. She'll be forty-three next month." Linda shook her head and tapped her fingertips on the edge of the table. "She doesn't want to listen. Who knows, it might be because her little beauty shop does great business so she probably figures she doesn't need a husband. I'm surprised she can afford all the stuff she buys and she has money set aside for Patrick's education."

"Does she get child support?"

"No. She won't tell me who Patrick's father is. I bet it's one of the guys that hang out at Marty's—probably married."

"Maybe he gives her money."

"Doubt it. She might not even know which one. Her favorites don't last that long. She likes your Dave."

Gwynn's eyes narrowed. "He's not my Dave," she said emphatically.

Linda cocked her eyebrows. "Whatever. But Dave's not interested in anyone that old."

Wanting to get back to her questions, Gwynn changed the subject. "How did Arne die?" she asked, hoping Linda might tell her more than Marilyn did.

"Hydrogen sulfide poisoning." Linda bit her lower lip. "So sad."

"He didn't have a gas monitor?"

"It wasn't working right. Turk came in the day after it happened. Boiling mad! Claiming the company should have inspected the gas monitors more often." She leaned closer and whispered, "Turk also said he wasn't buying it."

"Meaning?"

"He wouldn't elaborate. I thought it meant the monitor worked okay."

"Didn't Arne have it with him?"

"He had it. They found it at the well site."

"Foul play?"

Linda took a sip of her coffee and glanced around the café. Then, she raised her elbow to the table, rested her chin on her hand and said softly, "Don't like to talk about it, in case Turk's right. There could be a killer out there someplace. Will you keep this to yourself?" After Gwynn nodded, Linda continued, "Janice said Arne was up to something. Something that was going to make him a rich man, but he wouldn't tell her anymore. She thought it was illegal—maybe dealing in drugs or something like that. That might be what got him into trouble."

"Was he a user?"

"No. At least not around Janice and he never came in here stoned or out of it.

"Hydrogen sulfide isn't normally a weapon of choice to execute someone."

"I know. I know. That's what I told Janice, but she still thinks something wasn't right about Arne's death. His birthday was going to be in a few days. One of his buddies called Janice and asked her to keep him busy that afternoon so they could decorate his apartment. Too bad, he never got a chance to see it."

"He went out to a well after he left her place?"

"Yes, at dusk. The well pump wasn't working. He told her it wouldn't take him long to fix it. He planned on meeting her at Marty's later."

"Which friend called her about his birthday?"

"Don't know."

Three customers came through the entrance. "Be back in a minute," Linda said, rising to her feet.

Gwynn finished her sandwich while she absorbed everything Linda had said and pondered if Arne's death was the reason for her being in Bloomfield, New Mexico. He died a month before she arrived. Not everyone believed it was an accident and she knew Mike Drumlin's wasn't.

"I need to get back to work," Gwynn said, paying her bill.

Sitting at her desk, Gwynn searched through the computer system for payments coded to the equipment maintenance account and discovered no payments were made to repair a safety gas monitor. Then she thought they might have just discarded it, based on the cost. *Could it be in working order and given to the employee who replaced Arne?*

Gwynn hunted again for equipment assigned to Arne Boden. After clicking through numerous screens, she found the page.

"Gwynn, can you come to my office?" Hayes said, standing next to the reception counter.

"Sure." She hit the print screen button and then exited from that system.

Hayes's desk and credenza were covered with stacks of folders. He instructed Gwynn to close the door. "I've been searching high and low through the file room looking for the workover project files 306 through 314. Ash and Dave don't have them. It's like they vanished into thin air."

"All the invoices have been scanned into the system. Do you want me to recreate hard copies?"

"Are you going to the funeral on Thursday?"

"According to Mr. Prudell's speech, I thought he wanted us all to attend. Why?"

"His credenza looks as bad as mine," Hayes explained. "Sometimes he doesn't know what folders he has."

"You want me to go through them when he's not in the office?"

He nodded meekly. "Before we attempt to recreate the files I want to make sure no stone is unturned. Sometimes those folders contain notes that haven't been scanned."

"I won't stay long at the funeral. I can come back here and check for the folders." Gwynn recalled Ashton's procedures. "Wait a minute, he keeps his office locked when he's not here."

Hayes reached in a drawer and pulled out a ring of keys. "It's one of these," he said, handing it to Gwynn.

"I'll see what I can find."

Back at her desk, Gwynn threw the keys in her purse and mulled over what that was all about. She had seen Hayes in Ashton's office rummaging through files when Ashton was there. Those files could have been easily recreated. Workovers were performed often on existing oil wells to try to increase production. Nothing unusual about that. *Hayes is looking for something—but what?*

Gwynn took the document that listed the equipment previously assigned to Boden from her printer and looked it over. Feeling puzzled, she tucked a few strands of hair behind her ear, leaned on the armrest and scanned it again. No gas monitor.

CHAPTER 6

Thursday morning Gwynn was working on interest owner distributions when the blond officer who had visited her home the night of the *accident* walked into the lobby from the hallway that led to Ashton's office. He stopped at Marilyn's desk and chatted. Gwynn noticed him glimpsing in her direction a few times.

"See you at the funeral," Marilyn said as he stepped toward the door.

"Who was that guy?" Gwynn asked, slipping invoices into Marilyn's basket.

"Sam Young."

"Was he called for a special reason?"

Marilyn smiled. "No. No one has robbed Prudell. He just came in to talk to Mr. Prudell. They're good friends. He stops by occasionally or they meet someplace for lunch."

At noon the office closed for the funeral. Gwynn went to show her respect and give her condolences to Drumlin's family.

Upon returning to the office, Gwynn parked on the far side of the office building, out of sight from anyone driving by. She headed to the entrance, pulled out the key ring and tried various keys until one turned the lock. She had learned how to pick locks, but didn't want to use that ability unless it became necessary. *Low profile.*

On the way to Ashton's office, she stopped at her desk, laid out some papers and flipped on her computer so it would appear she came back to get some work done.

The first key she stuck into Ashton's lock opened his door. It took her less than fifteen minutes to thumb through the files stacked around his office—no project files. She couldn't control her urge to look through his cabinet and drawers, thinking she might run across something to do with Boden or Drumlin. She began with the file cabinet. None of the keys on the ring fit. Then she attempted the desk. Same thing—no key. She loosened her belt, slipped her fingers into a seam under it, plucked out her picks and went to work on the file cabinet lock. Within ten seconds, she was looking through the top drawer. She knew she had to move swiftly—Ashton could decide to return after the burial.

Nothing in the top two drawers caught Gwynn's attention. The third one was a different story. A folder near the rear of the drawer had "Arne Boden" handwritten on the tab. With a surge of excitement, she yanked it out, laid it on top of the extended drawer and opened it. The top page contained Boden's assigned equipment list. The fourth item down—H2S gas monitor—was highlighted. Wanting to copy the document, she glanced around the room and saw a fax and copy machine in the corner. She stuck the document under the cover and pressed the copy button. Biting her bottom lip, she anxiously stared at the machine as it took its time reproducing the image.

A minute later, she returned the original to the folder and continued flipping through it. The next five pages included Boden's employment information—his job application, references and notes from his interview along with the date he was hired for a pumper position. Gwynn knew that set of documents were copies since employee file tabs were printed, not scribbled by hand, and maintained in the file room.

Due to a potential time constraint, she breezed over the following handwritten pages about the wells assigned to Boden and various other jobs he had performed, like repairing well pumps, over the eight years he had worked for the company. A note at the bottom of one page read: "Arne can fix any piece of equipment at a well site."

Staring at the last page in the folder, she scratched her head and squinted at the circled name jotted down in the center of the sheet— Mike Drumlin. Nothing else was written on the page.

While Gwynn speculated about the significance of that sheet among Boden's documents, she put the folder back where she found it and moved to the bottom drawer. There she discovered the missing project files, picked-up the one on top and sat on the floor. Flipping through it, nothing struck her as being unusual, except on an engineer report the word 'increased' between potential and production was underlined and a question mark scrawled above it.

The snap of a door opening echoed through the structure. Gwynn dropped the folder back in the drawer, eased it shut and quietly rose to her feet. She placed the copied page under her blouse as she hurried out the door and closed it behind her. Heading toward the restroom, Gwynn came face-to-face with the intruder.

CHAPTER 7

"That guy wasn't easy to pin down," Ruben said, putting papers in his briefcase. "It took three weeks longer than I had anticipated."

"You suspected the first week," Gordon, one of Ruben's employees, commented. "He was clever." Taking clothes out of a hotel room dresser, Gordon smiled. "But not clever enough. When are you delivering the report?"

"Tomorrow, on my way to Bloomfield."

"Holly said last time she talked to Gwynn, she sounded pissed."

"She was. Probably still is. I think she's wondering if she has become a permanent Prudell Energy Company employee."

"Gwynn seemed excited to be the first team member sent out on an investigation, but she's not the first one who had to hang around waiting for the others to show. What's the record—four months?"

Ruben shook his head. "No. Five months. Other investigations came along that had higher priority. The client is aware of their standing. No one has ever dropped us because we were too slow and we've never had an unsatisfied customer."

"But there are some that aren't happy when we uncover the culprit."

"Especially when it's their child."

"Or a trusted friend."

"It's even worse when it's a group of them." Ruben stuck his laptop in his briefcase and clamped it shut.

"Have you told Gwynn yet anything about the investigation?"

"Not a hint. I'm almost surprised she hasn't been snooping around trying to figure it out. But after the situation she observed Friday, she isn't going to remain the dutiful employee very much longer." Ruben's employees worked in teams. They were not informed about an ongoing investigation that didn't involve them. That was a rule he wouldn't break, not even for Gwynn. She'd never know why it had taken him so long to finish his current investigation; the reason his 'soon' had dragged on.

"Will someone be picking me up at the airport or should I take a cab?" Gordon asked, locking his suitcase.

"Take a cab. Have a nice flight to Atlanta."

"Thanks. Say 'Hi' to Gwynn for me," Gordon said as both men left the hotel room.

Ruben took the parking garage elevator. His cell phone rang just as he climbed into his car. Plucking it out of his pocket, he closed the door and glanced at the familiar number that appeared on his screen.

"Ruben," he answered.

"Mrs. VanAusdell has a little problem she'd like you to handle," said her secretary.

"Let me call you right back." Ruben disconnected, took an N-phone from his briefcase and made the call, knowing it meant he wouldn't be joining Gwynn 'soon.' Mrs. VanAusdell was a very important client.

CHAPTER 8

"I didn't know you were here," Dave said, smiling at Gwynn.

"I wanted to finish checking some purchase orders," she said, feeling relieved it was Dave and not Ashton standing before her.

"Is Ash back?" he asked, looking at Ashton's door behind her.

"I thought I heard a noise coming from his office. I knocked. No answer," Gwynn said.

"What kind of noise?"

"A thump."

"He left the funeral before I did." Dave dug a key ring out of his pocket and went to stick one in the lock, but stopped and turned the doorknob. "It's not locked," he said, pushing the door open.

Gwynn quickly scanned the room and felt her muscles tense when she saw keys lying next to the copy machine. Trying to keep them out of Dave's sight, she slowly moved forward and swung around so the copier was behind her.

Dave walked around the room. "Nothing looks out of place. Ash always leaves files stacked everywhere. A bird might have struck the window," he said, waving his hand up and down in front of the floor-to-ceiling glass panels.

Gwynn inched back and grasped the keys in her fist. "Well then, I'll be getting back to work."

Dave stepped closer to her. "Are you sure that's what you want to do," he said, gazing at her with his shimmering eyes. "We're the only ones here." He took her arm and slid his hand down toward her palm where the keys were hidden.

Feeling his hot breath on her face, she gripped his moving hand. "I wouldn't have returned to the office if I hadn't planned on working."

The entrance door slammed shut, followed by heavy footsteps. Their heads swung toward the hall and watched Ashton come around the lobby doorway.

"What are you doing in here?" Ashton asked, glaring at them.

"Gwynn heard a noise. We checked it out," Dave said, leaving Ashton's office with Gwynn. "And Bro, you forgot to lock it."

"No. I didn't," Ashton snapped.

"Yes, you did," Dave said in a mocking tone.

Ashton closed his door, and Dave headed to his office.

Gwynn hurried to her desk and dropped the keys in the top drawer. Pulled out the page she had tucked under her blouse, wrote down the H2S gas monitor serial number and slipped the sheet into her purse. Wanting to know if the company still owned it, she clicked through several screens on her computer until she came to the asset list. From there she searched for Gas Monitors and the curser moved to that category. She scrolled down, looking for the serial number and found it. The column next to it was blank. In it should have been the monitor's location: the name of the employee it had been assigned to, if it was in storage or if the company no longer had it.

A metal storage building owned by the company sat half a mile down the road. Gwynn had driven by it, but had never been inside. She opened her top drawer, gazed at the keys and decided she needed a set in case she ran into a snag trying to pick the lock. Gwynn slipped them in her purse, cleared off her desk and headed to Farmington, thinking having the keys duplicated in Bloomfield could be risky.

It was 9:30 p.m. when she received the call—Ruben's 'soon' wasn't going to happen within the next week. He fabricated an excuse, but Gwynn no longer heard a word he said after he mentioned another project needed his immediate attention.

She grabbed a bottle of wine from the fridge, opened it with her new corkscrew, poured a glass and sat down at the table, wondering if Ruben treated all new employees poorly or if it was just her. He had arranged all her training and taken her with him on three jobs during the past year. Even though he had warned her she wouldn't get special treatment because of their personal relationship, she believed she would.

As she sipped on her wine, she thought about the skills she had acquired under Ruben's guidance and became confident she could handle this investigation alone. She peered out the window, pondering *what was the investigation?*

Gwynn got a notepad and listed the potential candidates. At the top she wrote Arne Boden's death followed by workover problem. Nothing else came to her mind. Mike Drumlin's murder occurred after she arrived so it couldn't be the reason for hiring Ruben's company. Yet, she decided to include it since she had first-hand knowledge about it and his name had been included in Ashton's file.

As she had observed Ruben do during each investigation, she summarized in writing everything she knew about the two deaths, which wasn't much. On another page she wrote down suspects; except for Marilyn and Debra, it included all of Prudell's Bloomfield employees and Sam Young, the police officer. She would be working under the assumption they were all guilty until she found a reason to cross their name off the list.

Gwynn walked into Hayes's office and handed him the key ring. "The project files weren't in any of the piles in Mr. Prudell's office. Among those keys, there wasn't one that opened his file cabinet so I couldn't check in it."

Hayes held up his hands in a stop motion with his palms facing Gwynn. "No. No. I didn't mean for you to look in the cabinet. That's where Ash keeps his personal folders. He'd never give anyone a key to that."

"I didn't know. Do you want me to recreate the folders now?"

"Yes. We have to have something even if it's not complete. Thanks for looking."

Dave had spent most of the day working at the downtown office. Right before quitting time, he strode into the lobby. "How about a beer?" he asked Gwynn.

"Can't," she said, pounding on the keyboard. "I'm working on recreating some misplaced files."

"What files?" he said, leaning over the short wall.

"Some workover projects."

He slightly tilted his head. "Lost, huh? I'm sure it can wait until Monday."

"I want to get it done."

"How about after you finish?"

"Then I want to soak in the tub."

He grinned. "Want company?"

"Remember?" She touched her engagement ring.

His eyebrows slanted in a frown. "Yeah. You comin' to the ranch tomorrow?"

Gwynn nodded.

"What time?"

"Late morning."

"See you there." Dave walked out the entrance without stopping at his office.

Gwynn continued working while she waited for everyone to clear out.

"Don't forget that when you leave the door will lock behind you," Ashton said, swinging it open.

"I won't."

An hour later, Gwynn pulled her oversized purse from under the desk and headed to the restroom. She changed into a black long-sleeved bodysuit with a scrunched turtleneck. She slipped on a thin raincoat on top to hide her outfit, the one she had acquired when she started working for Ruben. She thought it might be overkill to check out the metal storage building, but it always excited her to put that private eye investigator outfit on.

She drove about a thousand feet past the well lit storage structure and parked on the other side of two trees, which hid her vehicle from sight. Gwynn threw the raincoat in the backseat and attached a holster to her thigh and a sheath to her calf on the opposite leg. She slid her Beretta 9-millimeter, along with a knife into the holster and another knife into the sheath. She secured the backpack that held her night goggles, a flashlight, rope, rod and miscellaneous small tools. After Gwynn pulled on her gloves, she felt ready. She got out of the car and stood under a dark, cloud-covered sky.

At work, Gwynn had studied the information on the computer about the building and knew it had an alarm system with motion detectors, but no surveillance cameras. She memorized the location of each motion detector and the code to turn off the alarm system. She had learned how to disable an alarm system, but pushing in a code would make it simpler.

Moving stealthily, Gwynn approached the structure from the front in order to avoid a motion detector. She could have been easily spotted if someone drove down the street, but it was sparsely traveled at night. When she reached the door, she began inserting various keys into the padlock, searching for the right one.

It clicked open with the third key. She lifted the padlock out of the clasp, slid the bolt and put it back on the disengaged mechanism. Flipping on her flashlight, Gwynn opened the door and heard the alarm softly beeping. She had sixty seconds to enter the code. She rushed to the panel in the middle of the wall, punched in the code and the beeping stopped. Gwynn inhaled deeply and smiled—*so far so good.*

She was tempted to turn on the lights, yet feared the glow would illuminate under the doors—the one she entered plus the garage door in the center. Slowly moving the flashlight around the huge space filled with pipes, casings, equipment, tools, oil cans, lubricant sprays, hardware and other miscellaneous items, she analyzed where to begin. Going to the farthest corner, she slipped off her backpack and pulled out her night goggles. She forced them over her head and made the necessary adjustments.

As she dropped her backpack behind a shelving unit, the stock of a rifle caught her attention. She lifted it up, saw the initials AKB etched into the handle and wondered about Arne's middle name; she couldn't recall seeing it in the folder. Gwynn lowered it back down to its original position.

Small objects the size of gas monitors stood on shelves twenty feet from her. She made her way to them and began rummaging through the items. She stepped on a shelf to continue looking and discovered one H2S gas monitor, but couldn't make out the grease-covered serial number. Gripping it in her hand, she eased back down to the floor and headed to her backpack. From it, Gwynn yanked out a small container of moist wipes, pulled one out and cleaned around the area until the number clearly appeared. She shook her head, "Damn."

Brakes squealed. Gwynn hoped it didn't mean she was having company. She set the monitor on the floor, put on her backpack and as a precaution, hunkered down behind a stack of pipes.

"He didn't lock up!" a guy with a whiny, gravelly voice said as the door flew open.

"He forgot to set the alarm," Turk said. "What a dumb shit! Let me grab it and we'll be out of here."

Gwynn heard the crunch of leather boots on the concrete as Turk came closer. She covered her lips with her hand, preventing any sound from accidently escaping.

"I don't think you should give it to Janice's kid," the whiny-voiced guy said.

"Arne always let him use it," Turk said. "The kid's been asking me about it and the other guns for months."

"The man won't like it."

"Don't care. He can keep the rest in the shed, but this one's special."

"Does he know you took it?"

"Just got it yesterday. Probably doesn't know it's missing."

A loud thud, followed by the sound of metal hitting the cement floor rumbled through the structure.

"What happened?" the whiny-voiced guy asked.

"Tripped on this damn monitor," Turk replied, sounding irritated. "What's it doing here?"

"He knows where they belong."

"Tomorrow he'll have a few more things to clean up."

Heavy footsteps pounded across the cement floor. Gwynn peeked around the edge of a pipe and saw Turk standing in front of the alarm system. "It's set."

Gwynn watched as he closed the door behind him and heard the clang of the padlock being snapped shut. *Oh great! Here I thought this was going to be easy—a piece of cake.*

CHAPTER 9

After waiting five minutes, Gwynn scooted along behind the pipes until she reached the corner, the end of the stack. With her back pressed against the wall, she attempted to avoid the motion detectors, but knew she couldn't make it to the system pad without setting off the alarm—no sixty second delay. That only worked when the door was opened or right after the alarm had been set. Gwynn could still manage to stop the obnoxious sound once the alarm went off, but couldn't prevent the signal from going to a security office somewhere.

She also worried that Turk and his buddy might confront the person responsible for setting the system and locking the door at Marty's—sending him rushing here thinking an intruder might be on the premises. Time was not on her side.

She sprinted to the panel as the loud buzzing erupted around her and quickly entered the code. The room became silent. It wouldn't be long before someone showed up to check the building.

Gazing at the row of switches, Gwynn wondered which one opened the skylights and noticed two with small, protruding levers next to them. She flipped one of the switches and heard a humming, mechanical sound. Using her index finger she moved the first lever as three skylights opened, but they weren't on her preferred escape route. She wanted to slip out on the other side of the roof, further away from the road. After closing that set of skylights, she turned on another switch and slid the second lever. The other skylights slowly creaked and the windows rose.

Gwynn climbed up a bank of shelves under the opened skylights. When she reached the top, she stood approximately fifteen feet away from the nearest skylight. She pulled a rope, hook and an extendable rod out of her backpack and flung the end of the rope over the support holding the center rafter. It dangled below the skylight.

Gwynn secured the hook to the rod and managed to use it to pull the dangling rope to her. She tied both ends of the rope to the corner shelf post and began to retract the rod when she accidentally knocked a row of tools off the shelf. The crashing sound of metal hitting concrete rang out as each tool struck the floor. Shaking her head, Gwynn tied another piece of rope around her waist, looped it over the rope that stretched to the rafter and shimmied to the skylight.

Off in the distance, she heard a police cruiser siren and assumed it was headed her direction. Gwynn extended the rod again and hooked it into the frame of the skylight and lifted pulling herself through the opening. Before she cleared the skylight, her backpack hit the glass, spreading shards through the air.

Lying on the roof, she saw blinking red and blue lights approaching. Gwynn inched over to a protruding pipe and tied her last piece of rope to it. She grasped it between her glove-covered hands and glided to the end of it, six feet from the ground. Gwynn jumped and landed hard on the pavement. With a sore foot, she ran from the building and into tall grass. Hunkering down, she quickly moved toward her car, brushing pieces of glass from her clothing along the way. Looking over her shoulder, she caught a glimpse of the blinking light in front of the metal building.

Gwynn scooted into her vehicle, put on her night goggles and drove without headlights for two or three miles. She stopped at the side of the road next to an orchard. There, she changed back into the clothes she had worn earlier, raised her skirt and secured the knife sheath to her thigh. She stuffed her black outfit, raincoat and holster into a hidden compartment in the trunk and placed a duffle bag filled with exercise clothing and towels on top of it. Gwynn leaned her head forward, shook it and ran her fingers through her hair. Only a few slivers of glass tumbled out. Suspecting there could be more, she vigorously brushed her hair until she felt satisfied it was all gone.

Gwynn started the car engine again, continued on the road, in the direction away from the building. Within ten minutes, the asphalt ended and a gravel road stretched out in front of her. She stopped, pulled her cell phone out of her purse and clicked on GPS. She touched the screen a few times and her address appeared. In order to get there, it showed she had to turn around. She clicked on maps searching for another route—nothing.

Irritated with herself for not devising a better plan to search the storage building, she stared through the windshield and mumbled sarcastically, "Ruben certainly would be proud of my smooth, quiet, skillful escape."

Reluctantly, she made a U-turn and planned on making a detour on a road about 500 feet from the metal structure, the only road between her and the crime scene. She knew there was a risk her Mustang could easily be recognized if someone stood by the road. Gwynn contemplated whether she should park and wait for an hour or so. Suddenly, she saw blinking red and blue lights heading her direction without a siren blaring and assumed the police were looking for the intruder.

Not more than a few homes were on that stretch of road. They were set back at least one hundred feet. No cars were parked along the pavement. Stopping would only draw attention to her vehicle so Gwynn proceeded and watched the patrol vehicle zoom past her.

As she got closer to the building, Gwynn noticed Silverados parked on both sides of the street along with two police cruisers. Men and women wandered around. Suspecting someone had spotted her Mustang, she stopped behind a Silverado, climbed out of her car and crossed the road.

"What's going on?" she asked Turk.

"Someone broke into the storage building," he said.

"What are you doing here?" Dave asked, walking toward her.

"After I left work, I decided to take a little drive and wanted to know where this street went," she said, gesturing toward it. "It only leads to a gravel road, but I kept going and got stuck when I tried turning around."

"I thought you wanted to go home and soak in the tub?" he asked, furrowing his brow.

"I still do. Driving was just a way of winding down."

A thin woman in her mid-twenties with puffy, long, curly hair and wearing heavy make-up, slipped her arm into Dave's. "Come on, honey, let's go back and dance."

"Give me a minute, Penny," Dave said, lowering his arm. The woman's arm dropped to her side.

Gwynn glanced around. It looked like almost everyone from Marty's had come out to inspect the crime scene. "What was taken?"

"So far, they don't know. Nothing big." He scanned her face. "How did you get unstuck?"

"Some guy came by and helped me."

"What was he driving?"

"A blue Ford truck," Gwynn said and then popped her eyes wide open. "Do you think it might have been the guy who broke in?"

"Could be," Dave said. "That road isn't traveled much. Have you ever seen him at Marty's?"

"I can't recall." Gwynn turned around. "I'm going home to enjoy a bath. See you tomorrow."

Gwynn fastened her seat belt, glanced at the crowd and saw Penny wrapping her arms around Dave's.

CHAPTER 10

At 11:20 a.m., Gwynn drove down a private lane flanked on both sides with white fences that had a few horses peering over them. Getting out of her car, the air smelled fresh and she gazed at the warm and inviting Prudell ranch: a large, white two-story framed house with a wrap-around porch, a huge red barn that had two attached dressing rooms for the convenience of their frequent guests, an Olympic swimming pool next to a gazebo and shade trees scattered throughout along with beds of multi-colored flowers.

Gwynn headed to the dressing room to change into her pale blue bikini and ran into Brad on her way.

"Did you hear about the break-in?" he asked.

"Yes. Last night. Do they know what was taken yet?"

"Can't find a thing missing. Maybe the alarm scared the guy off. He sure made a mess getting out of there—broken glass, tools scattered all over the floor."

"Broken glass?"

"Yeah. Cops think he accidentally got locked in. Climbed out through a skylight. Left a rope strung from a shelf to the skylight." He chuckled. "Broke the glass escaping. What a dumb shit!"

Gwynn refused to show any emotion, but couldn't prevent her cheeks from turning red as she found herself agreeing with Brad, *He's right. How could I have been so stupid?* "It's good if he didn't get away with anything."

His head bent down toward Gwynn's duffle bag. "Going swimming?"

She nodded.

"See you in the pool."

After Gwynn changed into her swimsuit, two women walked into the ladies' dressing room.

"Hi, Carol," Gwynn said to Ashton and Dave's sister, a thirty-seven-year old woman, with light-brown, short hair. She was a married, stay-at-home mom, with two small boys, ages three and five.

"Hi, Gwynn," Carol replied, cheerfully and nodded toward the other woman. "This is my friend, Megan Gardner. She doesn't live far from here."

Megan was a slender, five-foot-six, attractive woman with a heart-shaped face, long blonde, wavy hair and dimples. She looked ten years younger than Carol.

After the two women greeted each other, Gwynn grabbed her towel and suntan lotion and strolled toward the pool. She heard chatting, laughing and water splashing before she reached it. Over a dozen people were in it, swimming, playing ball, or diving. She quickly scanned the area for any sign of Dave. Satisfied he wasn't nearby, she eased down onto a lounge chair and squirted lotion on her legs.

"Can I help you spread that out," Dave said from behind her.

Without looking at him, Gwynn rolled her eyes. "No. I can manage," she said, massaging it in.

"Hi, Dave," Megan said, scooting a lounge closer to Gwynn's.

"You just get back in town?" Dave asked.

"Yes. Europe was wonderful. You should have come."

"Busy working." Dave knelt next to Gwynn. "After lunch, I'm hooking up a wagon to a couple of horses. Want to go for a ride?"

"That would be fun," Megan said. "It's been a long time."

"Gwynn, do you want to come?" he asked.

"Sure."

A mischievous expression flashed on Dave's face. He rose and jumped into the pool, sending water flying everywhere. A few soaked sunbathers moaned and children yelled, wanting him to do it again.

"I understand you work for the company," Megan said, applying lotion to her arms.

"Yes," Gwynn replied. "I've been with them for over two months."

"You dating Dave?" she asked, sounding meek with a hint of jealousy.

"No. I'm engaged."

Megan gasped for air and threw her hands on her chest. "To Dave?"

"No. To Ross."

Briefly closing her eyes, Megan asked, "Does he work for the company?"

"No. He's in advertising and lives in New York."

"New York? How does that work?"

Gwynn filled her in on how she ended up in Bloomfield—inheriting her uncle's house. She went on, "Ross and I decided we want to live here. He plans on finding a job close by. He's just been too busy at work to even start to look.

"How often does he come to see you?" Megan asked.

Gwynn bit her bottom lip and inhaled deeply. "He hasn't had a chance to get away since I came here."

Megan cocked her brow and stared at Gwynn. "Over two months?"

Gwynn slowly bobbed her head up and down.

Megan leaned toward Gwynn and touched her arm. "You poor thing. How awful." Her eyes moved to the swimming pool. "Dave and I were once engaged. Neither one of us were ready to get married so it ended."

Gwynn sensed sadness in Megan's tone and wondered how it really ended.

The Prudells fed all their visitors. For lunch, they spread out cold-cuts, breads, salads and desserts on a long, redwood, picnic table covered with a red and white plaid table cloth. Guests served themselves. At dinner time, they barbequed hamburgers, spareribs or steaks for those who remained.

After lunch, Gwynn hurried to her car to grab her specially equipped binoculars under the pretense that she wanted to do some bird watching in the wagon. The binoculars could be used as a gun with a quick modification and they had a hidden slot that concealed a knife, the ideal weapon if you were scantily clad. Gwynn had slipped on a pair of shorts and a blouse over her swimsuit. Still, any normal weapon would have bulged through the clothing. She doubted she needed to protect herself at the ranch in broad daylight. Yet, she already had one situation in New Mexico when she wasn't properly armed and Ruben's rule had firmly been planted in her head since then, *Always be armed with a gun and knife.*

Dave announced he had the wagon ready to go. Seven guests, its capacity, headed to the other side of the barn. On the way, Gwynn noticed the double barn doors stood wide open. She caught a glimpse inside and saw three ATVs, two motorcycles and a motorized golf cart. The golf cart struck her as being a strange item to have at a ranch with gravel and dirt paths.

"Gwynn, why don't you sit up front?" Dave asked.

"I think it will be easier to use my binoculars if I sit on one of the back benches." Gwynn said, realizing that was a lame excuse, then looked at Megan. "Why don't you sit up there?"

Without hesitation, Megan climbed up next to Dave.

Gwynn noticed Dave's eyes glowed as he looked at Megan and suspected he still had feelings for her. *Maybe their engagement did end just like Megan had said—neither one was ready to get married.*

Turk scooted in the back first and sat behind Megan. Gwynn sat on the bench across from him. Ralph from Marketing and his wife, Courtney, climbed in next to her. Teenage kids sat in the other two places.

Gwynn's goal was to focus on Turk. She wanted to know more about him, thinking it could narrow down the suspects who helped him clean up the night he killed Drumlin. She heard Megan drilling Dave about what he had been up to and then Gwynn began talking to Turk.

"How long have you worked for the company?"

"A long time," he replied while he stared at something behind her.

Without turning around, she studied the area for something unusual so when they returned she could use her binoculars at the same spot and search for what had drawn Turk's attention. Gwynn noticed two tree stumps with a large boulder between them and then continued quizzing Turk—what schools he had attended and projects he was working on. All of his answers were only a few words. She learned very little about him and nothing that would help with the investigation.

Occasionally Gwynn lifted the binoculars to her eyes and once saw an eagle soaring. She also saw a black raven perched on a nest in an old oak tree.

Dave pointed out some places Gwynn might find various varieties of local birds. He took the wagon on a rough dirt lane that ran parallel to the corral filled with cattle. The wagon bounced and jerked along with the passengers on the wooden benches. He stopped to check the flow of water in the troughs.

When they returned to the smoother surface, Gwynn peered through her binoculars again, looking for anything unusual. She saw a couple of dilapidated shacks with trails branching off in different directions. Off in the distance were hills covered with junipers, wild grasses and sagebrush, but her eyes lingered on three mockingbirds sitting on an elm tree branch.

An hour later, Dave turned the horses around and they trotted back toward the barn.

Gwynn kept her eyes peeled for the tree stumps and thirty minutes later saw them. She adjusted her binoculars, searched through the trees and caught a sliver of a woodshed. *Was that what Turk had looked at earlier? Could something important to the investigation be stored in there?* Gwynn swung her head slightly back so it would appear she was looking toward the sky since Turk was close by. In the process, she spotted a road on a hill behind the woodshed. Slowly, she lowered the binoculars and glimpsed at the shed tucked among the overgrown trees. Resting them against her chest, she noticed Turk gazing at her and said, "Have you ever done any bird watching?"

He shook his head.

"Would you like to use my binoculars?"

"Yeah."

She pulled the strap over her head and handed them to him.

He held them in front of his eyes, moved his head around and occasionally stopped, focusing on something interesting off in the distance. "These sure are powerful."

"Yes," Gwynn said. "They're 8 by 56. Great for picking up bird detail.

"They sure are. Maybe I'll have to get me a pair like this," Turk said with a smile, handing them back to Gwynn.

Dave pulled back on the reins. The horses came to a halt next to the barn. As Gwynn stepped down from the back of the wagon, she saw Brad standing by the barn door.

"Turk," Ashton said loudly, walking up the gravel path toward him.

Gwynn hadn't seen Ashton earlier in the day, so she assumed he had just arrived.

"And Brad," Ashton said. "Can I talk to you guys for a minute?"

"Want to go horseback riding?" Dave asked Gwynn.

"No. I want to lay by the pool and absorb a few more rays before I leave." Strolling away, she heard Megan telling Dave she'd like to ride.

Moving down the path, Gwynn observed Ashton, Turk and Brad huddled by a small table under a large tree out of earshot from anyone heading to the pool. She sat her binoculars on the tile floor next to a lounge chair, slipped off her shorts and blouse and stretched out on the lounge, pondering about the woodshed.

Forty-five minutes later, she gathered up her belongs and moved toward the dressing room, catching sight of the three men still sitting at the table. A fourth man had joined them. Wanting to know who it was, she dropped her towel. Bending down to pick it up, Gwynn managed to get a better look at the fourth person: Ralph Hunter, the guy who sat next to her in the wagon and only spoke to his wife.

CHAPTER 11

On the way home, Gwynn stopped at the grocery store and at a drugstore. The sun had set by the time she reached her driveway and she thought she saw a light coming from inside her house. As she drove up the gravel lane, the light vanished. *Two people who worked for Prudell are dead. Had anyone spotted me last night?*

She parked behind an overgrown bush twenty feet from the front door, opened her trunk and secured the loaded holsters to her body. Gwynn raised her Berretta and flipped off the safety. With it firmly in her hand, she crept around the house, thinking if there was an intruder his car might be around back, but the yard was empty. She perked up her ears and slowly scanned the edge of the woods—nothing.

Gwynn unlocked the back door. It squeaked as she eased it opened. Leaning next to the outside of the doorway, she listened for movement inside the house. The only sound was the humming of the refrigerator. She cautiously entered, ready for a potential unwelcome visitor. With the glow of the moon streaming through the windows, she stealthily inched past the kitchen cabinets, with her eyes darting back and forth.

Reaching the doorway to the living room, she pressed her back against the wall and listened again. She sensed someone else was in the house and felt her pulse quicken and her muscles tighten.

Holding her weapon out in front of her, she edged around the door frame. Suddenly, someone grabbed her hand and hit the inside of her forearm with the side of his other hand, knocking her weapon from her grip. A loud thud echoed through the house as the pistol tumbled to the hardwood floor. As she veered down to scoop it up, his hand clasped onto her arm. Gwynn grabbed his wrist, twisted it and flipped the intruder to the floor. Her movements were rapid and concise as she flipped him again, hurling his body into a chair. He gripped her ankle and gave a jerky pull, landing her on her back. The attacker staggered to his feet. Gwynn leapt up and flung herself at him, sending him sprawling across the room. She bounced on him, drew her knife and held it next to his throat. Gwynn stared at the face of her attacker in the dim light, leaned down and smothered his lips with hers.

"I wanted to surprise you," Ruben said.

"I could have killed you!"

"That's why I took care of the pistol."

She held up the knife gripped in her hands. "How about this?"

"You would have wanted answers, not blood, since I wasn't brandishing a weapon."

"Why didn't you just say something?"

"Wanted to watch you in action." He wrapped his arms around her, pulled her closer and kissed her. "You did well!"

Gwynn knew Ruben could have easily overpowered her if it would have been a real fight. "Did I hurt you?"

"Just a little sore back, but your chair's a goner."

She glanced toward it and saw pieces of broken wood where it had once stood. "We could use more light," she said, sliding off Ruben and standing. She flipped the switch and her eyes sparkled as she gazed at the tall, handsome man with deep blue eyes and dark brown hair. "Your other project didn't take very long."

"I have to go back," he said, putting his arm around her shoulders.

"When?"

"Tomorrow."

"Only one night?"

He squeezed her shoulder. "Afraid so."

She looked up, bounced her eyebrows and gave him a flirtatious smile. "The bedroom door is right behind you. Let's take advantage of the new mattress."

"Have you eaten?" he asked.

"I don't need food."

"I picked up a bottle of your favorite wine, cheese and fresh rolls. I want to talk before we enjoy what your bedroom has to offer."

"Food! Groceries are in my car."

Twenty minutes later, they were sitting on the couch drinking wine and eating.

"Next time you decide to break into a storage building," Ruben began, "make sure you have thought out an escape plan that doesn't leave an unnecessary trail of debris behind."

Gwynn choked on her wine and began coughing, splattering it on her blouse. Ruben rubbed her back. "How did you know?" she said, gasping for air.

"After you called about the murder, I sent an employee to keep track of you."

"I didn't see anyone."

"He's good."

"Was he in the metal building?" she asked.

"No, but he was close by when visitors arrived."

"Did he follow me when I left?"

"Yes. He even watched as you changed your clothes."

"Peeping Tom!"

"Not exactly. He didn't see much."

That night ran through Gwynn's mind again. She recalled seeing a cloud of dust and a flickering light running parallel to the road, but off in the distance—too far away to see her, so she had assumed it was someone taking an evening ride on a dirt bike or an ATV.

"He must have some powerful binoculars."

"With zoom lenses," Ruben said.

"Any pictures?"

"A few. The one with you limping away from the structure concerned me. How's your ankle?"

"It wasn't that bad. I packed it in ice while I watched TV. Didn't want to raise any suspicion when I went to the ranch." She dropped her eyes to her blouse. "Let me change this."

"It's coming off soon anyway. Relax and enjoy your wine while you explain what was so important in that metal building that you felt it necessary to go against my orders and snoop around."

Gwynn took a sip, pondered if she should also tell him about breaking into the file cabinet in Ashton's office and decided it might not be a good idea to admit going against orders twice. "After Drumlin's death, I heard another Prudell employee had accidentally died a few months ago from hydrogen-sulfide poisoning," she said, stressing the word "accidentally." "Based on snippets of conversations I overhead, some people didn't think it was an accident."

Ruben held up his hand. "Stop there. Snippets?" he asked, raising his brows. "Who did you ask about it?"

Gwynn bit her lower lip and tapped her fingers on the armrest. "Okay," she said, reluctantly, "Marilyn at work mentioned the accident, but Drumlin's death was also believed to be an accident. I wanted to check it out and asked Linda at the café."

"You've told me about her."

"Her sister, Janice Robinson, hangs out at Marty's, flirting with all the guys. Arne Boden, the guy who died earlier, told her he had something going on that would make him rich. Janice thought the 'something' was illegal and didn't believe Boden's death was an accident. Neither did his friend, Turk Carlsen. He works for Prudell." She looked down and scratched her forehead.

"What?"

"Something else strikes me as strange. Linda said the day Boden died, a guy at work had called Janice, wanting her to keep him busy so they could decorate his apartment for his birthday. When he left her, to fix a well problem, it was dark."

"Who called her?"

"Linda didn't know."

"That doesn't explain why you were in the metal building."

"The H2S gas safety monitor. Everyone was told it had malfunctioned, but since then—no repairs or purchases of new H2S gas monitors. There isn't even one listed under the items assigned to Boden."

"Wouldn't it have been given to his replacement if it was working?"

"Yes, but there's a column to indicate what happened to it—transferred to, in storage, disposed, like all of Boden's other equipment. One should have been on his list, but nothing. I searched through the company records and located the serial number on a prior printout of Boden's equipment." *Found in Ashton's file cabinet.* "I looked through the computer screens that showed all company equipment. The monitor was there, but the column indicating its current disposition was blank. I thought it might be in the storage unit. If it was, I planned on having it checked."

"Did you find it?"

"No. I ran across one. It had the wrong serial number. I didn't get a chance to search the whole building, but it's organized so all the gas monitors should have been together. I bumped into a rifle in the far corner with the initials AKB etched in the handle. That's why Turk and a guy with a gravelly voice, Prudell employees, showed up—to get it. Turk plans on giving it to Janice's son, since Boden had let him use it and the kid had been asking about it. The other guy said 'the man' wouldn't like it. Then Turk said 'the man' could have the rest that were in the shed."

Ruben rubbed his chin with his knuckles, his eyes narrowed, and he mumbled, "Hmm."

"Are you going to tell me why I'm here?"

"Tomorrow. Before I leave."

CHAPTER 12

A crisp morning breeze whipped through the open window, causing goose-bumps to rise on Gwynn's exposed arm. Opening her eyes, she smelled the sweet aroma of bath oils lingering on Ruben's skin. She had poured them into the tub they had shared the night before.

Gwynn shimmied closer and slipped her cold arm under the covers and laid it on the bare muscular chest of the man she loved. She felt his warm breath as he rolled on his side and stroked her hair. Raising her head, they kissed and became entwined, enjoying the new mattress again.

Once Ruben and Gwynn disentangled again, he smiled and put his arm under her neck and she rested her head on his shoulder. "I've missed you," he said softly.

"Can you stay most of the day?" Gwynn asked, hoping he'd be close to her a little longer.

"I have to leave in a couple of hours."

"Do you know when you'll be back?"

"Soon."

Gwynn rolled her eyes and had the urge to shout "what does soon mean?" Yet, she resisted the impulse and remained silent.

"Let me fix you breakfast before I leave," Ruben said. "And we need to discuss business."

She lingered in bed and watched Ruben take a robe out of his suitcase. "Are you going to tell me who my bodyguard is?" Gwynn asked, knowing Ruben might not approve of her planned actions and now she'd have a hard time remaining under his radar.

"We'll discuss business after breakfast."

Gwynn sat at the table sipping on coffee while Ruben cooked eggs, bacon, hash browns and toast. She had offered to help, but he had insisted on doing it by himself.

Ruben felt guilty about leaving her alone for two months, seldom calling and almost completely ignoring her, but it was by design. He couldn't allow himself to worry about her any more than he would about his other employees. Emotions got in the way in his business. Gwynn had been given the best training available and now it was time for her to perform the job she wanted. He had to stifle the impulse to only give her the easy assignments, which, before the second death occurred, he had assumed this was one of those.

Assigning someone to keep track of Gwynn was something Ruben would have done for any of his employees if an event occurred that might put them in harm's way. Ruben's employees rarely became victims and he planned on keeping it that way.

Gwynn's stomach growled when Ruben brought over their filled plates. Within fifteen minutes, she had devoured everything on it and gazed at his handsome face while he ate the last piece of toast.

The two-bedroom frame house lacked a dishwasher. Not wanting to spend time washing dishes, she stacked them on the counter.

Ruben filled their coffee cups and sat down. "Ready?"

Feeling anxious to hear about the investigation, Gwynn adjusted herself in the chair and linked her fingers together. "Yes. Do I need a notepad?"

He shook his head. "No intricate details." Ruben leaned forward, placed his forearms on the table and scanned her face. "Have you figured it out yet?"

"I have two theories."

"Go on," he said as he nodded.

"Investigating the murder of Arne Boden or something to do with workovers."

"Workovers? Is that some kind of operation done to existing wells so they'll produce more?"

Gwynn nodded. "The goal is to increase production. Sometimes that doesn't happen."

"What made you think the investigation might be about workovers?"

"Alex Hayes, the CFO," Gwynn said.

"I know who he is."

"He's been looking for some workover project folders that are missing. He asked me to go through the folders on Ashton Prudell's desk when Ashton was at Drumlin's funeral. He gave me the key to Ashton's office. It didn't sit right with me."

"Did you?"

"Yes. The folders weren't there. All the workover invoices and the engineer reports have been scanned into the computer system. I'm in the process of creating new folders with hard copies."

"If those files can be recreated why was Hayes concerned?"

"That's just it—I don't know. He made some comment about notes in the files that weren't scanned into the system."

"Do you know how long they've been missing?"

"Not a clue." Gwynn cocked her head. "Is that what I'm supposed to be investigating?"

"The investigation is to determine who killed Arne Boden and why. Maybe the workovers play a role."

"And Mike Drumlin?"

"I suspect there's a connection there."

"Have you completely ruled out that Boden's death could've been an accident?"

"It wasn't. The well was tested the following day. The hydrogen-sulfide level wasn't high enough. Boden was very conscientious about checking his gas monitor and it would have started buzzing before the gas reached a dangerous level. Also, he had coins in his pocket and the copper pennies weren't discolored."

"If the color of the pennies didn't change, that level of hydrogen-sulfide couldn't have floated through the air." She pursed her lips. "It was administered through a gas mask?"

Ruben nodded. "A creative way to kill someone, but murder is murder."

"Did the police question it?"

"No. They just assumed it was an accident."

Gwynn wondered why the client didn't go to the police after the well test, but she knew from past experience that Ruben's clients almost never wanted the cops involved. "What specifically should I be doing?"

"Keep your eyes and ears open. Find out what you can about the workovers—interest owners, cost, who did the work, production, anything that might be helpful. Stay low profile. Understood?" he said firmly.

"Understood, boss," she said, putting her arms around his neck. Gwynn pulled him closer and kissed the tip of his nose.

He smiled. "Is that how you treat all your bosses?" he asked, referring to her Prudell employment.

"What do you think?"

He stroked her arms and flicked his eyebrows. "Maybe. If they'll give you information."

Gwynn lightly hit his shoulder. "No! I don't need to smooch with them."

Ruben placed his palm on her check. "You better not." He downed the rest of his coffee. "I have to get going."

"Some of the people I talk to at work and in town are beginning to act like my fiancé has dumped me. Can I tell them Ross Madison came to see me?"

"No. Let them think you're not smart enough to even suspect there's a problem. If they believe you're not very swift, they might not hesitate to talk in front of you."

"Got it."

"Any questions?"

"Can you tell me who the guy is that's watching me?"

"It's better if you don't know. You might be tempted to make contact and I don't want you to be observed talking to a stranger in town."

"Makes sense. Have any of the guys who work for Prudell been in trouble with the law?"

"Why?"

"Repeat performance."

"I'll have someone check on it. When they get the results, they'll call your cell phone and say Mr. Madison won't be able to call you this evening."

"But I've heard that before."

"Next time, it will be your cue to call me on the N-phone. Then, I'll give you their number."

"What if I'm at work?"

"Call when you get home."

Ruben kissed Gwynn goodbye and headed through the foliage that ran near the long driveway, with a duffle bag flung over his shoulder, to his car, parked on the edge of the road.

CHAPTER 13

As soon as Gwynn walked into the office, Marilyn repeated the same question she had asked every Monday morning for the past couple of months. "Did your guy make it in town over the weekend?"

"No," Gwynn said, sinking down into her chair. Out of the corner of her eye, she saw Marilyn looking down and shaking her head.

After Ashton entered the building and wandered past Gwynn's cubicle to check out her cleavage on the way to his office, she continued printing off documents for the recreated files. Even before Ruben's visit, she was already making an additional set for herself, but hers would include more information.

Shortly before lunch, Hayes went to Gwynn's desk. "How are you doing on those files?"

"They're finished," she said, lifting up the stack.

"I'll take the top one." He pulled project #306 from the group. "Just file the rest."

Gwynn headed to the file room and opened the cabinet drawer. Her eyes popped wide open as she gawked at the project folders #306 through #314, neatly placed where they belonged. She put her newly created folders on top of the file cabinet and began going through the originals, searching for clues. Nothing seemed suspicious except the Project #312 folder contained an underlined handwritten notation in the top corner—GOR. Gwynn knew that stood for gas-oil ratio. *Does this mean anything?*

She entered Hayes's office and saw him sitting at his desk eating a sandwich while he punched numbers on his 10-key calculator. "Whoever had the missing files, returned them."

"They're back where they belong?" he asked, with a flash of bewilderment on his face.

"Yes. Right where they belong."

He dropped his sandwich on a pile of papers and strode toward

Gwynn. "What a surprise!" he said, passing her on his way to the file room.

"What do you want me to do with these?" she asked, referring to the duplicates.

"Leave them on my credenza."

Returning to her desk, Gwynn wanted to do some research about the GOR's on the wells associated with Project #312, but she had neglected her other work for two days. In order to maintain her cover, she put that task aside and dug into getting caught up.

At 5:00 p.m., Gwynn made a detour on her way home to search for the road behind the woodshed that had captivated Turk's attention during their wagon ride. Based on the layout of the ranch, she thought it was located a mile or two from the barn. Gwynn hadn't planned on visiting the woodshed, but it was easier to find the road during daylight.

She drove forty minutes and stopped near the fork in the road, the place where she would normally turn left to reach the ranch house which was five minutes away. Gwynn turned right, guessing that section of the road could run behind the shed. As she continued moving along, she kept glancing over her left shoulder, looking for the ranch through the foliage.

Ten minutes later, she spotted a sliver of a red barn through the trees and pulled over to the side of the road to verify it was Prudells'. She hadn't seen a vehicle since she turned at the fork. Without hesitation, she crossed the road to get a better look. Prudells' barn had yellow doors and a large brass P attached to the front peak.

Gwynn stood near a six foot fence with barbwire running along the top. Since she wasn't dressed for a closer surveillance, she walked along the edge of the road, peering between the trees and bushes. Within five minutes, she caught a good glimpse of the P and the yellow doors.

The roar of a diesel engine approaching from further up the road pierced her peaceful solitude.

Gwynn hurried across the street and moved quickly toward her car. When she was only a few feet away from it, breaks squeaked and a truck stopped. Seeing the grey tailgate, she swallowed hard.

"Gwynn," Dave said, loudly. She turned. "What are you doing out here?"

"I forgot my make-up bag at the ranch on Saturday. I came out to get it."

Dave climbed out of the driver's seat. "You wear make-up?" he said, teasingly.

"Yeah." She smiled. "Hard to believe isn't it?"

He crossed the street. "At the fork, you should have gone left."

"I figured that was where I screwed up. I didn't see you at work today. Have you been working at the ranch?"

"No. We're planning on drilling another well by 26-10." He pointed up the road. "Been working with surveyors and the drilling company."

Gwynn recalled hearing that the Prudells became involved with the oil and gas industry when a reservoir was discovered under their land. "Is it far from here?" she asked, thinking it could give her a future excuse to be on that road.

"A twenty-five minute drive. Do you want to see the location?"

"Sure. The sun's still shining and I enjoy driving around. If I stay on this road will I be able to recognize the location—poles, markings, equipment."

"It's not right on this road. You have to travel on a dirt trail for a while." He glanced at Gwynn's car. "It'll be too rough for your Mustang. I'll take you."

"But you've been there all day. I can see it some other time."

"Don't mind. And I haven't been there all day. Only a few hours." He took a step closer. "You still got that boyfriend?"

Gwynn nodded. "Yes."

"He come see ya?"

She lightly shook her head.

"I'll take you anyway," Dave said with a crooked smile. He checked out her long legs, tight butt and well-proportioned breasts as he held onto her arm while she raised her leg over two feet in the air to reach the truck cab.

"A step would be helpful," Gwynn commented.

"Not rugged enough."

"But I've seen steps on the other trucks," she said sliding into the passenger seat.

He patted the side of his vehicle. "That's what makes this one special—no frills." Dave got into the driver's seat.

She gazed at the dashboard. "I wouldn't exactly call your Bose sound system, no frills."

"That's a necessity."

"How about the leather seats?"

"Necessity."

Gwynn wanted to ask him how his girlfriends liked climbing in here without a step, but decided it might sound too much like flirting.

Dave flipped the truck around and thought Gwynn was looking at him. Instead, she was focused on the area outside his window, searching for the woodshed. "Have I got food on my face or something?" he asked.

"No, why?"

"Just from the way you're staring."

"I'm looking at the ranch. You must love it out here."

"I've already got myself a spread not far from here. The house needs some fixin'. Hoping to change careers in ten years."

Gwynn saw the edge of the woodshed between thick bushes and noticed that part of the fence sagged a little and tree branches hung over it. *I might not need wire cutters on my return visit.* Out of the corner of her eye, Gwynn looked for other branches dangling over the fence just in case that wasn't a unique quality at that location. She didn't spot another one.

Fifteen minutes later, Dave turned off the paved road. The truck bounced up and down on the rough dirt surface riddled with potholes, jerking Gwynn around in the seat.

"You're right. My car couldn't have gone on this route," she said. "Is it going to be graveled before the drilling?

"Yeah. In a couple of days it'll be smoothed out with a blade and gravel spread. Then they'll start bringing in the equipment."

A couple of days. Gwynn knew she didn't have much time to check out the shed with the comings and goings.

Dave pushed on the brakes. "This is the spot. Not much to see yet." Two small pieces of equipment were tucked between some trees and the ground had been well trampled. Apart from that—nothing.

They climbed out of the truck and walked around. Dave pointed out the exact location of the well, the separators and where the gathering lines would run.

"What if it's a dry hole?" Gwynn asked.

"Not a chance," Dave said without the slightest doubt in his tone.

Getting back into the Silverado, Dave put his hands on Gwynn's waist and lifted her up. "Wasn't that easier?" he asked with a mischievous smile.

Gwynn had to admit it was, but a warning might have been nice before he grabbed hold of her.

The sun slowly sank behind a hill and darkness began to blanket the unpopulated area as they reached the road. "Would you like to stay for dinner at the ranch?" Dave asked. "I can whip us up some steaks."

"No. I don't want to impose."

"The folks went to Albuquerque for the night—a friend's birthday. It'll just be you and me."

She shook her head. "No. I better get home."

He leaned over and touched her arm. "I'll be on my best behavior. I don't want to drive back to the city tonight and I hate eating alone. You'd be doing me a favor." Dave lived in a small house in Bloomfield, but spent weekends and, occasionally, other days at the ranch.

Gwynn thought it might give her an opportunity to find out about the ranch security system. "Okay, but I have to leave right after dinner."

"Understood."

Dave pulled in behind the Mustang. She moved to her car and followed him to the ranch house.

He uncorked a bottle of wine and poured them both a glass. Gwynn was surprised by how polite and charming he seemed. Saturday at the pool, Megan had raved on about Dave. Now, Gwynn was beginning to understand what Megan had seen in the handsome cowboy. It wasn't just his looks.

"I need to look for my make-up bag," Gwynn said, remembering her excuse for being on the road. "Do I need a key?"

"No. Nothings locked."

"Aren't you concerned about theft?"

"I'll let the dogs loose after you leave. They're all the security this place needs."

Gwynn recalled seeing a dog pen between the house and the barn with four dogs inside, but she had never heard them make a sound. "The dogs out there are watch dogs?"

"Oh, yes. Got a poacher bad last month. The guy had to be hospitalized."

"But they don't bark."

"They don't need to. They're trained to get intruders. Sometimes they howl, especially after they've pinned someone down."

"Have they ever bitten a guest?"

"No, but we have had a couple chased."

"How often do you let them out of the pen?"

"They were out when we got here. I stuck them in while you pulled down the driveway." He pointed in the direction of the dogs. "Those are never out when we have company."

"Those. Are there more?"

"Yeah, out by the cattle."

"You must never get drop-in guests at the ranch."

"It's happened sometimes, but most drop-ins know to sit in their car and honk for one of us to come out." Dave flashed a boyish smile. "You plannin' on dropping by when the other employees aren't here?"

"No. Just curious how you handled that."

Mulling over the dogs as a formidable obstacle, Gwynn headed to the dressing room while Dave went to the grill, carrying the meat on a platter. She briefly looked around, and then returned.

"Did you find it?" he asked, adjusting the heat under the steaks.

"No. Maybe it's in the bottom of my duffle bag."

He raised a corner of a steak from the grill. "How do you like yours?"

"Medium. Can I help with anything?"

"No. Got everything under control," he said, filling her wine glass.

"No more. I have to drive home."

"There's plenty of bedrooms here."

"No. I have to go to work in the morning."

"I'll write an excuse for you."

She shook her head. "No."

As the aroma from the cooked meat penetrated the air, Dave dished up grilled potatoes, corn and the steaks.

"Sure smells and looks good!" Gwynn said, gazing at her plate and feeling her mouth water.

After they finished eating, Gwynn helped clear off the table. "Did they ever find anything missing from the metal building?"

"No. Damnedest thing. The cops think something spooked the guy so he took off—probably the alarm."

Gwynn wondered if Dave knew about Turk and another guy

visiting the storage structure earlier that evening. "Could an employee have scared him off?"

"Doubt it. No one goes there at night. Have the cops asked you any questions about the guy that helped you get unstuck?"

"No."

"I mentioned it. They might ask you some questions and they might not since nothing's missing."

Driving away from the ranch, Gwynn pondered about what her bodyguard had been doing while she had enjoyed a steak.

CHAPTER 14

During work the following day, Gwynn couldn't find any time to study her created folders since Hayes kept bringing her new items to work on. With each one, he made it a point to say it was a rush job. None of them struck her as requiring immediate attention. She did note the names of the vendors and purchasers in her notepad, so she could research them when she had a little down time.

From the drawn expression on Hayes' pale face and the intense look in his eyes, Gwynn suspected he was upset about something. Shortly before five, she asked him, "Was anything missing from the workover project folders?"

"No," he said, his chin drooped and shoulders slumped.

Gwynn had expected a reaction like that. Something definitely wasn't right with those projects, but *what?* She wanted to take her folders home, but the stack couldn't fit in her small purse. She removed the contents from project #306, folded the documents and stuck them under her sweater in her second drawer.

As everyone began clearing out of the office, Gwynn turned off her computer, wrapped her sweater around the documents and carried it along with her handbag out to her car.

She dropped off the documents at home, grabbed a quick bite to eat and changed into sweats—clothing easy to remove. She threw her backpack and the duffle bag that held her black outfit into the trunk of her car and drove to Farmington where she had reserved a black, 4-wheel drive vehicle to be picked up around 7 p.m.

When she arrived at the rental agency, all the paperwork was in order. She signed for the car under the name Marsha Wayman that appeared on the driver's license she presented and on the credit card.

By 7:15 p.m., she had transferred her backpack and duffle bag to the black Jeep and was heading to the ranch. Gwynn hadn't seen Dave all day, but did drive by the downtown office and saw his stepless Silverado parked by the building. She had memorized his license plate number the prior evening, while they had strolled around the planned well site.

She turned right at the fork, drove five minutes and pulled over to the side of the road. Stepping out of the vehicle, Gwynn felt a warm windy breeze cross her face as she scanned the area. The moon and stars were hidden behind thick clouds, preventing any ambient light from shining through. Off in the distance behind her, she saw a small incandescent glow and assumed it came from the headlight on her bodyguard's bike. To her right, the direction of the ranch house, she spotted a glimmer of light between a cluster of trees and bushes. In front of her and to her left, everything dissolved into the dark night.

Gwynn moved to the other side of the car—the side away from the road and opened the back door. No light inside the Jeep flicked on because she had already disabled all of them. She changed her clothing, pulled her night goggles out of her backpack, and slipped them on. A few minutes later, she climbed back into the driver's seat, dressed for her planned task.

When she saw the tree branches hanging over the fence, she turned the vehicle around and parked 200 feet ahead of the sagging section of the fence. Gwynn put on a ski mask, tugged on her gloves, clipped a can of mace to her belt and swung the backpack over her shoulder. She switched on her flashlight and moved toward the overhung branches. Next to them, she discovered a loop of wire secured the fence to a pole. With a tug and a yank, she lifted up the curved wire and dropped it to the ground. It gave her ample clearance to enter the Prudell property. She felt her pulse rapidly accelerating as she slipped the wire over the pole, closing the opening behind her.

Gwynn stood motionless, listening for the sound of dogs. She heard an owl hooting, branches swaying from the soft breeze and a slight clanging sound, like the wind hitting a metal object. She inhaled deeply, turned off her flashlight and put her night goggles on again. Gwynn crept toward the shed with leaves crunching under her feet. Every few steps, she stopped and listened —nothing. Reaching the side of the woodshed, she hunkered down, waited a minute for the pounding in her chest to slow and then stealthily eased around the corner. Staying low, she pulled her picks from her pocket and unlocked the padlock. Not wanting to take a chance on getting locked in, she laid the padlock on the ground, three feet from the door and covered it with leaves.

With trembling hands, Gwynn pulled a small container of clear fluid out of her backpack and held it firmly in her hand as she cautiously pushed open the door with squeaking hinges enough for her to slide in.

Inside the ten by twelve foot space, she squirted the door hinges with the clear liquid to prevent them from squeaking and shut the door without making a sound. Gwynn glanced around and saw an old wood stove in the corner, a boarded up window, a dirty, rickety cot and boxes covered with a thick layer of dust. Cobwebs were prominent in every nook and cranny. In the far corner, she spotted it—a two-foot tall cylinder with H2S printed in bold letters on the side along with a warning message. Staring at the label, only one thought ran through her mind: *The proof that Boden's death wasn't an accident.*

Stepping toward it, a surge of adrenalin rushed through her body. Gwynn suspected the cylinder could be covered with fingerprints. She took a kit from her backpack and began dusting it. Numerous fingerprints appeared. She covered ten of them with transparent tape. She spread out several sheets of paper, removed the tape from the canister and stuck each captured print onto the paper. Gwynn froze when she heard a soft humming sound off in the distance. She sat motionless and listened. The sound was gone.

She hurriedly nudged the sheets into a plastic bag, tucked it into a special compartment in her backpack, and brushed the remaining fingerprint powder off of the cylinder. Gwynn noticed three rifles leaning against the wall next to the canister and caught a glimpse of a small white card under a stock. Pulling it out, she assumed it was a business card and stuffed it into her pocket without further examination.

The snap of a branch startled Gwynn, sending an icy chill along the back of her neck. *Could it be the guy sent to keep track of me?* She forced herself to drop that thought because she might not take proper precautions if she believed no danger lurked outside and staring at the canister she knew she wasn't safe. She swiftly secured her backpack, yanked her gun from her holster and inched toward the door. Crouching down, she carefully pushed the door ajar, peeked out and perked up her ears, straining to hear the smallest unnatural sound.

The rustling of leaves, crunching of leather boots and snapping of twigs rumbled through the outside breeze, like it came from a short distance away.

Biting her lower lip, Gwynn opened the door wider and scooted out. She held her breath as she clicked the lock back on and slithered around the edge of the shed. With her back pressed against the building, she rose to her feet and listened. The prior noise had dissipated. She moved to a nearby tree surrounded by bushes and peered around it toward the front of the shed. Gwynn spotted a tall silhouette creeping among the foliage and feared she had tripped a silent alarm.

Hunkering down, she quickly made her way to the fence. She slipped the wire over the pole and heard heavy footsteps pounding the ground behind her. Gwynn sprinted to her car, leaving the fence drooping. Clasping her key, she leaped into the driver's seat, threw her backpack in the back seat and slammed the door shut. Her hands shook as she stuck the key into the ignition, revved the engine and sped away.

Gwynn yanked off the ski mask, took several deep breaths while her heart rapidly pounded. Her breath came in wild gasps as her headlights skimmed over the pavement. The car's dashboard seatbelt light flickered and beeped. Swallowing hard, Gwynn snapped the seatbelt on and glanced at her rearview mirror—only darkness lay behind the taillights.

Near the fork, she managed to get her breathing under control, but that quickly ended when she saw headlights approaching from the other direction. Gwynn executed a sharp left turn, floored the accelerator and heard tires screeching and the roar of a diesel engine less than a mile away. She zoomed along a flat section of highway with only private lanes leading to ranches and farms for the next twenty mile stretch. Gwynn's eyes darted back and forth between the windshield and the rearview mirror.

The truck behind her appeared to be traveling at her same speed—94 miles per hour. The distance between them didn't look like it was closing, nor did her speed leave the truck in her wake. A moment later that changed. The vehicle began gaining on her. Up ahead, she saw another set of headlights and felt her palms getting moist, wondering if the truck driver had enlisted recruits. Looking at her side view mirror, she caught sight of a headlight behind her pursuer. *Is it someone to help me or a buddy of the truck driver?*

Gwynn spotted an intersection ahead as the car approaching from the opposite direction whizzed by her. Her sweaty hands clasped the steering wheel tighter. She swallowed hard and nervously shook her head. *Calm down. This isn't a private road. Other cars travel on it.*

Next to the well-lit, 4-way stop intersection stood a patch of trees, blocking her view from cars entering from the right on the perpendicular road. Glancing up that road beyond the obstacle, she saw a sedan coming from that direction and estimated it would reach the intersection before her.

Gwynn had no intention of obeying the stop sign and kept glimpsing at the approaching car until it disappeared behind the trees. Without slowing down, she barreled into the intersection and swerved to avoid colliding into the sedan.

Behind her, brakes squealed and tires skidded. Checking her mirrors, Gwynn saw the sedan sliding through the intersection and the truck skidding off the asphalt behind it, sending dust swirling and rocks flying. The truck plunged down into the gulley that ran near the edge of the highway. The sedan came to a stop on the shoulder of the road. A single headlight still moved in her direction. She assumed it belonged to her friendly tracker. Hoping to get a better look at his motorcycle, Gwynn eased up on the gas pedal and waited for it to get closer. Instead, the light became smaller and the distance between them grew.

After making a right turn onto another road, she adjusted her speed to the legal limit and cruised toward Bloomfield. The traffic became heavier when she reached the outskirts of the town. She found a quiet street, parked a block from a light pole and changed her clothes without stepping out of the car.

Gwynn held up the business card that she had snatched from the woodshed floor and examined it. The card stock was crisp, not damaged from being there for years. Flipping it over, she discovered it wasn't a business card, but a dentist appointment reminder. The doctor's name appeared in bold print along the top. The date and time lines had been filled in with blue pen. There wasn't a place on it for the name of the patient. Gwynn opened her purse and slipped it in.

She continued to Farmington, dropped off the rental, left the keys in the night slot and climbed into her Mustang.

CHAPTER 15

Wednesday morning, Dave walked through the office building entrance door at 11:10 a.m. and strolled over to Gwynn's desk. "Ready for a rematch?"

"Sure," Gwynn replied, knowing he'd beat her again at pool, but hoping she might acquire additional information.

"After work?"

Gwynn bobbed her head up and down. "Have you been staying at the ranch?"

"No, just working in town. Planning on making a surprise visit?"

"Not with your dogs."

"Otherwise you would?"

"That's not what I meant and your parents are back from Albuquerque."

He put his elbows on the short wall and leaned closer. "You'll only come when we can be alone?"

Gwynn shook her head. "No."

"The folks decided to stay in Albuquerque for a few days in case you change your mind. I'll lock up the dogs."

"If you're not staying there, who's taking care of the animals?"

"A couple of guys. Not a problem." Dave liked her interest in the ranch. Maybe that would be his ticket to gaining the pretty accountant's affection, but she might be turned off if she knew there had been a problem at the ranch last night. Looking into her glowing hazel eyes, he became convinced she'd never go to any dangerous places.

"Employees."

"Of the folks, not the energy company."

Gwynn wanted to know who stayed at the ranch last night and briefly pondered how to ask without raising suspicion. "Do company employees sometimes help out?"

"Yeah. Do you want to help move cattle in a couple of weeks?"

"I don't ride that well."

"I'll work with you when you come on Saturday."

"Okay," Gwynn said, thinking someday she might need that skill.

"See you after work," Dave said and went to his office. Ten minutes later, he left the building.

On the way to get lunch out of the fridge, Gwynn paused at the counter. "Marilyn, last night I chipped a tooth chewing on popcorn, can you recommend a dentist?"

"Our insurance only covers three. I go to Richard Morris, the Prudells go to Jack Omer and I can't remember the name of the third. It should be in your health care pamphlet."

"Would you recommend your dentist?"

"I like him, but he's planning on retiring soon so maybe you should start out with Dr. Omer or the third one."

"What do you know about Dr. Omer?"

"Not much. His office always calls to remind Mr. Prudell or Dave about their appointments. Got a call this morning for Mr. Prudell. He forgot. Now, I have to reschedule a meeting he planned with one of the field guys. It sure would be nice if that man kept track of medical appointments on his calendar."

"Maybe I should ask him about Dr. Omer. Is he leaving soon for his appointment?"

"It's tomorrow. But he's working behind a closed door, so I wouldn't bother him. Wait until he has it opened or ask Dave about the dentist."

"That's what I'll do," Gwynn said and strolled to the break room.

Sitting at her desk, she took a bite of her sandwich and pulled the appointment card out of her purse. The night before, when she tucked it in there she had read the name Dr. Jack Omer along the top. The card stated the scheduled appointment was for Thursday at 2 p.m. She assumed that was Ashton's appointment. Still, Gwynn wanted verification since Prudell employees could only chose between three dentists, it might be another employee's appointment.

She went over to Marilyn and asked, "If I don't get a chance to ask Dave about it later, will Mr. Prudell be in tomorrow morning?"

"Yes. His appointment isn't until 2."

"Good."

Gwynn eased down on her chair, continued eating her sandwich and mulled over everything she had learned so far about Boden's murder. At least three guys were involved, maybe four. Finding Ashton Prudell's appointment card in the woodshed probably meant that he was 'the man' mentioned by the guy with Turk. The guy had a whiny, gravelly quality to his voice as did Brad Williams, but his didn't seem as dominant. She planned to pay more attention to his voice at Marty's. The other voice she heard the night Drumlin died didn't sound remotely like Brad Williams, or Ashton Prudell. She recalled her nerves were playing havoc on her that night and doubted she could've accurately picked out those sound qualities.

She pulled out the top workover project folder from her drawer and began looking at the production for the well before and after the work had been completed. The oil produced stayed almost flat between the two periods, yet the casinghead gas production spiked after the workover. Maybe that was the reason for the handwritten 'GOR', the gas-oil ratio, on a page in Project #312 folder. Gwynn started a spreadsheet to determine if all those wells had increased gas volumes, but not oil.

At 4:05 p.m., Gwynn's cell phone rang. She plucked it from her purse and looked at the number. It belonged to Ruben.

"Hi," she answered.

"Hello, Gwynn," he said in a formal tone. "I'm calling to let you know that I won't be able to talk to you this evening."

Gwynn hadn't expected Ruben would be the one calling to deliver that message and besides his rigid tone, she sensed an edge in his voice.

"Do you know when you can?"

"I need to get back to a meeting. Talk to you later," he said and disconnected.

Staring at the phone, she figured he wanted to talk to her about last night. Gritting her teeth, *the bodyguard has snitched.*

After Gwynn and Dave finished their beers, they headed to the single unused pool table. Dave racked the balls.

"Aren't Turk and Brad showing up tonight?" Gwynn asked.

"Brad's over there," Dave said, gesturing toward the bar. "Turk's next door at the garage, talking to his buddy about his truck."

Gwynn broke. A striped ball landed in a corner pocket. "See? I'm going to beat you tonight."

"Don't count on it," Dave said, smiling smugly.

She made an unsuccessful attempt to get another ball in and then stepped back from the table. "Is something wrong with Turk's truck?" she asked, suspecting it was his truck that landed in the gully the night before.

"Tried to straddle over too big a rock. It did some damage."

After Gwynn lost two games, she picked up her beer on the counter, turned around and saw Brad standing by their table. "Want to play?" she asked him.

"You giving up?"

"One more game and then I'm through."

"You a bad loser?" Dave asked, racking the balls.

"No, a realistic player. I know when I don't stand a chance."

"You just need more practice."

"What do you think, Brad?" she asked.

His eyes roamed down her body. "You've got some great moves. Practice will help."

Gwynn wanted to concentrate on Brad's voice, but, fearing what Ruben might say to her on the phone later, it became an impossible task.

"One more game and I'm through practicing for today," she said, stressing the word practicing.

The game lasted longer than the other two combined. Gwynn thought it was because Dave didn't want her to feel discouraged. Still, she knew he could have cleaned the table whenever he wanted to.

CHAPTER 16

Driving home, Gwynn dreaded the call she needed to make to Ruben. It had consumed all of her thoughts and haunted her for the past four hours—ever since he clicked off the phone. She knew Ruben fired employees who didn't follow his orders. Sometimes he forgave a valuable employee after he harshly threatened them and they pleaded for their job and promised it would never happen again. Gwynn was a relatively new employee and lacked that type of clout, but she was his girlfriend. *Would that count?*

She changed into her sweats and retrieved the N-phone from behind the kitchen drawer. After laying it on the table, she made a cup of tea, trying to stall as long as possible. She sat the steaming cup down in front of her, took a sip, turned on the phone and reluctantly punched in the number.

"What was last night's stunt all about?" Ruben snapped.

Gwynn swallowed. "I found the H2S canister," she said, tapping her fingertips on the edge of the table.

"Gwynn, what does low profile mean?"

"Not to draw attention to yourself," she said, her voice quavering.

"I had planned on overlooking the metal storage unit incident, but I can't overlook two infractions."

"Please, Ruben, I won't do it again. Please," she pleaded in an uneven tone.

"Do you have any concept of the danger you put yourself in? When you crept into that shed, the guy keeping track of you couldn't have helped if a problem arose. He was close by, but not close enough. The car chase! You were just lucky that another car approached that intersection. On a long, two-way, almost deserted highway like that, it doesn't matter how good a driver you are. You can't weave in and out of traffic, make fast turns, meandering through side streets. Nothing! The vehicle you rented didn't have a powerful enough engine to leave them in the dust. They could have shot out a tire! Then all they'd need to do would be to slip on a safety mask and give you a strong whiff of H2S. My guy couldn't have prevented that. He'd be lucky to escape himself. That's why when we go in search for that type of evidence, we go prepared—armed with safety equipment!"

"I'm sorry, Ruben," Gwynn stuttered. "It won't happen again. I promise."

"I know it won't," he said, harshly. "Tomorrow, you'll quit your job at Prudell. Give them a week's notice. After that, you'll go home."

"But … but." Water welled in her eyes. "Please, please, give me another chance," she sniffled, her voice trembling. "I've found some stuff. Please." Gwynn wiped her face while she anxiously waited for Ruben to say something.

After a long pause, he spoke, "What have you found?"

"I…I lifted some fingerprints from the canister. The guy who shot Drumlin is Turk Carlsen."

"How do you know that?"

"I recognized…his voice and asked…who he was," she stammered. "Also, his truck has a… badly dented tailgate."

"Tailgate?"

"Yeah. I know it's strange. He drove the first car. And I think it was Turk's truck that followed me last night. It plunged off the road into a gully. His truck is at a garage being fixed. I haven't had a chance to spend very much time checking the workovers."

"That's because you went scouting out the shed on Monday night so you could break into it on Tuesday. Right? Instead of working on the workover assignment. Have you found out anything about them?"

"There seems to be something wacky about their production. The oil didn't increase after some workovers, but the gas did. Strange."

"Thank you for gathering that information," Ruben said, solemnly. "I'll pass it on to your replacement."

Gwynn flinched. "Please, Ruben, don't do this," she sighed, helplessly, through quivering lips. "Remember, I'm your inside person. I know how their computer system works, files and most of the employees. Please, let me stay. I promise I won't do anything without your approval. Promise." She brushed away tears.

Another long pause. "Since you are well rooted in Prudell, we'll take this a week at a time, but one more problem and you are through. Do you understand?"

Gwynn briefly closed her eyes. "Thank you, boss. I won't disappoint you. What should I do with the fingerprints?"

"Send them to us," Ruben said and proceeded to give her the address. "You had asked about Prudell's employees' criminal records. The only employee that has one is Turk Carlsen. He never spent any time in prison. He was involved with helping and harboring an illegal alien on the run. Nothing violent."

"Besides checking on the workovers, is there anything else you want me to work on?"

"No. Just that. Remember, low profile."

"I thought about going to Prudells' ranch on Saturday. Will that be okay?"

"Yes, but unless you're in the dressing room, stay out in the open—where you can be easily spotted through binoculars. Tomorrow morning there will be a bug in your top desk drawer. It will be disguised as a brooch. Wear it all the time even on your swimsuit."

"It can get wet?"

"Water won't hurt it."

"Ruben, can I call my boyfriend?" she asked in jerky breaths.

"Tomorrow night. On your regular cell phone. Goodnight, Gwynn," he said and disconnected.

With trembling hands, she lifted her cold tea and sipped.

CHAPTER 17

Gwynn stared at the red, rosebud brooch, lying in her desk drawer, admiring its beauty. Picking it up, a gold chain trailed behind. Turning it over, she discovered the brooch could be worn as a pin or on a necklace. She clasped the chain around her neck, wondering if Ruben had really intended on firing her or if the awful phone call the night before was to force her into compliance. Whatever it was, it worked. Gwynn wouldn't do anything again without Ruben's approval. She had worked too hard to become one of his employees and, with two strikes already against her, didn't want to take a chance on being thrown out of his organization.

Carrying a cup of coffee, Gwynn returned from the break room. On the way to her desk, Marilyn stopped her and stared at the brooch. "What a beautiful necklace."

She raised it off her neck to give Marilyn a better look. "Ross sent it to me."

Marilyn ran her fingers over the rosebud. "It's just too bad he didn't deliver it in person," she said, sounding annoyed.

"He can't get away from work, but he wanted to let me know he was always thinking about me," Gwynn said with a big smile.

"Sure," Marilyn said in a tone of disbelief.

Gwynn sank down in her chair and worked swiftly all morning to get through her Prudell job assignments. At noon she went to the post office and mailed the fingerprints. When she got back to the office she dug into the workovers—setting up spreadsheets and downloading the information from the computer system.

Shortly before 2 p.m., Ashton stepped into the lobby and told Marilyn he'd be back in an hour. Then, he left the building for his dentist appointment. Gwynn lightly smacked the side of her head. *I forgot to tell Ruben about the appointment card.*

Gwynn copied all the documents onto a memory stick and stuffed the folders into her oversized purse so she could work on her assignment later.

Driving home, Gwynn felt tense, knowing she was under twenty-four-hour surveillance, even splashing in the shower would be overheard. She had worn a bug before, though she had never been required to have it on around the clock. Stepping out of the car, she decided to go for a run to clear her mind. She jogged a couple of miles every morning to stay fit as an investigator. After work and on weekends, Gwynn preferred to hike, but some of those places were secluded—not easy to be spotted by binoculars.

She changed into a short-sleeve, cool-mesh, gray top and a pair of slim fitting running tights and her running shoes. Gwynn stuck her pistol in a fanny back and strapped it around her waist with the pouch hanging in front and headed out the door.

With gravel crunching under her feet, she jogged down the driveway at a slow pace. Gwynn inhaled the fresh air and smelled evergreens as she took off up the road, a rhythmic pounding of her shoes on the asphalt. The cool breeze brushed against her face. She enjoyed the freedom of sprinting. The sound of a vehicle approaching from behind, forced her to leave the smooth paved surface and retreat into the rough graveled shoulder of the road. Returning to the asphalt, Gwynn stared at the tailgate of a grey Silverado in front of her. She touched her brooch and decided to keep going.

An hour and a half later, she walked up her driveway, sweating profusely and wondered if the driver of the grey Silverado was keeping track of her, since it had driven by three times. The license plate was smeared with mud. The driver wore sunglasses and a blue and yellow cap. Each time the truck got close to her, he managed to be looking the opposite direction. Gwynn thought she could spot the cap if she saw it again.

After she showered and ate, Gwynn set up her laptop on the kitchen table and inserted the memory stick. As she worked on the spreadsheets, her eyes occasionally glanced to the bottom right-hand corner of her monitor to check the time, thinking about calling Ruben and wondering if he was waiting to hear from his girlfriend. As the evening passed, she never picked up her cell phone.

The next day, while Gwynn worked on entering invoices into the computer system, she received an internal phone call from Hayes requesting her to come to his office. She sensed something was wrong. He had never before called her on the phone.

Walking into his office, she saw Hayes slumped in his chair. Strands of his hair stuck up around his ears and dark circles under his eyes stood out on his pale face. His wrinkled shirt clung to his chest, as if he had slept in it. Normally, Hayes always looked well groomed. His appearance told Gwynn something was seriously wrong.

"Are you feeling okay?" she asked.

"Yes," he said in a strained voice. "Can you shut the door?" He nodded toward it.

Gwynn closed it and sat in the chair facing his desk.

"I have to leave in a couple of hours for Michigan. My wife's father passed away yesterday."

"Oh, I'm sorry. Please give your wife my condolences."

"Thank you. He's been sick for a while, so his death wasn't unexpected."

"Is there something special you want me to do while you're gone?"

Hayes leaned forward, adjusted his elbows on his desk and linked his fingers together. "I don't know where to begin."

"Let me get a notepad," Gwynn said, rising.

"No. No. That won't be necessary. You'll remember." He paused. "I spent the night here going over all the details of the workovers again—who performed them, funds spent, production reports, looking for some logical explanation why the oil production didn't increase on any of the wells in the Cisco unit. It makes no sense to me. How can the casinghead gas volume go up and the oil production remain stagnant?"

Gwynn shifted in her chair and cocked her head. "Did the GOR change?"

"No. I had it tested last week by an outside group." He held up a document. "Here are the results."

"Outside? Why didn't you have a Prudell employee handle that?"

"I hate burdening you with this, but I'm at a loss," Hayes said, without answering her question.

"Have you mentioned your concerns to Ashton Prudell?" she asked, leaning on an armrest and clasping her hands together.

"I wanted to talk to Lewis, Ashton's father, but I just don't know," he said, his mouth quivering.

Gwynn slid her chair closer to the desk, reached over and touched his arm. "Go on. I'm listening."

"We had an employee die a few months ago, Arne Boden. He was the pumper that handled those wells. He started telling me about a problem. I didn't have the time to listen. I had to catch a plane. My wife and I were often called to Michigan when her mother thought her dad only had a few days left. I could have let Helen, my wife, go alone, but she doesn't do well traveling by herself. We were there for almost two weeks. Arne died the day we returned." His eyes dropped to the desk. "I never got a chance to talk to him again."

"Do you think the pumper reports for those wells are wrong?"

He nodded. "Yes. If not, the workovers never happened or they weren't successful, but then how could the gas production increase?"

"Which of the pumpers is currently handling those wells?"

"Brad Williams. The volumes on his reports are consistent with Arne's. I've checked all the oil transportation run tickets. They match the reports. Some interest owners have been calling wanting answers since they helped pay for the workovers and they're not seeing the fruits of their investment."

"What have you been telling them?"

"I'm checking into it. Now I've been saying that for over two months and working on it longer. In the middle, all the files disappeared."

"Who do you think took them?"

"I don't know. I suspect when they showed up some documents were missing or adjusted. I just can't pin-point the problem."

"But the documents were scanned into the system."

"Not all of them."

"How can I help?" Gwynn asked, bending forward with her palms braced on the edge of the desk. She studied his face and sensed he feared something to do with the problem. *What could it be?*

"If... if you could go over these files, search for something I might have overlooked."

"Production? Shouldn't you be talking to an engineer about that?"

"Before I do, I want to narrow in on the problem and exhaust any other potential justifications."

Gwynn wondered why it seemed he didn't trust the Prudell

engineers. *Does he know something about Turk or for that matter Dave?*

"I'll email you the schedules I've prepared."

"Should I contact any of the workover vendors?" she asked.

"Not yet. The invoices were all approved by Ashton or Dave. Only call them if an item doesn't make sense—like you're calling for clarification, not questioning the charge. Also, they were all paid before Arne had his accident."

"Besides the workovers, is there anything else you'd like me to work on while you're gone?"

"Pay the bills that can't wait. I should be back in a week." He glanced around his office. "I'll leave you my keys should you need anything in here."

"I'll get right on this," she said, standing up. Hayes handed her a stack of folders.

Gwynn sat them on a cabinet next to her desk and noticed Project #306 wasn't the top one. She skimmed through them to make sure they weren't out of order.

On her way back to Hayes' office, Gwynn heard him say, "Janice, I can't deal with that until I get back." He noticed Gwynn standing in the doorway. "Hold on," he said into the phone and covered the mouth piece.

"I don't have Project number 306," she said.

Hayes nodded toward his credenza. "It's over there."

She grabbed it and scurried out of his office, but lingered a minute in the hallway.

"I've sent it…no … I can't do that!" Hayes hissed into the phone. A second later, Gwynn heard the receiver slamming into its cradle and hurried to her desk.

Sitting in her chair, Gwynn felt relieved she no longer needed to pretend she was working on something else when she worked on Ruben's assignment. Before she dug in, she wanted to determine why Alex Hayes was so concerned—a production problem wasn't something a chief financial officer normally had to resolve.

Hayes stopped at Marilyn's desk and said a few words. Then he went over to Gwynn and dropped off his keys. "If something comes up that you don't think can wait until I get back, call my cell phone," he said, scribbling it down on a sticky note. He stuck it on the side of her desk and left the building.

Gwynn went over to the receptionist's counter, rested her

forearms on it and asked, "Marilyn, I don't know very much about Alex's family. I'd like to send a sympathy card and make it sound personal. How many children does he have? Do any of them live at home or work for Prudell?"

"He only has one daughter, Courtney. She's in her mid-twenties and married to Ralph Hunter."

"I saw her at the ranch. Courtney and Ralph were on the same wagon ride I took. Cute couple."

"Yes. It was fun around here when they were dating. She used to pop in and ask where Ralph was working that day so she could surprise him with a picnic lunch." Marilyn smiled. "Ralph worked in the field before he got his degree and moved into marketing. If Courtney got a whiff that Ralph was coming into the office, she'd find some excuse to visit her father at the same time. Oh and the crazy fingernails! She'd dress them up for every holiday—hearts, Easter bunnies, flags, witches. Courtney always asked if I thought Ralph would like them. What a sweetheart. They have two of the cutest little boys. The oldest one has bright red hair. It will probably turn into auburn, like Alex's used to be before the grey streaks appeared. Alex said when he was a youngster he had flaming red hair. Such a cute little family. There's a picture of them on Alex's credenza. You'll have to take a peek next time you're in there."

"I will. Thanks."

Gwynn recalled seeing Ralph huddled in a conversation with Ashton, Turk and Brad. She wondered if Hayes' concern had anything to do with his daughter. Keeping that thought in the back of her mind, she decided to look over the interest owners again.

Prudell maintained at least fifty-one percent ownership of their wells. A lot of their employees also had some interest ownership in various wells. She opened her ownership spreadsheet and saw Hayes' name on five of the Cisco wells. His working interest ranged between fifteen and twenty percent. Then Gwynn noticed Hayes' middle initial was a P and wondered what it stood for. Marilyn also had a small interest in some of the wells—a half percent. Gwynn wanted to know more about Hayes' holdings and raised her finger to tap on the curser to close down that spreadsheet when the name of another interest owner caught her eye—Patrick Robinson. *Is that Janice's son?* His interest was 3% on the same wells.

As Gwynn continued researching Hayes' interest, she discovered almost half of his interest came from bonuses given to him by Ashton's father. The rest he had purchased from other employees in small increments. His total revenue distribution, for those wells, had been significant. His share of the workover cost was being deducted from distributions so he hadn't received a payment since that project started and he still owed more. Based on the current net revenue from those wells, he probably wouldn't receive another distribution from those wells for at least a year.

Gwynn plowed through other screens, trying to determine if Hayes had interest in any other wells and found he did in the Lander unit. Her eyes popped wide open when she saw his share of revenue. He could have easily paid off his portion of the workover costs for the Cisco wells from the Lander distribution.

She clicked to see if other Prudell employees had interest in the Lander unit wells and found Turk Carlsen, Brad Williams and Ralph Hunter on the list. The estates of Mike Drumlin and Arne Boden were also included. Gwynn assumed that meant their estates hadn't been settled yet. Staring at the screen, she noted that Ashton Prudell held an interest share in his name. Besides the company's 51% interest, two other people were listed: Kevin Whitehead and Janice Robinson.

Boden's interest was greater than Hayes'. Gwynn speculated whether the revenue from that unit could have been what Boden referred to when he told Janice he was going to become a rich man. Still, that didn't explain why he was killed unless someone who would benefit from his death knew about it. *Inheritance?*

Janice had a quarter of a percent interest. Gwynn wondered if Janice had mentioned it to Kevin Whitehead, her current boyfriend. *Maybe that somehow enticed him to buy a piece of the action.* She printed the screen, stuffed the page in her purse and planned on asking Ruben to have someone check on Boden's will. Next, she searched for the date Boden had acquired the interest. It happened three months before his demise.

Gwynn's office phone rang, startling her. "Hello," she answered, forgetting to say Prudell Energy Company.

"Hi, Gwynn," Linda said. "I have the night off at Marty's. How about a movie?"

Gwynn gazed at Janice's name on the list of interest owners. "Sounds good," she said, thinking it might give her an opportunity to question her about Janice.

They agreed to meet at the Town Café after work, have dinner and then hit the theater.

At 9:10 p.m. Gwynn and Linda strolled out of the theater and ran into Janice's son, a 5-foot-11, thin, 16-year-old with auburn hair that hung below his ears.

"Have you ever met Patrick?" Linda asked.

"No," Gwynn replied, smiling at him.

After the introductions, Gwynn asked him, "How's school?"

"Some classes are great and others suck."

"Hey, Pat!" a heavy set teenager said, holding the theater door open.

Patrick nodded toward the guy. "Gotta go," he said to Linda and Gwynn.

"See you tomorrow," Linda said and watched him disappear through the doors. "I'm glad to see him going out. He spends almost all of his time in front of his computer screen. You should see his bedroom. Looks like a computer lab. But he keeps up on his homework. Gets almost straight A's."

"That's great. He seems like a nice kid."

"He's a real sweetheart. It's still early. Do you want to go to Marty's? They have a good group playing tonight."

"Okay, but I don't want to stay longer than an hour or so."

"Not a problem."

When they walked into Marty's, Gwynn was surprised to see such a huge crowd. The dance floor was packed. "I don't see any empty tables. Maybe I'll just head home."

"Patience," Linda said, holding up her hand with her palm facing Gwynn in a stop gesture. She made her way through the horde of people with Gwynn close behind. "We'll sit at the bar until someone invites us to their table."

"You sure that's going to happen?"

"Positive," Linda said and ordered two beers.

Gwynn and Linda were sitting on bar stools sipping their beverages when a rugged-looking, forty-year-old guy wearing a cowboy hat approached.

"Didn't see you come in," he said to Linda.

"Hi, Walt. Do you know Gwynn?"

"Seen her in here a few times. Never been properly introduced."

"Walt, this is Gwynn. She works for Prudell. Gwynn, meet Walt. He's a mechanic and works next door."

"Always glad to meet Linda's friends," Walt said. "Do you ladies want to join me and a few buddies at our table? It's right by the dance floor."

"Sure," Linda said.

"Have you got enough room?" Gwynn asked.

"Always got room for a couple of pretty gals," Walt said. Gwynn and Linda picked up their glasses and he led them through the crowd.

Turk was sitting at Walt's table, along with another man and a woman. Walt introduced the couple as Sam and his wife, Candice. Four empty chairs stood at the table. Gwynn guessed they were taken by people dancing.

Without hesitation, Linda settled in one of them. "Gwynn," she said, tilting her head toward an empty chair.

Gwynn reluctantly sat down and took a sip of beer. As she placed the glass on the table, her eyes met Turk's. He gave her a smile and kept looking at her. She felt a strange vibe coming from him and pondered if he was the guy who had driven up and down her street the prior night while she jogged.

The music ended and the dance floor crowd headed to their tables as another tune began.

"Wanna dance?" Turk asked.

"Yeah," Gwynn said, thinking she might find out something.

Turk took her hand and they stepped out onto the hardwood floor. A hand from behind her gripped her forearm.

"When did you get here?" Dave asked.

"Ten minutes ago. I came with Linda."

Dave's eyes moved to Turk. "This is my dance."

"Thought I could squeeze one in before you noticed she was here," Turk said.

Dave smiled. "Sorry, buddy."

Turk sat back down at the table.

Dave slipped his arm around Gwynn's waist and held her hand in dance position. The music was slow and the song romantic. He pulled her closer, so close she could hear his heart beating and felt his pecs through his shirt. Gwynn enjoyed dancing with Dave, but not this close, not this intimate. After all, she supposedly had a fiancé.

Dave released her hand, moved his hand to the back of her head and stroked her hair. She felt his warm breath on her cheek, but did nothing to escape his hold.

"Hey, you two," Linda said, leaving the dance floor with Walt. "The band is taking a short break."

Dave's arm dropped from her waist. Gwynn walked to the table without looking at him. She eased into a chair, grabbed her beer and took a swig.

Dave stood and chatted with Linda and Walt. Then he pulled up a chair and sat next Gwynn. He rubbed her hand. "You okay?"

"Just thinking about Ross," Gwynn said and noticed Dave rolling his eyes.

"When do you think he'll get around to visiting?" Dave asked.

"Soon." Gwynn glanced at Linda and saw a sympathetic smile on her face. She picked up her glass again and slowly sipped the beverage, thinking I wouldn't believe it either. A fiancé who doesn't visit for two and a half months, can't be too interested in his girl or about getting married. She wished she didn't have to keep his only visit a secret so she wouldn't look like such a gullible idiot, but she had a role to play. It was part of the job.

Dave touched her necklace. "Did he send you this?"

"Yes."

"Does that make-up for being an absentee boyfriend?" Dave asked, mockingly.

"He's been busy. He hasn't had a chance to come see me," Gwynn justified.

Dave cocked his brow then turned toward the other people sitting at the table. "Does everyone want another round? I'm buying."

Heads bobbed up and down and Turk said, "Yep."

Dave raised his arm and motioned to the barmaid. She scooted through the horde, carrying a tray full of empty glasses. "Another round," he said, swinging his arm over the table, gesturing toward everyone seated there.

The barmaid added the drained glasses and bottles to her tray, verified what each person's drink order was and headed to the bar.

Gwynn felt a little disappointed that she hadn't had an

opportunity to pry any information about Janice out of Linda and wanted to leave, but she had told Linda she'd stay for an hour. With twenty minutes to go, she asked Linda, "Are you working tomorrow?"

"Only in the morning. After that, I'm going to help Janice paint a bedroom."

"Is she here?" Gwynn asked, looking around.

"I haven't seen her," Linda said.

"She's here," Dave said, glaring at his bottle. "Saw her on the dance floor."

Clanging of the musical instruments and a high pitched squeal from the mike brought everyone's attention to the small stage as the band prepared to start another set. They began with a fast number.

"Ready for another dance?" Dave asked Gwynn.

She nodded and Dave led her out to the dance floor. She danced with him until they played another slow tune. "It's getting late and I'm getting tired," she said, picking up her purse.

"How about one more dance?" Dave asked.

"Not tonight. I really need to get going. See you tomorrow at the ranch."

"Wear or bring jeans for your horseback riding lessons."

"Will do."

CHAPTER 18

Under an overcast sky, Gwynn arrived at the ranch, wearing jeans and a t-shirt. She strolled around looking for familiar faces and saw several Prudell employees along with their families, including Ralph and Courtney at the pool, but didn't see Ashton, Turk, Brad or Dave. Gwynn watched a three or four-year-old boy with red hair splashing around in the kiddy pool and assumed he must be one of Hayes' grandsons.

She wandered toward the barn and heard Dave's voice when she got close to it. Stepping through the double doors, she saw Dave saddling up a black horse. "Hi!"

"I planned to look for you after I got Marco and Sweetpea saddled."

"Let me guess," Gwynn said with a smile. "I'll be riding Sweetpea?"

"You got it." He stroked the side of the black horse. "Marco would be too hard for you to handle."

"Where's Sweetpea?"

Dave pointed to a light brown horse with white patches in the next stall. "Right there."

Gwynn noticed the horse was a foot shorter, if not more, than Marco. Gwynn walked over and gingerly touched the horse's nose.

"You don't need to be afraid of her," Dave said. "She doesn't bite."

Gwynn stroked Sweetpea's nose until Dave threw a blanket and saddle over the horse's back. She backed up so he could get the job done.

"I want you to wear this," Dave said, lifting a helmet down from a shelf. "Inexperienced riders sometimes fall off or bump their head on a low branch."

"No problem," Gwynn said, securing the helmet strap under her chin.

Dave held onto the reins and led the horses out of the barn. "Have you ever ridden a horse?"

"Once. When I was twelve. Does that count?"

He smiled and helped her get seated into the saddle. "Hold onto the horn," he said, pointing to the front of the saddle. "I'll hang onto the reins for awhile."

Dave climbed into his saddle and the horses slowly trotted away from the barn. "Let me know if you feel like you're going to fall?"

"Okay," Gwynn said, firmly gripping the horn with her hands.

Dave took them to a fenced in area, handed Gwynn the reins and proceeded to give her instructions. She followed them and moved the horse around in the area with Dave riding next to her.

An hour later, the sky grew darker as a thick layer of grey clouds covered the sun. Lightning flashed and the sound of thunder spooked Sweetpea and she leapt. "Aaaah!" Gwynn yelled.

Dave galloped toward her. "Whoa. Whoa," he said, leaning over and taking the reins from Gwynn's hands.

The clouds opened and it began to rain. Thunder echoed through the valley and lightning lit the sky. "We better get back," Gwynn said, urgently.

"I don't think it will last long. There's an old chicken coop not far from here. We'll wait out the storm there. Hang onto the horn," he said, walking the horses toward the opening in the fence.

Gwynn's palms were moist. She wiped them on her jeans and hung on for dear life, as Dave galloped down the lane, going at a much faster pace than she thought necessary. He stopped under a metal awning near an old shed, badly in need of repair and dismounted. He tied the reins to a pole and held onto Gwynn as she climbed down from Sweetpea. Inside the structure, Dave went to close the door.

Gwynn touched his arm. "No, leave it open. I like seeing the rain hitting the ground and the small streams of water it makes," she said, remembering she had to be seen through binoculars.

"You did good," Dave said, unhooking her helmet.

"I don't need to wear that anymore?"

"Not in here." He lifted it off her head and took a step closer to her.

She stepped back. "Remember, I'm engaged."

He wrapped his arm around her waist and pulled her body next to his. "How can I forget? You keep reminding me." Dave kissed her forehead. "How much longer are you going to keep that ring on?"

Gwynn moved her hands between them, trying to put a little distance in the middle of them, especially since a guy with binoculars tracked her every move. "Always. I'm planning on marrying Ross."

Dave slightly released his hold on her. "His plan and your plan might not be the same. You realize that, don't you?"

"What are you saying?"

"He might not see the ring as an always thing."

Gwynn found herself without words. What possible reasonable explanation could she give for Ross' neglect? Also, as hard as it was to admit, she liked Dave's closeness. "I'm sure he does. He wouldn't have given it to me if that wasn't what he meant."

Dave gave her a sly smile. "Whatever." He moved away from her and stood looking at the water running off the edge of the awning that shielded the horses from the rain.

While they waited for the storm to end, neither one of them spoke. They just watched the water pour from the heavens. Fifteen minutes later, the clouds broke up and a sliver of the sun shined through.

Dave and Gwynn rode to the barn with a clear, blue sky above them. This time Gwynn dismounted without Dave's help.

"I'm going to change into my swimsuit," Gwynn said.

"Why don't we eat lunch first?"

Gwynn rubbed her thighs. "I want to get out of these damp jeans. Just give me a minute and I'll slip on my swimsuit." She hurried to her car, grabbed her duffle bag and binoculars and speed walked into the dressing room. After stepping into a stall and closing the door behind her, Gwynn emptied her duffle bag then removed her boots with her pistol and knife concealed inside, stripped out of her clothes and stuffed them into her bag. She put on her black, one-piece swimsuit, sandals, a long blouse and slipped the binocular strap around her neck. She quickly ran a comb through her hair, put on lipstick and flung the duffle bag over her shoulder. Walking out of the dressing room, Gwynn stopped in her tracks when she heard Turk's voice.

"She's trouble," Turk said in an angry tone.

"I can handle her," Dave said.

Some giggling, laughing kids playing ball ran past, interrupting her eavesdropping.

"…help you out," Dave said.

"It'll be gone in the next week," Turk said.

"Hi, Gwynn," Carol said, heading to the dressing room. "You just get here?"

"No. I've been riding with Dave."

Dave stepped around the corner of the building. "You must be starving," he said to Gwynn. "I am."

Three hours later, Gwynn pulled into her driveway. Taking the duffle bag out of the trunk, she noticed a small broken branch on the side of the path leading to the front door. Someone had been there. She wondered if Ruben, or perhaps an intruder, waited for her inside.

Cautiously, she went around the exterior of the house, looking for anything out of place. The back screen door stood ajar. She specifically remembered latching it. Before she left the ranch, she had changed out of her swimsuit and put her damp jeans, t-shirt and boots back on, hiding her weapons inside. Gwynn bent down, pulled out her Berretta and eased up the steps. She listened at the back door, unlocked it and slowly pushed it open. She stealthily moved from room to room in the dim light, without seeing or hearing any unusual sounds.

She flipped the light switch in the bedroom and glanced around. Nothing appeared to be out of place. Gwynn turned on the living room light. Her eyes swept over the space. She returned to the kitchen, lit up the room and a cold chill washed over her—the folders on the table were gone. She knew somehow, somewhere, she had screwed up. *What did I do that drew attention to me?*

A spasm of panic struck. *Is anything else missing?* She rushed to the bedroom to check her other weapons and a few gadgets. Gwynn shimmied under the bed, looked up and opened a concealed compartment in her box springs. A sigh escaped her mouth. Nothing had been taken. Gwynn pulled out her scanning device and scooted out. She went to the kitchen and made sure the intruder hadn't found her N-phone. It was right where it belonged. Gwynn opened the bottom kitchen drawer, removed utensils and the false bottom. Her equipment hadn't been touched. Next, she went to the bathroom to verify her documents and cash hadn't been discovered. She raised a small section of the tile floor—nothing missing.

Gwynn wanted to scan for bugs, but knew it would be a useless task as long as she wore the brooch. Going against Ruben's orders, she took it off and left it in the bathroom while she ran her electronic scanner over the walls, furniture, telephone, picture frames and even the floors. Nothing. She moved her brooch into the living room and scanned the bathroom. Inhaling deeply, she slipped the gold chain around her neck again.

After making a cup of tea, she sat at the table, sipping it and ran over everything in her mind that could've alerted someone to her alternative agenda for becoming a Prudell employee. Her face scrunched and she rubbed her forehead with her fingers when she realized where she might have screwed up. *The woodshed. I didn't check for a silent alarm or a surveillance camera. How could I have been so stupid!*

Given the condition of the shed, Gwynn had just assumed it would be an easy mark. Now it all made sense—the guy checking out the woodshed at the same time she happened to be there; the grey Silverado keeping track of her as she jogged; Turk's strange behavior toward her.

Then Gwynn recalled she wore a ski mask. Even if she had been picked up by a surveillance camera, she couldn't be positively identified. Turk could suspect—nothing more. Hayes wanted her to go through the workover folders. If someone confronted her about them she had a legitimate reason to have them in her possession.

Gwynn knew she should contact Ruben about the break-in at her place. Even if she didn't explain how she screwed up, he'd figure it out. She wasn't equipped to handle another strike against her on this investigation, since it would be her last. Mulling over her mistakes, she made another cup of tea.

CHAPTER 19

It was a dismal morning. The sky was blanketed with dark grey clouds and rain was expected. The day amplified the way Gwynn felt—disappointed that Ruben hadn't contacted her over the weekend to find out why she hadn't called Wednesday night. The guy who did call was Dave to invite her to the ranch for barbeque ribs. The role playing seemed to get harder by the day and she found she wanted to take Dave up on his invitation. Yet, she could only handle so much closeness with another man while her boyfriend ignored her.

Walking into the building, Gwynn greeted Marilyn and waited for her Monday morning question: Did your fiancé visit? To her relief, the question never came.

After getting a cup of coffee in the break room, Gwynn settled in at her desk, clicked on her computer and opened the workover spreadsheets. Within a minute, Ashton entered the building and made his usual detour to her desk to check out her cleavage, and then he proceeded to his office.

During morning break, Gwynn decided she needed a haircut and called Janice's place.

"JR Salon," Janice answered.

"Hi, Janice, this is Gwynn. I haven't had my hair cut since I moved to Bloomfield. I really could use a trim. Do you have any appointments available this week?"

"Let me see." A pause. "I could squeeze you in tomorrow around three. Would that work for you?"

"Yes, that works. See you then." Gwynn clicked off, hoping Janice wouldn't scalp her. Though, her desire to acquire additional information outweighed a possible bad haircut.

At 2:30 p.m., Dave bolted through the door with a hostile, furious expression on his face and strode over to Gwynn's desk. "I want to see you in my office. Now!" he snapped and headed to the hallway.

Gwynn had never seen Dave angry before. Rising to her feet, she speculated about the cause for his rage and followed him into his office.

"Sit," he growled.

He pushed the door shut, moved to the other side of his desk and plopped down in his chair. His eyes bore into hers. "What were you doing with some of the workover files?"

The word 'were' immediately caught Gwynn's attention. With the rosebud brooch attached to her blouse, she knew someone was listening to this conversation and had to find a way to avoid discussing the break-in at her house since Ruben didn't know about it.

"Alex asked me to look at them and seemed anxious about it. He had me make another set of the project files number 306 through 314. I took them home, thinking I might get a chance to work on them over the weekend," she said with her lips quivering and attempting to sound meek. "Is there a company policy that files should never leave the office?"

Dave's expression softened as his eyes roamed over her face. "No. No policy." He leaned forward and rubbed his chin. "What was Alex concerned about with those workovers?"

"He couldn't understand how none of the wells generated an increase in oil production, but the gas production increased and the GOR didn't change."

"That is strange," he said, squinting. "I normally only look at the total production numbers and they're increasing. Are the original files at your desk?"

"Yes."

"Let me see them."

Gwynn went to her desk, feeling relieved that he never mentioned how the workover files were brought to his attention.

As she set them down on his desk, Dave grabbed her hand. "I'm sorry if I came across a little irritated earlier. I didn't mean to upset you. It's just that Turk somehow has it in his noggin that you're spying for our opposition." He shook his head. "As if we have all these trade secrets. Last week, someone broke into a woodshed at the ranch and he thought it was you." He chuckled.

"What about your dogs?"

"They weren't loose yet."

"Woodshed? Do you keep valuable stuff in a woodshed?"

"Not my stuff. Turk's borrowing it. He's storing some guns and few things there while his place is being remodeled."

"Does he think I want his guns?" Gwynn asked, sounding bewildered, leaning her hips against his desk.

"Do you even know how to shoot one?"

"A little."

"Like you knew how to ride a horse?"

Gwynn smiled. "Something like that."

"I'll tell Turk his guns are safe from you. But I must admit he had me going when he mentioned the workovers and…"

"You don't need to say anymore," she said, interrupting him, fearing what he might disclose. "I understand." Gwynn looked down at the folders. "There are production reports in each file. I didn't print the disposition report for the unit. Do you want me to wait in here while you go through them?"

"No. It might take me awhile." He gazed at her face. "Can I make amends by taking you to dinner?"

"That's not necessary." Gwynn patted his hand. "You're forgiven."

"I'd still like to take you. How about it?"

She studied him a few seconds. "Okay."

Gwynn and Dave left shortly after 5 p.m. in his Silverado. He wanted her to try a seafood restaurant in Farmington. As they drove, they talked about the workovers.

"Those numbers don't make sense to me anymore than they did to Alex," Dave said. "Any idea why he didn't discuss them with Ash or me?"

"He planned on doing that when he got back. He just wanted me to check the workover costs and production numbers to make sure there wasn't anything he missed."

"What brought it to his attention?"

"An interest owner called about it."

"Ash normally gets those calls. Brad's the pumper for those wells. Before I talk to him, I'm going to the well sites." He caressed Gwynn's arm. "It's about a forty-five minute drive. Do you want to come?"

"When are you going?"

"Tomorrow afternoon."

"I planned on taking a late lunch to get my hair trimmed. I have an appointment with Janice at three."

"Janice? Are you sure she's the right person for the job?"

"She must be good because Linda says her salon does great business."

"It does?" he said, furrowing his brow.

"Anyway, I'm going to give her a shot."

Dave flipped a few strands of Gwynn's medium-length, brown hair. "Don't let her take it all."

"I won't."

"How long do those appointments last?"

"Less than an hour."

"Then we could be on the road by four if you want to go."

"What about work?"

"I have an in with the boss," he said with a lopsided smile.

"Okay, I'll go."

The restaurant was a rustic looking structure made of rough-cut cedar poles, situated between two hills and surrounded by scrub oak. The interior had exposed, dark, aged timber walls and only four small windows to bring in a little natural light. The white linen table cloths and a single red rose in a vase on each table added to the dimly lit romantic atmosphere. The maitre d' seated them at a cozy table near the far wall.

"Do you come here often?" Gwynn asked.

"No, but the food is great!"

The server came to take drink orders. Dave asked Gwynn, "Did you like the wine you had at the ranch?"

"Yes. It had a nice, bold, robust flavor."

Dave ordered a bottle.

Gwynn began looking at the menu. "Anything you would suggest?"

"The salmon, but everything on the menu is good."

After drinking a bottle of wine, eating great meals and decadent desserts, they left the restaurant. Driving back to Bloomfield, Gwynn wondered what Ruben would think about the evening. *Would he be a little bit jealous?*

Dave pulled into Prudell's parking lot, cut the engine and walked around to give her a hand getting out of his truck. When both her feet landed on the ground, he wrapped her in his arms and smothered her lips with his.

It happened so quickly, Gwynn didn't have a chance to turn her head to avoid the kiss. "I'm engaged," she said, sounding irritated.

"Was it that bad?"

"That's not the point."

"What is?"

"Dave, I like you, but I've already committed myself to someone else. I want to spend the rest of my life with Ross."

Dave gave her a doubtful look and shrugged his shoulders. "It's dark here. I'll wait until you drive off." He tucked her hair behind her ear and gave her a triumphant smile. "Don't want anything to happen to you so you miss your hair appointment."

Gwynn climbed into her car and drove out of the parking lot. She watched Dave through the rearview mirror until he was out of sight.

CHAPTER 20

At 2:55 p.m., Gwynn cut to the curb in front of JR Salon. It was two blocks away from the down town office space leased by Prudell. Earlier in the day, when she told Marilyn she had an appointment with Janice, Marilyn mentioned several of the employees went to her for haircuts, including Mr. Prudell.

No customers were in the salon when Gwynn walked through the doorway.

"Right on time," Janice said.

Gwynn eyed the space. It looked like it had recently been remodeled. Black and white diamond-shaped panels covered the walls. The large picture windows, facing the street, appeared new, along with all the black and chrome fixtures in three workstations.

Janice motioned for her to take the salon chair farthest from the door. "Do you want me to cut it any special way?"

"No. I just want a trim," Gwynn said, holding up a handful of hair. "Maybe a little over an inch off."

Janice washed Gwynn's hair and towel dried it. While she combed and began separating Gwynn's hair with clips, she asked, "When you getting hitched?"

"We haven't set a date." Gwynn noticed a huge diamond on Janice's finger. "What a beautiful ring," she said, pointing to it.

"I was engaged to Arne," Janice said in a sad tone. "Have you heard about him?"

"Yes. I didn't realize you had been engaged to him."

"We were planning a small, intimate wedding," she said as she continued working on Gwynn's hair. Her eyes dropped to the floor and she sighed. "We would have been so happy together. I'll miss him forever."

"Oh, I'm so sorry. Did you get a chance to spend any time with him the day of the accident?"

"All afternoon. It was wonderful! His friends were decorating his apartment for his birthday. He never got to see it."

"Did he die on his birthday?"

"No. A few days before. They wanted to surprise him."

"Was a party planned?"

"Yeah. I was going to go with him to his place after he got back from working on a well. Arne would've been so surprised."

"I can't imagine how hard that must have been for you—losing the man you loved."

"Oh, it was, but Arne's friends helped me out a lot."

"Were his friends Prudell employees?"

She nodded. "Turk was his best pal. They'd known each other since elementary school."

"Did he plan the surprise party?"

"No. Brad planned it all. I'm sure Turk helped with stuff."

"Are you doing okay now?"

"It'll never be the same. Every day is a struggle. Going to Marty's helps."

Gwynn thought *can she spin a yarn* and wondered what Linda would say about Janice's bleeding heart. "It's a fun group that goes there. Have you thought about seeking any grief counseling?"

"Not yet. A few friends have talked to me about it." She flipped on the blow dryer and used a brush to get the ends of Gwynn's hair to turn under. Five minutes later, she turned off the dryer. "How does that look?"

"Great," Gwynn said and meant it. After she paid for the haircut, she gently touched Janice's shoulder. "Try to take good care of yourself."

"I have to stay strong for my son," Janice said, looking like she was on the verge of tears.

"Thanks for the cut," Gwynn said and left.

Gwynn drove two blocks to Prudell's downtown office where Dave was working. They had planned on meeting in the parking lot at 4 p.m. She showed up fifteen minutes early and parked in a stall to wait.

A moment later, Dave walked out the door and went to her Mustang.

"I'm early," she said, climbing out of her car.

"Only a few minutes. I saw you from window. Have you ever

been in this building?"

"No."

"You'll have to come by sometime and take a tour." He took a hold of her shoulder and twirled her around. "Janice did a good job."

"Yeah, she did," Gwynn said, opening the trunk. "I want to bring my binoculars. Never miss an opportunity to do a little bird watching."

Dave went to help her into his Silverado. "No, I can do it by myself," Gwynn said. "I'm starting to get the hang of the giant two foot step." She raised her leg, grabbed a handle on the side of the seat and hoisted herself up.

Gwynn buckled in and said, "Janice told me her heart wrenching story about how much she missed the love of her life."

"And who's that?" Dave asked, pushing on the gas pedal.

"Her fiancé."

"Her what?"

"Arne Boden, the guy she was going to marry."

Dave chuckled. "They were never engaged."

"I saw the ring."

"That's only because Arne left it at her house."

"It was all a lie?"

A muscle tightened in his jaw. "Janice is famous for that."

Gwynn laughed. "Linda had already told me about Arne and Janice. I had a hard time keeping a straight face the way she went on."

Dave looked at her and smiled. "You knew? You really do know how to keep a straight face—had me going."

Forty minutes later, Dave turned onto a gravel road, drove five miles and then veered to the left, onto a dirt lane riddled with potholes. He maneuvered around them as the Silverado jerked back and forth along with the passengers inside.

"Do tankers drive on this?" Gwynn asked.

"No. Flow lines bring the oil to storage tanks in an accessible location," Dave said, stopping fifty feet from a well.

After they climbed out of the truck, Dave paced the area. "This is the separator," he said, gesturing toward a huge cylinder, lying horizontal to the ground. "It separates the oil and the casinghead gas. Over here is the gas pipeline. The wells in the Cisco unit aren't individually metered. The gas volume is measured when it leaves the unit and allocated back to the wells, based on well tests."

"And the oil volume?"

"It's measured at the Bamberg tank battery and allocated back."

"The battery?"

"We have six storage tanks there," he said, checking the separator and connections. "The gas is sold where we meter it. Just past our meter is the purchaser's meter and there hasn't been a discrepancy between those two volumes. Alex is right—there should be more oil volume."

"What do you think happened to it?"

He shrugged. "I'm going to walk the flow line to the top of that hill and see if anything looks unusual. Then we'll go to the next well."

"I'll come with you," Gwynn said, following him away from the well site and into tall wild grasses. She had worn casual slacks and athletic shoes to work, not her usual attire, in anticipation she might be doing some hiking out in the field. Her binoculars bounced against her chest with every step she took. She had also anticipated that and slipped on her bullet-proof vest under a bulky cotton sweater before she left the office to give her the padding she needed.

"So far so good," Dave said, looking into a gulley. "We'll drive along the flow line after we've checked the wells if we still have daylight."

A gunshot rang out.

"What the…," Dave said as another shot hit a pile of rocks within ten feet from where they stood.

Gwynn grabbed Dave's arm and yanked him toward a large boulder not far away. A violent eruption of dust clouds rose near their feet and the sound of gunfire echoed through the air.

"Aaah," Dave moaned as a bullet struck his leg. He buckled over.

Using all her strength, Gwynn pulled him behind the boulder while he grimaced and blood squirted from his wound. She wanted to modify her binoculars into a gun, but she wasn't ready to give up her cover. Also, she knew that gun would be no match to the powerful rifle used by the assailant. He had to be a significant distance away from them since she hadn't been able to pinpoint his location. A minute earlier, she thought she was the shooter's intended victim. Now, she wasn't sure. *Is the gunman trying to silence both of us? Why? The flow lines?*

Dave clamped his teeth and briefly closed his eyes in a determined effort to control the pain rippling through his leg.

"Give me your keys," she ordered, lifting off her binoculars and placing them on the ground.

Without hesitation, he plucked them from his pocket while the pinging of slugs striking the boulder bellowed out.

"I'll be right back," she said, scurrying away, hovering close to the ground. When she reached a cluster of junipers thirty feet from Dave, she leapt to her feet and sprinted erratically toward the Silverado as the gunfire continued. She ducked down next to the Silverado, opened the door and shimmied in, remaining below the windows. She turned the key and stepped on the gas. The engine roared to life. Staring out the very bottom of the front windshield, Gwynn tore through grass and bushes that stood in her path as she plowed toward Dave.

She skidded to a stop next to him. Using the boulder for cover she managed to help him scoot into the passenger seat. After grabbing her binoculars, Gwynn jumped into the driver's seat and slid them behind it. She leaned over, snapped Dave's seatbelt on, buckled herself in and peeled off, whirling dust in her wake. She spun the Silverado around and headed toward the well site as bullets struck the vehicle's metal frame.

The truck swerved when it hit the dirt road. Bouncing up and down, she revved the engine and became airborne over some of the potholes. Reaching the gravel road, Gwynn could only see a cloud of dirt and dust behind the tailgate as she sped through the rocks. "How are you doing?"

"Okay," he said, clenching his teeth.

"Do you know where the closest hospital is?"

"Take me to the one in Bloomfield."

"The bullet struck your calf, right?"

He nodded, reeling in pain.

While she continued moving along, Gwynn reached under the sleeve of her sweater, grabbed her blouse sleeve and, after several attempts, managed to tear it off. "When we get to the paved road, try to tie this right below your knee."

Groaning, he nodded again.

Gwynn would have preferred to stop and help him, but that wasn't an option. She skidded onto the highway, sending rocks flying everywhere and almost clipping a car. Glancing at her side mirror, she saw a grey truck less than a thousand feet away. She slammed on the accelerator and passed three vehicles ahead of her, going over a double-yellow line on the last one, but given her speed she knew she'd be back on her side of the road before hitting the curve.

When she came to a straight stretch of road, she looked out the rearview mirror and saw the other Silverado keeping pace.

"That looks like one of our trucks behind us," Dave said, leaning on the door and staring at the side mirror. "If it is, they'll help." He fished his cell phone out of his pocket. "Slow down a little so I can see the last number of the license plate."

"Dave, I think it is one of your trucks. I also think it's being driven by the person who shot you. I'm not slowing down."

"But who?" he asked, sounding confused.

"You can figure that out after your leg has been taken care of."

"I'm calling 9-1-1."

"No, put away your phone. You can't give them a location and we're not stopping to wait for an emergency vehicle. We'll only pull over if we see blinking red and blue lights right behind us."

They zoomed by a sign that indicated sharp curves ahead. The tires screeched as Gwynn navigated the road, only slightly slowing down so the truck wouldn't plunge into the ravine abutting the pavement. Though, Dave's Silverado didn't escape without the front bumper scrapping the edge of a guard rail around the last bend.

"Sorry about that," she said, flooring the accelerator again.

As they came closer to Bloomfield, the traffic increased. Yet, the assailant did not relent in his pursuit. Gwynn spotted a green light ahead and hoped to make it to the intersection before it changed. No such luck. It flicked to yellow. The Silverado didn't stop when it turned red. She blew through the intersection. Horns erupted around them. Looking out the rearview mirror, she saw their pursuer had stopped at the light and slowed down to 10 miles above the speed limit.

"Where do I turn for the hospital?" she asked her wounded passenger.

"Go right at the second light."

Gwynn hit green lights at both intersections, executed the turn and saw the hospital ahead. She followed the sign directing her to the emergency entrance and stopped by the curb behind an ambulance. "I'll get help." She opened the truck door, jumped out and sprinted into the hospital. "My friend needs help," she shouted after clearing the double doors. "He's been shot."

Her last sentence brought people scurrying around. Within a minute, Gwynn led a gurney, pushed by two men dressed in blue scrubs, out the door.

She gripped the handle of the truck door and swung it open. The two men moved Dave onto the gurney and rolled him through the emergency entrance while Gwynn held his hand. As they wheeled him through another set of doors, a woman approached Gwynn and told her she needed to complete some paper work.

Filling out the forms went smoother and quicker than Gwynn had anticipated. After she gave the female hospital employee Dave's name, the employee pulled up his medical information on her computer. Then the woman asked how Dave's wound occurred and Gwynn filled her in on the details.

"Can I see him?" Gwynn asked.

"He's in room five, through those doors," the woman said, indicating the double doors down the hall.

Walking into room 5, Gwynn saw Dave had been hooked up to a monitor. His jeans were cut off right above the knee. His shoe and sock sat on a table near the bed. A young-looking doctor stood bent over him, checking his leg and a nurse was adjusting his bed. Dave appeared calm and relaxed—the pain gone.

"Did they give you morphine?" Gwynn asked, stroking his arm.

"Something like that," he said with a weak smile.

Gwynn wanted to talk to him about the shooting, but since she had already demonstrated skills that accountants aren't expected to possess, she decided to wait for him to bring it up. "Do you want me to call your family?"

"Call Ash. I don't want to upset the folks."

"Can you give me his number?"

He pulled out his cell phone. "It's in here."

"I'll call him in the hall," Gwynn said, taking the phone.

She turned it on and discovered the battery was almost dead. Gwynn flipped to Dave's contacts, scrolled down to Ashton's name, and entered his number in her phone. She clicked on it and pushed send. Bridget, Ashton's wife, answered. Gwynn had talked to her on the phone a few times at work and recognized her voice, but had never met her. "Is Ashton Prudell at home?"

"Is this a solicitation call," Bridget snapped.

"No. This is Gwynn Wagner. I'm calling about his brother. He's had an accident."

"Ash, Dave's been hurt," Bridget said, loudly.

"Hello," Ashton said, sounding breathless.

"This is Gwynn. I was with Dave checking some wells. When we were there, someone shot at us and a bullet hit him in the leg."

"How bad?" Ashton asked, anxiously.

"It doesn't look that bad, but I don't know. He's at the hospital."

"In Bloomfield?"

"Yes."

"I'll be right there," he said and disconnected.

Gwynn strolled back into Dave's room. "Your brother's on his way. How bad is your wound?" she asked, sliding a chair next to the bed.

"Doc, can you tell her?"

"Do you want to know in technical terms or layman?" the doctor asked, still examining Dave's leg.

"Layman."

"The bullet penetrated the side of his calf, making a deep laceration. Another doctor is on his way to stitch it up."

"Why can't you stitch it up, Doc?" Dave asked.

"That's out of my line of practice."

Gwynn looked at the young doctor and suspected he was an intern.

"Dr. Sands will be with you soon," the doctor said and stepped out the door.

"Are you comfortable?" the nurse asked Dave. He nodded. "Buzz if you need anything." She handed Dave the end of a cord with a button prominently positioned at the tip.

"Did you get the last number of the license plate?" Dave asked.

"No. Sorry."

Dave stared at the wall for a minute. "You might not know much about riding a horse, but you sure know how to handle a car. Were you a race car driver before you became an accountant?"

Gwynn smiled. "No. I was a teenager, needing to get to work on time."

"And you drove like that?"

"It was a necessity."

"Ever get stopped by the cops?"

"Once. Got by with a warning."

"A warning?"

"Didn't want those insurance rates to go up," she said, crossing her legs with a pleased expression on her face.

A lean, short man with gray hair, dressed in a white lab coat entered. "Hello, Mr. Prudell. I'm Dr. Sands. Have you been taken good care of since you arrived?"

"Yes."

Loud footsteps came pounding down the hall and Ashton rushed in. "Dave, who did this?" he asked, his face creased with concern as he hurried to the bed.

"Don't know, Ash."

"How's his leg?" Ashton asked the doctor.

"I was just about to exam it," Dr. Sands said.

"You haven't looked at it yet?" Ashton said in an irate tone.

"His leg has been looked at, but not by me," Dr. Sands clarified.

"Go ahead," Ashton said, pulling up a chair next to Gwynn.

Ashton's eyes remained fixed on Dr. Sands as the doctor checked Dave's leg. "It doesn't appear too serious. I want to have it x-rayed before I stitch it up," Dr. Sands said, putting a bandage over the wound. "You two might be more comfortable in the waiting room while Mr. Prudell is taken to the lab."

"We'll wait here," Ashton answered, without consulting Gwynn.

Five minutes later, a man wearing hospital scrubs wheeled Dave out of Room 5.

"Start at the beginning," Ashton said. "What well site were you and Dave at and why?"

Gwynn briefed him, but gave an ambiguous 'why' answer saying, "Dave just wanted to check it out and asked if I wanted to come along since I hadn't been to a well site before."

"He never mentioned why he wanted to check it out?"

Gwynn shrugged her shoulders.

"I better call the folks," he said and began to rise.

"No," Gwynn said, touching his arm. "Dave didn't want to upset them. Why don't you wait until after the x-ray?"

"I'll wait, but I'm calling Sam." He stepped out into the hall.

Gwynn assumed Sam was Officer Sam Young. The policeman who visited Ashton and one of the two officers that showed up on her front porch the night of Drumlin's fabricated crash.

Shortly after Ashton returned to the room, Dave was pushed in. "How did it go?" Gwynn asked.

"Smooth. Didn't have to wait."

Dr. Sands entered again followed by a nurse. "Your x-rays look good," he said, as the nurse pulled out a tray with a medical pack on top, opened it and spread out the supplies.

When the doctor finished stitching the wound, he said, "You're set to go home. Get these filled." He lifted two prescriptions out of his pocket. "Take as directed and come back in ten days to have the stitches removed."

"Can I walk on it?" Dave asked.

"Try not to put any weight on it for a few days. Pick up a pair of crutches in the pharmacy. Give me a call if you notice any swelling and a liquid discharge around the wound."

"Pus?" Dave asked.

"Yes."

"Do you want me to take you home?" Gwynn asked just as Officer Sam Young walked through the doorway.

"Dave, why don't you come to my house? Bridget will make sure you stay off that leg."

"That I know," he said, smiling at his brother.

"The shooting took place outside my jurisdiction," the Officer said. "The county sheriff is sending over a detective. I've arranged to be involved with the case. When he gets here, he wants to ask you a few questions."

"Sam, can he do that at my place?" Ashton asked.

"I'm sure that won't be a problem. I'll wait here and take him there."

Gwynn stood. "I'll leave your truck at the downtown office and pick up my car," she said to Dave. "I'll give Ashton your keys tomorrow." She bent down and kissed him on the forehead.

"I don't deserve more than that after taking a bullet?"

She slowly shook her head and smiled.

CHAPTER 21

It was 11:35 p.m. when Gwynn stepped out of the shower and slipped on her nightshirt. She climbed under the covers, turned off the nightstand light and immediately dozed off. The buzzing sound of the doorbell woke her. She raised her eyelids and glanced at the clock. 12:45 a.m. Last time someone rang her doorbell around midnight, it was Officer Young and another policeman after Drumlin's bogus car crash. *It's probably him wanting a statement about the shooting. Couldn't he wait until daylight?*

She dropped her feet to the floor and forced her body to stand, then put on a robe, stuck her pistol in the pocket, and shuffled to the front door while the buzzing continued. She pushed the curtain aside, then quickly unlatched the door and pulled it open.

Gwynn hugged her late night visitor, one of Ruben's employees. "I didn't know you were coming," she said, starring at Holly, a thirty-three year old, brown-eyed woman with shoulder length auburn hair, wearing a bright purple Fedora hat—her trademark.

"Neither did I, until five hours ago," Holly said, setting down her suitcase.

"Were you out there long?" Gwynn asked, nodding toward the front porch.

"A while. I was about to pick the lock, but that can be dangerous when there's a loaded gun on the other side." Holly held up her index finger to her mouth. She reached down, pulled out a bug sensor from the side of her suitcase, glanced at Gwynn's necklace with a bug concealed inside and motioned for her to go into another room.

Ten minutes later, Holly came into Gwynn's bedroom and gestured for her to go into the living room. Gwynn sat on the couch and waited.

"All clear," Holly said, plugging in an electronic jammer. "It doesn't sound like they're so sophisticated we'd need this, but it's good to take precautions. Let me get the rest of my stuff out of the car and then we can talk."

"Do you want some coffee or tea?"

"Coffee," Holly replied, stepping out of the house.

After three trips to the car, Holly had all her stuff inside and sat her large computer monitor on the coffee table. "I'm going to need a desk or a table I can sit at."

"The kitchen table," Gwynn said, pouring coffee.

"No. I like to leave stuff spread out."

Holly was a computer expert and hacker, plus skillful in weapons and fighting. Last time Gwynn worked with her, Holly had three tables, three computers, a printer and a scanner.

"Since you didn't know you were coming here, were you still on a job?" Gwynn asked, sitting down at the table.

Holly dropped a teaspoon full of sugar in her cup. "I was traveling to another assignment when Ruben called."

"What about that assignment?"

Holly shrugged. "Ruben will figure it out."

"Fill me in on what Ruben told you," Gwynn said and took a sip of steaming coffee.

"He called right after Paul reported the shooting."

"Paul?"

"Yeah. The guy who's keeping track of you. Ruben didn't tell you?"

"I just didn't know his name."

"Ruben suspects you might have been the target, but the assailant wasn't a very good marksman."

"Why would he think that?"

"The woodshed. The silent alarm you tripped and your face-covered image captured on the surveillance camera."

Gwynn took a deep breath and her shoulders sagged. "He knows about that?"

"He told me he talked to you about it," Holly said with a confused expression.

"About the break-in. I didn't know he knew about the silent alarm and camera. I didn't want him to know."

"It's impossible to keep secrets from him."

"Last time I talked to him, I thought he was going to fire me." Gwynn lowered her head and stared at the table.

Holly put her hand on top of Gwynn's. "Ruben has never had a newbie employee before."

"I know. Everyone he's ever hired has had at least five years experience. He sent me to the best places to be trained and he worked with me, but I'm still the new kid and I've been screwing up."

"First, Ruben shouldn't have left you here alone so long and second, you should have obeyed his orders."

"I'm minding him now and I won't do anything without his approval."

Holly rose and filled their cups. "My role is to play your cousin, Susan, from your father's side of the family, his brother's child. I just lost my job as a bank teller due to downsizing so I thought I'd see what it would be like living in a small town. Bottom line, I'm supposed to be with you all the time."

"How about work?"

"I'll see if I can get a job there."

"Doing what?"

"Still working on that."

Gwynn leaned forward, placed her elbow on the table and rested her chin on her knuckles. "What's the plan for the investigation?"

"Finding the who and why behind Boden's murder which, after today, appears to include determining what happened to the missing oil."

"Have the fingerprints I sent been analyzed?"

"Yes. Brad Williams', Mike Drumlin's and Ashton Prudell's were identified. Two other sets weren't on file in any databases. That doesn't necessarily mean those guys were involved in Boden's death. It just means they touched the canister. Did you see any safety masks in the woodshed?"

"No. There were some boxes covered with a thick layer of dust. It would've been difficult, if not impossible, to stick them in those without showing any signs of disturbing the dust." Gwynn nervously chewed on her lower lip and pondered about revealing the last thing she discovered in the shed. *Will Ruben fire me since I didn't tell him?* She swallowed hard. "I found a dentist appointment card on the floor."

"Does Ruben know?"

Gwynn lowered her eyelids and shook her head.

"Gwynn! Are you anxious to lose this job?"

"No. I just wanted to follow a lead on my own and then tell Ruben when I really had something, so I could prove I was competent."

"We work as teams. Everyone knows what's going on. No surprises among team members."

"But I was the only team member."

"No. Ruben is always a team member, even if he isn't on site. Understood?"

Gwynn sighed. "I screwed up again."

"Let's get to the card. Whose appointment was it?"

"There was only a time and date on the card, no patient name. Ashton Prudell had an appointment with that dentist at that time."

"He's moving up the list as a prime suspect."

"He was on the top of mine, but things aren't adding up. You should have seen Ashton at the hospital. His concern for his brother showed all over his face. He looked like he'd change places with Dave if he could. He'd never hurt him or allow anyone else to do it."

"But if you were the intended target, Dave should have been safe. The problem was the marksman." Holly drank the rest of her coffee. "Anything else you haven't shared with Ruben?"

Gwynn inhaled deeply. "Yes, but I didn't know about it until after I talked to him."

Holly rolled her eyes. "Go on."

She filled her in on the interest owners for the Cisco unit, which included Alex Hayes and her suspicions about his relationship with Janice.

"Wait," Holly said, holding up her hand. "Cisco unit, that's where Dave was shot, right?"

Gwynn nodded. "Yeah, at one of the unit wells." She went on and told Holly about the size of Hayes' income from the Lander unit and gave her the names of everyone who had an interest in that unit.

"Are the Cisco and Lander units close to each other?"

"Yeah, real close."

"What happened to Boden's and Drumlin's share?" Holly inquired.

"Their names have 'The Estate of' in front, so that interest is probably tied up in wills or probate. I had planned on asking Ruben to find out about Boden's beneficiaries, just in case that had a bearing."

"Was his interest as much as Hayes'?"

"More. I printed that page. Let me get it." Gwynn went into the bedroom, returned and handed the document to Holly.

Holly's brows bounced as she studied it. "I'll check into Boden's estate."

"Hayes seemed real worried about the missing oil from the Cisco unit and he didn't want to discuss it with Dave or Ashton. I think he's trying to protect someone."

"His son-in-law, Ralph Hunter?" Holly asked.

"Maybe. Or it might have something to do with Janice Robinson or her son, Patrick."

"I'll find out what Hayes' middle initial, P, stands for. Auburn hair." She lifted up a few strands of hers. "Do you think I might be one of Hayes' kids?"

Gwynn smiled. "Possibly."

"Let's move on to the shooting," Holly said and yawned.

Gwynn glanced at the clock on the wall. It read: 3:15 a.m. "Can we finish this tomorrow? I need some sleep before I go to work."

"No. I want to get caught up," Holly said. "Take part of the day off. Call in and say you were so upset about the shooting you didn't get very much sleep. You need a few more hours."

"Yes, Mother. Can you do it for me?" Gwynn said, resting her elbows on the table and cradling her head in her palms.

"I'll get you up so you can make the call. Okay, focus on today."

"Did Paul see the shooter?"

"Paul spotted him in the trees about 200 yards from you. He couldn't make out his features. The guy wore a cap. Paul thinks the marksman was around 5-foot-9. He got the license plate number. I'm planning on checking that out tomorrow."

"Unless you hack into Prudell's computer system, all you'll find is the truck's registered to the company. Give me the number. I can find out who's assigned that vehicle." Gwynn stood and took a notebook and pen out of a kitchen drawer.

Holly pulled handwritten notes out of her pocket and scanned through them, then scribbled the number on the notepad. "What are your thoughts about today's outing?" She glimpsed at her watch. "I guess it's yesterday's outing now."

"Dave either mentioned to someone we were going there or we were followed. While he drove, I kept checking the side mirror. No grey Silverados. I suspect Dave told Turk. Turk was involved with Drumlin's murder, but I doubt he played a role in Boden's. At the same time, whatever is going on with the oil problem puts him on my list of suspects."

"Do you think Turk could be the shooter?"

"He's at least five inches taller than 5-foot-9."

"That was just Paul's guess," Holly said. "The guy could be taller."

"Five inches?" Gwynn said, skeptically. "Turk hangs out all the time with Dave. He acts like they're best buds. I can't believe he'd shoot him."

"Would he shoot you?"

"Possibly. But the way those bullets were flying, either Dave or I could have been hit. If he's after me, I don't think he'd risk injuring Dave in the attempt."

"Any other suspects come to mind?"

"Brad Williams. He's about the right height."

"And his fingerprints were on the canister," Holly remarked. "Does the company store safety masks in the metal building?"

"On my visit I didn't notice any. I can check the inventory. Thinking about breaking in?"

"Yes, to get fingerprints. I realize other prints might also be on those, but it would be interesting if the same ones appeared. Have they upped the security system since your adventure there?"

"I'll check."

"Let's summarize. Your jobs for tomorrow are to find the name of the employee assigned to the truck used in yesterday's shooting, determine if safety masks are stored in the metal building and to check on its security system. Anything else?"

"I have the keys to Hayes' office," Gwynn said. "I want to search through his desk and cabinet before he returns."

"Good idea. Can you do it without being observed?"

"Alex gave me permission to get stuff out of his office if I needed something. It's okay if I'm seen in there. I'll be careful going through his desk." Gwynn hit her forehead.

"What?"

"One more confession."

Holly shook her head. "I can't believe this. Fess up."

Gwynn proceeded to tell her about breaking into Ashton's file cabinet and seeing the missing workover folders and files on Boden and Drumlin.

"All companies have files on their employees," Holly said.

"Not like these. The tabs were handwritten. That's where I found the serial number for Boden's gas monitor."

Holly flopped back in her chair and looked at the ceiling for a minute. "Gwynn, is there anything else you have forgotten to tell me," she said, slowly enunciating every syllable.

"No. That covers it."

"When you lay down in your bed and something else comes to mind, I want you to rush into my room and tell me. Okay?"

Gwynn nodded and then stared straight ahead. "Oh no," she said, squinting.

"Go on," Holly said, tapping her fingertips on the table.

"This house was broken into."

"I already know about that."

"How?"

Holly smiled. "I've already told you—some things you just can't keep a secret from Ruben. He wasn't happy that you took off your bug to scan, but he understood it was necessary."

Gwynn's eyes darted around the room. "Where are the cameras?"

"Hidden. It's unfortunate they weren't installed until after the folders were taken."

"We're being watched?"

"In here and in the living room. The bedrooms and bathroom are private."

"Will I still have a job tomorrow?" Gwynn asked in a heavy voice, sounding helpless.

"Neither one of our cell phones have rung. That's a good sign."

"But Ruben heard everything I said?"

"He did. Live feed with video."

Gwynn hung her head and sighed. "Ruben must still be absorbing it. He'll probably call before I go to work."

Holly leaned forward and stroked Gwynn's arm. "Don't look so gloomy." She took a deep breath. "I'm dropping fast. I need to get to bed. Is your guest bedroom all made up?"

"Yes. Sheets and blankets are on it." Gwynn held onto the table as she stood and looked at the clock. It read: 4:55 a.m. "You don't need to wake me. Sleep in. I'll set my alarm, call and go back to bed. Are you coming with me to work tomorrow?"

"No. I'm going to buy a table and get my stuff set up. Paul will be closer than usual. If you notice a guy on a motorcycle hanging around, don't be concerned. Don't talk to him either. And try not to leave the building."

Worrying about her job, Gwynn climbed under the covers and thought she'd have a hard time falling to sleep, but in a flash, she drifted off.

CHAPTER 22

The sunlight filtered through the bedroom curtains, making it impossible for Gwynn to go back to sleep after calling the office. She gave up trying and staggered out into the kitchen to make a pot of coffee. Measuring the coffee grinds, she caught a glimpse of herself reflected on the shiny chrome toaster and thought she should have showered, combed her hair and put on make-up before she stepped out of the bedroom. In the kitchen, someone watched and filmed her every move. Gwynn fastened the top button of her robe and was half-tempted to stand in the center of the room and wave, but decided against it, realizing she was on shaky ground with Ruben.

She sank down in a chair, stared at the coffee machine and waited for it to finish brewing. After the last drop fell into the carafe, she filled a mug, poured a bowl of cereal and added milk.

As she sat and ate, her cell phone rang—the sound she had feared. Reluctantly, she hurried to her bedroom, picked it up and with quivering lips said, "Hello."

Ruben's voice came through static, "Unplug the jammer."

Gwynn moved into the living room, pulled the device out of the outlet and sat down in the kitchen in front of her coffee. "It's unplugged. Should I pack now?" she asked, feeling discouraged.

"I tried reaching you at the office and I was told you weren't coming in until later."

Gwynn smiled, Ruben was playing fiancé. It wasn't her boss calling.

"Are you sick?" he asked.

"No. A lot of stuff happened at work yesterday and I couldn't sleep. I'm going to work soon. My cousin, Susan, came to visit. Do you remember her?"

"The one with the auburn hair?"

"That's her. When are you coming?"

"I'm hoping to get there soon."

'Soon,' whatever that means.

"I need to get back to a meeting," Ruben said. "I'll call over the weekend and we can catch up."

"I love you," Gwynn said.

"I love you, too," Ruben said and hung up.

Gwynn rested her head back against the chair and her body relaxed, the tension gone. Ruben hadn't fired her. She felt reborn as she ate the rest of her soggy cereal and drank coffee.

At 10:20 a.m., Gwynn walked into the office building, carrying a lunch sack.

"I didn't think you'd be in until this afternoon," Marilyn said. "Ross called to talk to you."

"He reached me at home."

"Are you still engaged?"

Gwynn held up her ring hand. "Oh yes. He's coming to see me soon."

Marilyn shook her head as the phone rang. "You poor thing." She picked up the receiver.

Gwynn expected that type of response, but after talking to Ruben earlier, it didn't bother her at all. She booted up her computer and searched through the company trucks and located the one with the right license plate number.

Marilyn ended her call and walked over to Gwynn's desk. "On the phone you said you couldn't sleep because of the shooting. How did you hear about it?"

"I was with Dave when it happened."

"You were?" Marilyn asked, scrunching her face in confusion.

Gwynn nodded. "He asked if I wanted to see a well site, so I went with him after I had my haircut."

"Are you okay?"

"Yes. Feeling pretty lucky. The way the bullets kept coming at us, it's amazing we got out of there alive."

Marilyn's eyes opened wider. "Tell me everything," she said, moving around the short wall, easing down into the chair next to Gwynn's desk and clasping her hands together.

After Gwynn spilled all the details, she asked, "Have you heard how Dave's doing this morning?"

"Mr. Prudell says he's doing real well. Dave's staying at their place." Marilyn stood. "Do you know what else happened?"

"Something else happened?" Gwynn asked, squinting.

Marilyn nodded. "The downtown office was broken into—computers smashed, documents stolen."

"When?"

"Around 11 p.m."

"That was right after I dropped Dave's truck off there."

"Does Mr. Prudell know about the truck?"

"I mentioned at the hospital I'd be leaving it there and picking up my car. Why?"

"Mr. Prudell said when the police arrived the parking lot was completely empty. No sign of the burglars or anyone."

"They might have only been referring to people—not that the parking lot was literally empty. Isn't there an alarm system there?"

"Yes, but someone forgot to turn it on."

"Surveillance cameras?"

"Two in the parking lot. They were both damaged. The police are looking at the tapes, hoping something was captured before the cameras were destroyed. Mr. Prudell is at that office now. I'm going to call him about Dave's truck." Marilyn went back to her desk and placed the call.

Gwynn closed her eyes and tried to envision how the parking lot looked last night. She recalled seeing another company truck parked three stalls from her car and glancing at the building before she left. It looked pitch black inside. The exterior was well lit. Doubting the robber's goal was to damage the computers since everything on them would've been automatically backed up in the network, she wondered about the stolen documents. *Could they have anything to do with the Cisco or the Lander unit?*

She went back to her assigned investigation tasks and clicked on the shooter's Silverado. It didn't surprise her when Brad Williams' name appeared in the assigned column. With the first assignment finished, Gwynn pushed on several keyboard buttons, until the inventory listing popped up on her monitor. Scrolling down several pages, she stopped on safety masks. Six were listed: five in the storage building and one in Ashton Prudell's possession. *Interesting.*

"Dave's truck is gone," Marilyn said loudly, standing by the counter.

"Gone?"

"Stolen."

"The tailgate was riddled with bullet holes. If someone wanted a Silverado, they could have found one in better shape."

"Beats me." Marilyn shrugged. "The company trucks are pretty easy to spot. Mr. Prudell wants me to tell you that Officer Young and a Detective Marsden will be over soon to take your statement about the shooting. "

"I expected they'd be over sometime today. Last night after I got home, my doorbell rang and I thought it was Officer Young, but it was my cousin." Gwynn smiled and her face glowed. "I was so happy to see her!"

"Your cousin's come for a visit? That's nice. How long will she be staying?"

"Awhile. She just lost her job—downsizing. She decided to come and see what the job market was like here. I wish Prudell had something available for her."

"What did she do on her last job?"

"Bank teller."

"I'll keep her in mind if I hear of any job openings."

"Thanks."

Marilyn returned to her own desk and Gwynn proceeded with her next assignment—metal building security system. She clicked through several screens and attempted to open the one she wanted, but was abruptly stopped by a message flashing across her monitor 'Access Denied.' She leaned over the short wall. "Marilyn, has the system security been upgraded again?"

"Yes. Mr. Prudell mentioned it right after you left yesterday. Our computers went down at four. He said if we were denied access to a system we needed, to let him know. Did you run into a problem?"

"I accidentally clicked on a program, but I don't need to get in it. The denied access thing just surprised me."

"Increasing security has become a big thing with Mr. Prudell. After last night's break-in, they'll probably be installing security cameras in here, like they're planning on putting in the storage building."

A spasm of panic ran through Gwynn's body. "Maybe they'll do them at the same time. I hate working around construction. Do you know when that will be?"

"The storage building is scheduled for tomorrow, so they could show up in here, too. I hope they do, since Prudell has had two break-ins. It'll make me feel better if something comes up and I have to work late."

"Good point." Gwynn sank into her chair, leaned on the armrest and thought about breaking into the metal building. It had to be tonight or it would be more complicated. She touched the brooch around her neck and knew Holly had heard every word said.

Feeling disappointed that she was blocked out of the security system program, Gwynn worked on Prudell's invoices while she waited for Officer Young and Detective Marsden.

Two hours later the Officer, Ashton and a stocky, bald, well-dressed man walked into the building. Ashton came over to Gwynn's desk. "Good afternoon, Gwynn," he said as his eyes dropped to her chest.

Gwynn smiled without showing it, knowing the break-in didn't deter him from checking out her cleavage.

"Marilyn told me you had a rough night trying to sleep after the shooting," Ashton said.

How true Gwynn thought.

He continued, "Are you feeling better now?"

"Yes, a lot better. Marilyn said Dave's doing well."

"He is. Dave wanted Bridget, my wife, to take him to the downtown office so he could see the damage, but she's keeping him in bed."

"Is it okay if I give him a call later?"

"Of course. Call my landline."

"Did Dave lose his cell phone?"

"No. Some of the guys have been calling him about the break-in and he doesn't know his truck's been stolen. Bridget is screening his calls." He glanced at the two men. "We didn't know his truck was missing until Marilyn called. I had completely forgotten you said you were leaving it there and not here. Detective Marsden and Officer Young would like to talk to you."

Gwynn stood and went with Ashton over to the two men. After he introduced her to Detective Marsden, he said, "They're going to talk to you about yesterday's shooting in the conference room."

Ashton led them to the room. Gwynn sat on one side of the table and the Detective and Young on the other side. Young pulled a small, spiral notepad out of his pocket.

Detective Marsden took a folder out of his briefcase and opened it, revealing a pad of lined paper. "This interview is regarding the shooting that took place yesterday afternoon at a well site in the Cisco unit," Marsden said. "Can you tell us about it, beginning with Dave Prudell driving to the location?"

Gwynn related the details again ending with the pursuit to the hospital.

"You didn't get a good look at the driver?"

"No. I was trying to stay as far ahead of him as possible. I know I broke the speed limit."

"Mr. Dave Prudell mentioned that and a damaged front fender."

"With all the bullet holes in his truck, I can't imagine anyone wanting to steal it."

"That might be the reason it was stolen."

"They wanted a bullet riddled truck?" Gwynn asked, cocking her brows. Though, that same explanation had already occurred to her.

"The crime scene has been searched. Every bullet and cartridge was gone. The site had been swept clean."

"Not one bullet?"

"It's being checked again, but so far—nothing. We suspect bullets might have been lodged in the vehicle frame. Without a bullet or cartridge, we can't determine what type of weapon was used."

"It wasn't a rifle?" Gwynn said, attempting to sound naive.

"We're certain it was a rifle, but we need to know the type to begin looking for the weapon."

"Maybe it was one you took hunting."

"Let's move on," Marsden said. "Even if you couldn't identify the driver, did you notice a hat or cap?"

Gwynn shook her head. "It has to be someone that has a company truck. Maybe you could ask those guys where they were yesterday afternoon."

"We've already started that process, but there is one truck not assigned. It's parked behind this building. A couple of technicians are going over it from top to bottom. One final question—do you know anyone that would want to harm you?"

"Me?" Gwynn asked, wrinkling her nose. "No."

"I've been told your fiancé hasn't been to visit you since you arrived in Bloomfield. Any problems there?"

Her mouth fell open. "You think Ross wants to kill me?"

"We're looking for a motive. No stone will go unturned."

"Ross and I are going to be married. He's been busy. It's not his fault he couldn't come and see me." Her eyes became moist. "He'd never hurt me," she sniffled.

Officer Young leaned over and patted her shoulder. "We didn't mean to upset you, but these questions have to be asked."

Gwynn stood, got a tissue from a box on the side table and wiped her eyes. "I know it's just part of your job."

Marsden closed his folder, dropped it into his briefcase and rose to his feet. "Thank you for your time, Miss Wagner," he said, shaking her hand. He pulled a card from his breast pocket. "Call if you think of anything else."

"I will," she said, taking the card. The three walked out of the conference room. Gwynn headed to her desk and the two men went into Ashton's office.

Marilyn looked at Gwynn dabbing her eyes. "Are you okay?"

"They think someone is trying to kill me."

Marilyn rushed to Gwynn's side and put her arm around her shoulders. "I'm sure you understood that wrong." She led Gwynn to her desk and eased her down into the chair. "That's general police procedure to ask victims if they have enemies. Don't you watch any police shows on television?"

"I do. I guess I'm just overreacting."

"Let me make you a cup of tea," Marilyn said and went to the break room.

Within five minutes, Marilyn set a filled mug on Gwynn's desk. "That will make you feel better."

"Thank you," Gwynn said. She took a sip and decided to call Dave since she didn't want to go to Hayes' office while the two men were still in the building.

After she identified herself to Bridget, Dave came on the line. "I'm glad you called," he said. "I feel like I'm under house arrest, but worse—confined to this bed and my calls are screened."

"It sounds like Ashton's wife is taking good care of you."

"Too good. Breakfast and lunch in bed, any video I want to watch, a wide assortment of beverages and snacks. I guess I shouldn't complain."

"Can I join you?" she asked, teasingly.

"Sure. Come on over. King-size bed. Plenty of room for two."

"Seriously, how are you doing?"

"Not bad. My leg doesn't even hurt."

"Drugs?"

"A variety."

"Did Detective Marsden ask you if someone wanted you dead?"

"Not in those words. But he did ask if I had any known enemies. Why?"

"He just talked to me and asked a question similar like that. I wanted to know if that was standard procedure. Marilyn thinks it was."

"It is. Don't worry about it. I'm the one that got shot."

Gwynn watched Ashton say something to Marilyn and walk out of the building with Young and Marsden. "I'll let you get back to your videos. I came in late so I need to catch up."

"Late?"

"Yeah. I slept in."

"Must be from yesterday's excitement."

"Probably. I'm glad you're feeling okay."

"Call me tomorrow. The Gestapo might not let me have my cell phone."

Gwynn smiled. "Okay. Talk to you tomorrow."

Marilyn came over to Gwynn's desk. "They found some bullets at the site," she said, sounding excited.

"They did?"

"Yes. Mr. Prudell told me. Detective Marsden just got a call about it. They're going to catch the guy."

"That's great," Gwynn said.

After Marilyn headed back to the counter, Gwynn grabbed a notepad and took her empty mug into the break room. On the way back to her desk, she made a detour to Hayes' office. She wanted to search Hayes' desk before Ashton returned. There wasn't a key on the ring that fit the lock. Gwynn pulled her picks out of her belt and took care of it.

She breezed through the center and top drawer—nothing worth lingering over. Hayes' checkbook was in the second drawer. Gwynn flipped through it and saw numerous checks written to Janice Robinson. Laying it back in the drawer, she noticed a small ledger and took it out. The columns had headings: payee, date, amount, accumulation. The initials JR appeared in the first column. The dates consisted of the first day of every month. The amounts never changed. Gwynn thumbed through the ledger and discovered it included payments for sixteen years—always the first of the month and always the same amount. The amount seemed in line with child support payments. Sixteen years. Any question she had about who was Patrick's father vanished.

Gwynn moved to the third drawer, pulled out a folder labeled Lander Investment and laid it on the desk. Opening it, she saw the top document—an agreement between Arne Boden and Alex Hayes. Gwynn sank down into the chair and jotted down the terms in her notepad. Boden had sold part of his interest in the Lander unit wells to Hayes for $70,000. It was signed two weeks before Boden's accident. In the margin a handwritten note read: "He's marrying Janice – good for Patrick."

Under that document was a torn notepad page with a tally of how the money would be spent. Gwynn noted it wasn't Hayes' handwriting and assumed it was Boden's. The items scribbled on it were: ring - $15,000, fixing salon - $35,000, wedding - $6,000, honeymoon - $10,000, miscellaneous stuff - $4,000. Gwynn thought it was strange that Hayes would have received a summary on how the funds would be spent, but maybe Boden was known for not being able to manage money. Also, Hayes' goal might have been to give Boden money to get married and not because he believed it was a profitable investment.

Hearing talking in the foyer, Gwynn quickly slipped the folder back in the desk, jumped up and went to the file cabinet. She inserted a key in the lock, turned it and pulled out the second drawer just as Ashton peeked into the room.

"You are here," he said. "I thought you might have gone home."

"No," she said, lifting out a folder. "Alex said he'd be back in a week, but I wasn't sure if that meant this Friday or Monday. Do you know which day?"

"Monday. Everything going okay in his absence?"

Gwynn nodded. "So far so good."

CHAPTER 23

When Gwynn returned home she found the living room transformed into an office—two tables, two computers—a desktop and a laptop, an office chair, a printer and some other pieces of equipment Gwynn hadn't seen before. The couch, chair, end tables, coffee table and television had been pushed against a wall. Holly was busy pounding on a keyboard.

"Did it take you all day to get this set up?" Gwynn asked.

"Yes, but that's only because I didn't get out of bed until noon. You did good in your interview with Marsden and Young." She smiled. "But don't worry, your fiancé isn't trying to kill you."

"What a relief," Gwynn said, making her way to the couch. "Let me fill you in on what I found out." As she sat down, Holly swiveled her chair around. "The police discovered some bullets at the crime scene."

"I heard. Remember your brooch," Holly said. "Paul had pried some out of the truck when it was parked at the hospital and thought he'd give the cops a hand."

"So the shooter wasn't careless?"

"He was careless—shooting at you." Holly lifted her elbow to the arm of the chair, raised her hand and leaned on it. "I got into Prudell's system. I already know the truck was assigned to Brad Williams. There is a chance he wasn't the driver. Not likely, but a possibility."

"Then you probably also know about the safety masks."

"Haven't gotten there yet. I've only been on the computer for twenty minutes."

"There are six—five are in the storage building and Ashton Prudell has one."

"Mmmm," she said, pressing her lips together.

"I couldn't get into the program that shows the security system.

Only those that need to know have access now."

"I can take care of that. And I also heard your conversation with Marilyn about the security cameras. You're probably feeling beat, but we need to move on that tonight. I can fix the cameras so the same image appears for a while, but it can get tricky right after an installation—people might be watching the monitors closely. Did you get a chance to search Hayes' office?"

"Only his desk, but I got the answer to my question about Patrick. Ran into Hayes' checkbook and ledger. He pays Janice the same amount of money the first of every month."

"That points more to the possibility he's Patrick's father, but not absolutely. Who knows, she could be blackmailing him over something else."

"Guess I jumped to that conclusion too quickly."

"You're probably right, but we like airtight conclusions. Anything else?"

"Found an agreement. Hayes paid Boden seventy-thousand dollars for part of Boden's interest in the Lander unit wells. Hayes had written in the margin that Boden was marrying Janice and it would be good for Patrick. There was also a handwritten note how the money would be spent."

"Hayes wrote it?" Holly asked with narrowed eyes.

"No. It wasn't his handwriting. Probably Boden, but I'm not certain—not airtight."

"How was it to be spent?"

"A ring, fixing up a salon, wedding, honeymoon."

"Do you think Hayes bought it so Boden could get married?"

"That's what it looked like to me."

"A note? It's odd that Boden would give Hayes details about how he planned to spend the money. Maybe Boden had money troubles, or it was something Hayes required. Who knows? A lot of crimes occur around money issues. I'm going to check on Boden's finances." Holly stood and stretched. "I've made some lasagna. It just needs to be cooked. We'll leave for the storage building right after we eat. Try to take a little snooze before dinner."

"Good idea," Gwynn said, meandering around the furniture to get to her bedroom.

At 8 p.m. Gwynn and Holly headed for the metal structure. Earlier, Holly had been able to get into Prudell's security system and discovered the password had been changed. The new one wasn't listed. Gwynn parked behind a group of trees, the same spot as the last time she broke into the building.

"When we're inside, Paul will bolt the door and snap on the padlock," Holly said, approaching the door.

"We'll be locked inside?" Gwynn asked, sounding confused.

"Only temporarily. Just a precaution if someone should drop by to get something. Tonight will be their last opportunity not to be observed."

"Yeah. By now, everyone working for Prudell in Bloomfield probably knows about the security camera installation."

"Paul will call if a car stops next to the building."

"Do you want me to put the alarm system out of commission?" Gwynn asked.

"In case someone else shows up, it's better if we don't have to do that. If we can figure out the new code, they'll just think someone forgot to set. It'll also be quicker to reset if we have enough time."

"How are we going to come up with the code?"

"Two attempts," Holly said. "Enter the same code you used last time, but raise the last two digits by one. If that doesn't work, increase the first two numbers by one. If that still doesn't work, I'll disarm it."

"Do we have that much time?"

"Sixty seconds is longer than you think."

After slipping on gloves, Gwynn unlocked the padlock with her duplicated key, slid the bolt and put on her night goggles. "Ready?" she asked. Holly nodded.

Opening the door, Gwynn heard the soft beeping sound coming from the alarm, rushed to the middle of the wall and punched in the code. Adjusting the last two numbers didn't work. Holly was prepared to disarm it as Gwynn tapped on the pad, upping the first two numbers by one. The beeping stopped and 'System Disarmed' flashed on the alarm monitor followed by 'Ready to Arm.' "Good guess."

"Most people when they adjust codes try to make it easy on themselves," Holly said. "Where are the safety masks?"

Gwynn's eyes swept around the room. "Over there," she said,

pointing. "On the same shelf as the gas monitors."

The women took off their backpacks and pulled out fingerprint kits.

"You do those two," Holly said, gesturing. "I'll do the other three."

Fifteen minutes later, they were finished and moving toward the alarm pad when the roar of a diesel engine came from outside. Holly's phone vibrated. She yanked it out of her pocket and glanced at the screen. "Someone's here. Turn on the alarm and we'll go behind those pipes." She motioned.

Gwynn pushed the alarm button, hurried to the stack at the rear of the building and hunkered down next to Holly while she listened to the soft beeping sound and heard noise at the door.

Holly touched her arm and whispered. "The beeping will end before the door swings open."

"How can you be sure?"

"Paul's delayed them a couple of minutes."

"How?"

"He put goop on the padlock. The key can't go in until they clean it off," Holly said and then the room fell silent.

The door flew open and the beeping began again. Holly and Gwynn watched through cracks between the pipes.

"What did that kid have on his fuckin' hands when he closed that lock," Turk said, pounding on the alarm pad. Brad shrugged. Turk went to the sink and washed his hands while Brad moved to the shelving unit where Holly and Gwynn had acquired fingerprints.

"Don't just stand there," Turk snapped. "Get to work!"

Brad picked up a safety mask and began wiping it with a bluish-green cloth.

"You have got to be the dumbest shit I know," Turk said, gritting his teeth. "Put on your gloves! What's the point in cleaning off fingerprints if you're not wearing gloves? Dumb shit!"

Brad reached in a bag and pulled out a pair of yellow, rubber gloves. "Turk, I told you I was sorry about what happened," he said, tugging them on. "I thought she'd be an easy mark out there. You know, I'm a pretty good shot—hit the bull's-eye all the time. People would just think it was a stray bullet since they were so close to a prime hunting area. Got a deer there last year."

"Dumbass. It's not hunting season!" Turk said, wiping a safety mask. "And you didn't only shoot one bullet. How do you explain over fifty going astray?"

"Everything got cleaned up. No one knows there were that many."

"You haven't heard?"

"Heard what?"

"They found four slugs?"

"No. I cleaned it up good."

"Not good enough!"

"But you told me that Dave said the police didn't have any leads. They won't know it was my rifle. No one saw my license plate number. With so many company trucks, it can't be pinned on me."

"God, what have I gotten myself into," Turk said, shaking his head. "This whole thing has turned out to be a nightmare. You could have killed Dave!"

"But I didn't. I'm a good shot!"

"If you were that good, you wouldn't have hit him. The chase. What were you thinking?"

"Just trying to get them away from there, so I could clean up."

"But you chased them almost all the way to town!"

Brad picked up another safety mask and began scrubbing it.

"What did 'the man' say?" Turk asked.

"He's madder than you are. He doesn't want her dead before we question her about what she knows." Brad's eyes darted around the space. "I guess we can't meet in here anymore."

"The break-in screwed us up. Most of the stuff in here is pretty expensive."

"Wouldn't surveillance cameras outside have been enough?"

"Probably, but the security company recommended putting them in here also."

"Can we meet in the downtown office?"

"They're also installing them there because of last night's break-in." Turk looked at Brad as he put a mask on the shelf.

"That was agreed," Brad said.

"Where's the sixth mask?" Turk asked.

"It's got to be there."

Turk searched that shelf and all the ones in that section of the structure. "Don't see it anywhere."

"Did you check the list?"

"No, but there's no reason one would be missing," Turk said. "I'll check it tomorrow and find out what happened to it."

"I need a beer," Brad said. "Let's go."

"I'm hitting the john first. Meet you in the car."

Brad walked out the door and Turk ducked into the restroom, but immediately came out. He hurried to the corner, close to Gwynn and Holly and rummaged through miscellaneous items on a shelf. He lifted down a toolbox, raised the lid and top tray and took out a black bag. Turk unzipped it, pulled out a pistol, stuck it under the back of his belt and covered it with the bottom of his t-shirt. He reached in the bag, took out a box of bullets and put it in the sack he had carried into the building. Then, he stuffed the bag and tray back in the box, closed it and tucked it behind some items on the shelf.

Turk grabbed the sack and set the alarm.

After she heard the lock snap into place, Gwynn asked, "What do you think that was all about?"

"Turk thinks Williams is a loose cannon. And based on the conversation, I'd have to agree with him. He's going to be armed and ready."

"I wonder if that was the pistol Turk used to shoot Drumlin."

"Probably, since it was hidden. He might have put it there the night of the shooting just in case someone noticed a bullet hole in the charred remains of the victim. Let's get out of here. We can talk on the way back to the house." Holly pulled out her cell phone and punched numbers. "We're ready," she said into it, disconnected and slid the phone back in her pocket.

Two minutes later, the door opened and the beeping began again. Gwynn glanced at the exit, hoping to see her tracker as she sprinted to the alarm pad and entered the numbers. "Paul's not coming in?"

"No. He just needed to open the door to give us sixty seconds to turn off the alarm. Otherwise, it would have gone off as soon as we were spotted by one of the motion detectors. Remember your last outing in here?"

"I do," Gwynn said and waited for Holly to reach the door. She punched the activation button and left the building.

As Gwynn drove away, Holly said, "It makes reporting to Ruben a lot easier since you're wearing a bug. He already knows everything that was said in the storage building."

"And he was right—I was the intended target. But I still can't figure out how anyone knew I was the one that broke into the woodshed. My face was covered. I didn't think they'd be all that concerned about the earlier break-in since the fingerprints on the safety masks by themselves aren't that damaging. The ones on the canister are a different story."

"I'm starting to think that one of the assailants is either very good with computers or has a friend who is."

"Why?"

"If they traced all your computer moves at work—the data you checked; it would have made them nervous and then when the woodshed was broken into by a woman—obvious connection." Holly smiled. "Tomorrow, I'll find out if that happened and the IP address of the perpetrator. I'd do it tonight, but I want to go to bed after I scan in the fingerprints and send them off."

"I thought you were going with me to work tomorrow."

"I am, but I'll bring my laptop. My purse is big enough to hide it."

CHAPTER 24

Gwynn scrutinized Holly's appearance. Her curled shoulder-length hair, her heavily made-up face, a large earring dangling from each ear and her outfit: a black and white, extremely low cut, ruffled neckline blouse, black skin-tight slacks and five-and-a-half-inch stilettos. "You know you look like a floozy. Are you sure you don't want to tone it down just a bit?"

"Is this how Janice dresses?"

"Even she's more conservative than that."

"Good. Then I'll have one up on her."

"You'll certainly draw the attention of all the guys."

"That's the plan."

"Can you walk in those?" Gwynn asked, staring at Holly's shoes.

"This isn't the first time I've had to wear heels like this. Have you been able to avoid it?"

"So far. I can't manage more than four inches."

"I suggest you practice."

The two ladies entered the office building and Marilyn's eyes sprang wide open. "Is..Is," Marilyn stammered, "this young woman your cousin, Gwynn?"

"Yes. Let me introduce you two. Marilyn this is Susan Wagner. Susan, this is Marilyn Bentner, Prudell's receptionist. She knows everything that goes on around here and she keeps track of the boss."

"And that isn't easy some days," Marilyn said and looked at Holly. "Have you put in any applications?"

"Not yet. Gwynn really likes working here so I thought I'd check if Mr. Prudell had something available."

"We don't have any openings."

Gwynn went to her desk while Holly chatted with Marilyn,

knowing Holly would find some way to hang around.

"How about part-time while I look for something else?" Holly asked.

"There just isn't anything available. Mr. Prudell has talked about maybe putting on another field worker, but I don't think that's anything you'd be interested in."

"What do they do?" Holly inquired.

"For a starter position, mainly grunt work—stuff the other guys don't want to do. Mr. Prudell probably would be looking for a guy to fill that position."

"Is he in?"

"No. I expect him to walk through that door any minute," Marilyn said, nodding toward it.

"I'll just sit on the couch and wait."

"I think you'd make better use of your time if you went to the employment agency on Main Street. They might be able to find you something."

"I want to talk to him first."

"Okay," Marilyn said, shrugging her shoulders. She straightened up some pamphlets on the counter while Holly sauntered over to the couch.

Holly was flipping through a magazine when Ashton walked through the doorway. His eyes immediately fixed on her. She lowered the magazine and gave him a good peek at her cleavage.

"Good morning, Mr. Prudell," Marilyn said.

Holly laid down the magazine and inched up into a standing position.

"Good morning, Marilyn," he said as he continued gazing at Holly.

Holly moved to his side, "Hello, Mr. Prudell," she said, stretching out a hand. "I'm Susan Wagner, Gwynn's cousin."

"I'm happy to meet you, Susan," he said, shaking her hand. "Are you here visiting?"

"No. I want to live in Bloomfield, so I'm here looking for a job. Gwynn likes working for Prudell so I was hoping you'd have something available for me."

"Let's talk about it in my office," he said and walked with Holly into the hallway.

Gwynn almost felt a little disappointed he didn't make his usual detour by her desk, but Holly's attire put her low cut blouse to shame.

Ashton gestured for Holly to take the chair on the other side of the desk. He watched her slowly ease down into the seat. "What did you do in your prior job?"

"I was a bank teller."

"How long did you work at the bank?"

"Almost two years."

"And before that?'

"A receptionist, a file clerk, a special assistant—all office jobs, but I could work outside. Do you have any outside jobs, like telling the guys were to pick up oil and stuff like that? I could do that. I could pump gas, too. I didn't see any gas pumps. Where are they?"

"Oil and gas, as it comes out of the ground, isn't ready to go into vehicles."

"Well, maybe I could get it ready."

Holly noticed Ashton rolling his eyes, yet she maintained a serious expression.

"The oil has to be refined…at a refinery."

"Do you have any openings there?"

"We don't own any refineries. We sell our oil unrefined."

"People buy it like that?"

"Companies buy it like that."

"Mmmm," she mumbled. "Do you have any openings for sales people?"

"No."

"Have you got anything?"

"You said once you were a file clerk?"

Holly nodded.

"How long?"

"Boy, I had that job for over a year. I'd still be there if my boyfriend hadn't wanted to move."

"Boyfriend?"

"Yeah. I dumped him along with a few others before I came here. They were all stupid! Didn't know how to take care of a woman." Holly leaned forward, providing him with a closer view of her chest. "I bet you know how to treat a lady."

Ashton gazed at her for a minute. "I have been thinking that some of our old stored files should be discarded, but first we need to verify that all the documents in the folders have been scanned into the system. Have you ever worked on a computer?"

"Yes. That's what we always used at the bank."

"This won't be a permanent job. It will only last long enough to verify what documents are in the system and scanning those that aren't. Do you want that type of a temporary position?"

"Oh, yes. I want to work for Prudell."

"It's only temporary."

"Oh, thank you!" Holly rose to her feet, walked around the desk and took his hand. "Thank you. I'll just be the best employee you have."

"Remember this isn't a permanent position."

"Maybe something else might open up here while I'm doing that job."

"Doubtful, but there's always a possibility."

Ashton stood. "I'll have Marilyn get you started."

Marilyn's eyes popped wide open when she saw Ashton stepping into the lobby with Susan in tow.

"Susan will be working here temporarily," he said.

Marilyn clasped her hands together and cocked her eyebrows. "What will she be doing?"

"The files in the file room are jam packed to the brim," Ashton said and proceeded to explain Holly's created position.

"Where will she sit?"

"Set her up in the conference room."

"And the computer?"

Ashton leaned his elbows on the counter and lowered his eyes. "Is Debra coming in today?"

"No."

"For today, let's have Susan sit at Debra's desk. I'll check with Dave and see if she can use his computer for a few weeks. He has another one at the downtown office."

"Wasn't it damaged in the break-in?" Marilyn asked.

"Yes. New ones are being delivered this morning. A tech will be there this afternoon to install the software. That office will be back in business tomorrow."

"Great."

"Have Susan fill out employment forms first," Ashton said.

"And salary?" Marilyn inquired.

"The same hourly rate as a new field worker. I need to make some calls," he said and turned toward Holly. "I hope you enjoy working here."

"I know I will," Holly said and watched Ashton disappear down the hallway. She received a stack of forms to complete and sat down at Debra's desk.

Gwynn walked into Debra's cubicle and whispered, "I can't believe you pulled that off."

Holly's brows bounced. "The outfit."

CHAPTER 25

Shortly after 2 p.m., Ashton checked on Holly's progress for the sixth time, said a few words to Marilyn and then left the building.

Carrying an armful of papers, Marilyn strolled over to Holly. "Mr. Prudell wants me to do some filing in his office while he's gone. I'll be in there if you need me."

"Okay."

Marilyn went to Gwynn's desk. "I'm going to be working in Mr. Prudell's office for awhile. I can answer the phones in there, but if someone should stroll into the lobby, which I doubt, can you come and get me?"

"Sure," Gwynn said and waited for Marilyn to be out of sight. She stood and saw Holly setting up her laptop. "Can you watch the lobby while I visit Hayes' office?"

"Uh-huh," Holly mumbled as she plugged in her computer.

Gwynn headed into Hayes' office and began looking through his file cabinet for anything that might pertain to the investigation. The bottom drawer held documents relating to the Lander unit. Gwynn took out a stack, sat them on Hayes' desk and plowed through them. The first bundle only contained production numbers. Since she could acquire that information on her computer, those documents were set aside.

In the second stack, Gwynn ran across purchase agreements applicable to the Lander unit and discovered most of them were executed three months prior to Boden's death. Various individuals were listed as the sellers, not Prudell Energy Company, and Hayes wasn't a party to any of the transactions. She wondered why he had them and how he had acquired them. The company would have received notification of an interest owner change, but not the details of the sale. Thinking Ashton could return any minute, Gwynn decided to copy the documents and study them later. She headed to the copy machine in the file room.

On her way back to Hayes' office with her arm full of agreements, Holly rushed past her and went into the restroom. Putting the stack on Hayes' desk, Gwynn heard a thumping noise, stepped out into the hallway and saw Dave wobbling on crutches. "You were allowed to get out of bed?"

"Only for a few minutes, just long enough to pick up a folder," he said as a slender woman with bright blue eyes peeked around the corner.

"Dave, your few minutes are almost up," she said with a warm smile.

"Gwynn, have you met Bridget?"

"No," Gwynn said, eyeing the attractive, forty-year-old woman.

As soon as Dave finished introducing the two women, Marilyn came out of Ashton's office. "Hello, Mrs. Prudell," she said, cheerfully.

"Hello, Marilyn. Is my husband hiding in there?"

"No. He went to check on the progress of the surveillance camera installations and to see how everything is going at the other office. He's probably there now. Do you want me to check?"

"No. I was just going to say hi—nothing important." Bridget looked at Dave. "You have less than a minute left." Then her attention turned back to Marilyn and they chatted about the break-in and Dave's missing truck while he shuffled to his office with Gwynn right behind him.

"How's the leg?" she asked.

"Better." He sank down on his chair and pulled out a drawer.

"When will you be coming back to work?"

"Monday, but not here."

"You could have called. I would've brought you what you needed."

"What I needed was to get out of the house. The kids want to lay next to me on the bed and watch movies."

"Oh, poor baby."

He gave her a crooked smile. "The problem is they don't like the same type of shows I do. You can only watch so many animated movies and silly teenage flicks."

"It must be terrible for you."

"Time's up," Bridget said, standing in the doorway.

Dave held up a folder. "Got it."

"I'll take that," Bridget said and lifted it out of his hand.

"Come by the downtown office on Monday," Dave said to Gwynn as he moved toward the door.

"I will." Gwynn watched Dave and Bridget go into the lobby, heard the sound of the main door closing and then opened the restroom door. "You can come out now."

"They're out of the building?" Holly asked.

"Yes."

"I certainly didn't want Ashton's wife to see me."

"I understand. You probably wouldn't be working for Prudell tomorrow. How did you know it was her?"

"All I saw was a woman helping a guy get out of a car and handing him crutches. I assumed it might be the wife, hightailed it in here and listened at the door."

Gwynn leaned closer and whispered, "Have you found out anything yet?"

"Yes, but this isn't the place to discuss it," she whispered. "Sometimes walls have ears."

"Do you want to go to Marty's after work?"

"Sure do. I want to get as much use out of this outfit as possible."

Gwynn smiled. "Have you got others?"

"Yes, but only a few. We'll have to go shopping over the weekend."

"I need to get back to filing some documents in Hayes' office."

At 5:05 p.m. Gwynn and Holly left the office with their purses stuffed with documents. They climbed into Gwynn's car and stopped at the house to drop off the copied pages along with Holly's computer. Then they proceeded to Marty's.

The eyes of all the customers fell on Holly as the two women entered the establishment. Men gawked; women sneered. They took a table and before they had an opportunity to order, Turk approached.

"Okay if I join you, Gwynn?" he asked.

"Sure. Turk, this is my cousin, Susan Wagner. Susan, this is Turk Carlsen. He works for Prudell."

"Are you visiting?" Turk asked, eyeing Holly up and down as he sat down next to her.

"No. I just started working at Prudell today."

Turk squinted. "Doing what?"

"Pumping gas," Holly giggled.

Turk chuckled. "Are you really a Prudell employee?"

"What can I get you to drink?" the barmaid asked, interrupting the conversation.

After everyone ordered, Holly said to Turk, "Yes. I'm working on going through some files before they're shredded."

"Full time job?"

"Temporary, but I'm hoping something else opens up."

"We sure could use a receptionist in the downtown office."

Holly slightly leaned forward. "Can you tell that to Mr. Prudell?"

"I sure will," he said as his eyes dropped to her bosom.

The barmaid delivered their beers. "Put that on my tab," Turk said.

Holly put her hand on Turk's. "Well, aren't you sweet!"

"Thanks," Gwynn said. "Do you know if Dave's going to be able to make it over here?"

"Not tonight. He said he'd try to escape the bed tomorrow."

"How will he get here? Have they found his truck?"

"No. If he can leave the house, I'll pick him up. It's probably going to be a few weeks before he can drive. The bullet hit his right leg."

That hadn't even entered Gwynn's mind.

"Gwynn told me about the shooting. She's so brave. I'd go to pieces if I had to go through something like that." Holly said, grabbing Turk's arm.

Gwynn sat quietly, sipping on her beer and enjoyed observing Holly in action.

Turk patted her hand. "Don't worry. They'll catch the guy."

Brad strolled over to their table from behind Holly. "Turk, aren't you going to play pool?"

"In a few minutes. Susan, do you play?"

"Well it depends on what the game is?" she said in a seductive tone.

Brad took another step and saw Holly from the front. "You new around here?" he asked, staring with wide bulging eyes.

"Susan is Gwynn's cousin," Turk answered for her. "Susan, meet Brad. He also works for Prudell."

"Hello, there," she said, giving him a shy smile. "I just started working for Prudell today."

"Doing what?" Brad asked, and Turk filled him in.

"Susan, do you play pool?" Turk asked again, emphasizing 'pool.'

"I know how to tap a few balls around," Holly said and ran her tongue along her top lip.

Turk took a swig of his beer. "Do you want to give it a try?"

"Sure." She rose gingerly and picked up her glass.

"Gwynn, do you want to play?" Turk asked.

"No. I'll just watch." She followed them and sat down next to the pool tables.

"It's been awhile since I've played this game." Holly put her glass down by Gwynn. "I hope I don't disappoint you," she said, standing in front of Turk, her face a couple of inches from his.

"You won't. It takes practice to be a good pool player."

"We're rotating?" Brad asked.

"We'll rotate," Turk said. "I'll play against Susan and you'll play the winner. How does that sound?"

"Fine." Brad said, thinking he could wait a few more minutes to play Turk. "I'm getting another beer. Anyone else want one?"

"I do," Turk said. Holly and Gwynn declined.

Turk racked the balls. "Why don't you break, Susan?"

"Sure." Holly lifted her cue up to the table and scanned the pockets. She slowly swayed her hips into place, leaned forward and struck the white ball. To everyone's surprise, she knocked in three striped balls.

"This is fun," she said, positioning herself for another shot.

Brad handed Turk a beer, took a chair next to Gwynn and kept his eyes on Holly as she arranged her body against the pool table for each shot.

Holly didn't miss pocketing a striped ball until only one remained on the pool table. Gwynn thought Holly missed that one intentionally.

"Are you a pool shark or something?" Turk asked. "I didn't think I was going to get a chance to step up to the table."

"Once, I travelled around the country with this guy that played pool to make money. That was how we lived. He taught me a few tricks, but I haven't played for a long time."

"You haven't lost your touch," Turk said and began clearing the table, but he didn't get all the solid colored balls in.

Within two minutes, Holly had won.

"Never been beat by a girl before," Turk said.

Holly stroked his arm. "You're not mad at me, are you?"

"No. I like challenges. I'm looking forward to our next game."

Brad racked the balls. Holly insisted that he break since she did it last time. Just like the game with Turk, it didn't take her very long to win.

Turk began gathering the balls.

"I can't play anymore," Holly said. "Gwynn and I need to do some shopping."

With those words, Gwynn walked over to Holly.

"Are you ladies coming here tomorrow evening?" Turk asked.

"Oh, yes," Holly said. "Gwynn mentioned there's a live band on Friday nights. I just love to dance." Her eyes darted between Turk and Brad. "I hope one of you guys ask me."

"You can count on that," Turk said.

"Me, too," Brad echoed.

"That was impressive," Gwynn said, sliding into the driver's seat. "You are a pool shark."

"I won trophies in high school and play whenever I can to keep it up. When I was on the police force, the guys hated playing me." Holly shook her head. "Guys, right? I guess it's an ego thing, a woman beating them."

"You were a police officer?"

"Yes. A member of a special investigation unit."

"Why'd you leave?"

"Ran across a little corruption in the department and reported it to the wrong person."

Gwynn cocked an eyebrow. "You were fired?"

"No, but it became difficult to work there. People ignored me. I started being assigned the crappier jobs, so I quit."

"Is that when you started working for Ruben?"

She bobbed her head up and down. "He heard about me through a friend and asked if I'd be interested. Best decision I ever made."

Gwynn felt a tinge of jealousy. She was an accountant when she met Ruben. At that time, he was investigating her best friend's murder. After she helped him solve the crime, she had pleaded with Ruben to work for him, and he had sought out Holly.

"I'm not the only one of Ruben's employees he's recruited," Holly said. "He knows what his organization needs and goes after a person with those skills."

Gwynn pulled into the driveway and stopped in her usual place.

"Wait here," Holly said, getting out of the car.

"What?"

"Someone has been here." Holly pulled a pistol out of her purse and released the safety.

"How do you know?"

"The front doorknob."

Gwynn looked at the door and saw a reddish-orange streak on the doorknob. She raised her pant leg, leaned down and yanked out her weapon.

Holly stayed close to the tall bushes and foliage surrounding the house as she crept toward the door. She moved to the side of the house and kept her back against it as she inched along while her eyes scanned the area. Without touching the doorknob, Holly looked at it, raised her arm and motioned for Gwynn to come.

With her pistol at the ready, Gwynn cautiously edged toward her as she checked both sides of the driveway.

"Go that way," Holly said, gesturing. "I'll go the other way and meet you in the back.

Gwynn stealthily eased around the corner of the house, looking for anything unusual and intently listening for sounds that didn't belong.

Holly saw Gwynn and announced, "All clear."

"Are you sure?"

"Yes. Someone attempted to enter the front door and received a shocking surprise."

"Electrical shock?" Gwynn asked.

"Yes. I rigged it last night."

"But it could have been us," Gwynn said.

"No. There was a turn off lever. I hit it earlier when we dropped off our stuff."

Gwynn saw Holly unlocking the back door. "How are you so sure it's clear inside?"

"Whoever was here came at least two hours ago based on the

doorknob color. Had someone just touched it, the color would be bright red. As time moves on, it turns orange."

"But they could have hung around some place, waiting for us."

"The back door hasn't been touched. They would have attempted another way in--breaking a window, hitting the back door with an object, something."

"Whoever it was probably expected it to be easy, like when the workover files were taken."

"Right," Holly said. "Before we go in, let me show you how to turn the mechanism on and off."

Gwynn moved up to the porch.

"See this small wire," Holly said, indicating a piece sticking out the side of the door frame. "When it is up, current will be sent to the doorknob if someone touches it, down—it's off."

"And the color?" Gwynn asked.

"The knobs have been coated with a clear substance. An electrical current turns it red. Now I need to scrub it off the front doorknob so I can apply a new coat."

"What about going out of the house? Is there a turn on and off inside."

"No. The inside wasn't rigged." Holly walked into the kitchen and dropped her purse on a chair. "After I get out of these clothes, should we see who it was or eat first?"

"I'm hungry. I vote for food first," Gwynn said.

After dinner Gwynn helped Holly reposition the television closer to the couch, she placed her beer on the side table, set a bowl filled with popcorn in the center of the coffee table and stretched out her legs on it.

Holly connected her computer to the television, then grabbed her mouse and the remote, curled up on the other side of the couch with her legs tucked up next to her body and clicked on the television set. The screen lit up. It was divided into four sections, one for each corner of the house. "What you're seeing is outside at 5:30 p.m. I think the aspiring burglar arrived sometime between 5:30 and 6 p.m."

"That's because you suspect it's the same person I do."

"And he showed up at Marty's around 6:20 p.m. If I'm wrong, we'll be watching longer or I could do a quick scan."

"This is kind of exciting," Gwynn said, picking up the bowl. "Do you want some?"

Holly took a handful of popcorn.

Gwynn munched on a few pieces. "Look!" she said, seeing a figure in the bottom right hand quarter.

Holly clicked on it and that section covered the whole screen. "He isn't even attempting to be inconspicuous. He probably saw your car pull into Marty's parking lot and headed right over here."

They watched Brad grip the doorknob and laughed as he stumbled down the stairs. His eyes darkened with rage. He glared at the house, opened his mouth and his lips moved.

"It's too bad we don't have sound," Holly said. "But I can imagine what he's saying."

"So can I," Gwynn said, still laughing.

Brad trudged away.

"He didn't even go to the back of the house," Gwynn said. "And how was he planning on getting in. Even without the shock, the door would have been locked."

"I suspect he has a key. Williams took the doorknob with his left hand. His right was partially in a pocket. Also he doesn't seem like the kind of a person that would know how to pick a lock. His job wouldn't require it."

"My keys must have been copied at the ranch. Sometimes I had to leave my purse locked up in a locker. Never did trust my stuff was safe in those lockers since I felt certain the Prudells had another set of keys for them."

"Lockers?"

"Yeah. There's a whole row of them for their Saturday guests to use."

Holly stood. "I'm going to look at the video again on my computer, pause it at one of the good front views of Williams and print it."

"I might as well get started reading through the purchase agreements and make notes. Oh, what did you find out about the computer thing… did someone trace my moves?"

"Yes. I've got the IP address. After I get a good image of Williams, I'll locate the street address."

"Have you searched for Boden's will?"

"Haven't had a chance to spend very much time looking for it."

"Something about Janice's story, her being told to keep Boden occupied so his place could be decorated for his birthday, never struck me right. His birthday was almost a week away. I could understand it if there wasn't another weekend before the event, but I've checked the calendar and there was."

"Janice does have an interest in the Lander unit even if it's small. She might be a player, especially if she had something to gain from Boden's death. If I could get the address where the checks to his estate are mailed, that will help speed up the process—give me the city, state. Narrow the search."

"Do you want me to get that for you at work?"

Holly glanced at the clock. It was 9:40 p.m. "Yes. If Ashton doesn't leave the building, he'll keep popping by and tomorrow it'll be easier for him since I'll be in the conference room. I'd look for it tonight, but I don't want to get to bed late. It takes Susan a long time to get ready to go to work."

"I can hardly wait to see what Susan will be wearing tomorrow."

CHAPTER 26

Holly styled her hair and fixed her make-up like the day before. She wore a pair of skinny jeans, a red silk blouse that draped low in the front and five inch heels.

"I located the street address for the IP last night," Holly said. "I want to drive by during lunch."

When they arrived at work, Gwynn introduced Holly to Debra. Like everyone else, Debra's eyes moved over the outfit. "I'm sure you'll like working here," she said without any enthusiasm in her tone.

"It's only temporary, but maybe something will open up at the other office," Holly said, thinking about the reception position Turk had mentioned.

Dave's computer had already been moved into the conference room along with the folders Holly left on Debra's desk the day before. Holly found the most comfortable chair out of the assortment in the room and got to work.

"I see you're settled in," Ashton said, stepping into the room. "Has Marilyn answered all your questions?"

"Yes. She's been great."

"Good. I better get to work."

At noon, Gwynn and Holly climbed into the Mustang. Holly gave her the directions to the location of the IP address. It led them to a well-maintained, two-story, red brick house with an attached three-car garage situated in a nice, upper-class neighborhood. They stopped on the other side of the street, three houses down.

"Something seems familiar about this address," Gwynn said.

"This isn't what I expected," Holly said. "I thought the IP address would be located in an office building.

"Do you know the name of the owner?"

"No. It was late when I got the address," Holly said, pulling out her cell phone. She pushed numerous buttons, occasionally pausing. A look of utter disbelief crossed her face. "The owner is Janice Robinson. There's no way she could afford this on her income. I checked her tax return. Also, I searched for Hayes' middle name. The P stands for Patrick. To maintain her life style, Janice needs money from Hayes."

Gwynn shook her head. "I doubt those payments would be enough to carry that house. She's getting money from somewhere else. I wonder if that revenue stream from Hayes will end when Patrick's older."

"It probably depends if they have an informal child support agreement between them or if Janice is blackmailing Hayes. Blackmail won't end."

Gwynn rested an elbow on the rolled down window. "There is a possibility that Hayes has told his wife about Patrick."

"Janice's house," Holly said, tapping her fingertips on her leg. "I can't imagine she's that knowledgeable about computers. Whoever is, must be working out of her place."

"Patrick!" Gwynn said, recalling a conversation. "Linda said Patrick spends all of his time in front of a computer screen…that his bedroom looks like a computer lab."

"Teenagers can be pretty savvy when it comes to computers. But to hack into Prudell's system and trace where you had been, takes an expert." She gazed at Gwynn for a minute. "Do you have any gloves in your car?"

"Yes, in the hidden compartment in the trunk. Are you thinking about checking it out?"

"Patrick should be in school and Janice is probably at her beauty salon."

"I could call her salon to make sure," Gwynn said. "I've got her home phone number, but she might have caller ID."

"Call her salon. Then I'll call the house."

Gwynn lifted her cell phone from her purse and punched in the salon number.

"JR Salon," Janice answered.

"Hi Janice, this is Gwynn. Did I by any chance leave a pair of sunglasses there?"

"I haven't run across any. Hold on and I'll look around."

The sounds of drawers opening and closings, the rustling of papers, and heels clicking on a hard floor came through the phone.

"No," Janice said. "There aren't any here."

"Thanks for looking. Bye." Gwynn disconnected.

"Instead of calling, I'm going to ring the doorbell. Patrick would have no idea who I am. I can easily pretend I've got the wrong house." Holly stepped out of the car, crossed the street and went up the sidewalk to the front door. She pushed the doorbell and waited. Then she pushed it again, stood on the porch for a minute, and returned to the car.

"I only have one pair of gloves," Gwynn said. "Since my heels are over an inch shorter than yours why don't I check it out?"

"No. I'd better. After seeing his room, if I suspect he's the culprit, I want to look at a few things on his computer. You can watch and call my cell phone if someone approaches the house."

Holly went to the front door and picked the lock. Within a few seconds, she was inside and heard the beeping of an alarm system. She located the pad by the back door and disconnected it. Assuming Patrick's room was on the second floor, Holly bolted up the stairs. The first door was locked. After quickly glancing into the other rooms, she returned to the locked door, picked the lock and pushed the door open. Immediately, she knew it belonged to a person who liked computers. Equipment surrounded the bed.

Holly noticed a pile of papers sitting by the printer. She looked at the top page. The heading said: Turk Carlsen and the dates of the past week. The report consisted of three pages and listed all the programs, locations and sites he had visited. Under that report was one for Ashton Prudell. Holly thumbed through the stack and discovered a report for every employee who worked in one of Prudell's offices.

Holly sat down at the computer and turned it on. It was password protected. She began pecking on the keyboard and got past the password. After making a mental note of his software, she clicked on his email, managed to get around that password and opened the list of his recent emails. There were several that had numbers and digits in place of a name. She clicked on one, took a blank sheet of paper from the printer and wrote down the senders email address.

Holly's cell phone vibrated. She plucked it out of her bra, glanced at the number and pushed a button. "Who's coming?"

"A black civic pulled into the driveway."

"Can you see the driver?"

"Patrick just got home."

Holly glanced at her watch. It showed 12:50 p.m. "What time do kids get out of school?"

"Not this early. Maybe he came home to pick up something."

"I'm not finished," Holly said, stuffing the sheet under her belt. "I need to connect the alarm." She turned off the computer, shut and locked the door, ran down the stairs and hooked the alarm back up. Unlatching the back door, she heard a key in the front lock and moved outside. She went to the corner of the house, planning on going to the front, but found a six-foot fence. Wearing skinny jeans, Holly didn't want to climb. She went to the other side of the house, saw a gate and attempted to open it, but it wouldn't budge and assumed it was locked from the other side. Without going into the house or climbing the fence, the only way out of the backyard was through the door into the garage. In there, she'd have to open the garage door and suspected the mechanism could be heard from inside the house.

She moved to a tree at the rear of the yard, out of view from anyone inside and called Gwynn. "I'm in the backyard. I can only leave if I climb a fence and I don't want to ruin my jeans."

"What can I do?"

"Pick the lock on the gate, which is on the same side of the house as the kid's bedroom. It could squeak when it opens. Do you have any liquid in your car?"

"A small bottle of lotion."

"Good. Bring it when you come to break me out, but first turn your car around and park on this side of the street with the motor running. That will help drown any noise we make. And walk normal getting here. If a neighbor notices someone creeping around they might get suspicious, think you're a burglar and call the cops."

"Got it. What side of the house is the gate on?"

"It's on the right, not the garage side."

"Patrick's room is upstairs, right?"

"Yeah."

"I'll get there as fast as I can," Gwynn said and disconnected. After she parked again, she walked across the lawn to the edge of the house. Then she moved cautiously, staying next to the wall in case Patrick should look out the window, she wouldn't be spotted. A gravel path ran along that side of the house to the backyard. Two garbage cans stood in front of the gate. Gwynn slid one aside, causing a grinding sound. It was too large for her to attempt to lift so she tilted it and pulled it forward. It still made a scrapping noise along the rocks, but not as loud as before. When that one cleared the gate she repositioned the other one.

"Can you hear me?" Gwynn asked, leaning on the fence.

"Yes."

"I'm throwing the bottle," Gwynn said and heaved it over the gate.

"Got it."

Gwynn proceeded to pick the padlock and removed it. She inched the door slightly open and heard a loud screech. "Pour more lotion on the hinges."

"I've used all of it," Holly said.

The roar of a diesel engine came from the front of the house. It sounded like a truck had pulled into the driveway. Gwynn quickly pushed the gate open. "Nothing could possibly be heard over that sound. I just hope it isn't someone from the company who can recognize my car."

Holly closed the gate behind her. Gwynn snapped the padlock on. They each took a handle of the garbage cans and lifted them back into place. They scurried to the front corner of the house. Holly peeked around it. "It's not a company truck. It's twenty years older. Probably one of Patrick's friends. Let's get out of here."

At a normal pace, they walked to the Mustang and climbed in. Gwynn pushed the gas pedal and maintained a slow speed as she drove out of the neighborhood. "What did you find out?"

"Next to his printer was a pile of reports. One for each of Prudell's office employees, including Ashton Prudell, indicating all the sites and programs they entered for the past week."

"So he is the culprit."

Holly nodded. "I wanted to check out his computer. It was password protected so it took me a few minutes to get in. I went to his email. That was also password protected. Several of the emails didn't indicate the name of the sender, only numbers and digits. I wrote one down. If Ashton leaves the office, I'll get back into

Patrick's email."

"You can't exactly set up your laptop with him checking you out at least once every hour," Gwynn said.

"Then I'll do it tomorrow. My Saturday research list keeps growing." Holly looked at her watch. "We're almost an hour late from lunch and I'm starving."

"There's a sandwich place a couple of blocks from the office. I'll stop there."

At 2:05 p.m., they entered the office.

"Where have you two been?" Marilyn asked. "Mr. Prudell has been looking for you."

"Car problem. I had another flat tire," Gwynn said.

"Another one?" Marilyn asked.

"Yes. Now all of my tires have been changed. I'm starting to think the ones that were on the car when I bought it were all inferior."

"I'll explain it to Mr. Prudell," Holly said and headed into the hallway.

"They'll be a live band at Marty's tonight, right?" Holly asked as they drove home after work.

"Yeah. Every Friday night."

"Then I want to change into a pair of heels that are an inch shorter before we head to the Towne Café."

Linda spotted Gwynn as soon as she walked through the door, hurried over to her and gave her a brief hug. "How are you doing after that shooting?"

"Fine, but I jump with the slightest strange noise," Gwynn said, "I guess that's normal."

Linda patted Gwynn's shoulder. "Sweetie, you're holding up great. Turk told Janice all about it and she filled me in. Oh, the car chase. We're just happy that Dave's going to be okay and you weren't hurt."

"Thanks. So am I," Gwynn said and gestured toward Holly. "Susan came into town the following day and having her in the house helps. Oh Linda, this is Susan, my cousin. Susan, this is Linda, the nicest person in town."

Linda's cheeks turned red and the two women greeted each other.

"I've got to get back to work," Linda said. "Why don't you two take the booth next to the window and I'll bring you some waters."

When Linda placed two glasses of water and the menus on the table, Gwynn asked, "Are you going to Marty's tonight?"

"Can't. I wasn't scheduled to work here tonight, but Betty's sick. I have to fill in. Doing a double shift. I need to deliver some orders." She hurried to the kitchen.

"She's Janice's sister?" Holly asked for verification.

Gwynn nodded. "They don't look or act anything alike."

"Do you think she has a clue about anything going on?"

"Not a lot. I get the impression she knows more than she's mentioned to me. I can't believe after sixteen years she doesn't know who Patrick's father is. Janice doesn't strike me like a woman that could keep a secret that long."

"If she's blackmailing Hayes, she might be a little hush about that."

Linda strolled back to their table, "Ready to order?"

"We'll both have the special," Gwynn said without consulting Holly.

"Good choice. Anything to drink besides water."

"No."

"I'll have that right out," Linda said and disappeared into the kitchen.

"Janice wouldn't tell her sister about blackmailing Hayes, if that's what it is," Gwynn said. "She'd probably call it child support. On another matter, do you think you could finagle Turk to take us to the Bamberg tank battery?"

"That's where the oil for the Cisco unit is stored and picked up, right?"

"Yes. And the Lander unit. I thought about asking Dave under the pretense I wanted to know more about the company operations, but it'll be a while before he can drive and feel comfortable walking around on the site."

"What are you thinking?" Holly asked.

"I just want to go there and check it out. I have the legal description and know the general location, but not how to get to the specific site. Asking one of the guys to give me the directions is a little too obvious."

Linda returned to their table carrying two plates of chicken fried steak, mashed potatoes and string beans. She put the plates down in front of them. "Let me know if you need anything else."

"Looks good," Gwynn said.

Linda left to seat more customers.

Gwynn went on, "It has about a million calories and worth every one of them."

The ladies ate in silence for ten minutes. "This is good," Holly said, between bites. "Why do you want to go to the battery?"

Gwynn glanced around and noticed how the café was filling up. She didn't recognize any faces, but at the same time someone not affiliated with Prudell could be involved. "I'll tell you later."

Holly's eyes darted around the room. "I didn't realize how crowded it was getting in here."

"It's a popular place."

CHAPTER 27

At 7:20 p.m., Gwynn and Holly walked into Marty's. They looked around for familiar faces. Gwynn spotted Dave with his leg propped up on a chair next to the dance floor. She touched Holly's arm and pointed. "Over there."

"You were allowed out?" Gwynn asked him.

"Yes, but I have a curfew," he said with a smile.

"Curfew?"

"Ashton and Bridget still think I need looking after and they don't want me getting back there too late. Probably worried about having a drunk cowboy in their house." He nodded toward the empty chairs. "Sit."

"With the drinks on the table it looks like someone is already sitting there."

"The guys can pull up other chairs." He eyed Holly. "You must be Susan, the gal that beat the crap out of Turk and Brad at the pool table."

"It wasn't like that," Holly said. "They were close games."

"That's not how the guys tell it."

"I'm sorry, I should have introduced Susan," Gwynn said.

"No need," Dave said. "I knew who she was as soon as you two walked through the door." He stretched out his hand. "Susan, I'm Dave and you've probably already heard that I work for Prudell."

Holly shook his hand. "Yes. I've heard something like that. It's too bad you're not going to be able to do any dancing with that leg."

"Yeah. I'll have to make it up by drinking," he said and took a big gulp of his beer.

"Ashton and Bridget might have cause to worry about a drunk cowboy," Gwynn said.

"I ain't driving," Dave said. "But I wish that bastard who took my truck would return it."

"The back of it was riddled with bullet holes," Gwynn said. "We were just lucky one didn't strike a tire."

"The way you were driving, you still would have gotten us out of there," Dave said, taking Gwynn's hand. "You ladies need a drink." His head moved around the space. "Connie," he yelled, raising his arm and motioning to the barmaid.

Connie made her way through the people that were milling about. "What can I get you?" she asked.

Dave ordered three pitchers of different types of beer and a bowl of nuts.

Turk stepped up to the table. "Susan, ready for a rematch?"

"When does the band start playing?" Holly asked.

"In about fifteen minutes," Turk said.

"Sure," Holly said and walked with Turk to the pool tables.

"Slide your chair a little closer so I can pretend you're my date," Dave said.

"But I'm not,"

"Give a wounded man a break."

Gwynn smiled and move her chair next to his, thinking that might be his way of keeping the other gals at bay. He probably isn't up to any serious flirtation. *Can't take any of the gals home if you're staying at someone else's house.*

The barmaid brought the pitchers and glasses, poured one for Gwynn and filled Dave's.

"How you doin', baby?" Janice said, standing behind Dave and putting her hands on his shoulder.

Dave reached up and moved her hands. "Good. Where's your lover boy, Kevin?"

"He's not here yet. Can I sit down by you guys?"

"Sorry, all the chairs are taken. A new gal's playing pool. Maybe you should watch her and learn something."

"Well, if that's the way you're going to be." Janice turned and marched off.

"That wasn't very friendly," Gwynn said. "We could've pulled up another chair."

"Have her sitting here all night—no thank you," Dave said with a frown.

Gwynn had the urge to pry about Dave's relationship with Janice, but didn't want to take a chance on creating any animosity. "Are you all caught up on silly teenage flicks?"

"Not yet. Corinne, Ashton's daughter, already has some more picked out for us to watch later or tomorrow. I can hardly wait," he said in a monotone.

"This is probably fun for the kids, having their uncle visit."

"Yeah, too much fun."

A loud static sound echoed through the room as a band member checked the microphone.

"What do you know about the group?" Gwynn asked, pointing to the band.

"They're good. They play here about once a month."

The music began, a fast song, and a few couples ventured out onto the dance floor.

Holly, Turk and Brad returned to the table.

"How'd it go?" Dave asked.

"The lady's got style and moves," Turk said, pouring beer.

"I take it Susan beat you again?" Dave asked.

"She beat him and clobbered me," Brad said.

Dave smiled at Susan. "You need to take it easy on these boys. Having a pretty gal like you beat them can be embarrassing. We'll have to play when the doc says it's okay."

Gwynn thought, *Dave's already honing in on Holly; maybe he's already planning his next conquest.*

"Wanna dance," Turk asked Susan.

She took his hand and they stepped onto the dance floor.

"How about it?" Brad asked Gwynn.

"You guys just going to leave me sitting here alone?" Dave asked.

"I won't dance the next one," Gwynn said and went with Brad.

Holly took turns dancing with Turk and Brad. Gwynn occasionally danced with one of them, but spent most of the time sitting next to Dave. After an hour, the band took a break and the ladies headed to the restroom.

"I got us an invitation to go to the field," Holly said. "I'll explain more when we get home. Turk introduced me to Janice at the pool table. I saw a guy with a goatee dancing with her. Is he Kevin Whitehead?"

"Only one person in here with a goatee. That's him."

"I want to dance with him," Holly said.

"Janice won't like it."

"That's what I'm hoping."

As they walked toward the table, Holly noticed Whitehead at the bar. "You go ahead," she said, "I'm going to make a detour. If anyone asks, tell them I saw a person I recognized."

Holly didn't waste any time. She pushed her way through the people, lingering around the bar, to Whitehead. "Do I know you?" she asked in a seductive tone as she moved closer, until her voluptuous breasts touched his arm.

Whitehead turned and his eyes dropped from her face to her chest. "I don't believe we've ever met. I'd remember someone like you."

"Are you sure? Nebraska. Lincoln, Nebraska?"

"I've never been there."

"You sure look like that handsome guy I met there."

The music started again, a slow song.

Holly closed her eyes and tilted her head back. "Don't you love this song? How about a dance, so I can just pretend you're that guy from Nebraska. We had a couple of great nights together."

"Why not?" he said and followed Holly.

Gwynn saw them going out on the dance floor and had to press her lips together to hide a smile when Holly snuggled against his body.

"Susan knows Kevin?" Brad asked.

"He must be the one," Gwynn replied. Suddenly, she felt a slap on the back of her shoulder. "Owww!" She flipped her head around and saw Janice leaning down. "What was that for?"

"Janice, what are you up to!" Dave snapped.

"Your gal's hussy cousin is dancing with my guy."

Turk rose to his feet and grabbed Janice's arm. "Now you wait a minute. There's no reason for name calling. Susan knows him."

"She's a bitch!" Janice said, gritting her teeth. "Can't you guys see that! An A-1 bitch hussy! Open your eyes and look at the way she's dressed."

Turk yanked Janice away from the table and took her toward the back of the establishment while she shouted obscenities.

Gwynn looked at Holly and Whitehead still dancing and wondered if they hadn't heard Janice's outburst or if they had both decided to ignore it. Her question was soon answered when the song ended and she saw the rage on Whitehead's face as he headed in the direction Turk had taken Janice.

"I heard some commotion at the table," Holly said, timidly. "Was Janice mad about something?"

"She slugged me," Gwynn said. "You were dancing with her boyfriend."

"Are you hurt?"

Gwynn tilted her head toward her shoulder and rubbed it. "It's sore. I think she bruised it."

"Let me see," Dave said, pulling down Gwynn's blouse.

"Dave!" Gwynn said, holding up her blouse.

"Sorry. I wasn't thinking about that, just wanted to look at your shoulder. It's red."

"I didn't know Janice had a bad temper," Gwynn said.

"She's started a few cat fights in here," Brad said. "Once, a customer called the cops."

"And she wasn't banned from the place?" Gwynn asked and caught a glimpse of Dave staring at the floor.

"I didn't see her for a week and some of the guys thought she was," Brad said, "but then she showed up again. Janice dresses up the place and the guys like her." He glanced at Dave. "Well, most of the guys like her."

Another tune came over the speakers and Brad asked Holly to dance. Turk returned to the table. No one asked him how it went with Janice. Gwynn didn't dance the rest of the evening, using the excuse that her shoulder hurt.

Shortly before 10 p.m., between songs, Dave asked Turk, "Ready to take me back to Ashton's?"

"Sure," Turk said and looked at Holly. "Will you be here when I get back?"

"It's been a long day. Gwynn and I are going to leave after I have another dance with Brad," Holly said. "But I'll see you on Sunday."

Dave and Brad's brows creased as they looked at Turk.

"Two-thirty?" Turk asked.

"Sounds good."

Half an hour later, Gwynn and Holly walked into their small white house. Holly opened her purse and pulled out a plastic bag with a beer glass inside. "Fingerprints."

"How did you manage to get that?" Gwynn asked.

"That one was easy." Holly lifted out another bag containing a beer bottle. "This one was hard."

"Whose are they?"

"Glass—Turk Carlsen's, bottle—Kevin Whitehead's. I wanted to get Dave's too, but he never left the table and kept his glass close by. Couldn't grab it out of his hand. Then the barmaid picked it up along with the other empty glasses as Dave was leaving with Turk. If the two I got aren't the unidentified prints from the canister, I'll find away to get Dave's on Monday."

"Do you suspect Dave?"

"Based on the conversation we heard in the storage facility, Williams did the shooting on his own. It wasn't sanctioned by whatever group we're dealing with and 'the man', whoever that is, was mad about it. Williams didn't think a bullet would strike Dave. Remember, he believes he's a great marksman. Hits the bullseye all the time. So getting shot doesn't automatically remove Dave as a suspect."

"But he doesn't have personal interest in the Lander unit, like Ashton."

"We don't know that has anything to do with Boden's death. All we have right now are assumptions."

"What couldn't you tell me at Marty's about Turk taking us to the battery?"

"I told Turk I wanted to see the site where the shooting took place. I figure from there, I'll talk him into going to the Bamberg battery. If something strange is going on there and he's somehow involved, I didn't want him clued in. Who knows who he might mention it to. He wasn't happy you were coming... third wheel. I said you'd been real nervous since the shooting so I didn't want to leave you home alone. He was very sympathetic. Still, I had to add a little frosting."

"What?"

"I'm going to have a drink with him, alone, when we get back."

"But I thought we were glued at the hip."

"You'll stay in the house and Paul will be close by. Now tell me why you want to go to the battery."

"I checked production reports for the Lander unit. That unit's oil production increased the same time as the workovers were completed in the Cisco unit."

"Did Lander have any workovers?"

"One. So there is a chance I'm barking up the wrong tree. I originally thought the run tickets, which show the volumes transported from storage tanks, might be wrong and the production was taken from a different storage tank—Cisco's instead of Lander's. But the volumes are fairly consistent and different tanker drivers pick up the oil. That's still a possibility, but then several drivers would have to be in cahoots, besides the pumper, since there are numbered seals on all the storage tanks."

"So what do you think is happening?"

"Just a theory—flow lines. I told you when Drumlin was killed I found documents in his truck, but I only got away with the cover sheet labeled 'Flow Line Layout Adjustments.' The project folder in the file room doesn't say anything about adjustments."

Holly squinted. "Flow lines?"

"Surface pipes that carry oil from the wells to the storage tanks," Gwynn explained.

"Would you know if they were screwed up by looking around the storage tanks?"

"Probably not, but it's worth a shot. Dave would know. I wanted to find a way to talk to him about it, but if he's a suspect…"

"We just don't know yet. Let's see if we run across anything on Sunday. Also, I'm planning to work on the computer all day tomorrow: researching Kevin Whitehead, Boden's will, Patrick's emails …"

"Oh," Gwynn interrupted. "Boden's will." She pulled a sheet out of her purse. "His estate and Drumlin's are being sent to the same address." She handed the page to Holly.

Holly glanced at it. "Interesting."

"I thought you needed to do some shopping tomorrow," Gwynn said.

"That has to be thrown in the daily mix too."

"Kevin Whitehead. One time when I was at Marty's, Ashton was there talking to Janice in a booth. They appeared real friendly, just hand holding, not kissing or anything. When Ashton headed toward the door, he ran into Whitehead and from my angle, it looked like the two men were glaring at each other for a minute. Then Whitehead went and sat in Janice's booth. After, I thought it might have something to do with Janice, but now I'm not sure."

"You're thinking they have history?"

"Yeah. I asked Linda if Whitehead ever worked for Prudell and she said no, but some of Prudell's guys used to work for the same oil company Whitehead works for in Farmington. That's how he started hanging out at Marty's."

"Do you know which guys?"

"No. If you can find out the name of the company where he works, I can check the employee files on Monday."

"Okay. Anything else?"

"Why did you want to make Janice angry?"

"I did a little research on Marty's to find out if they had any problems with the police. They had very few, but in one of the reports, I ran across the name of Janice Robinson. Some kind of a fight, so I suspected she had a short fuse since she fought in public. I just wanted to cause friction between her and Whitehead, in case her son is compiling the information for him. Just a hunch, but glancing through that stack in Patrick's room and seeing a report for everyone who works in one of Prudell's offices, that only leaves Brad Williams, Kevin Whitehead and Janice Robinson that have interest in the Lander unit. I can't imagine that Williams or Robinson are smart enough to think about looking through the computer to check if anyone is snooping around, so that leaves Whitehead."

"That's under the assumption that has something to do with Boden's death, right?"

Holly nodded. "We have to cover all the potential angles. We might be dealing with two completely separate crimes. I feel beat. Not used to all that dancing. I'm going to hit the sack."

CHAPTER 28

Sunday afternoon, Turk's light grey Silverado pulled up in Gwynn's driveway. Holly and Gwynn had been watching for the truck since they didn't want him to get a look inside at the makeshift office. As he walked toward the door, they came out.

Turk studied Holly's outfit: a pair of tight jeans, low, scoop-necked t-shirt and four-inch heels. "You might want to bring a pair of athletic shoes if you want to walk around."

"Gwynn said the same thing. Give me a minute." Holly went back inside.

Turk opened the back door of his extended cab for Gwynn. She held onto a handgrip, stepped on the rail and saw Dave sitting inside. "I didn't know you were coming," she said, easing down on the seat next to him.

"It was my duty. I couldn't let Turk take two pretty ladies by himself."

"Can you walk around out there?"

"I'm not planning on doing that, just coming along for the ride."

"Is this better," Holly said, climbing into the front passenger seat.

Turk looked at her shoes. "Yes, but that's the first pair of athletic shoes I've ever seen that have high heels."

"It's only a two-inch heel."

Turk started the engine, drove out the driveway and headed toward the Cisco unit.

"Are you still staying at your brother's?" Gwynn asked Dave.

"Yeah. Ash thinks I should stay there until I can drive. It's tough. I don't have to do any work and the cooking is great. I'd still rather be at my own place, but he can be pretty persuasive. It's almost like he feels guilty I got shot. There wasn't any security system he could've had installed out there. He sure has upped it in the storage building and the downtown office. Next week cameras are going in the main office."

"Yeah," Turk said. "You won't be able to pick your nose without someone watching."

Everyone in the car laughed.

"Any new leads on the shooter or the burglars?" Gwynn asked.

"Sam says they're following up on some, but he's pretty hush-hush about it." Dave adjusted himself on the seat. "Would you mind if I put my leg on you?"

"Is it bothering you?" Gwynn asked.

"It doesn't hurt. It just feels a little uncomfortable."

Gwynn moved her hands away from her lap. "Raise your leg."

"We have to change sides. Can you climb over me or should Turk stop?"

"I can climb over." She snapped off her seatbelt and raised her hips over Dave as he slid under her.

Dave leaned into the corner of the cab, strapped in and lifted his right leg onto Gwynn's lap.

"Comfortable?" she asked.

"Yeah. Thanks."

Gwynn realized Dave planned to get as much mileage out of his injured leg as possible. She was in the hospital when the doctor told him to try and stay off it for a couple of days, not five. Then she recalled Ruben's bullet wound. How he wouldn't stay down for twelve hours. As soon as he could move, he went back to work. Thinking about him, she faced the window and briefly closed her eyes as she reminisced about the last time they were together. She longed to be back in Ruben's arms.

"See anything interesting?" Dave asked.

Snapping out of her reverie, Gwynn sat up straight. "Just looking for birds. Haven't seen one since we left Bloomfield."

Turk turned onto the gravel road and the truck jostled, jerked and gyrated as he drove around chuck holes and navigated through the rough terrain. He stopped next to the well where the shooting had occurred. Dave opened his window before Turk turned off the engine. Turk, Holly and Gwynn scooted out of the Silverado and walked around while Turk explained to Holly the pieces of equipment on the well site.

"The rock up there," Gwynn said, pointing to a boulder surrounded with yellow crime scene tape. "That's the one Dave and I had to hide behind." She gestured toward a wooded area. "The shooting came from over there." Wanting to see the damage the rock had sustained, she trudged through the trampled grass to the boulder with Holly and Turk right behind her.

"Will you look at this," Holly said, touching the chips in the boulder. "There must be at least a hundred here. Was the guy using a machine gun?"

"No," Gwynn said. "The bullets didn't come in a rapid session. There were slight pauses. Probably a semi-automatic."

"You know about guns?" Turk asked.

"My dad was a big hunter. I went out with him a few times. I hated it, but I learned a little about rifles."

"He made you go?" Turk asked.

Gwynn nodded. "Only child. Didn't have a boy to take."

"My brother and I could hardly wait for hunting season," Turk said.

"Where does this go?" Holly asked, stepping toward the flow line. "It looks like a fat hose, bigger than a fireman would use."

Turk stood next to her and put one arm around her shoulders. "The flow line goes to a storage tank. From there, it's trucked to a pipeline."

"I don't see anything sticking out of the ground," Holly said. "What does a storage tank look like?"

"You can't see them from here," Turk said. "They look like giant cans, big round cylinders. We'll go to a place where we have a few, so you can see one."

"I'd like that," Holly said. "I want to know everything about Prudell so I can be a great employee. Have you had a chance to talk to Mr. Prudell about a receptionist?"

"Not yet, but I'm planning on doing that the next time he comes to the downtown office."

"That's so nice of you," Holly said, stroking Turk's arm. "Gwynn, do you want to see any more?"

She shook her head. "No, I've seen enough."

They headed down the hill. Gwynn opened the truck door. "Are you bored in there?" she asked Dave, scooting into the backseat.

"No. I've been busy staring at the woods. I should've brought some binoculars."

"I've got some," Turk said, reaching into his glove compartment and pulling out a pair. He handed them to Dave. "Here. I got that pair right after I looked through Gwynn's at the ranch, the ones she uses for bird watching. They're 8 by 56, just like hers."

"Driving here, I wished I had taken mine," Gwynn said. "Even though I didn't see any birds near the highway, we might run into some interesting ones around here."

Dave looked through Turk's binoculars. "They sure are clear. Gwynn, I see a bird on that electrical pole."

"Let me look," she said and Dave handed her the binoculars. "It's a bluebird. I haven't seen one of those since I arrived in New Mexico."

Starting the engine, Turk said, "Susan wants to see what a storage tank looks like. I'm going to the Bamberg battery." He glanced over his shoulder. "You doing okay back there, buddy?"

"Yeah."

Turk drove back to the paved road and headed south for half-a-mile and turned left onto a well maintained gravel road, with no potholes or bumpy ridges. He pulled into a clearing between six storage tanks. Three stood on each side with a wide space between them, large enough for a tanker truck to make a U-turn.

Everyone piled out except for Dave. "Those three belong to the Cisco unit," Turk explained, motioning to the ones on our left. "The oil from the well we were at flows into one of those tanks."

"They're huge," Holly said, walking around one.

Gwynn moved to the other side of the tanks, looking for something that was out of place, like a flow line from the north going into the tanks on the south or reverse, but she couldn't see anything that obvious. She wondered if she could spot anything through the binoculars and went back to the truck. Dave held them against his eyes, searching for birds.

"Dave when you're through, can I see the binoculars?" Gwynn said. "There's a bird on the pole off to your right. I want to get a better look."

Dave lowered the binocular. "Sure," he said, handing them to her through the opened window.

"Thanks." She moved closer to the pole, raised the binoculars to her eyes and saw the bird perched on it. "It's a hawk. I want to check for birds in the trees off in the distance. Can I keep the binoculars for a few minutes?"

"Be my guest."

Gwynn headed to the other side of the storage tanks and scanned the area through the binoculars. She noticed something shiny among the trees and focused on it. A man partially hidden in the foliage, held a rifle with the barrel aimed toward them. "Get on the other side of the truck!" she yelled, sprinting to it. "Dave duck down!"

"What?" Turk said as he hustled with Holly around the tailgate.

"Look there," Gwynn said, handing Turk the binoculars and swinging her fingers toward the junipers.

"I don't see anything," he said.

"Let me see," Holly said and took the binoculars. "Someone is in that group of trees over there and pointing a rifle in this direction."

"Let me see them again," Turk said, grabbing the binoculars. "I still can't see anything."

"Give me the binoculars," Dave said, loudly from inside the truck.

Turk cautiously moved toward the windows, staying below the hood of the truck and slid them through the window.

"I see it," Dave said. "But the person is behind that branch. I can't even make out if it's a man or a woman. Turk, do you have your rifle in here somewhere?"

"The toolbox." Turk lowered the tailgate, leaned forward and keeping low, edged into the truck bed.

A shot rang out, followed by a clanging sound. The aluminum siding on a small storage building a hundred feet away fluttered and Gwynn saw the indentation left by the bullet.

"Oh, shit!" Turk yelled, lying in the truck bed.

"Turk, stay put," Gwynn said. "I'm getting us out of here. Where are your keys?"

"In the ignition."

Holly zigzagged over to the small shed.

"Susan, where are you going?" Dave yelled from the backseat.

Holly dropped to the ground. "I'm hiding," she said in a quivering voice.

Gwynn jumped into the driver's seat and started the vehicle.

"Susan, get in the truck!" Dave shouted.

"I'm so scared," Holly said as she sprinted to the truck and leapt into the passenger seat.

"Buckle up," Gwynn said. "Turk, hold on."

Gwynn backed the truck up, flipped it around and drove a half a mile away from the storage tanks and stopped. She flung open her door and stepped out of the Silverado while Holly sat trembling in the passenger seat.

Turk opened his tool box, pulled out a rifle and a box of bullets. He slammed it shut, jumped out of the bed and closed the tailgate.

"That had to be the same guy that shot at Gwynn and me," Dave said, poking his head out the window. "But he didn't spray us with bullets like last time. Maybe that was because of the storage tanks. I'm calling Sam." He yanked his cell phone out of his pocket.

"Shouldn't you be calling Detective Marsden?" Gwynn asked.

"Sam can relay on the info. His number is programmed into my cell phone." Dave zoomed through his cell phone's contact list and clicked buttons.

"I need to make a call, too," Turk said and walked ahead of the Silverado as he stuck his hand in his pant pocket and lifted out his cell phone.

While Gwynn listened to Dave's report to Young, she went around to the other side of the truck. Her eyes swept over the surrounding area for any signs of movement and opened Holly's door. "Are you okay?" she asked, knowing Holly had been playing the role of a damsel in distress.

"I don't know," she said, biting her lower lip. "That was so scary."

"Compared to the time Dave and I were shot at before, that was mild," Gwynn said. "But I probably won't be able to sleep tonight."

Dave tucked his phone back in his pocket. "Sam's on his way."

"When you were talking to him, you mentioned something about the prior shooting," Gwynn said. "Have they got a lead?"

"They've discovered which company truck was used."

"What was that?" Turk asked, approaching the Silverado with a worried expression. "They know who did the shooting?"

"Soil samples. They checked all the tires. Only one truck had soil on it that matched."

"Whose?" Turk asked.

"Sam wouldn't say."

"Does he want us to wait here for him?" Gwynn asked.

"No. He has to contact Detective Marsden. I described the location where we saw the shooter. Sam wants us to stay away from the area until Marsden and his men have had a chance to check it out."

"Did you call Ash?" Dave asked Turk.

"Yes, but he didn't answer. I left a message," Turk said.

Gwynn doubted that was true unless he placed two calls. She had seen his lips moving and pausing like he was carrying on a conversation with someone.

Turk got into the driver's seat and put his hand on Holly's knee. "You okay?"

She fidgeted with her fingers. "Better."

"You could probably use a stiff drink."

"Yeah. I could. A double."

Fifty minutes later, Gwynn and Holly were dropped off. Holly and Turk had made plans to go out later.

Inside the house, Holly reached in her pocket and pulled out the bullet she had snatched from the ground next to the small storage shed. "I want to compare this bullet to one from the other shooting."

"You have one?"

"Paul retrieved five from Dave's truck. We kept one."

"You don't think the shooter was Brad?"

"No. He might not be the smartest guy in town, but he isn't the dumbest. Since Turk chewed him out and 'the man' wasn't happy about the prior shooting, he'd have to be a complete idiot to try it again. I'm not saying that isn't possible, but it isn't likely."

"I don't get it. From what Dave said, the police have identified the truck, Brad's truck and they haven't questioned him about it."

"Maybe they have," Holly said, placing the bullet under one side of a comparison microscope. She pulled out another bullet from a bag on the table and put it on the other side.

"But then why wouldn't Young tell Dave whose truck?"

"I suspect the cops are going after a search warrant for Brad's place. If that's the case, Young shouldn't have said anything to Dave about the truck. People talk." Holly leaned down, looked through the microscope and saw the bullets side by side. "These weren't shot by the same rifle."

"Can I see?" Gwynn asked.

"Sure."

Gwynn peered into the microscope. "Even I can see that and I've only had an hour class on forensic ballistics."

"Brad still could've been the second shooter and used a different weapon. Does anyone else come to your mind?"

"Maybe today's shooting was for Turk's benefit," Gwynn said, "hoping he'd believe it was Brad and go after him. Turk could have mentioned he retrieved a pistol at the storage building to someone, another accomplice—someone else whose fingerprints are on the canister."

"I'll see if Turk has anything he wants to get off his mind tonight?" Holly picked up her cell phone and punched a number. "Coming now." She disconnected and held up the bullet. "I'm running this bullet out to Paul so he can take it to the battery site. The shooter would have already searched for it, so it will be safe there for the police to find."

Shortly after dinner, Holly left to meet Turk and Gwynn decided to work on a summary of known facts in the case and speculations.

At 8 p.m., Ruben called Gwynn's cell phone and to support her cover, he played the role of Ross, her fiancé. They talked like lovers and expressed how they really felt about each other. In case her phone was being tapped, the listening would indeed believe she was engaged. Before the call ended, he said, "Say hello to your cousin for me. I can't call you tomorrow night because I have a meeting at 7 p.m." Ruben stressed the time.

Gwynn wondered if that meant anything as she said goodnight and hung up. She was getting ready to go to bed when Holly walked through the front door. "How did it go?" she asked, walking out of the bathroom.

"Couldn't get him to say too much, but he definitely was upset about something. I did learn that Brad has not been questioned again by the cops. They only talked to him when they talked to the other guys with company trucks."

"Ruben called."

"Did you talk to him on an N-phone?"

"No. He called as my fiancé, but he did say something strange after he wanted me to say hi to my cousin from him."

"What did he say?"

"That he couldn't call me tomorrow night because he had a meeting at seven. That's the first time he's mentioned a specific time."

"He wants us to call him at seven." Holly turned on her computer.

"There's one more thing I want to research before then."

"I want to check on the GOR's, that's the Gas-Oil-Ratio, for the Lander unit and try to determine if it's possible that unit could have that much production. I also want to go out and walk the flow lines to see if I can figure anything out there, but now that will have to wait until after we've talked to Ruben.

CHAPTER 29

Hayes was talking to Marilyn when Gwynn and Holly walked in. After Gwynn introduced Susan to Hayes, she went with him into his office.

"Marilyn filled me in about the shootings," Hayes said. "Working for Prudell is becoming dangerous for you. Don't go out in the field anymore until the person responsible for the two shootings is behind bars."

"I won't," Gwynn replied, shaking her head with her hands clasped on her lap.

Hayes leaned forward, resting his elbows on his desk. "Getting back to work, were you able to find out anything enlightening about the workovers?"

Gwynn briefed him on how Dave had discovered she was looking at them. When she had mentioned Hayes' concern to him, Dave decided to check into the production problem.

"I had planned on discussing it with either him or Ashton when I got back in town. Whatever is going on, it's not an accounting problem. What does Dave think about it?"

"He suspects something isn't right."

"Was that the reason you went out to a Cisco well site?"

Gwynn bobbed her head up and down. "Yeah."

He rubbed his chin. "I wonder if that was the reason you were shot at."

"That's what I'm thinking."

"Besides that problem," Hayes said, "did anything else arise while I was gone?"

Gwynn proceeded to tell him how the work-week went.

Shortly after lunch, Marsden and Young came to interview Holly and Gwynn about the shooting. They talked to each of them separately. During the interviews, Marsden claimed they had a prime suspect, and they were getting close to bringing in that person, but he wouldn't give any additional information.

At 6:55 p.m., Holly hooked up her N-phone to her laptop while Gwynn got two bottles of water out of the fridge and sat them on the table. Holly placed the call.

Ruben answered, "Right on time."

Gwynn looked at his image on the screen and wished she could touch him.

Ruben's eyes glowed as he smiled at her. "Gwynn, let's begin with you. What did you find out about the purchase agreements?"

"The oldest ones were Kevin Whitehead's purchases from numerous interest owners. He bought 40% of the ownership interest in all the wells in the Lander unit for $380,000. Those agreements were executed four to six months before Boden's death. A month after Whitehead acquired that interest, he sold a portion of it to Boden, Carlsen, Williams and Drumlin, giving them each an eight percent interest in the wells."

"How much did they pay?" Ruben asked.

"Each paid a hundred thousand."

"Boden sold a portion of his to Hayes for seventy thousand," Ruben commented, raising his brow. "He recouped 70% of his investment for 37.5% of his interest. Not a bad profit."

"Two weeks later, out of Whitehead's remaining interest of eight percent, he sold a portion to Ralph Hunter and Janice Robinson really cheap. Hunter paid $500 for a two-percent ownership interest and Robinson paid twenty dollars for a half percent."

Ruben jotted down notes.

Gwynn continued, "Checking in the computer system, I discovered Ashton Prudell acquired his five-percent personal interest in those wells seven years earlier."

"Anything else?"

"When I pulled out the documents from Hayes' file cabinet, I didn't realize the bottom one wasn't a purchase agreement. It probably doesn't have anything to do with Boden's death, but I found it interesting."

"What was it?"

"A child support agreement between Hayes and Robinson. It had been drawn up by an attorney, so she wasn't blackmailing him. It accounts for the routine, consistent payments he made to her."

"That is interesting." Ruben rubbed his chin with his knuckles. "When will the payments end?"

"On Patrick's eighteenth birthday. There wasn't anything in the document about college expenses or any other payments outside of that."

"How old is he now?"

"Sixteen, but I don't know his birth date." Gwynn took a sip of water.

"Were you able to do the research on the GOR's you mentioned last night?"

"It was difficult, since today was Hayes' first day back in the office, but I managed to complete a spreadsheet based on that information and the gas production. The results were the same as the Cisco unit, except going the opposite direction. Unless the GOR's are wrong, the Lander unit wells couldn't have produced that much oil."

"Anything more?"

"No. You know everything else." Gwynn propped her elbows on the table and linked her fingers together.

"Holly, what did you discover during your research on Saturday?"

Holly looked at her notepad. "Boden's will was signed three months before his death. All of his assets go to Janice Robinson. He has a brother who's contesting the will on the grounds Boden owed him some money. It appears it is slowing down the process, but currently his brother has not been able to present any documentation about the debt.

"The same attorney who drew up Boden's will also did one for Drumlin and it was executed at the same time. All Drumlin's assets go to his two children, except his interest in the Lander unit wells, which goes to Kevin Whitehead. As of Saturday, no one was contesting the will, so his estate should be settled soon."

Ruben's eyes dropped and he glanced at a document. "Eight percent goes to Whitehead. That makes his total interest in that unit thirteen-and-three-quarters percent. Go on."

"Kevin Whitehead is a landman for Brawny Oil and Gas Company, located in Farmington. He's been with that company for three years and before that he worked for a company in Texas."

"What's a landman?" Ruben asked.

"Gwynn," Holly said, lifting her bottle of water.

"A person who negotiates with landowners for drilling leases, land options, pooling agreements, stuff like that," Gwynn said.

"Obtaining the interest in the Lander unit was right up his alley," Holly commented. "Whitehead has been married twice."

"Any children?" Gwynn asked.

"No." Holly flipped over the page. "He doesn't have any type of police record, has good credit and little debt, an upstanding citizen. Gwynn mentioned that Whitehead and Ashton Prudell had glared at each other at Marty's. I checked if they had any history and discovered Whitehead had attended the same university as Ashton Prudell. They were in the same class and in the same fraternity. That's where Prudell acquired a police record, so I dug deeper. At the fraternity house one night a girl overdosed. Prudell and some of the other guys ended up spending the night in jail. The next day they all got bailed out. Prudell beat the rap, but it was a complicated case—an attorney, court appearances and the process dragged on for months."

"How was Whitehead involved?" Ruben asked.

"I was getting to that. Based on Prudell's statement, he had returned to the fraternity house when the cops were there, after the girl was dead. Prudell's car had been parked behind the building all evening. He claimed he had taken a drive, because he had just broken up with his girlfriend, to clear his head. Whitehead had loaned him his car because Prudell's was blocked by other vehicles. Whitehead insisted that never happened and he was the one driving around, not Prudell. Prudell had no witnesses so the cops took Whitehead's story as being accurate since it was his car. Whitehead was off scot-free without ever being booked. But I suspect somehow Prudell got even with him because Whitehead left that university shortly after the case was settled. Prudell graduated."

"That explains the glaring," Gwynn said.

"It might even go deeper than that." Holly turned to another page in her notepad. "I did a little more research on Prudell. His wife, Bridget, was raised in Texas and moved to Bloomfield after she married him. They might have met at some oil function, because her brother is the CEO of Critten Energy Company, the company Whitehead worked for in Texas. I haven't been able to locate any information as to why he left there four years ago."

"You're thinking that Prudell might have played a role in his departure?" Ruben asked.

"Just speculation, but yes."

"Moving on. What did you find out about the emails?"

"I got the location of the IP for the email address I acquired at Robinson's. It's in the condo building where Whitehead lives. Before I read a couple of the emails, I thought he was the one calling the shots, now I'm at a loss."

"What did they say?"

"Patrick's responses: 'He says you can't have that yet.' 'Any more trouble you'll never get it.' 'He doesn't like the way you did that.' Snippy. That just isn't how you would respond to 'the man.'"

"Good point. What had Whitehead requested in the emails?"

"Documents. They were short: 'Need number 5.' 'When will you have 4 ready?' Probably codes they had made up so not very much info would be sent across the airwaves. I'm going back into Patrick's email to see if I can find an email that might lead me to 'the man'."

"Ashton?" Gwynn asked. "Holly, remember Dave saying he thought Ashton felt guilty about his injury. And he seemed pretty friendly with Janice that one evening. Maybe it was because her son is working on a project for him. Even if he had earlier problems with Whitehead, maybe they reconciled and the glaring at each other had something to do with what's going on. Ashton's fingerprints were on the canister, he had the workover documents, the other guys work for him and the company wouldn't suffer because the company gets fifty-one percent of everything."

"It isn't Ashton Prudell," Ruben said, firmly.

A light bulb went off in Gwynn's head, Ashton Prudell was the client. Since most of Ruben's clients wanted to remain anonymous, he only shared that information with the one of his top investigators. Even Holly wasn't that high up in his organization.

"Anything else, Holly?" Ruben asked.

"No. That brings you up to speed. What did you find out about the fingerprints I sent you?"

"Whitehead's prints matched a set from the canister. Carlsen's prints didn't. Drumlin's, Williams' and Whitehead's were among those you lifted from the safety masks."

"Should I get more?" Holly asked.

"Not yet." Ruben thumbed through his notebook. "This investigation has to be over in a week."

Holly and Gwynn glanced at each other.

Ruben continued, "I have other assignments waiting for both of you."

That brought a smile to Gwynn's face.

"This is how we are going to proceed. Bev's flying in for a few days. She'll be going with Paul. Paul, are you listening?"

Bev was one of Ruben's employees whom Gwynn had been with on a previous investigation.

Then came a deep baritone voice, "Right here, boss."

"You two will be investigators."

"I think I can play that role," Paul said, chuckling.

"The company name will be Strait's Investigations. Paul you'll be Max Strait and Bev will be Betty Kent. Have a few business cards printed in Farmington. You'll talk to Turk Carlsen. He appears like he's ready to break. Gwynn, Bev is about the same size you are. I want Carlsen to believe she was the one that broke into the woodshed.

"Paul, Bev will make first contact and set up an appointment under the façade of a proposed settlement of Boden's life insurance policy. She'll make an excuse and apology for being so late contacting him."

"Will Carlsen believe Boden would name him as the beneficiary?" Paul asked.

"They were best friends since elementary school, went off to college together and were roommates until Boden dropped out. Carlsen will buy it. Bev's setting up an office at the place we talked about earlier. She'll call Carlsen from there and try to make an appointment with him for Wednesday. Tell Carlsen you know about the canister. Even if his prints aren't on it, he knows about it. Paul, you and Bev can proceed however you want. When you're through, you should have acquired everything he knows about Boden's death. If it involves the Cisco and Lander units, get that information also. Meet Bev there tomorrow evening to go over your strategy."

"Any restrictions?" Paul asked.

"No, but I don't want him to leave needing medical attention. After Carlsen has been interviewed, Holly and Paul will be federal agents. Do you both have your badges with you?"

"Yes," Holly and Paul said in unison.

"Holly, wear the padding."

She wrinkled her nose. "Do I have to? I hate looking thirty pounds heavier."

"Yes. You're going to question Patrick. In case he describes his visitors to anyone, I don't want one of them to resemble Susan."

"Got it," Holly said.

"You're going to tell him you know about his hacking and the feds have known for a while. Scare him. Tell him if he tells who he's providing the information to, he won't be brought in—something like that. He's a kid. He won't know about his rights. Make up whatever you want."

"Where and how should we approach him?" Paul asked.

"Just show up at his house. He is supposedly on his computer every minute he's not in school. It shouldn't be hard to catch him at home. Take him to the same office space used to question Carlsen."

"Is there anything I should do?" Gwynn asked.

"Keep Janice in her salon during the time they're with Patrick. If she discovers Patrick isn't home and his car's there, it could cause problems when he's being dropped off. Any questions?"

Gwynn and Holly shook their head. "No."

"Gwynn, call your fiancé on the regular cell phone after Holly and Paul have questioned Patrick. Tell him Susan has a new boyfriend. Then I'll be expecting a call on the N-phone in one hour or 7 p.m., whatever is later."

"Okay," Gwynn said.

"Talk to you all then," Ruben said and clicked off.

CHAPTER 30

Two police cruisers were parked out in front of the building when Gwynn and Holly returned from lunch.

"I don't like the looks of this," Holly commented. "Why don't you go in and find out what's going on. I'm going to stay in your car."

Gwynn was well aware that Ruben never liked to get the police involved with any of his investigations, and she had been questioned twice about shootings and Holly once. She couldn't imagine the police were here because of something they had done, but Holly did break into Robinson's house in broad daylight.

The foyer buzzed with activity. Two uniformed police officers, Marsden, Young and Ashton were all talking at the same time. Marilyn and Debra were running around gathering documents and copying them.

Gwynn caught up with Marilyn in the file room. "What's going on?"

"Brad Williams. The police went to bring him in last night for questioning; something to do with the shooting at the well and he was gone. Someone else has been shot, but I don't know who or any details. Detective Marsden wants all the personal information we have on Brad."

"He was gone? They couldn't find him? Had he packed up and left town?"

"I don't know," Marilyn said, grabbing a pile of copies. "They need these." She hurried back into the lobby.

Gwynn stood there for a minute, staring at the copy machine. *Shot, who?*

She moved past the talking group and headed to the Mustang for Holly. "They're here about Brad Williams. He's missing." Gwynn relayed all the information she had obtained from Marilyn.

"He shot someone?" Holly asked, squinting.

"Yeah."

"When we get inside, I'll hang around your desk, listening."

As they entered, a police officer's head swung around and he gazed at Holly until she stopped at Gwynn's desk and turned away from him.

"Some guys just can't keep their mind on business," Holly said.

"I'm going to look up how much Brad had currently been paid on his interest in the Lander unit to find out if he had enough to disappear for a while," Gwynn said.

"Go ahead. I'll just stand here and pretend we're talking about something."

Gwynn punched on her keyboard until she reached the screen where Williams' name appeared. She clicked on it and went to the column that showed accumulative distributions. "He has enough to hide for at least five, six years, maybe longer if he makes good investments."

"Is he paid by check?" Holly asked.

Gwynn clicked through a few more sites. "No. It's electronic fund transfers to his bank. The bank name isn't here, but the routing number and his account number are."

"Print the screen or write it down," Holly said.

Gwynn pushed the print key. When the sheet came out of her printer, she handed it to Holly. "Have you been able to pick up a name yet?" she asked, referring to the person shot.

"No. But it's a he and he works for Prudell."

"Turk?"

"That's who I'm thinking. I'm going to the conference room and do a little snooping on the company's computer."

Gwynn's attention turned to the men in the lobby. Now, the only one speaking was Young. "Ash, we'll let you know as soon as we learn anything about his whereabouts. In the meantime, I'm going to have the area around here patrolled until the security cameras are installed in this building."

"They didn't prevent the shooting," Ashton commented, his features lined with concern.

"No, but they did help Karl. Don't worry, we'll get him," Young said and walked out with the other men.

The only Karl who worked for the company was Karl Lee, the guy who takes care of the storage building and does other miscellaneous jobs. *He was shot? Why*? Gwynn rose to her feet and went over to Ashton. "What happened?"

"It's a mess," Ashton said, leaning an elbow on the counter. Marilyn stood listening on the other side. "The police wanted to question Brad Williams about his truck, the company one. Apparently, the tire treads and dirt around the rim match those found near the location of the shooter, when Dave was shot. Brad wanted something out of the storage building. With our increased security, he didn't have the code to turn off the alarm system. He had Karl go with him there. Inside the building, Brad picked up a large bag stuffed in the back corner and Karl asked him what was in it. Brad went into a rage and pulled a pistol out of his belt and shot the poor kid."

"How's Karl doing?" Marilyn asked.

"He's stable. It's good those surveillance cameras were being monitored."

"Where was he shot?" Gwynn asked.

"His stomach."

"Can I go and visit him?" Marilyn asked.

"No. Only family for now."

"Do you want me to send flowers?"

"Yes, a nice bouquet."

During the afternoon, Gwynn had attempted to talk to Holly, but each time she headed in that direction she saw Ashton in the conference room.

At 5 p.m., Gwynn and Holly walked out the main doors. "Do you want to go to Marty's?" Gwynn asked.

"No. I want to do some more research." She smiled. "Marty's will just have to survive without us tonight. I know it will be hard on the guys, but then they'll be more excited to see us tomorrow."

"Do you think the place will still be standing after we're gone?" Gwynn said, teasingly.

"As sad as it is, they'll be other babes to take our place." Holly looked around. "Where are you going?

"Grocery store. We need milk."

Gwynn glanced out her side mirrors. "I don't see a motorcycle anywhere around. Has Paul deserted us for Bev?"

"Fraid so. Paul called right before quittin' time and said he was going to have dinner with Bev. She's set up the appointment with Turk for tomorrow afternoon."

"How does he call you?"

"On my regular cell phone. I recognize his number. He didn't talk in those exact words. He said something like—my girlfriend just came in town so I'm taking her to dinner since she has to leave tomorrow afternoon."

"Who does he say he is?"

"My brother, John."

"I wonder what my next role will be." Gwynn said, pulling into a parking lot.

An hour later, Gwynn stopped in front of the house and carried in a sack. Holly headed to the bedroom to change while Gwynn went out to bring in the rest of the groceries.

Gwynn bent down to get another bag out of the trunk when she was grabbed from behind and felt a pistol pressed against her head. "Stay quiet and you won't get hurt," the assailant said. He yanked her necklace off and threw it. "You won't be needing that."

Gwynn thought she could free herself, but there was a chance she could be injured in the scuffle, so she decided to wait for a better opportunity. He wanted something from her or she'd already be dead.

"Hands together," he ordered.

She stretched them out in front of her.

Keeping the pistol aimed at her head, he used his other hand to secure a plastic handcuff around her wrists. "This way." Brad nodded toward the foliage behind her. As she turned, he pushed the barrel of the gun into her back, shoved her between bushes and trees and led her through the woods to a company truck. "Get in and don't try any funny business."

She climbed in and he slammed the door.

Brad slid into the driver's seat and sped further up the road away from town, aiming the weapon at her all the time, without saying a word. Fifteen minutes later, he pulled down a dirt lane and stopped next to an abandoned house.

A green Dodge truck was parked on the other side of the

structure and Gwynn wondered who was waiting inside. Williams got out, moved around to the passenger door and jerked it open. "Get out."

He pushed her inside the house, to a folding chair that stood close to two others in front of a boarded up window.

Looking for the owner of the green truck, she scanned the barren, dirty room with an inch of dust covering the floor and an old table across the room. The door on the other side of the room was wide open. She expected someone to walk through that doorway. No one did. She perked up her ears and listened for any sign of another occupant. Nothing. "What do you want, Brad?"

"Information?"

"What information?"

"Why you're here? Who sent you? Where we can find them? You can either tell me or wait until someone else arrives."

"Who?"

He gave her a sinister smile. "Let's start with my questions." He yanked on her hair, forcing her head back. "I can see why Dave likes you. Are you any good in bed?"

"Is that part of the information you want?"

He gripped her jaw. "No, but it could buy you some more time."

"What do you mean by that?" she asked as a chill swept over her body.

"Figure it out. You can't be that dumb. Maybe you are, thinking your boyfriend actually cares about you, but never shows up. Are you really that fuckin' stupid?" His face darkened with rage.

Williams' cell phone chirped. He yanked it out of his pocket, glanced at the screen and answered it. "Why aren't you here?" He kept his eyes on Gwynn while he moved to the other side of the room. "She … yeah … I can handle that … I'm ready … later." Williams tucked the phone back into his pocket, strolling toward Gwynn. "Ain't never beat up a girl before," he confessed. "But you're responsible for the fix I'm in." He flung out his hand, hitting her across the face.

Gwynn pressed her lips together to suppress any moan from escaping. Her eyes moistened as the pain rippled through her jaw. "Brad, I don't know what you're talking about. I came to Bloomfield because I inherited my uncle's house; otherwise, I wouldn't be here. No one sent me. Honest." A tear trickled down her cheek.

"Then why did you break into the shed out at the ranch? Why were you checking out the production of the Cisco and Lander units? Why did you want Dave to take you there? Why did you take those workover files home?"

"I didn't break into any shed," she said, shaking her head. "What do you think I am? Some kind of a spy?"

He slugged her in the arm.

"Oww!" She rolled her shoulder and swallowed hard. "Why did you do that?" she asked in an uneven tone.

"Because you're a fuckin' liar."

"Alex asked me to look into that production," she sniffled. "He couldn't figure out why none of the Cisco unit wells production increased after the workovers. I mentioned it to Dave so he was going to check it out and I went with him. That was all. No big spy thing."

His eyes bore into hers. "What's wrong with that production?"

"I don't know."

"It's not going where it should," he said with a smirk, knowing she'd never be able to tell anyone.

"Why did you throw away my necklace? My fiancé gave that to me."

"Don't give me that lame excuse! It's a tracking device. You don't think I notice a motorcycle showing up whenever you're in trouble. That asshole was right behind me each time I chased you."

"Each time?"

"Yeah. In the rented Jeep and in Dave's truck."

"Rented Jeep?"

He slapped her face again, but not as hard as the first time.

Gwynn raised her bound hands and rubbed her cheek as she twisted her jaw.

"You know, we ain't stupid."

She took a deep breath. "Brad, I'll make you a deal."

"Go on."

"I'll answer your questions if you answer mine first."

He leaned down and glared at her. "What you wanna know?"

"Who killed Arne Boden?"

"So that's why you're here," he said, straightening his spine. "I knew we shouldn't have done it. Arne was a nice guy, but he broke the rule."

"What rule?"

He raised a corner of his upper lip.

"Who helped you kill him?" she pressed.

"Drumlin. You going after him?" he smirked.

"Anyone else?"

"Yeah. One more guy."

"Who?"

"That's enough. Who sent you?"

"One more question?"

"What?"

"Who's 'the man'?"

Brad clenched his jaw and raised his fist to swing at Gwynn. She leaned back and kicked him with both her legs, sending him stumbling backwards. She leapt to her feet while the chair tumbled to the floor.

"You bitch!" he yelled and lunged for her.

She went on the attack, clutched her bound hands together and knocked him on the side of his head at the same time as she swung a foot out, hitting him hard on his ankles. The floor creaked as he sprawled across it, landing on his back. Gwynn delivered a kick between his legs. Brad moaned, winced and curled up in pain. She didn't relent and struck a blow between his shoulder blades, forcing him down on the wood planks.

Gritting his teeth, he rolled over with the barrel of his gun aimed at her. She darted to the side as a bullet sailed past her, penetrating a crumbling, deteriorating wall. Gwynn bent down and yanked her Beretta from the holster under her pant leg while she watched Brad out of the corner of her eye. She leapt toward the desk just in time to avoid another bullet. It landed in the wall, sending debris through the room. Gwynn raised her weapon toward her assailant. "Put down the gun," she ordered.

He whirled his pistol toward her. She pressed the trigger.

Another slug spiraled into the air from Brad's weapon as he grabbed his chest. A horrible cry came from his throat. His gun dropped with a thud. His head smacked against the wooden floor.

Gwynn knelt next to him. Brad gripped her arm for a second and then his hand fell to his bloody chest. She touched his neck, searching for a pulse and briefly closed her eyes. Gwynn knew she couldn't linger since any minute someone would be arriving. She fished in Brad's pocket for the truck keys and his cell phone. She hurried to the Silverado, climbed into the driver's seat and drove away from what was planned to be her final destination.

As she headed toward the house with her hands still bound, Gwynn glanced at every vehicle she passed that was traveling up the road, wondering if it belonged to 'the man.' Not one looked familiar and they zoomed by too fast for her to get a good glimpse at any of the faces.

When the truck pulled into the driveway, Holly spotted Gwynn behind the wheel, charged out the house and ran toward it. She pulled open the driver's door. "What happened?" she said, her brows creased with worry.

Gwynn inhaled deeply and turned toward Holly.

"Oh, my God!" Holly yelled, seeing Gwynn's bruised face.

"I'll explain everything later. We need to get the truck back," Gwynn said. "Get in my car and follow me, but first can you cut this?" She held up the plastic handcuff, securing her hands together.

"My knife's in the house and so are the car keys," Holly said and sprinted up to the porch. A couple of second later, she came out carrying a pair of snippers and locked the door. "I thought these would be faster." She clipped the handcuff. "I need to call Paul." Holly punched in his number. "She's here… okay… tell you later." She clicked off.

With her hands free, Gwynn turned the Silverado around while Holly climbed into the Mustang. She drove back to the abandoned house. The only vehicle outside was the green truck she had seen earlier. Gwynn stopped in the same spot where Williams had parked and hurried to her car. "Open the trunk." She took out wet wipes and returned to the truck.

"Who brought you here?" Holly asked as she helped Gwynn wipe down the cab.

"Brad Williams."

"Where is he?"

"Inside," she said, nodding toward the house. "Dead. We need to hurry. He was expecting company."

"Were you in the backseat?"

"No."

"How about in the house?"

"Only a chair. I can take care of it." Gwynn rushed inside, quickly wiped off the chair lying on the floor and tried to avoid looking at Williams' body surrounded by a puddle of blood.

Within five minutes, Gwynn and Holly were in the Mustang and heading back to the house.

"What happened?" Holly asked

"Brad grabbed me when I was getting groceries out of the trunk."

"You couldn't get away?"

"Not without possibly getting shot."

"Then you did the wise thing and waited for the right time." Holly looked at Gwynn's face. "That didn't happen until he slapped you around?"

"No," Gwynn said, even though she knew she could have taken him earlier, but she wanted information.

"It's too bad we're not closer to Dr. Kozlov," Holly said. "He'd take care of those bruises."

"His miracle cream," Gwynn said, remembering having it applied to her face and waking up without a black and blue mark anywhere.

"I wish he'd sell it," Holly said. "Go on. Tell me what happened next."

"He took me to that place and wanted to know who had sent me to Bloomfield. I told him the cover story. Nothing more. But he did confess to the murder of Boden."

"We need to call Ruben the minute we step into your house." Holly drove along the driveway. "I'll put the speaker on and you can tell us both everything at the same time. Your necklace is on the table."

"You found it?" Gwynn said, getting out of the car.

"It wasn't hard with the GPS." Holly unlocked the door.

"Are you going to hook up the N-phone to your computer?" Gwynn asked, filling a plastic bag with ice cubes.

"No. Ruben won't be expecting the call, so he won't be in front of a webcam." Holly poured two cups of coffee and sat them on the table. "You could probably use something stronger, but I just made this before you showed up."

"Does Ruben know I was missing?"

"No. Paul's been driving around with Bev looking for you."

"Where?"

"Any place you've gone in town. They were headed out to the well. We thought it would be better if I stayed here in case the cops or someone came by with news about your whereabouts." She took a sip of coffee and then picked up the N-phone.

Gwynn's hands trembled as she added sugar, stirred her coffee and took a drink. She leaned her elbow on the table, raised the ice bag in her palm and rested her cheek on it.

"What went wrong?" were the first words out of Ruben's mouth.

"Brad Williams was going to be picked up last night by the cops for questioning—the tire match. He took off," Holly said. "They couldn't find him, but he found Gwynn."

"Is she missing?" Ruben asked, sounding upset.

"She was for a while," Holly said, "but she's here now."

"Why didn't you call me?"

"It was before seven. Paul and Bev went looking for her and I stayed here. We were going to call you and then she showed up."

"Are we on speaker?"

"Yes."

"Gwynn, what happened?"

"I was taking groceries out of the car and Williams grabbed me. He held a gun against my head. The way he was holding me, I couldn't get away without possibly being shot."

"You followed procedures and waited for a better opportunity."

"Yes. I figure he wanted information based on what was said in the storage building. Otherwise, he would have just shot me."

"I just tapped into the surveillance camera. Move your face around. Look at the cabinets."

Gwynn followed his instructions.

"Explain. Start with why you weren't wearing your brooch."

"Williams yanked it off my neck, threw it into the bushes and told me I wouldn't need it."

"Did you discover his reason while you were held captive?"

"Yes."

"What happened after he grabbed you and tossed your brooch?"

"He put a plastic handcuff on my wrists and took me to an abandoned house. There he wanted to know why I was in Bloomfield and who sent me. I told him the cover story—nothing more."

"Were your arms and feet tied to a chair after you arrived at the house?"

"No."

"And you never had an opportunity to escape until after he had slugged you? Raise your head." Ruben studied her face. "He hit you more than once. Between those slaps and punches you never had a chance to get out of there?" he said, sounding doubtful.

Gwynn shook her head. "No, boss, I didn't."

The line went silent for ten seconds. "What did you find out while you were under his control and unable to escape?" he asked.

Gwynn knew he wasn't buying her story. "I found out that he was one of the people responsible for Boden's death. There were three guys. Another one was Drumlin. Williams wouldn't tell me the name of the third. Williams was expecting someone else to come to the house. That person called him on his cell phone while I was there. I snatched his cell phone when I left."

"Have you got it now?"

Gwynn pulled it out of her pocket and held it up. "Right here."

"Does it have a GPS?"

"I don't think so. The police could have located him if it did."

"Holly, check it."

Gwynn pressed her lips together, hoping she hadn't screwed up again. When she took it, she hadn't even thought about GPS.

Holly examined it. "No GPS."

Gwynn sighed.

"Did you find out anything else?" Ruben asked.

"Williams thought my necklace was a tracking device because each time he chased me in the Silverado he noticed a motorcycle behind him."

"Each time? So he knows you rented the Jeep?"

"I told him he only chased me once. He smiled like he didn't believe me and didn't say anything else about it. The Jeep must have just been a guess." Gwynn didn't want Ruben to know that she hadn't covered her tracks well enough when she rented the vehicle.

"Normally, Paul never gets spotted, but it's difficult during a car chase and impossible on a two-lane, sparsely travelled highway. Also, I'd told him to stay close so Williams could have seen him on other occasions. Any other discoveries?"

"No."

"After you escaped, how did you get back to the house?"

"In Williams' company truck," Gwynn said, timidly.

"What aren't you telling me?"

"I struggled with Williams when I was trying to get away. He kept firing his pistol at me. I shot him. He's dead."

"With your gun?"

"Yes. He never searched me for weapons."

"Did you also have your knife?"

Gwynn hesitated. "Yes."

"I want to make sure I have this straight," Ruben said with an edge to his voice. "You had your weapons after you had been captured. You were not tied to a chair. Only your hands were bound and you never had an opportunity to escape until after he had slugged you around and you had acquired some information. Have I got that right?"

"Yes, boss. That's how it was." Gwynn could feel him fuming. At the same time she knew her story was feasible, not likely and only slightly possible, but with enough room for doubt. She met Holly's eyes, squinting at her and saw she didn't believe it either.

Holly broke the silence. "What should we do with Williams' body?"

"Nothing," Ruben responded. "Whoever he was expecting has already arrived. He's either called the cops or he's disposing of the body. Gwynn, did you fire more than one shot?"

"No."

"You need to change weapons. Don't carry that gun any more on this assignment. Understood?"

"Yes."

"Where's Williams' truck?"

"Holly followed me back to the abandoned house," Gwynn said. "We removed the fingerprints and left it there."

"Did you take care of your prints inside the house?"

"Yes. Everything I touched got wiped off."

"Now we need to be more vigilant. The third guy knows Gwynn got away, but he doesn't know she was the one who shot Williams. Since Williams knew about Paul, I suspect the third man does too. Holly, check the last call Williams answered and tell me if it's Whitehead?"

Holly punched the cell phone. "There's only a number. No name. I can quickly research it on my computer. Do you want to wait on the phone when I do it or should I call you back?"

"Call me back in half an hour," Ruben said. "While you're at it, also skim through his other calls, see if you run across someone unfamiliar."

"Should I be doing anything?" Gwynn asked.

"Lie down and cover your face with ice packs while I plan how we'll proceed." Ruben disconnected.

Holly headed to her computer. Gwynn put ice cubes into another plastic bag, stretched out on the couch and covered her cheeks with them. "Do you think Ruben is mad at me?" she asked.

"What do you think?" Holly asked as she clicked away on her keyboard.

"Yes." Gwynn was well aware of Ruben's main rule: never put yourself in harm's way unless there was no way you could prevent it, and then get away as fast as you can. She knew Ruben's organization handled numerous dangerous investigations, but everything was carefully laid out, minimizing potential harm to any of his employees. Suffering with her freezing face, she hoped he'd forgive her transgressions.

"I can't stand this anymore," Gwynn said, pulling off the ice bags. She felt her cheeks. "My face is frozen in place. I don't think I'm even going to be able to smile."

"Just as well," Holly said, still working on the computer. "Right now, I'd say you don't have anything to smile about."

Gwynn rose, went into the bathroom and looked in the mirror. Bruises were on both cheeks and under her eyes. Her nose looked red. She wiggled it with her fingers. Nothing broken. She felt grateful it never bled; otherwise, she would have left DNA inside the abandoned house.

"Gwynn, it's time," Holly said from the kitchen.

Gwynn sat down across from Holly and watched Holly place the call.

Ruben answered, "What did you find out?"

"It was Whitehead's cell phone number. He had some unfamiliar cell numbers, but so far they belong to various women. A few of the names looked familiar. I might have heard them at Marty's."

"They're probably not important," Ruben said. "Who does he talk to the most?"

"Carlsen, followed by Whitehead, Dave and several to Robinson... Janice, not Patrick. I didn't run across one call to Ashton, Hayes or Hunter, the other interest owners in the Lander unit."

"Finish checking the other unfamiliar numbers and see if Carlsen called him after the shooting on Sunday, while you were parked on the gravel road.

"Good point," Holly said, "I'll do it right now." She went and grabbed the cell phone lying next to her computer. She returned to the table, tapping it. "Yes, he did and the call was received."

"He wasn't Sunday's shooter," Ruben said. "Carlsen probably knows who it was. Paul and Bev will get that information from him tomorrow. Gwynn, did you keep ice on your face?"

"As long as I could stand it."

"You're not going to be able to go to work tomorrow. The meeting with Carlsen isn't until the afternoon. This is how the day will go: Gwynn will call sick. Paul will stay with her during the morning while Holly goes to work. Holly, right after lunch you'll get ill—maybe you just caught whatever Gwynn has and go home. Once you arrive at work, stay in the building until you're going home."

Holly nodded. "Okay."

"Whitehead might think you helped Gwynn escape, seeing Williams grabbing her in front of the house and following them to the place."

"What about Paul?" Gwynn asked.

"Won't you protect him when he's there?" Ruben said, jokingly.

"Ruben, you know what I meant. The motorcycle."

"Paul won't be riding it any more during this investigation. No one has seen his face. He always wears a helmet. Let's move on to questioning Patrick. Gwynn, on Thursday you will have to go to work. Put on heavy make-up. I want you to stay there, inside the building, while Holly and Paul question Patrick. From your desk, call Janice and chat with her while Patrick is being picked up."

"How about when he's being dropped off?" Gwynn asked.

"Holly, you and Paul will have to play that by ear. If there is commotion around the Robinson house, drop him off down the street. Give him some kind of excuse."

"Got it. We'll come up with something," Holly said.

"That covers everything. Any questions?"

Gwynn shook her head and Holly said, "No."

After they hung up, Gwynn said, "Do you think he sounded mad?"

"No."

"Then I'm going to have something to eat. I'm starving."

CHAPTER 31

Gwynn applied a thick layer of make-up so she wouldn't look too awful when she met Paul. Afterwards, she sat in the kitchen enjoying a cup of coffee and watching Holly buzz around, getting ready to leave for work. The doorbell rang.

"I'll get it," Holly said.

Gwynn stood and walked to the doorway leading to the living room, feeling anxious to meet Paul, the man who had shadowed her since Drumlin's death. The man who watched her change clothes after the first break-in at the metal storage building. The man who chased Williams' truck while Williams chased her.

The door opened and Holly greeted a tall, broad-shouldered man with a dark-complexion and deep brown hair. As he stepped over the threshold, she said, "Like your buckle."

He touched the large silver, engraved belt buckle. "Got it in Bloomfield."

Gazing at his denim vest, Gwynn suspected it concealed a weapon.

"Gwynn, this is Paul," Holly said.

"Nice to finally meet you," Gwynn said.

Holly smiled at Paul. "You already know her."

"Sure, do."

"I need to get going," Holly said, heading out the door. "See you around one."

"Would you like some coffee?" Gwynn asked Paul.

"I could use another cup," he said, strolling into the kitchen.

"You hungry?"

"No. Just ate."

When they were both settled at the table with coffee, Gwynn asked, "How long have you worked for Ruben?"

"Eight years."

"What did you do before then?"

He gulped some coffee. "Best not to talk about that. Things in my past might make you feel uncomfortable."

Gwynn tried not to stare at him as she wondered what that was all about—*uncomfortable. Had he been in prison?* "I understand you're an expert at disguises."

"Yes, I am. Did you ever see me at Marty's?"

She scanned his face. "I can't recall ever seeing you before. Were you there?"

"Sure was. Sat with a gal at the table next to you one night, the night Dave had his leg on a chair, the night Janice's temper rose."

Gwynn thought for a minute and recalled seeing a couple at the table. The guy had light brown hair, wore glasses and was a little overweight. "That was you with the woman wearing a blue sweater."

"Sure was."

"How did you meet her?"

"Picked her up at the bar. Thought it would be better than sitting alone."

"You're right about that. Alone, guys at tables tend to stand out." She leaned an elbow on the table. "I'm sorry you had to give up your motorcycle."

"I didn't give it up. Just put it aside for a few days."

"Are you ready for Turk this afternoon?"

"Yep."

Feeling like she was interrogating him with the all the questions, Gwynn decided to sip her coffee and wait for him to speak.

He held up his mug and motioned toward the coffee machine. "Sure."

Paul filled her cup and his. They sat in silence as they both looked out the window and drank.

The doorbell rang, startling Gwynn.

She glanced at the clock. It read: 9:40 a.m. "Who could that be?" She headed toward the door with Paul right behind her, pulling a pistol out from under his vest.

He moved to the edge of it, against the wall, where he couldn't be seen from outside.

Gwynn slide the door curtain aside and saw Young. She latched the chain and eased the door open. "Hello, Officer Young," she said, her voice dragging to sound sick. "What can I help you with?"

"I tried to reach you at work," Young said. "I was sorry to hear you weren't feeling well."

"Thank you," she said, softly.

"Do you think you're up to answering a couple more questions about the shooting?"

"Not today." Her eyes moved behind him, looking for the detective. "Is Detective Marsden with you?"

"No. He asked me to check on a few things. It shouldn't take very long."

"I'm sorry, but I'm just not up to it." She gripped her stomach with her hands. "I've got to go. Sorry." Gwynn closed the door and loudly stomped out of the room.

Standing in the kitchen, she saw Paul looking through a small slit between the living room drapes.

Gwynn crept toward him. "Is he still there," she whispered.

Paul nodded.

Easing down on the couch, Gwynn pondered if he knew something about Williams getting shot or maybe the break-in at Robinson's house.

Five minutes later, Paul straightened up. "He's gone."

"Why do you think he was hanging around?"

"Talking to someone on his phone in the car."

"Got any ideas why he was here?"

Paul shook his head. "If it had anything to do with Williams' death, Holly would've called."

"Why?"

"Prudell. Someone there would have mentioned it."

Holly returned at 1:05 p.m., twenty minutes later than expected. Paul walked out the door to meet her just as a patrol car turned toward the house.

Gwynn adjusted the drapes, leaving them an inch open and watched Holly get out of her car and stand next to Paul.

Officer Young climbed out of his cruiser and approached them. "Holly, I missed you at work. I wanted to ask you a few more questions regarding the shooting," Young said, eyeing Paul.

Holly put her arm across her stomach and covered her mouth. "Officer Young, I just can't talk now."

Paul put his arm around her shoulder.

"And who are you?" Young asked Paul.

"Stan Woods, Holly's boyfriend."

"Not anymore," she mumbled through her cupped hand and pushed Paul's arm away. "I need to go in." She shuffled into the house.

"Are you staying in town?" Young asked Paul.

"Yeah."

"Where?"

"Just got in. Don't have a place yet."

"Where's your car?"

"Don't have one here. Got dropped off by a cab."

"Where's your luggage?"

Paul gestured toward the house. "Inside."

Young gave Paul a suspicious look as he climbed back into his cruiser. Paul went into the house.

"I need to get going." Paul said, looking out the crack in the drapes.

"How can I help?" Gwynn asked.

Paul saw the cruiser leave. "He's gone out the driveway, but I think he's lingering on the road. He's up to something. Holly, did you hear anything this morning?"

"Just that Williams is still missing and Karl Lee is doing better. How are you going to get out of here?"

"You two—grab a couple of towels and drive out the driveway, pretending to head to a clinic. When you reach the road, check for his patrol car. Then call me."

"Got it," Holly said as Gwynn ran to the linen closet and took a stack of towels.

Gwynn climbed behind the steering wheel and Holly scooted into the passenger seat. "Why the towels?" she asked, turning the key in the ignition.

"Remember, we're supposed to be sick. Can't keep anything down. It has to go somewhere."

As they moved onto the asphalt, they saw the cruiser. Gwynn drove toward town and noticed it following them.

Holly plucked her cell phone out of her purse. "How you doing, Babe? … Your friend's trying to get close to me. You have all the freedom and I'm stuck with him … sure, hon, call later." She clicked off.

"That one I got," Gwynn said with a smile.

"That wasn't too creative," Holly said. "But what can you do in a pinch? Turn left at the next intersection and drive around for ten minutes and then head back."

"What if Young shows up?"

"He probably will. Just tell him I threw up so we couldn't go to the clinic. Maybe we'll attempt it again later. Something like that."

As Holly stepped into the house, she asked, "What did you guys have for lunch?"

"Sandwiches," Gwynn said. "You didn't eat?"

"No. I was too sick to my stomach to get anything down," Holly said with a smile. She opened the fridge and pulled out lunch meats.

The front doorbell buzzed again.

"It's him," Holly said.

Gwynn went to the door. "Officer Young, can't the questions wait until tomorrow?" she asked, breathing slowly with droopy eyes.

"I saw you drive into town so I thought you were feeling better."

"Susan and I tried to go to the clinic, but she threw up all over—down her blouse and pants, so we came back. If the heaves slow down, we might try to go again."

"This will just take a minute."

"Not now."

"Can I talk to her boyfriend?"

"She kicked him out. He's gone."

"How?"

"Don't know. He didn't have a car. He walked down the driveway, carrying his duffle bag. You might be able to catch him on the road." Gwynn lowered her head and held onto her stomach. "I'm sorry, I need to lie down." She closed the door and walked out of the living room.

"If he rings that bell again," Gwynn whispered. "I'm going to motion through the window for him to get lost. I'm not opening that door again."

"He is definitely up to something. It's almost like he wants to come into the house. I could almost understand his curiosity if Williams had mentioned he got zapped at the door, but Williams wouldn't have told that to a police officer: I was trying to break-in and I got shocked. If Young had anything solid, like us breaking into

Robinson's, he would've showed up with another officer and brought one of us in, whether we were sick or not. We'll have to watch ourselves around him and see if he tips his hand."

"Are you going to work on anything this afternoon?"

"I still wonder how Janice can afford that house," Holly said. "What you told me she receives in child support wouldn't be enough to sustain Patrick and her. He drives a late model Civic and she has a Volvo."

"Maybe her salon does great business."

"Doubt it," Holly said. "I thought I'd do a little snooping and see if any of the other guys are also paying child support. It could have a bearing on someone needing more money."

"How are you planning on doing that?"

"Routine deposits, checks, stuff like that."

"If I watch television, will that bother you?" Gwynn asked.

"Not as long as it isn't too loud."

Holly stood and stretched. "I'm starting dinner."

"What did you find out?" Gwynn asked, sitting up straight on the couch.

"Janice does have another benefactor. Ashton Prudell."

Gwynn scrunched her face. "Really?"

Holly nodded. "Pays Janice a lot more than Hayes does."

"They've worked together for such a long time, you'd think somewhere along the line they'd share notes."

"It might not be child support she's getting from Prudell. The payments aren't the same amount or consistently timed."

"Ashton wouldn't have acted so sweet toward her at Marty's if she were blackmailing him. And Linda said they had a thing going."

"Blackmail seems unlikely. But if it is child support you would think that either Hayes or Prudell would've had the kid tested. Janice doesn't have a reputation for being a puritan."

"I suspect Hayes did check it out since he entered into a legal agreement with Janice. Maybe Prudell would rather pay than taking a chance of being exposed."

"Possibly. Prudell had only been married a short time when Patrick was born. While I'm cooking dinner, look at Hayes' agreement for the name of the law firm."

"Would they have it?"

"Maybe."

"When will we know how interviewing Turk went?"

"Paul will be here sometime this evening, but he won't be coming to the front door with Young possibly lurking around somewhere. Also, he'll be staying here until the investigation is over."

"Where will he sleep?"

"We'll figure it out."

When Gwynn and Holly were eating, they heard tapping on the back door.

CHAPTER 32

"That must be Paul," Holly said, standing and lifting her gun from her holster.

"Who's there?" she asked loudly, with her weapon raised.

Paul's voice came through the door, "It's your boyfriend."

Holly holstered her gun, unlocked the door, opened it and hugged Paul as he stepped in. Gwynn had assumed the boyfriend thing was just a cover, but now she wasn't sure.

"You hungry?" Holly asked.

"Just ate, but that meatloaf sure looks good. I could probably manage a small slice."

Holly smiled, loaded up a plate and placed it down in front of him. "What happened to your knuckles?" she said, rubbing them.

"The interview. I'll tell you about it after dinner."

"Is Bev gone?"

Paul nodded.

"Did you see any sign of Young?" Gwynn asked.

Paul swallowed his first bite. "No, but I suspect he'll be back." He cut another piece. "What did you tell him about me?"

"That I kicked you out," Holly answered.

"What about transportation?" Paul asked.

"We watched you walk off into the sunset," Gwynn said, snickering.

Raising his fork to his lips, he said, "That works, even if it was broad daylight."

They finished eating, cleared off the table and Gwynn began washing dishes.

"Do you want coffee?" Holly asked.

"Yeah," Paul said. "I can make it."

"No. Here," Holly said, handing him a plastic bag. "Fill it with ice and stick your hand in it."

He complied and then sat at the table with his hand submerged in the bag. Within five minutes, the coffee was on the table and Gwynn and Holly joined him.

"The interrogation," Paul began. "Since I was detained here, Bev had to keep Turk Carlsen occupied for fifteen minutes before I showed up. I called—she knew I'd be late. Won't go into details. A group was formed three months before Boden's death. Called the Brotherhood. Their only goal was to make money by stealing oil. Members had to follow a set of rules. The first rule: no one could tell anyone about it."

"That should have been understood," Holly said. "Did they need a rule for that?"

Paul took a drink of his coffee. "They attached consequences if a member of the Brotherhood broke a rule. It makes sense. Possible jail time and all."

"Did Boden break that rule?" Gwynn asked.

Paul nodded.

"The consequence was death?" Holly said with wide opened eyes.

"Fraid so."

"Who would agree to that?" Gwynn asked, shrugging her shoulders.

"The Brotherhood."

"How many members?" Holly asked.

"Five."

"According to Williams," Gwynn said, "three killed Boden. Where was the fifth?"

"The fifth didn't believe anyone would really die if they broke a rule. Carlsen wasn't invited to the killing or even know about it, until he heard of Boden's death."

"Carlsen and Boden were best buddies," Gwynn explained.

"Carlsen knew the hydrogen sulfide story was a cover-up for murder. He wanted to go to the police immediately, but he didn't have any proof and he feared the same consequence or jail time because of the Brotherhood's activity."

"Who are the five?" Holly asked.

"Boden, Drumlin, Williams, Whitehead and Carlsen."

"Turk Carlsen shot Drumlin. Did Drumlin break a rule?" Gwynn asked.

"Nope. Carlsen had been upset with the group ever since Boden died. He was gathering info to protect his hide. Drumlin saw some of the documents in his truck. Caused a confrontation. Carlsen thought he had it smoothed over, until he found Drumlin on his tail as he headed up the road out here." He tilted his head toward the street.

"That explains why Carlsen's tailgate had been damaged," Gwynn said, tapping her fingers on the table. "I was looking for a truck with damage in the front."

"Protect his hide?" Holly said. "Carlsen thought he was in danger?"

"Yep. Didn't trust the guys after what happened to Boden. Wanted a bargaining chip."

"Where was Carlsen going that night?" Holly asked.

"An abandoned house he owns." Paul looked at Gwynn. "Probably the same place Williams took you."

"Carlsen could be nailed for Williams' murder," Holly suggested.

"Carlsen doesn't know Williams is dead," Paul said. "My theory is that he was going to be nailed for Gwynn's murder."

"We heard Carlsen giving Williams a hard time in the metal building," Holly said. "You think it might have been a setup by Williams and Whitehead?"

"Sure do."

"All the members of the Brotherhood have been accounted for and Whitehead isn't 'the man' so who is?" Gwynn asked.

"Maybe the person Boden told," Paul said, rotating his hand in the bag of ice.

Holly gazed at Paul and squinted. "You couldn't get Carlsen to give you the name?"

"Not without putting him the hospital."

"Is he afraid of him?" Gwynn asked.

"Apparently."

"Well, 'the man' has to be one of the other interest owners in the Lander unit." Gwynn raised her hand. "Sorry, I'm jumping ahead. The oil theft is stealing it from Cisco, right?"

"Yep," Paul confirmed. "Just like you suspected. Flow lines. They disconnected and reconnected so Cisco's oil flows into Lander's storage tanks and Lander's, which have a much smaller volume, flows into the Cisco's, except for one well. Lander's highest producing well flows into the right tank. The change to the flow lines is a distance from the battery. Not easy to detect."

"Instead of the Brotherhood, they should have called themselves the Cisco Bandits," Holly said.

"Cisco Bandits?" Paul rubbed his chin. "I like that."

"Besides the company," Gwynn said, "there are only four other interest owners left in the Lander unit who could profit from the Cisco oil theft. Ruling out Alex Hayes and Ashton Prudell, that leaves Hayes' son-in-law, Ralph Turner, and Janice Robinson. Ralph Turner sure doesn't strike me as being tough or ruthless enough to be 'the man'."

"The guy isn't an interest owner. Gets paid twenty percent of the Brotherhood's proceeds. He doesn't want his name listed on anything and he doesn't want anyone to speak it. That's why he is referred to as 'the man'."

"Three of the five are dead. How is he going to get a share of that?" Holly asked.

"Wills. The Brotherhood members were to will their interest to Whitehead. Whitehead was the original organizer. Some of the guys didn't have enough cash to get into the group. He put together a payment plan for them. High interest. Nothing in writing."

"Boden?" Holly said.

Paul nodded. "He left everything to Janice Robinson. That's the reason his estate hasn't been settled. 'The man' contacted Boden's brother and got him to contest the will. That's all Carlsen knew about it."

"I can trace the money," Holly said.

"He's paid in cash."

"That's a sizeable amount to be carrying around," Gwynn commented.

"How does that work?" Holly asked.

"He knows the well production. He knows when Prudell sends out the checks or makes electronic fund transactions. He knows the amount."

Holly scratched her forehead. "Must be getting that info from Patrick."

"Carlsen doesn't know about him." Paul pulled his hand out of the ice and stretched his fingers.

"Interesting. Whitehead does," Holly said.

"That was probably set up before 'the man' came onto the scene," Paul said, going over and pouring another cup of coffee. He held up the carafe. "Want some?"

Holly nodded. Gwynn shook her head.

"The shootings at the well and the battery, did you ask him about those?" Gwynn asked.

"Yep. He confirmed the first one was Williams, but he wasn't the one at the storage tanks. Carlsen called Williams right after it happened and Williams was watching a game on television; he heard the background noise. He suspects it might have been Whitehead."

"Why do they want to kill me?" Gwynn asked.

"The video when you broke into the storage shed. Even without seeing your face, they're convinced it was you. Williams chased you. He got part of the license plate number. A black Jeep with those same digits was rented by a woman in Farmington late that afternoon and returned to the rental agency before it opened the next day."

"Patrick probably did that research," Holly said.

"But who told Patrick to do it?" Gwynn asked.

"Whitehead," Paul said. "Williams reported the break-in and his suspicions about you to him. He would have been the one to contact Patrick. If the second shooter was Whitehead, Carlsen figured it was a scare tactic because they didn't want you dead before they get info from you."

"That's what Williams wanted," Gwynn confirmed.

"Getting back to 'the man', how do they give him the money?" Holly asked.

"They make cash withdrawals and hand it over to him at a specified location."

"Does the location change?" Holly asked.

"No."

"Too many people are becoming aware there's a problem with that production—Hayes, Dave, the Cisco interest owners and Ashton has to suspect," Gwynn said. "That crime can't go on forever. What's he planning on doing, killing anyone who inquires about it?"

"I asked Carlsen a similar question," Paul said. "It was planned to be a twelve month deal. They figured they could make up excuses about production for that long and a few other things to stall them. If too many people got suspicious, they'd talk about shortening the time. As far as Carlsen knows, that's still the plan, but he's worried about it. The only one at the company right now that is going gung-ho over the problem is Hayes. Whitehead suspected early on that

Hayes might be a problem since he's Prudell's CFO and he has interest in the Cisco unit. He took care of that by having his son-in-law become an interest owner in the Lander unit. Since Hayes doesn't know the whole scheme, he won't blow the whistle for fear his son-in-law might be involved."

"I assumed that's who he's protecting," Gwynn said. "Especially since his interest, along with the others, was purchased about the same time the production became a problem and Hunter got his share cheap.'"

"Did you find out any other information?" Holly asked.

"Nope. That's it."

"Ashton has a personal interest in that unit. I can see Dave protecting him," Gwynn said. "But I think Dave will still research the production problem and eventually figure it out."

"If they stay with the twelve month period, don't they have seven months to go?" Holly said.

"Yeah, that seems about right. I'll verify that tomorrow." Gwynn tapped her fingers together. "I sense Whitehead's initial interest in the whole thing is to screw Ashton. Think about it: Prudell workers maintain the flow lines, the wells, check the storage tanks. Whitehead wasn't involved with any of that. The only one left out of the Brotherhood to say Whitehead played a role is Carlsen. If he's gone, Ashton could very easily be left holding the bag. Who knows, Whitehead might even find a way to turn him in… revenge."

"That's exactly what I was thinking," Holly said. "Carlsen's days might be numbered. Whitehead is probably contemplating how to get rid of 'the man'."

Paul looked at Holly. "We're on the same brain wave."

"Whitehead knows someone is snooping around, but it's not the cops," Holly said. "Maybe he still thinks he can pull it off. The only hard evidence we have against him is his fingerprints from the canister and safety masks. The safety masks have been wiped clean and by now the canister probably has too. We can't prove that's where we got the fingerprints. Also, we don't get involved with the cops." Holly's eyes darted from Gwynn to Paul. "Got any ideas?"

"A couple," Paul said. "The kid might be able to provide something substantial. Tomorrow evening, we'll discuss our concerns with Ruben."

"Ready for your FBI role?" Holly asked.

Paul gazed at her and his face creased with a crooked smile. "I'm ready for my boyfriend role."

"So am I," she grinned.

Gwynn felt like a third wheel. "I'm going to hit the sack. I need to get up early to work on my make-up."

"Your face doesn't look that bruised today," Holly said.

"You didn't see how much make-up I put on this morning. I'm surprised my face doesn't look caked."

"It's good you did, with Young making a few unexpected appearances," Holly said.

"I'll make you up," Paul said.

Gwynn smiled. "Thanks. I could use your expertise."

"Paul, why don't you get your stuff before Gwynn goes to bed? I think we all need to be alert whenever the door is opened."

"Good point," Paul said and moved to the back door.

"Do you want my help?" Holly asked.

"The car's parked up the road. We'll be going through the woods. You okay with that?"

Holly nodded. "More than one trip?"

"No."

"Gwynn keep your pistol handy. We'll be coming through this door." Holly looked at Paul. "Will you be listening?"

"Yeah." He stuck an earplug in. "I'll know if there's a problem."

Holly and Paul went outside and Gwynn eased the door shut.

Earlier Gwynn had wondered why Holly was vague when she asked her where Paul was going to sleep; now she knew the answer. She thought it was nice how Ruben tried to put couples together whenever he could. But she also knew he wouldn't do that if it interfered with the way they performed their jobs. Then she recalled Paul saying he was at the next table at Marty's and pondered if Holly knew or if his disguise deceived even her.

"It's us," Holly said, inching the door open. She entered with a large duffle bag hanging from her shoulder. Paul followed with a suitcase and a duffle bag.

"Did you get everything?" Gwynn asked.

"Yes. This is it," Paul said.

"I get to use the bathroom first to get ready for bed," Gwynn said, walking toward the hall.

CHAPTER 33

The lobby was unusually quiet when Gwynn and Holly strolled into the office building. Marilyn wasn't at the counter. Then a loud crashing sound echoed through the structure and a moan drifted from the hallway.

Gwynn and Holly ran in the direction of the noise and found Marilyn in the file room buried under a shelving unit and a pile of boxes. They began yanking the heavy containers off her.

"My head," Marilyn murmured.

"Do you think you can stand or should I call 9-1-1?" Gwynn asked.

With a pale face, Marilyn raised her arms and swung them to the side. "Can you help me get up?"

Gwynn and Holly each took an arm and raised her off the floor.

Marilyn tilted her body around. "I think I'm okay."

"Let's get you to your desk," Gwynn said, holding onto Marilyn's arm.

"Are you sure you're okay?" Holly asked. "I could drive you to the clinic."

"No. Just give me a few minutes," Marilyn said, easing down into her chair. "It was just the shock of having that whole shelf tip over." She looked at Holly. "Thank goodness Mr. Prudell is having Susan work on getting rid of some of those files."

"Can I get you some coffee or something?" Holly asked.

"Coffee would be nice."

Holly went into the break room.

"What were you looking for?" Gwynn asked. "I can get it."

"The Cisco unit documents—engineering, plans, maps. Dave can't find them at the downtown office. He's thinking they might have been among the stuff stolen during the break-in. They're not in the computer system. I can't figure that out. We scan in all that stuff. He wanted me to check if by any chance they were here."

Holly came out with a steaming cup of coffee and sat it down on Marilyn's desk.

"Thanks," Marilyn said as a black-and-blue mark began forming on her chin.

The entrance door swung open. "Good morning, ladies," Hayes said, stepping into the lobby. He stopped at the counter. "Is something wrong?"

"A shelving unit fell on Marilyn," Gwynn said.

His features lined with concern. "Marilyn, are you okay?"

She nodded.

"In the file room?"

Marilyn nodded again.

"Half that stuff in there should have been tossed years ago." Hayes said, shaking his head. "It's a mess in there."

"I'm working on that," Holly said.

"Marilyn, you take it easy today." Hayes headed toward his office. "What a mess," he said from the hallway. "Do you want me to help clean it up?"

"No, thanks," Gwynn said. "We can manage." She touched Marilyn's shoulder. "Let me know if you change your mind about a visit to the clinic."

Marilyn picked up the cup of coffee. "I will, but really everyone is making too much of a fuss over this."

"I'll see if I can find those documents," Gwynn said, "and clean up the file room."

"I'll help," Holly said and followed Gwynn into the hallway.

Gwynn and Holly righted the shelving unit and looked through each box before they put it back on a shelf. No Cisco documents. Gwynn opened a file drawer to make sure the folder "Project #112: Cisco Unit Flow Line" wasn't missing. Gwynn sighed when she saw the manila folder was right where it belonged.

Since Patrick would be out of school at 2:30 p.m., Holly pretended to be ill again right after lunch and went back to the house to get ready for her FBI performance.

Gwynn wondered why Young hadn't been in to talk to her after he seemed so anxious yesterday, but she anticipated he could show up any minute. Her cell phone rang.

"Call her now," Holly said and disconnected.

Gwynn punched in Janice's salon number.

"JR Salon," Janice answered.

"Hi, Janice. This is Gwynn."

"What do you want?" she snapped.

"I was feeling a little bad about what happened on Friday night," Gwynn said. "I've talked to Susan. She promises she won't dance with your boyfriend any more, unless you break up with him."

"She said that?" Janice said in a tone of disbelief.

"Yes. She doesn't want to make any trouble."

"Does she like one of the other guys?"

"Turk. He took her out Sunday night. She's talked a lot about him since then."

"She likes Turk?"

"I think so. She said he really knows how to treat a lady."

"He does?"

"Yes. Susan thinks he's quite the gentleman."

"There was a time I was interested in him, but it didn't work out," Janice said.

Gwynn suspected Janice had slept with all the Prudell guys who hung out at Marty's. She was surprised that Turk might not have fallen under her loose and free charms.

"So we can be friends again?" Gwynn asked, thinking Patrick should have been picked up by now.

"Yeah. Marty doesn't like squabbles at his place," Janice said. "Are you going there tonight?"

"No. I missed work yesterday because I had that twenty-four hour bug. I'm taking it easy tonight, but I'll be there tomorrow. You going to be there?"

"Never miss a dance," Janice said. "See ya."

Gwynn hung up and wondered about the interview with Patrick, hoping they'd find out who 'the man' was. If they had to wait until after interest owners were paid, that would delay things eleven days. She wanted to see Ruben and knew he wouldn't be physically joining the investigation. Also, she couldn't see how the investigation could end by Monday—the end of the week ultimatum Ruben had mentioned during the conference call.

At 5 p.m., Gwynn began looking out the front office windows for

CHAPTER 34

"Did Paul make it in last night?" Gwynn asked, finishing her morning coffee.

"Yes, around eleven-thirty," Holly said. "After Carlsen got home around ten, Young showed up in his cruiser, got out and looked around, but he didn't knock. He went back in his car and didn't leave. Since the cops have the place staked out, Paul came here."

"Is he gone?"

"Yeah. He left around six. He wants you to have his cell number." Holly proceeded to give it to her as Gwynn punched the numbers on her cell phone.

When they walked into the office building, they found Hayes behind the counter.

"You're just the person I want to talk to," Hayes said to Gwynn. "Do you know where Marilyn keeps her date stamp?"

Holly briefly greeted Hayes and then proceeded to the conference room.

"I'll show you," Gwynn said, dropping her purse off at her desk. She went behind the receptionist's counter and opened a drawer. "Here, it is." She lifted it out. "Where's Marilyn?"

"Her back ached when she woke up. Her husband has taken her to the clinic."

"Probably from yesterday morning."

"That's what she thought," Hayes said. "You can't have a shelving unit filled with boxes fall on you and not sustain some kind of injury. I thought she was moving pretty slowly yesterday afternoon. I tried to get her to go have herself checked out, but she can be stubborn. When you get settled in, come and see me."

"Okay."

Gwynn turned on her computer and grabbed a notepad. On the way to Hayes' office, she stopped in the conference room where Holly was working. "Hayes wants to talk to me about something. No one is in the foyer. Can you sit at Marilyn's desk until I get back or until Debra gets here?"

"When is she coming?"

"Around ten."

"Sure," she said, standing.

Gwynn went into Hayes' office. "Do you want the door closed?"

He nodded. She pushed it shut and sat across from Hayes.

"Has Dave found out anything about the Cisco unit yet?" he asked.

"I haven't talked to him since Monday, but Marilyn was looking for Cisco unit documents when the shelf fell on her."

"They're not at the downtown office?"

"No and they're not here. They were probably among the documents stolen during the break-in."

"We can print off another set," Hayes said.

"No. They're not in the system."

Hayes' eyes opened wide and his forehead creased. "How can they not be in the system?"

Gwynn shook her head. "Marilyn said that was why she was looking for them. After I went through the boxes in the file room and helped clean it up, I searched through the system and couldn't find them anywhere."

Hayes leaned on his elbow and rubbed his chin. "That's not possible. No one has access to erase them. They're 'read only'."

"Well someone did or they were never on the system."

"They were there. I checked over two months ago."

"Did you print any of them?" Gwynn asked. "It might help Dave."

Hayes nodded, stood and went over to the file cabinet. He unlocked it and opened the second drawer. He pulled out all the hanging folders and files and laid them on his credenza. From the bottom of the drawer, he took out a legal size folder.

Gwynn realized that she had not done a very good job searching his file cabinet, since it never occurred to her that anything would be hidden under the hanging files.

"I've got another one," Hayes said, handing the folder to Gwynn.

He proceeded emptying out the third drawer and taking out another file.

"Can you make a copy and give me these back?" he said. "Lately, things have a way of disappearing around here."

"I'll do that right now," she said and marched across the hall to the file room. Some of the documents were large so it took her time to copy and tape pages together. She made two copies, hiding one set behind a file cabinet.

She walked into Hayes' office. "Done," Gwynn said, giving him back his folders. She held up the copied folders. "I'll make sure Dave gets these or do you want to deliver them?"

"I'd rather you take care of that," Hayes said.

"With Marilyn not here, I hate to leave right now. Will it be okay if I drop them off at lunch?"

He nodded. "Hand them to him personally."

"I will. Was there anything else?"

"No. That was it."

On the way to her desk, Gwynn retrieved the hidden copies. She stepped into the lobby and saw Holly flipping through a magazine. "Sorry that took so long. Were you bored?"

Holly nodded. "All the stuff I'm working on is stacked on the conference table."

"Ashton isn't in yet?"

"He's here. He chatted for a few minutes while he gave me the once over, but he must be busy because he didn't hang around all that long. Did Hayes say anything interesting?"

Gwynn bent closer to Holly and said softly, "He wanted to know how Dave was doing on checking the Cisco unit. Hayes had a set of the documents I was looking for yesterday; the ones Marilyn was initially searching for."

"The Cisco unit stuff?"

Gwynn bobbed her head up and down.

"So there was a set here," Holly said.

"No. He printed them from the computer system."

"They were on the system?" Holly said, squinting and tapping the counter.

"'Read only'. The project folder for the Cisco unit flow line is still in the file room, right where it belongs. It has a small map of the flow line layout in it. Whoever snatched the other Cisco documents must have overlooked that folder."

"I'm going to find out who erased the documents from the system," Holly said, putting the magazine back on the coffee table. "For that, I can use the company computer."

Gwynn raised two folders. "During lunch we have to deliver these to Dave."

"Good, that will give me a chance to let Turk invite me to dinner," Holly said. "Call Linda now so we make sure we coordinate." She moved around the counter. "Oh, Debra won't be in until eleven."

"Can you just stay one more minute while I call Linda?"

Holly nodded reluctantly.

Gwynn placed a call to the Café. Linda got off at 6:30. They made plans to eat there and then go to Marty's. Linda asked about Susan and sounded relieved when Gwynn told her Susan wouldn't be joining them for dinner.

"Linda's set," Gwynn said, carrying a stack of invoices to the counter. "I'll work here until Debra shows."

"Okay. I'm heading back to the conference room, " Holly said and stepped into the hallway.

A young man in his early twenties, dressed in a khaki uniform walked through the entrance. In his hands, he carried a clipboard and a sealed, green and white, ten-by-fourteen envelope.

"Can I help you?" Gwynn asked.

"I have a special delivery for Ashton Prudell," the man said.

Gwynn stretched out her hand. "I can take it to him."

"No. It can only be delivered to him personally."

"I'll get him." Gwynn headed to Ashton's office and knocked on his closed door.

"Yes," he said, loudly.

"Mr. Prudell, there's a special delivery for you," Gwynn said, through the door.

"Take it."

"The man says it has to be hand delivered to you." She heard banging and footsteps and then the door flew open.

"What's this all about?" Ashton said, sounding irritated.

Gwynn followed him back to the lobby.

"Who's it from?" Ashton barked.

The man looked at the envelope. "The name of the sender isn't on it."

Ashton grabbed the envelope from the man's hands.

"Sir, I need a signature," the man said, raising a clipboard.

Ashton scribbled his name on the line and hurried back to his office.

Gwynn watched the young man get into a green, unmarked van as she wondered what was so important in the document that it had to be hand delivered. *Could it be a legal summons or subpoena?*

She glanced at the multi-line telephone and saw Ashton's light go on. As she worked on the invoices, she noticed several times it went off and immediately went back on. He was placing numerous calls.

Forty-five minutes later, Ashton came into the foyer with a face drained of color and drooping eyes.

"Mr. Prudell, are you feeling okay?" Gwynn asked.

Ashton handed Gwynn a sheet of paper. "Make motel reservations for these men for the weekend and don't mention this to anyone."

"Beginning tonight or tomorrow?" Gwynn asked.

"Tonight."

"Do they need airline tickets or anything else?"

"No, just motel rooms. The same place they always stay." Ashton walked back into the hallway and turned the opposite direction from his office.

Gwynn wondered if he was going to Hayes' office. Glancing at the list, she recognized the four names from payroll and knew those men worked out of the Artesia office. While she looked through Marilyn's file for the name of the motel from prior travel itineraries, Ashton passed the lobby door, heading toward his office. She found the name of the motel and made the reservations. Then a thought occurred to her and she quickly went into the file room, opened the cabinet drawer that contained the folder "Project #112: Cisco Unit Flow Line." The folder was gone.

Sitting back down at Marilyn's desk, she believed Ruben had conveyed to Ashton the theory of Whitehead's plan. It made sense that Ashton wouldn't know which of his local workers he could trust. Gwynn mulled over whether or not he had discussed it with Dave. If Dave seemed tense when she dropped off the documents, then he must know about the problem.

Debra entered the building. "Sorry, I'm late. I had to deal with some stuff at school."

"No problem," Gwynn said, moving toward her desk. "You'll have to sit at Marilyn's desk and answer the phone."

"Where's Marilyn?"

"She injured her back yesterday when a shelving unit in the file room tipped over on her."

"Geez, is she going to be okay?"

"She worked the rest of the day, so she didn't break any bones, but she probably should have had herself checked. Today she's suffering for it."

At noon, Holly and Gwynn left for the downtown office.

"I hope they haven't already gone out for lunch," Holly said.

"Dave told me he goes at twelve-thirty every day, in case some time I wanted to join him."

"Maybe we should let the guys take us to lunch," Holly said. "One more opportunity to get close to Turk."

Pulling into the parking lot, Gwynn saw a Silverado and assumed it was Turk's, since he was the only one now in that office with a company truck.

As Gwynn and Holly entered the office, Turk and Dave stopped working.

Dave looked at Gwynn and said, "Did you decide to take me up on that lunch invitation?"

"Actually I'm here to drop off these folders," Gwynn said, putting them on Dave's desk.

Dave glanced through them. "Where did you get these?"

Since Hayes had stowed the documents under hanging files, she doubted he'd want anyone to know he had been hiding a set. "Yesterday when I told you they weren't in the file room, I hadn't notice a couple of boxes. That's where I found them."

"This is great. I know the robbers got away with the originals. I still can't understand how they missed being scanned in."

"I made another copy. I'll have Marilyn scan them tomorrow."

"I can do that," Holly said.

"Then I'll give them to you after lunch."

Dave held up a large envelope. "Can you put this in my office when you get back?" he asked Gwynn.

"Sure," Gwynn said, taking it from him.

"You ladies don't want to go with us to lunch?" Turk said.

"Of course, we do," Holly said, moving closer to Turk. "What happened to your face?"

He touched his bruises. "Had a flat tire. Went to remove the car jack and it sprang up and attacked my face."

Gwynn held her lips tightly together, hiding her smile. He had used one of Holly's excuses.

Holly gently stroked his face. "Does it hurt?"

Turk smiled at her. "It already feels better."

"There's a new Italian place not far from here, Turk and I were thinking about trying it," Dave said. "How does that sound?"

"Good," Gwynn said and since Dave seemed his usual cheerful self, she suspected Ashton hadn't mentioned anything to him about his special delivery letter or that he had sent for some employees who work in Artesia.

During lunch, they talked about Williams still being missing. Turk hadn't heard a word from him and thought he had gone to Mexico. Dave couldn't figure out why he had shot Karl and Turk acted like he didn't know either. Then Dave and Turk chatted about a planned, new well site that needed to have one measurement retaken because it didn't make sense on the layout.

"Turk, I promised Bridget I would stay off the leg." Dave smiled. "She's given me a pass to the dance tonight at Marty's. Don't want to push my luck."

"Dave," Gwynn said. "In the hospital the doctor only said to stay off your leg for a few days. It's been over a week."

"I told Bridget that. She called the doc for verification." He shook his head. "Doesn't trust me. He told her the few days was the minimum. She took that to mean I needed more time. I'm walking around with crutches. I won't be able to dance, but my foot won't need to occupy a chair."

"How long are you going to stay at your brother's?" Holly asked.

"The way Bridget takes care of me, I'm thinking of making it a permanent home." Dave grinned. "Only until I can drive."

"Want to go check a measurement with me?" Turk asked Holly.

"What would I need to do?"

"Just hold one end of the tape."

"I can handle that," Holly said. "But what about work?"

"That is work," Dave said. "I'll check with Ashton, but I'm sure it won't be a problem. You'll be on the clock."

"What time were you thinking about going?" Holly asked.

"In an hour," Turk said.

"How long would we be gone?" Holly asked.

"A couple of hours. Why, do you have a hot date?" Turk asked.

"No. I was going to take you out to dinner. Gwynn's meeting Linda and I didn't want to eat alone."

Turk gave her a boyish smile. "I certainly wouldn't want you to eat alone."

"Can I go to the well site in what I'm wearing?" Holly asked.

"The shoes," Turk said. "We could swing by your place and you could get another pair."

"Why don't you ever invite me to dinner?" Dave asked Gwynn.

Gwynn held up her engagement ring. "Remember."

"Why don't we all go to dinner Saturday night," Holly suggested. "I saw a steak place on the edge of town."

"Dave, Gwynn, you in?" Turk asked.

They nodded.

CHAPTER 35

Leaning over the short wall by Gwynn's desk, Holly whispered, "Paul will follow Turk and me for ten or twenty miles, just long enough to make sure no one else is. Then he'll come back to keep track of you so don't leave the building."

"I won't," Gwynn said. "Ashton said it was okay for you to go?"

"Yeah. He sure has something on his mind today, hasn't been to check me out since he arrived. Turk's on his way over. I'm going to wait outside."

Gwynn saw the Silverado pull into Prudell's parking lot and Holly climbed in. Then she remembered the envelope Dave had given her. She went into his office, laid it on his desk and froze when she saw a blue and white cap sitting on his credenza. Gwynn picked it up and stared at it, convinced it was the cap worn by the man who had driven by her numerous times when she jogged along the road. She squinted. *Could Dave be 'the man'?*

She bent down and attempted to open a desk drawer. It was locked. While she intently listened for footsteps in the hall, she got out her picks and unlocked the desk. She carefully began looking through the drawers, trying not to make any noise. In the second one she saw a DVD labeled: "Break-in at woodshed." She didn't find anything else suspicious in his drawers. She wanted to search his file cabinet, but knew she could easily be discovered any moment. Reluctantly, she locked his desk and went back to her cubicle.

She gazed at her computer screen as Dave consumed her thoughts. Of all the guys she knew in Bloomfield, he was the one she had least suspected could be involved.

"Miss Wagner," Officer Young said, standing by her desk.

Gwynn was so busy concentrating on 'the man' that she hadn't even noticed Young entering the lobby. "Good afternoon, Officer Young," she said. "Did you come to talk to me about the case?"

"Downtown," he said. "Detective Marsden will meet us at the police station so the interview can be recorded."

"Recorded? Why?"

Young shrugged his shoulders. "That's what Detective Marsden wants. The county does a few things differently than we do. Just between us, Detective Marsden should have brought his recorder when he talked to you here."

Gwynn agreed.

"He also wants to ask questions about the disappearance of Brad Williams," Young said.

"I don't know anything about that."

"He's looking for confirmation. General police procedure."

"We could use the conference room if he can come here," Gwynn suggested, since she wasn't supposed to leave the building.

"No, he wants to do it downtown."

"Do you want me to go to the station right now?"

"Yes. I'm here to pick you up."

Gwynn thought that would be safer than driving alone since Paul wasn't close by. "Let me tell Alex. How long will this take?"

"I'm not sure. I would think you'd be gone less than two hours."

After Gwynn told Hayes, she climbed into the front passenger seat of the police cruiser.

"That seatbelt sticks." Young leaned over her to grip it. The button of his cuff got caught in her necklace chain. They both attempted to free it, but the chain broke. "I'm so sorry," Young said, holding it. "Let me get this fixed for you."

Gwynn reached for it. "No, I can take care of it."

"No, I insist," Young said, slipping it into his breast pocket. "There's a jewelry store next to the police station. I'll drop it off there on our way in. You'll have it back before you leave."

Gwynn wondered if Young had an alternative motive for wanting to keep her necklace. *Did he know about the bug?* She decided she'd retrieve the brooch when he dropped it off. If he didn't drop it off, she'd know he was up to something.

Young yanked on her seatbelt strap, pulled it over her shoulder and hooked it.

"That was stuck," she said.

"It needs to be replaced," Young said, sounding irritated. "I've taken it to the shop twice and each time they claim it's fixed. It is for a few days, but then this happens again."

Young cut to the curb in front of the police station. "I don't see Marsden's car. If there's a problem I'll take you back to work. Stay here," he said, getting out of the cruiser. He went into the jewelry store and then headed into the station.

Gwynn snapped off the seatbelt and walked at a fast pace into the jewelry store.

"A police officer just dropped off a necklace," Gwynn said to the clerk.

"Yes," the store clerk said, holding it up.

"Can I have the brooch?" Gwynn asked.

"Miss," the clerk said. "I don't know this is your necklace. I can't give it to you. Have Officer Young come and get it. The jeweler will be back soon and it won't take him long to fix it."

"Okay," Gwynn said, disappointed, and left the store.

Young stood by the cruiser. "Was your necklace already fixed?"

"No. I just wanted the brooch."

"It will be safe there," he said with a smile. "Sally, the clerk, said I could pick it up in half an hour. Getting back to Marsden, he wants to question you at their office in Aztec. It's a short drive."

Not wanting to draw to much attention to her necklace, Gwynn slid back into the passenger seat. Young tugged on her seatbelt and secured it around her as she pondered if they were really going there or if he had other plans. She clutched her purse on her lap, knowing her cell phone had GPS, Paul could locate her.

As they drove toward the county facility, Young's cell phone rang.

"Young," he answered. "There? ... Not the main location ... okay, we'll go there."

While Young was on the phone, Gwynn pulled her cell phone out of her purse and tucked it into her bra, so she could keep it within her reach regardless of their destination.

"Marsden's going to do the interview at their substation. Dealing with the county folks isn't easy."

Young steered off the main highway and drove along a less traveled road. He stopped near a row of six attached offices in need of maintenance. The parking lot had weeds growing through cracks in the asphalt. An old, worn sign hung above the end unit: "Police Substation." The structure appeared unoccupied with the exception of the office at the other end. Two cars were parked by that entrance door.

"Marsden's not here yet," Young commented. "Let's go in."

They walked to the door and Young fished a key out of his pocket.

"You have a key to a county office?" Gwynn questioned.

"Yes, Marsden gave it to me."

Gwynn saw through his lie, wondered how long he had planned this day and wanted to know why, as she stepped into the office. Scanning the room, she saw the barren walls—not one picture, a wood desk without a single item on it and four chairs, badly in need of refurbishing. "An employee isn't stationed here all the time?"

"No," he said, locking the door behind him. Young turned around with a pistol protruding from his hand, aimed at her. He lifted a silencer from a slot in his belt and screwed it on the tip of the barrel.

"What are you doing?" she asked, raising her eyebrows.

"Weapons," he said. "Lay them on the desk."

"I don't have any," Gwynn said.

"Yes, you do," Young said, glaring at her. "All investigators are packing."

"What makes you think I'm an investigator?"

"Don't play naive with me. No games. You broke into the woodshed at Prudells' ranch." He tilted his head toward the desk. "The weapons?"

Gwynn surmised it would be a waste of time arguing against his allegation. Though she believed she could disarm the man who stood before her, she wanted information.

"So it's going to be that way." Young frowned. "Hold out your arms."

Attempting not to be searched, Gwynn said, "I have a gun in a holster on my calf. Can I bend down and get it?"

Young nodded. "Two fingers."

Gwynn lifted a pant leg and with her thumb and index finger, raised her Beretta.

He grabbed it from her and dropped it on the desk. "Any more?"

"No," she said, hoping he wouldn't frisk her other leg and discover her knife.

"Dump your purse on the desk."

She emptied out the contents.

Young rummaged through the items. "Where's your cell phone?"

Gwynn stared at the pile. "It's not there?"

Young felt around inside her purse. "Where is it?" he snapped.

"I must have left it at work."

He ran his hand over her waist and down her hips while the tip of the pistol never wavered away from her chest. "Sit," he said, gesturing toward a chair and pushing her into it. "Give me your hands." He slipped a plastic handcuff on them, took a rope from a desk drawer and tied her to the chair by wrapping it around her waist and then secured her ankles to the front chair legs.

"What do you want, Officer Young?" Gwynn asked, meeting his eyes.

"Information." He laid his weapon on the desk, pulled a chair in front of her and sank into it. He moved his right ankle onto his left knee and folded his arms across his chest.

"Who do you work for?"

"You're not a policeman?" she asked, studying his face.

"Of course, I am."

"This isn't the way policemen ask questions."

"I'm not on duty," he said with a smirk. "This is my part-time job."

"Are you 'the man'?"

His expression hardened and his eyes darkened with rage.

Gwynn felt relieved he didn't strike her, but knew he had no intention of allowing her to leave this room alive.

"Where did you hear that?" he asked with a clenched jaw.

"Brad Williams."

"Where is he?"

She furrowed her brow. "You don't know?"

He gritted his teeth. "Where is he?"

"Ask Whitehead."

He flung the back of his hand across her face. She cringed as her head spun from the blow and every muscle in her face ached. Blood trickled from her nose. "You hit harder than Brad did," she said, inhaling deeply.

"When did you see him?"

"How about a deal?" she asked as her temples pounded.

"Do you think you're in a position to negotiate?" he asked with a sneer.

Her eyes darted over her bindings. "No, but I have information that will help you survive."

He lowered his leg to the floor and leaned closer to her. "Help me survive?"

"Yes, you have dangerous enemies."

"Go on."

"Not until we have a deal. You can easily kill me, but then you won't know who you should fear."

"What do you want?" Young asked, his cold eyes boring into her.

"My investigation is about Boden's death. I don't care about the Cisco unit theft."

He cocked his head. "How much do you know about that?"

"Enough, but that isn't my concern. I wasn't hired for that, just stumbled across it checking on Boden. You must be one smart guy to take over the operation after Whitehead had it in place."

He gave her a smug look. "Brains. They needed my legal expertise to keep them out of trouble. Everything was going smooth until Williams decided to do some shooting outside my jurisdiction."

"I am curious about one thing ... how did you find out about it?"

"Two ways, Boden and Patrick, Janice Robinson's kid."

"Boden told you he was going to engage in an illegal activity?"

"Arne and I went way back. He asked if I wanted to be a member of the Brotherhood, thought it would be good for the group—having a police officer involved. He told me what they were doing wasn't on the up and up, but I don't always walk a straight line. Arne never told me exactly what it was. He gave enough hints that I knew it had to do with stealing oil." He shifted in his chair. "Now it's your turn. Who questioned Boden's death?"

"The truth is, I don't know. It's an anonymous client. The person sent a request and our reply went to a P.O. Box. The client mailed a retainer in cash. Invoices go to that box and we're always paid in cash."

"You do business like that?"

"Yes, if there's a large enough benefit."

"Give me the P.O. box number?"

"No, but I can tell you who is after you."

"Who?"

"Williams and Whitehead."

"Williams questioned you?" he asked in a tone of disbelief.

Gwynn nodded.

"How did you get away?"

"A colleague."

"Where did he question you?"

"At an abandoned house further up the road from where I live."

"Mmmm," he said. "How did your colleague know you were there?"

"He followed us."

"How did it go down?"

"My turn. Patrick?"

"After Arne died, Patrick came to see me. Once before, he got into trouble for hacking. I cleared up the mess. He had some questions about the reports he was putting together for Whitehead. Arne had hooked him up with Whitehead. Whitehead had told him he had some investments with Prudell and suspected fraud. Before he went to the authorities, he wanted to make sure. That's how everything started falling together." He tapped his fingers on his thigh. "What did Williams and Whitehead tell you about me?"

"They didn't expect me to escape, so they talked freely," she replied, knowing that was the same reason Young didn't hesitate answering her questions.

"What did they say?" he growled.

"They referred to you as 'the man' and said you didn't deserve a piece of the action because they had done all the work and born all the risk. Whitehead planned on taking care of you after he devised a plan that wouldn't lead anyone back to him."

"An accident," Young said, rubbing his jaw with his knuckles. "Who do you work for?"

"Why do you care? Our investigation is over. We just need to wrap up a few things and we're out of here. When our mysterious client learns about Williams and Whitehead's involvement in Boden's death, I suspect you won't have to worry about them anymore."

Young bent forward, wearing a look of contempt and glared at Gwynn. "I don't want those bastards killed. How the fuck do you think I get paid!"

"Oh, I hadn't thought about that."

Young grabbed Gwynn's shoulders and shook her. "Who do you work for?"

"Strait Investigation Company," she said, giving him the fictitious company name Paul had used when he questioned Turk.

Young stopped shaking her, but he didn't release his hold. "Who are you working with?"

"I can't tell you that."

"You are one dumb broad," he said and slapped her again.

Pain soared through her jaw and nose.

He continued, "You need a man to come to your rescue. It ain't going to happen here. I took care of your necklace."

Gwynn squinted. He had just confirmed what she already suspected, but wondered who told him.

"Yeah. I know about that," he said, sounding pleased with himself. "And I know that Williams is dead. Do you think I'm an idiot? Williams was one dumbass. Why Whitehead picked him, I'll never know. Your colleague slowed down my payment. Now I have to wait for that interest to fall into Whitehead's hands and I know that bastard wants me out of the way."

Young pulled back his elbow and formed his hand into a fist, ready to strike. Gwynn was fed up and quickly pushed her upper torso back, tipping over the wooden chair. A back leg of the chair snapped off. She twisted and squirmed until she gripped the broken leg in her bound hands. Young reached for his pistol. She thrust the sharp end into his calf.

He buckled over in pain. "You bitch!"

Gwynn jerked around and retrieved her knife from under her slacks and sliced through the rope that held her waist and ankles to the chair.

Young grabbed his pistol and aimed the barrel at Gwynn as she raised her hands and flung the knife into his shoulder. A bullet discharged from his weapon, lodging in the wall less than a foot away from her.

Wincing in pain, Young yanked out the protruding knife while he continued clutching the pistol in his other hand. Blood flowed from the wound, saturating his sleeve.

Gwynn leapt on him, sending him sprawling across the floor. Another bullet sailed through the air and pierced the wall next to the back door. Young staggered to his feet. With her bound hands, she struck him in the head. He stumbled backwards, but quickly regained his footing and delivered a powerful blow to her stomach. Air spurted from her lungs. Ignoring the pain, she went on the attack and slammed her fisted hands into his cut shoulder. His face contorted as he clenched his wound. The pistol tumbled from his hand and slid under a chair. Summoning all her strength, Gwynn swung her leg around and forcefully struck his upper body. He swayed and keeled over, smashing into the floor. She moved toward the desk to retrieve her Beretta. A hand grabbed her ankle and yanked. She landed on the floor, taking a hard blow to her side.

Grimacing, Young started rising to his feet. She lifted her foot and rammed the heel of her shoe into his groin. An excruciating cry came from his throat as he dropped to the floor, reeling in pain.

Gwynn stumbled toward the desk and gripped her weapon in her bound hands. "Get up," she said as she released the safety and pointed the pistol at the injured man.

He gasped for air as he crawled to a chair and held onto it for support while he raised his body and flopped into it. "What are you planning on doing with me?" he mumbled.

"I'm going to find out," she said, reaching into her blouse and pulling out her cell phone. She searched for Paul's number and out of the corner of her eye she caught a glimpse of Young drawing a gun from his boot. Gwynn flung herself to the floor and heard the sharp, crackling roar and the shattering of wood as the projectile bore into the desk she had stood against a second earlier.

"Put down the weapon!" she yelled, aiming her Beretta.

Young swung his pistol in her direction. She discharged her gun. A moan rang out, along with the sound of bones splintering as the bullet drilled into his body. Young's chair tilted and he hit the hardwood floor with a thud.

Biting her bottom lip, she gazed at the motionless body and shook her head. Then she inched along the floor to the window and peered out the bottom for any sign of people. No one was in sight. She held onto the ledge and pulled herself up. She went to Young, crouched down next to him and felt his neck. No pulse. She searched his bloody pockets for keys and pulled out a ring of various sizes, along with a single key.

Gwynn moved to the door, unlocked it and peeked around the frame to the other end of the building. The cars she had seen in the parking lot earlier were gone. The only one that sat out front was Young's cruiser. Gwynn closed the door and slumped down by the wall. Her cell phone lay on the floor six feet from her. She scooted to it and grasped it in her palm. She looked at the display again, located

Paul's number and clicked on it.

"You weren't in the jewelry store. I'm headed toward your cell phone. Can you stay put?" Paul asked.

Gwynn breathed heavily. "Yes. Don't worry about the vehicle parked out front."

"Be there soon."

Resting her elbows on her legs, Gwynn cradled her head in her hands and her eyes watered. "I've killed another person," she mumbled and wept.

CHAPTER 36

Ten minutes later, Gwynn raised her head and inhaled deeply. She slowly trudged to the desk, picked up her tissues and wiped her face. She stuffed all of her belongings back into her purse and eased her gun into its holster. She scanned the floor for her knife, found it under a chair and swiped the blade on Young's shirt before sliding it back where it belonged. She went into the attached restroom, rinsed off her face, and wiped it with a paper towel from the roll hanging next to the sink.

Gwynn unlocked the back door, moved into the door frame and looked around the area. An industrial-sized garbage bin stood by the far corner of the building and a large open field lay behind it. Off in the distance she saw large structures, but no houses.

A light tapping came from the front door.

Gwynn closed the back door and moved to the front of the office. She glanced out the window, saw Paul and turned the key.

He stepped in and looked around. "What happened?" He gazed at her. "Are you okay?

"Yeah. Young tried to kill me. He was 'the man'."

"Officer Young?"

Gwynn nodded and stretched out her bound hands.

Paul pulled a 3-inch oblong device out of his pocket and pushed one of the three buttons on it. It sprang open and became a clipper. He snapped the plastic handcuff off of Gwynn.

"Thanks," she said, rubbing her wrists.

He collapsed the gadget and dropped it in his pocket, then he put on a pair of gloves and handed a pair to Gwynn. While she was slipping them on, he checked Young for a pulse. "His car keys?"

"On the desk."

Paul peered out the back door. "I'm driving the cruiser around here. We'll put his body in the trunk and then clean up in here."

"Okay."

"I'm putting your purse in my car," he said, picking it up.

When Paul entered through the back door, he took off his shirt and hung it over a chair. "The trunk's open."

Paul gripped Young's upper body while Gwynn lifted him by his calves. They tucked him into the vehicle and Paul slammed the trunk.

Back inside, Paul washed his chest with a damp paper towel and put his shirt back on.

Ignoring the blood stain on her blouse, Gwynn glanced at her watch. It read: 4:55 p.m. "We need to hurry. I'm meeting Linda at six-thirty and I don't want anyone to suspect Young is missing, or worse, dead."

"Why?"

"I'll explain when we're driving."

"Not enough time right now for a good clean up—just quick and dirty. We'll come back tomorrow if we can." Paul's eyes darted around the room. "There's a bucket under the sink in the bathroom. Start wiping everything you touched above the floor, disregard the two chairs lying on it."

Gwynn ran water over several paper towels and went to work on the door handles, the desk and the bottom of the window frame. Paul filled a bucket with water and dumped it on the chairs. Then he filled another one and dumped it on the floor.

"Throw the used towels in this," he said, referring to the empty bucket. Moving quickly, Paul grabbed a handful of towels and wiped the arms of the wet chairs and the floor, dropping the used towels as he went along.

"With your timeframe, we can't do any more," he said, picking up the bucket. He opened the back door, moved to the dumpster and poured the contents of the bucket into it.

"Those paper towels had blood on them," Gwynn said. "Won't anyone notice?"

"Not over the weekend. Monday possibly. Here," he said, handing her his car keys. "Lock the back door after me. Go out the front, lock it and then follow the cruiser."

After taking off her gloves, Gwynn adjusted the driver's seat and mirror, rotated the key in the ignition and pushed the gas pedal. She drove behind the patrol car down the highway, onto a gravel road. Paul turned the cruiser around and stopped in the weeds next to a fence, hiding the vehicle, from the main road, behind a clump of trees.

He walked over to his car. "Pull the trunk lever." From it, he took a box of moist tissues and wiped the patrol car's passenger side door, seat, seatbelt and dashboard. "Did you touch anything else in there?"

"No."

Gwynn scooted to the other side of the car and Paul got behind the wheel. He moved the car slowly to the pavement and then gunned the engine.

"I would've rather driven it longer, into a more secluded area," Paul said as they sped along, "but that wasn't possible with your timeframe. After you get cleaned up. I'll fix your face."

"Will the cruiser be noticed there?"

"Yes, but I think it will be okay for a few days. It's the weekend. Young might not be missed until Monday, depending on his schedule."

The time on the dashboard read: 5:36 p.m. "I'm calling Holly," Gwynn said, pulling out her cell phone.

Holly answered on the first ring. "Gwynn, are you still with Marsden and Young?"

"Hayes told you?"

"Yes. I've been waiting for you to get back to Prudell's. And why aren't you wearing your brooch?"

"Long story. I'm with Paul. He's taking me to the house so I can wash up before meeting Linda. I've got my car keys and we don't have time to drop them off. Can you take a taxi home?"

"I've got a set for your car. I'll meet you at the house."

"Can you turn off my computer and stack my papers so it looks like I came back?"

"Sure."

"Thanks." Gwynn disconnected.

"Explain," Paul said.

Gwynn filled him in on everything that happened after Young picked her up at work under the false pretense that Marsden wanted to talk to her about the shootings and Williams.

"I'll get your brooch tomorrow," Paul said. "Besides the fact that you killed him, is there another reason why you don't want anyone to know Young is dead?"

"I think Ashton Prudell is working on fixing the flow lines. When

Whitehead hears about Young, he might panic and immediately expose him, thinking someone is getting too close to discovering the truth."

"What makes you think Prudell is working on that?"

"He received a special delivery this morning—a letter. Shortly after that, he had me make motel reservations for four of his men that work out of the Artesia office. They're going to be working over the weekend."

"You're thinking someone tipped him off."

"Yeah."

"Would you have known about that if Marilyn would've been in today?"

"Probably not, since she's the one that makes reservations." Gwynn tucked her hair behind her ear. "Some of the blood on Young was mine."

He eyed her up and down. "Bloody nose?"

"Yeah. He knows how to throw a wicked punch!" She raised her brows and wiggled her jaw back and forth.

Paul smiled. "You just bring out the best in these guys. Do you have another weapon so you can replace the one in your holster?"

Gwynn nodded. "One more, then I'm out of guns that size." She grinned. "If I stay here much longer I'll be toting a rifle over my shoulder."

Paul drove into the driveway and glanced at the clock on the dashboard. "You only have twenty minutes."

"I need to call Linda," Gwynn said, walking into the house. She placed a call.

"Hi, Linda. Ross called as soon as I got home from work and I just hung up, so I'm going to be a little late. Will that be okay? ... Ten minutes ... See you then."

"What happened to you?" Holly said, moving her eyes over Gwynn's blood stained clothing.

"Paul can fill you in while I'm in the shower. What time are you meeting Turk?"

"Seven."

"I wish I had that much time," Gwynn said, entering the bathroom.

Twelve minutes later, Gwynn had showered, dressed, brushed her hair and was sitting at the table while Paul worked on her face.

"I can't believe Young was 'the man'," Holly said. "No wonder Patrick thought he was doing something sanctioned by the law. Do you think they'll have the flow lines repaired by Monday?"

Gwynn nodded.

"Sit still," Paul said.

Gwynn raised her hand and formed a circle with her index finger and thumb.

"I wonder if Ruben will be surprised," Holly said. "Sometimes he has an uncanny way of knowing who the culprit is even from a distance."

"Done," Paul announced, putting down the make-up brush.

Gwynn rushed to the bathroom to check out her face in the mirror. "You do great work." She picked up her purse and went to the front door. "Holly, how are you getting to the cafe?"

"Turk's picking me up."

"Call when you arrive," Paul said to Gwynn. "I'd follow, but I need to wash up and get ready for later. Plant a seed."

"I will."

CHAPTER 37

Linda sat in a booth against the window and when she saw Gwynn, she stood and waved.

Gwynn's ribs ached as the two women briefly hugged. "Sorry I'm late, but he doesn't call that often," she said, easing down onto the bench, trying not to bend any more than she had to.

"I understand."

"I might have left my curling iron on," Gwynn said. "I'm going to call Susan." She pulled out her cell phone and pushed buttons. "I think I left my curling iron on. Can you check? ... Thanks." Gwynn zipped up her purse and adjusted herself on the seat.

"When's Ross coming to see you?" Linda asked.

"There's a problem."

Linda reached over the table and touched Gwynn's hand. "Honey, he'll never stop having problems. You really need to consider getting rid of him."

"No. It's okay. It's just that he got a raise and now he's wondering if he really wants to leave the company."

Linda cocked her head. "And you're okay with a long distance relationship where you never see him?"

"No ... no. He wants me to go back to New York."

Linda squinted. "You're going to leave Bloomfield?"

"I don't want to. I like my house and job. Ross and I are going to talk about it some more on Sunday. Maybe I can still persuade him to come here so don't mention it to anyone. Okay?"

"I won't."

Gwynn knew Linda wasn't good at keeping secrets. While she mulled over how long it would take the news to spread, the waitress came and took their order.

"Janice told me you gave her a call," Linda said.

"I like Janice and I didn't want any hard feelings."

"After she slugged you, she should have apologized," Linda said. "Janice has a terrible temper. Sometimes it's gotten her into serious trouble." Her eyes drifted behind Gwynn. "Susan and Turk just walked in."

"Yeah, Susan said they were going to eat here since it's so close to Marty's and she doesn't want to be late to the dance. Do you and Walt have anything going?"

Linda smiled and her eyes sparkled. "Sometimes." She took a sip of water and changed the subject. "Is there anything new about the investigation? Have they found Brad?"

"No, he's still missing. Turk thinks he's gone to Mexico."

"That makes sense."

"Today, Officer Young picked me up so Detective Marsden, the county detective, could ask me some more questions about the shooting."

"Hasn't he already done that?"

"Yeah, but he wanted my answer recorded."

"Why?"

"Beats me."

"Here you go," the waitress said, delivering their meals. "Will there be anything else?"

Linda looked at Gwynn and then at the waitress. "No, that's everything, Dawn. Thanks."

"Mmmm, does that smell good," Gwynn said, cutting into a slice of meatloaf.

Linda slathered butter on a roll. "Did Sam and the Detective question you at the police station?"

"No," Gwynn said between bites. "That was our first stop, but the Detective didn't show. Officer Young called him and was told to take me to the county offices. On the way there his cell phone rang and he had to go back to the station. Never did get questioned. I sure think Sam Young is weird."

"He is," Linda said. "He used to hang out with Arne sometimes. Talk about opposites."

"At Marty's?"

"Yeah. He was a regular. He still comes around sometimes, but not very often."

"Maybe he has a girlfriend."

"Could be. He was sweet on a gal, Millie. She worked at the

drugstore, but got a better job in Farmington. She's another strange person—never tips, acts high and mighty and is so demanding, everything has to be perfect. Those two go together. He probably is still seeing her."

"I thought he liked Janice," Gwynn said, picking up her glass.

"Why would you think that?"

"One time I saw him arguing with Kevin and that was right after I noticed him eyeing Janice at the pool table, so I just assumed."

"All the guys at Marty's eye Janice. That doesn't mean anything. Arguing with Kevin Whitehead?"

"Yeah. They were right in each other's faces and they both growled."

"Loud?" Linda asked, raising an eyebrow.

Gwynn had managed to peak Linda's curiosity. "No, but I was close by."

"Did you hear anything?"

"Something like 'That's enough' and 'That's the way it's going to be.' But like I said, I thought it was about Janice."

"Now that you mention it, I've seen them talking sometimes and Kevin always looks pissed, like he has a beef with Sam."

As Gwynn walked into Marty's with Linda her eyes darted around the establishment and she saw Janice sitting on a stool talking to the bartender. Dave sat at his favorite table, next to the dance floor, with three pitchers of beer in front of him. Gazing at him, she wondered how she could have ever thought Dave could be 'the man.' She felt grateful she hadn't shared her suspicion with Holly or Paul after she spotted the baseball cap in his office. They could've viewed it as showing how inexperienced she was and she had already been doing a bang up job of proving that.

Dave motioned for Gwynn and Linda to come to his table.

"You here by yourself?" Gwynn said, slowly sinking into a chair.

"Yeah," Dave said, pouring her and Linda a glass of beer. "No one invited me to dinner."

"Poor baby," Gwynn said and held up her glass. "Thanks."

"Is it okay if I ask Walt to join us?" Linda asked.

Dave replied, "Sure."

Linda headed to the bar.

Gwynn noticed Dave staring at her as he rubbed his chin. "What's wrong?"

"Your face looks a little swollen."

She softly stroked her cheeks. "I bumped into a cabinet door when I was pulling out my curling iron. Boy, did that smart! Does it look bruised?"

Dave's eyes drifted over her face. "No, just swollen. It might bruise up over night."

"Then I'll look black and blue for dinner."

"Couldn't you cover it up with make-up?"

Gwynn swallowed. "I'll try. You don't want anyone to think you slapped me around?" she asked with a smile.

He shook his head. "I've already got an undeserved reputation regarding women. Don't want that one."

"Undeserved?"

Dave held her arm. "If you'd dump your boyfriend, you could find out for yourself." His eyes dropped to her chest. "Where's your necklace? Did you finally dump him?"

"No. Officer Young got it caught on his button, broke the chain and he's having it fixed."

"His button?" he asked, tilting a brow. "What were you two doing?"

"Not anything friendly. He was taking me to the police station and the seatbelt in his car sticks so he leaned over to pull it down."

"Bringing you in, huh? For Brad's disappearance?"

The image of Brad's bloody body suddenly flashed through Gwynn's mind. "No," she said, gripping her hands in her lap to prevent them from trembling. "Detective Marsden wanted to question me about the shootings again, but he never showed, so Young drove me back to work."

Holly and Turk sat down at the table and Dave talked to them about the well site they measured. Linda and Walt joined them at the table just as the music started.

"This is a slow one," Dave said to Gwynn. "Let's give it a shot."

"Are you sure you should be doing that on your leg?"

"I think I've babied it long enough."

On the dance floor, Dave pulled Gwynn tight to his body. She closed her eyes, not from enjoying the feel of his muscular chest, but trying to hide the pain that rippled through her torso from her bruised stomach being pressed against him.

She sighed when he released his hold and they walked back to the table.

"How did it go with the leg?" Gwynn asked, holding onto the arm of the chair as she sat.

"Not bad. We'll have to try it again when they play another slow song."

Gwynn picked up her glass and took a big gulp, believing it was going to be a long painful evening and she had to make sure her injured body didn't betray her.

CHAPTER 38

The morning sun streamed through Gwynn's bedroom. She stood, put on a robe and shuffled into the bathroom to freshen up. Gazing at her face in the mirror, she was surprised it no longer looked swollen and the bruises didn't appear all that bad, but she doubted she could hide them with make-up.

When she walked into the kitchen, Holly was making coffee and Paul was eating a bowl of cereal.

"Did the pills help?" Paul asked her.

"Yes. Thanks. I slept through the whole night," Gwynn said. "Are you still keeping track of Turk?"

Paul pointed to a monitor on the table. "Yeah. He's not out of bed yet." He scratched his forehead. "Don't touch the beer bottles in the living room."

"Why?"

"Fingerprints."

"Whose?"

"Whitehead's."

Holly brought over three mugs and filled them at the table. "We have work to do," she announced and then looked at Gwynn. "Are you up to anything?"

Gwynn ran her hands over her stomach. "Yeah, but we can't fight with anyone today if that's what you have in mind."

"No. You're the only one that fights around here. A few other things."

"What?"

"First, we have to finish the clean up job you and Paul started at that office and patch the hole in the desk. We don't want a trace left that you and Young were ever there."

"But when Young pulled in two cars were in the parking lot."

"Was anyone outside?"

"No."

"Even if someone spotted a police cruiser there, it would be very unlikely they wrote down the license plate number."

"Right."

"We'll take my rented Accord," Holly said. "It won't stand out like your Mustang. After that, we're going to scout out Whitehead's place to see what type of security system, if any, he has there."

"But he'll be home," Gwynn said.

"No," Paul said. "He was flying out to get signatures on some land deal—part of his company job. Whitehead told Janice he'd be back on Sunday."

"Then you don't need to track Turk?" Gwynn asked.

"Whitehead's plane isn't until noon," Holly said. "Checked it. Wanted to make sure he wasn't giving a line to Janice so he could meet up with another babe."

"And my brooch?" Gwynn asked.

"It'll be here waiting for you," Paul said.

"Paul's going to look for a place to move Young's car," Holly said. "We don't want to do that until after we've had dinner with the guys. Now I wish I hadn't arranged that."

"When do you think we can leave Bloomfield?" Gwynn asked.

"Ruben will let us know when we talk to him," Holly said. "Oh, the time's been changed."

"Talked to him last night," Paul said. "Got moved to midnight."

"Did you tell him about yesterday?" Gwynn asked.

"No, brief call. He was busy."

Turk's voice came from the monitor "Where the hell did I put that?"

"Need to go," Paul said, kissed Holly and charged out the front door.

Wearing jeans, t-shirts and bandanas wrapped around their hair, Gwynn and Holly filled the trunk of the Accord with supplies and drove to the abandoned office.

Holly stopped behind the building. They got out of the car and looked around the place. There was no sign of anyone in the other offices or the surrounding terrain.

"This might have been a substation once," Holly commented,

"But the police department abandoned it years ago."

"It was probably easy for Young to get access to it."

Gwynn slipped on her gloves, stuck the key into the doorknob and attempted to turn it. "This key doesn't work in this lock. Should I pick it?"

"Just run around and unlock the front door," Holly said, taking two buckets filled with supplies out of the trunk.

After Gwynn got in through the front door and let Holly in, they wiped down the damaged chairs, took them outside and threw them in the dumpster. Gwynn pried out the slugs in the walls, patched the holes and washed the doorknobs and window ledge again along with the wall she had leaned against. Next, she started scrubbing the blood splatters off the other walls and then moved to the floor, emptying the bucket often while Holly worked on the desk with a hammer, nails, glue and wood putty.

"You are quite the carpenter," Gwynn said.

"On the job training."

"Haven't had that yet."

"Talk to Ruben about it."

"These blood stains aren't coming off."

"After you finish scrubbing the floor, get the blue bag out of the car and mix the contents with water. Put some in the spray bottle and squirt the walls. It will take care of the remaining blood splatters. Then wash the floor again using that solution. There'll still be part of that huge stain, but it won't be identifiable as blood."

"How did you learn that?"

"A few times I've had to be a cleaner. It can be pretty gross, but it's part of the job. If we were in a bigger city, Ruben would have a crew take care of this."

"Yeah, I've been with him when he's called them."

"There's a strong possibility no one will even look here for clues regarding Young's death, but we never leave a mess behind."

"How about the abandoned house?"

"Couldn't clean it with Whitehead on his way. We removed fingerprints. It's lucky Williams didn't give you a bloody nose or wound."

"No one has my DNA," Gwynn commented.

"Not yet. But it's not good to leave it behind, in case there's a future match."

When the women finished, they gazed at their handiwork. "Looks good," Holly said.

"Sure does," Gwynn said.

"We'll have lunch and then head to Whitehead's place."

Pulling out of the parking lot, Gwynn threw the key into the dumpster and removed her gloves.

In a gas station restroom, Holly and Gwynn changed into clean jeans, conservative knit tops and applied make-up. Gwynn's bruises showed, but since they wouldn't be running into anyone from Bloomfield, she didn't worry about it. Then they put on blonde wigs and headed to a restaurant.

Whitehead lived on the third floor of a five-story, well-maintained condominium complex. It was a white-brick structure with balconies protruding from each unit, and it had unmanned security gates.

Holly parked across the street and watched a few people come and go from the building. "Too bad it's broad daylight," she said. "We'll have to walk around the building—anywhere we can go without a key card." She opened the trunk, handed a backpack to Gwynn and slipped one on.

It didn't take long to discover they couldn't go far without running into a security gate. The ones at the side of the building were set back five feet from the front of the structure.

"Now what?" Gwynn asked.

"Stand by the edge of the building, blocking me. I'll take care of this gate."

Gwynn followed Holly's instructions and heard tapping on metal behind her.

"Got it," Holly said, opening the gate.

They strolled along the edge of the building until they reached a door. It also needed a card key.

An elderly woman approached from the parking lot. They stepped closer to the gate. A few seconds later, the door behind them clicked open.

"I forgot something," Holly said, rushing toward it. She grabbed the door right before it slammed shut.

The elevator was ten feet from where they entered. They took it to the third floor. Stepping out of it, Gwynn asked. "What's his unit number?"

"Three-ten."

They made their way down the hall, passing a couple of people along the way. Whitehead had a corner unit, at the end of a hallway that ran perpendicular to the main hallway.

As a precaution, Holly went to his door and knocked, while Gwynn waited two doors away. She ducked down so she couldn't be seen through the peep hole and planned on rushing away if she heard noise in his unit.

Lowering her backpack to the floor, Holly motioned for Gwynn to join her. "I'm going to check for surveillance cameras. I doubt if Whitehead would have installed any, but we have to be careful." She pulled out a flat disk attached to a thin wire on a reel with a digital reader and forced the disk under the door. She released more wire as her eyes remained on the reader.

"If he has one it isn't in that room," Holly said. "He does have an alarm system with a motion detector. Hopefully, the panel will be close to the door."

"We're going in?" Gwynn asked, thinking they were only on a scouting mission to determine his security system.

"Yes, but we're not going to take anything. Not today. Stand where the two hallways meet and let me know if anyone's coming." Holly pulled a pair of gloves out of the front compartment of her backpack and yanked them on.

"How?"

"Cough if you see someone."

Gwynn nodded, moved down the hall and saw a man walking toward her. She cleared her throat and prepared to cough. The man stop at a door, unlocked it, and then disappeared inside. She bit her lower lip and breathed deeply. Her eyes darted between Holly and the two hallways as she sat down her backpack and took out a pair of rubber gloves.

When Holly was out of sight, Gwynn put on the gloves, hurried to Whitehead's condo and slipped inside, hearing a peeping sound. Holly was five feet from the door, disconnecting the alarm system.

"That didn't take long," Holly said, straightening up. "We're looking for the documents Whitehead received from Patrick."

"But we're not going to take them?" Gwynn asked.

"No. We don't want Whitehead to suspect we know about them,"

Holly said, searching the kitchen cabinets. "Whitehead might know Patrick was questioned by the FBI, but Patrick didn't divulge any information. He's probably relying on Young to keep the legal forces at bay or at least warn him, since Young has a stake in it."

Gwynn glanced around the furniture and saw only one spot large enough for the computer printouts, headed to the television console and opened a drawer. "I found them. They're in here.

"Are they all there?" Holly asked.

"Let me check," she said, lifting them out. "One group a week?"

Holly knelt on the floor and began looking through them also. "The set I saw at Patrick's was for a week, but that might not be consistent."

Thumbing through them, Gwynn said, "They all cover a week, but if they started when Lander's production increased they're not all here. These only go back three months."

"Let's keep searching," Holly said.

The condo had two bedrooms. Gwynn took Whitehead's bedroom and Holly scrounged around in the other one.

Combing through his nightstand, Gwynn saw a pistol and held it up to examine it closer. It appeared new and held a full magazine, ready for unwanted nighttime visitors. She rummaged through his other drawers. No documents. In the closet, she saw two rifles leaning in the corner. "Whitehead has a pistol in his nightstand drawer and two rifles in his closet, but there aren't any documents in his bedroom."

Holly came into the room and peered into the closet. "I suspect one of those rifles was used when we were at the storage tanks."

"Wouldn't he have gotten rid of it?"

"Not if he thinks he's not on anyone's radar."

They sifted through the laundry room, linen cabinet and hall closet.

Holly shrugged. "They're not here. I had hoped we could avoid searching Young's place, but that's no longer an option."

"Young was a policeman. He knows about evidence. Would he leave that type of stuff lying around?"

"Those reports have to be somewhere, unless they were destroyed, which is exactly what would happen if they sensed someone was hot on their trail, but then we wouldn't have found any here. And, if they are at Young's house, it could lead whoever investigates his murder right to Prudell. We need to check out Young's place."

"Now?"

"Yes," Holly said. "Young's body could be discovered at any time—not likely, but possibly. Time is not on our side." She began reconnecting the alarm.

Gwynn peeked out the door and gave Holly the all clear sign. Holly attached the last wire and they hurried out.

"What about a key card?" Gwynn asked when they reached the building exit.

Holly took a small square metal device out of her backpack and moved it over the key pad. "I'll make one before we return."

"You have more gadgets than I do," Gwynn complained.

"Talk to Ruben about it."

Heading back to Bloomfield, Holly turned right two blocks from the police station and drove for ten minutes. Then she veered left onto Young's street. His single-story, light-brown, frame house was sandwiched between a large Victorian and a two-story brick with a deep front porch.

She parked the Accord two houses away. "Let's see what his backyard looks like," Holly said, reaching for your backpack.

They waited a few minutes for a woman to finish unloading groceries from her car in the adjacent driveway. Then they hurried to Young's backyard and found tall trees and bushes surrounded it and his back door was under a covered patio.

"This isn't too bad, much more private than I had anticipated," Holly said, slipping on gloves. She pulled out her disk attached to the reel, inched it under the door and kept track of the digital display as she moved it forward. "No surveillance cameras, but he has an alarm system."

With her gloved hands, Gwynn picked the door lock while Holly put away her disk. The two women entered and saw the alarm panel on the wall leading to the kitchen. Holly quickly disarmed it.

"If you see anything here applicable to Prudell, take it," Holly said and the search began.

Gwynn started in the kitchen and Holly went into the living room. Gwynn was still fishing through the cabinets when Holly moved into the master bedroom.

"They're on top of his dresser," Holly shouted. "What a dumb cop. He never struck me as being swift, but I didn't think he was a complete idiot." She stuffed them into her backpack."Keep looking, we might find other stuff."

They picked up more documents as they continued searching. When they were in the final room, the back bedroom, the doorbell buzzed. They abruptly stopped and looked at each other, motionless and listened.

A knock echoed through the house, followed by a soft rattle.

"Keys," Holly said. Both women crept, without making a noise, to the far side of the bed and stretched out on the floor, since hiding in closets gave no escape route.

"Sam, are you here?" a woman's voice rang out.

Footsteps moved down the hall. "Sam?" she yelled again.

Looking under the bed, Gwynn and Holly saw the woman's feet, clad in brown loafers, standing in the hallway.

"Sam?" she said again.

The crunching of box springs and a tapping sound came from the master bedroom. Holly mouthed, "She's making a call."

"Sam, it's me," the woman said. "Where are you? I'm at your house. I'll watch television until you show up."

After additional footsteps, they heard the television blaring through the house.

"We can't stay and wait for Sam," Holly whispered with an amused expression. "If she's sitting on the couch, she can't look into the hallway. We're going to have to sneak out the back door, but I need to hook up the alarm so no one will know it's been tampered with."

Gwynn inched toward the door with Holly behind her and peeked around the door frame. "Clear."

Holly took the lead. They tip-toed down the hallway to the kitchen doorway. She spotted the back of a woman, raised her hand and motioned for Gwynn to back up farther into the hallway. "She's doing something at the counter," Holly mouthed without letting a sound escape.

Gwynn's cell phone vibrated. She eased it out of her pocket and glanced at the number. She didn't recognize it and pocketed the phone.

"Who?" Holly mouthed.

Gwynn shrugged.

They heard the fridge door open and close. Holly peeked into the kitchen, tilted her head toward the door and snuck across the kitchen floor. Since the television volume was blasting through the house, she opened the back door without worrying about preventing a squeaking sound and they hurried out.

"I still need to hook up the alarm," Holly said.

"I'll go to the front door and think of something to say to the woman that will keep her occupied," Gwynn said and scurried around the house. She stepped on the porch and pushed the doorbell.

The door opened. "Can I help you?" a short brunette asked.

"I'd like to talk to Officer Young. Is he home?"

"He's not home yet."

"When will he be here?"

"I don't know."

"I live just a few blocks away and I was hoping he could do something about my neighbors."

"If this is a police matter, you should call the station. They'll send someone out."

"I have and last time Officer Young came. I just thought it would be easier if I came and got him, instead of calling the station."

"No. You need to call the station whenever it's a police matter. You shouldn't come to his house."

"But I looked up his address and everything," Gwynn said as she saw Holly out of the corner of her eye.

The woman's face became hard. "You need to call the station. That's how legal matters are dealt with and Officer Young isn't here."

"I'll come back later."

"No, call the station," the woman said through gritted teeth.

"See you later," Gwynn said, stepping off the porch and hearing the door slam shut.

CHAPTER 39

At 5:30 p.m., Gwynn and Holly returned home. Gwynn's brooch and its gold chain were lying on the kitchen table, just where Paul had said it would be. He wasn't in the house.

"I'm thirsty," Holly said, pulling a beer out of the fridge. "Want one?"

Gwynn nodded and checked her cell phone for the call she had received at Young's. The unrecognized number had left a message. She clicked on it.

"Gwynn this is Alex. Could you give me a call when you receive this message?"

"Who was it?" Holly asked between sips.

Gwynn pondered if something had happened at work after she left on Friday. "Hayes. He wants me to call him." She clicked on his number.

Hayes answered, "Gwynn, I'm so glad you called."

"Is there a problem?"

"I wanted to know if you could work tomorrow… a special project."

"Yes. I guess I can come in. What time?"

"Nine, or is that too early for a Sunday?"

"Nine's okay,"

"Thanks, I appreciate it."

"See you tomorrow," Gwynn said, then disconnected and took a swallow of her beer.

"What was that about?" Holly asked.

Mulling over the conversation, she said, "Hayes wants me to work tomorrow on a special project."

"It's good you have your brooch back."

"There wasn't anything you wanted me to work on, was there?"

"No. I'm going to be checking some stuff on the computer."

A couple of minutes after 7 p.m., Turk's Silverado came down the driveway. Holly and Gwynn walked out the door before he had a chance to climb out of the driver's seat.

Turk opened the truck door for Holly while Dave pushed the back door open for Gwynn.

"Anything new on the investigation?" Holly asked.

"Which one?" Dave asked.

"Any—the shootings or the break-ins?"

"They're piling up," Turk said. "Two break-ins and two shootings. It would just be simpler if Sam could handle all of them, instead of dealing with that Detective Marsden."

"You don't like Detective Marsden?" Holly asked.

"He's okay, but we all know Sam," Turk said.

The restaurant they went to was a converted fire station. Two oversized garage doors were raised and inside stood long wood tables with benches. Customers seated themselves on a section of a bench and then a waitress took orders.

After they ordered, Turk said, "This place isn't very fast. It'll take at least fifteen minutes before we're served. There's horseshoes out back if anyone is game."

"I am," Holly said.

Turk rolled his eyes. "Don't tell me you're an expert at that, too?"

"Well, I can hold my own," Holly replied with a mischievous smile.

"Let's see how bad you can slaughter me at that sport," Turk said and left with Holly.

"You didn't think you could play with your leg?" Gwynn asked Dave.

"Maybe, but I want to find out something,"

"What?"

"I heard you were thinking about leaving Bloomfield."

Gwynn cocked her brow. "Linda. I haven't decided what I want to do. Ross doesn't know if he wants to live here."

Dave took Gwynn's hand. "Would it be that bad if you stayed without him?"

"Dave, I've been engaged to Ross for over two years. He's part of my life."

A brief flash of dismay crossed his face and his eyes narrowed. "I sure would hate to see you leave."

From Dave's expression, Gwynn suspected he thought Ross was just stringing her along since he hadn't showed up at her doorstep once since she'd been in New Mexico. She had the urge to set him straight, but her engagement was just a cover, nothing more. "I like Bloomfield. I just need to figure it out."

After they had eaten their steaks, the guys ordered dessert. When their pie a la mode was almost gone, Holly's phone rang.

"Sorry, I should have put it on vibrate," Holly said, taking it out of her purse. She glanced at it. "It's my sister. She never calls so I better take this." Holly answered and moved away from the table.

A moment later, Holly returned with moist eyes.

"What's wrong?" Turk asked.

"My…" She swallowed hard. "My father's had a stroke," she sniffled.

Gwynn stood and put her arm around Holly's shoulders, though she knew that was Holly's excuse to leave town in a hurry without drawing any suspicion and Holly's father died years ago. None of Ruben's employees had living parents. "Uncle Ben? Oh, no! Did Lucy say how he was doing?"

"They don't know yet, or maybe she didn't want to tell me over the phone." Holly pulled a tissue out of her purse and dabbed her eyes.

"Let me get you home," Turk said, standing up.

"I'll pay the bill and meet you at the truck," Dave said.

Soon after they arrived at the house, Gwynn and Holly waited until the truck was out of sight, then left in the Accord to meet Paul at Young's cruiser.

Turning off the highway onto the gravel road, they saw a man dressed in a police uniform standing next to the patrol car. With the exception of his height, he bore no resemblance to Paul.

Holly rolled down the car window. "Are you all set?"

"Everything's ready." Paul stepped closer to the Accord. "Gwynn, drive my car and follow at least a mile behind Holly. Don't get too close. We don't want this to look like three vehicles are traveling together. Holly, the license plate."

Gwynn headed to Paul's car and noticed a dark substance, like mud, smeared all over his license plate, making it unreadable. In Paul's gloved hand, he held a grimy looking rag, swiped the Accord plates with it and threw it in a sack in Holly's trunk.

The cruiser eased onto the main road, followed by the Accord and Gwynn trailed behind. As they drove further away from town, Gwynn spotted a vehicle behind her that had strobe lights on top and slightly eased off the gas pedal, wanting to make sure it was a patrol car before she alerted the drivers ahead. It was. She pushed a button on her cell phone.

"Yeah," Paul answered.

"There's a patrol car behind me."

"Maintain the speed limit, so far nothing to worry about."

The vehicle drove by her. Panic struck when she saw red blinking lights ahead and feared the cop had recognized Young's car. *Maybe the cop had been searching for it.* She slammed the accelerator to the floor and sped past the Accord and the two patrol cars.

A siren erupted behind her as she drove swiftly along, wishing there was more traffic on that stretch of the road. She saw an intersection ahead. Her tires skidded as she made a sharp turn. The blinking red lights kept pace and the siren still blared.

Ahead were two cars, one going in her direction and the other going the opposite way. She zoomed past the one and only avoided colliding with the approaching vehicle by a couple of feet. Tires screeched and a cloud of dust rose behind her. The red lights were no longer visible in her rearview mirror, but she knew they were just temporarily hidden. At the same time, she knew the driver couldn't see her tail lights so it was her opportunity to become invisible and she flipped them off. She drove with only the light of the stars and moon reflecting on the pavement. Up ahead she caught a glimpse of a wooded area and glanced at her rearview mirror. No blinking lights were in sight. She eased off the gas pedal and stopped next to the trees, then softly pressed on the accelerator and moved over the rough terrain behind the trees and turned the car so the hood pointed toward the asphalt.

Gwynn punched Holly's number.

"Good job," Holly answered.

"I just felt I needed to do something."

"I planned on doing that as soon as the cruisers pulled over to the side of the road. We'll talk at home. Is everything good with you?"

"Yeah."

"If you decide to drive my friend's car, make sure the license plate is clean. He always drives through the muddiest places and once I got stopped just because the number couldn't be seen."

"Got it. See you at home."

Gwynn opened the trunk, pulled out a container of wet wipes and cleaned off the license plate. After climbing behind the steering wheel, she moved the car forward with the headlights off, watched a couple of cars drive by and made her way back onto the pavement. Gwynn drove back the same way she came, not exceeding the speed limit. She saw a sedan and a cruiser parked along the side of the road. The front fender of the car was dented, but she didn't notice any damage on the patrol vehicle. A policeman, standing by the side of the road, gazed at her as she went by, but didn't flag her down or show any sign of concern.

As she continued making her way home, Gwynn saw two other police cruisers, which was unusual for that stretch of road and became convinced they were looking for Young's car. *Maybe the driver of the other cruiser had radioed it in.*

It was 11:20 p.m. when she arrived at the house. Paul and Holly walked through the door twenty minutes later.

"How did it go?" Gwynn asked.

"All taken care of," Paul said.

"What happened to the beer bottles that were in here," Gwynn said, referring to those standing on the coffee table earlier.

"Just needed fingerprints," Paul said. "Got 'em. The bottles are in the recycle bin."

"We already had Whitehead's prints. Why did you need more?"

"Transferred them to the cruiser."

"You can do that?"

"Sure," Paul said.

"It's pretty simple if you have the right equipment," Holly commented, setting up the computer and N-phone on the kitchen table.

"I made coffee if you guys want some," Gwynn said.

With a steaming cup in front of her, Holly placed the call to Ruben.

Gwynn stared at Ruben's handsome face. Her skin tingled with anticipation that they could be together soon. She missed him so much, but she had been warned about the possibility of long periods where they didn't see each other.

"I assume you all have things to report. Let's start with Gwynn's Friday adventure."

Gwynn filled him in on the time she had spent with Young.

"I suspected it could be him or he had a connection," Ruben said. "Most cops don't want to hone in on another jurisdictions investigation like Young did on the shootings. He would have gotten involved when the office break-in occurred in his jurisdiction, but not until then."

Gwynn thought a hint might have been nice, but since her colleagues didn't speak up she kept her mouth shut.

Ruben continued, "That would have been a point of discussion today if nothing else materialized. Anything else, Gwynn?"

"When I was having dinner with Linda, I mentioned that I had seen Young and Whitehead having a disagreement."

"Did she ask what it was about?"

"Yeah. I told her I thought it was about Janice since it happened right after Young had been eyeing her, but then Linda said she had noticed some friction between them."

Ruben gave her smile. "You planted a seed."

"Also, my excuse for being late to meet her was because I was talking to Ross. He might not want to live in Bloomfield, so there was a chance I'd be moving back to New York."

"Another seed," Ruben said.

"That's it," Gwynn said. "Holly and Paul can do a better job filling you in on the other stuff."

"Paul go first and begin with the cruiser."

Paul briefed him on moving it twice and adding Whitehead's fingerprints. "I left six of Whitehead's business cards at various places in the cruiser since his prints aren't on any police records. And Gwynn did a great job getting that cop with his blinking strobe lights off my tail." He rubbed his jaw. "I drew his suspicion when I didn't respond to the radio call."

"He was probably looking for Young," Ruben said. "And the bullet?"

"It was a messy job, but with that device it was a snap to retrieve," Paul said.

This was the first Gwynn had heard that Paul went after the bullet lodged in Young's body.

"Good. I'll have to get more of those. Gwynn, that Berretta can be used again." Ruben briefly looked down. "Paul, did you run across anything interesting when you searched Carlsen's place?"

"A pistol and two boxes of ammo in his dresser, a rifle in his closet and a knife under his mattress. He's prepared for unwelcome visitors. Outside of that, only a few bills and bank statements. No other documents."

"Holly?" Ruben said.

Holly briefed him on searching Whitehead's place and Young's.

"Anything new to report on Carlsen's calls or from hanging around with him?"

"No. His calls were chitchats to his friends, nothing out of the ordinary. Since I started monitoring his cell phone calls, there hasn't been one to Whitehead or Young. And I also planted a seed by having Paul call me when Gwynn and I were at a restaurant with Turk and Dave. I told them it was my sister reporting that my father had just had a stroke."

"Good." Ruben's head slowly turned, looking at each one of them. "Before I get started with the next steps, is there anything else I should know?"

Gwynn proceeded to tell Ruben what happened at work on Friday morning that led her to believe Ashton Prudell was working on fixing the flow lines.

"That's interesting," Ruben said, without showing any sign that he had sent the letter to Ashton.

"Hayes called yesterday and he wants me to work tomorrow on a special project. I'm thinking it might have something to do with that."

"On a Sunday?"

She glanced at the clock on the wall. "It's late, nearly two in the morning, so I'll be going there later this morning."

"Let's finalize this investigation," Ruben said. "Monday morning, Holly, call the office and quit your job. Don't go in. You and Paul will go to Whitehead's place and get the documents. Then you'll go to Robinson's and erase everything on Patrick's computer that has any connection to Prudell. Holly, is there any special software Prudell can add to their computer system so that won't happen again?"

"Yes," she said and gave Ruben the names of a few software programs.

"By two p.m., I want you to be ready to leave for the airport. We'll talk privately after this conference."

Holly nodded.

"Paul, you'll have to keep track of both Gwynn and Turk today. Gwynn will be at the office, so that shouldn't be a problem. If it becomes one, have Holly help. Monday, when you get back to the house with Holly..." He leaned forward and kneaded the bridge of his nose. "Call me at 7 p.m. I want to know why Gwynn went to work today before we proceed."

"Do you still want me to call you after this conference call?" Holly asked.

"Yes," Ruben replied and disconnected.

Holly unhooked her N-phone from the computer, stepped into the bedroom and closed the door.

"I wonder if you'll be leaving tomorrow," Gwynn said to Paul.

"Probably not until Whitehead is in custody," Paul said. "He might go after revenge if he discovers the flow lines have been repaired. Most likely, he'll think Carlsen tipped off Prudell."

"How about me?" Gwynn asked.

"Doubt if you're that high on his list. Carlsen would be in the top spot especially if Whitehead suspects Carlsen has learned about Williams' death. They were good buds and Carlsen's already upset about the Brotherhood."

"You're right and Turk's such a nice guy. Boy was that stupid of him to get involved."

"Prisons are filled with nice guys who made stupid mistakes."

"I'm going to bed. I need to get up in five hours."

"See you when the sun comes up," Paul said as Gwynn headed out of the room.

CHAPTER 40

At 8:57 a.m., Gwynn walked into the office building and saw Hayes waiting for her in the lobby. "Good morning, Alex."

"Good morning," he said, locking the entrance door.

"Is that necessary?"

"Yes. We're the only ones here and Ashton told me to keep the door locked. Come to my office and I'll tell you what this is all about."

Gwynn stopped at her desk, picked up a notepad and followed Hayes.

Hayes situated himself in his chair behind the desk. "As you know I've been concerned about the Cisco unit workovers."

Gwynn studied his face and demeanor. His cheeks looked a little rosy, his eyes shined and the tension she had noticed in his jaw and shoulders was gone. "Yes. Did Dave figure out the problem?"

"No. Ashton did and talked to me yesterday morning. I won't bore you with all the details, but around the time of the workovers, the flow lines leading to the Bamberg battery needed maintenance. There was a screw up. The flow lines didn't end up connecting to the right storage tanks."

"The Lander and Cisco units?"

"Yes. The Cisco oil production flowed into the Lander storage tanks and Lander into Cisco's except for one Lander well, which went to the right tank."

"What would you like me to do?"

"Ashton has some men working on the flow line problem right now. It will be fixed sometime today. He wants us to adjust the revenue distributions applicable to the two units. We're going to have to calculate figures since that one well was hooked up correctly."

"It would have been easy if we could just switch the production and revenues of the two units."

"I agree. There's not a problem with the gas production. I've started calculating the oil production based on GOR's back to when Lander's oil production spiked. Based on that number I've computed the sold volumes."

"How are we going to get the money back from the Lander interest owners?"

"Over time. Ashton doesn't want us to send out invoices requesting the money be returned since it was a company screw up. He wants us to compute each owner's overpayment and then reduce their future revenue until it has been recouped."

"And we'll pay the Cisco interest owners?"

"Yes. He wants those payments to go out as soon as possible, along with a letter stating that not all of the production had been accounted for in their earlier revenue distributions."

"Who's signing the letters?"

"Ashton."

"Most, if not all of those interest owners get paid electronically."

"All the better. We'll pay them and enclose their payment summary with the letter. Get started with the first two months." He handed Gwynn a sheet containing the oil production sales numbers.

"We could get a software program to compute this," Gwynn said.

"Ashton wants to keep this quiet until the Cisco interest owners are paid. We'll do it on spreadsheets and enter the adjustments. Since there aren't that many interest owners in either unit, it shouldn't take us that long."

"I'll get right on it," Gwynn said and went to her desk.

Within five hours, all the reversals and adjustments had been posted into the system for the two units, the electronic transfers had been completed and a check had been issued to the one interest owner who hadn't signed up for electronic deposits. The letters had been printed and ready for Ashton's signature.

"Are we going to send anything out to the Lander interest owners?" Gwynn asked.

"They'll get a letter in the regular distribution cycle."

Normally, Gwynn would have thought that wasn't fair since those interest owners might have been relying on a large distribution. At the same time, she knew most of them had been involved in the scam, so delaying their notifications was probably for the best.

"Thanks for helping," Hayes said, unlocking the door. "And

letting me spoil your Sunday."

"You didn't spoil anything. I didn't have any plans for the day. See you tomorrow."

When Gwynn walked into the house, she saw boxes and bags on the floor and Holly's tables were all cleared off except for her laptop computer.

"Getting ready to leave, huh?" Gwynn asked.

"Yeah," Holly said. "It takes a little while to get everything packed up, especially since it will be shipped. I won't be taking it with me. It's easier if you can just throw the stuff in a trunk." She finished taping up a box. "Have you had lunch?"

"No," Gwynn said, moving toward the kitchen. "I thought I'd make a sandwich. Have you eaten?"

"An hour ago," Holly said. "I just made another pot of coffee. I'm sure you could use a cup, since you didn't get much sleep last night. How are you feeling?" She sat down at the kitchen table.

"Better, but my whole mid-section is black and blue." Gwynn opened the fridge and pulled out bread, lunchmeat and condiments. "After lunch, I'm taking a pill and a nap."

"Good idea. What did you work on?"

"Adjusting all the revenue for the Lander and Cisco units, based on the right production numbers."

Holly grinned. "Whitehead is going to love that!"

"Yeah," Gwynn said, making a sandwich. "I almost wish I could see the expression on his face when he finds out."

"How is Prudell going to get the money back?"

"Through future distributions. No bills will be sent for the overpayments."

"So what they have, they get to keep. They just won't be getting any more for a long time … maybe years."

"And with the delay in payments, I'm sure he's planning on getting a share of last month's revenue," Gwynn said, pouring coffee. She carried her sandwich and coffee to the table.

Holly leaned on her elbow. "Delay?"

"Yes. April oil sales are billed and Prudell gets paid in May. The interest owners get paid in June. It's about six weeks after the end of the production month."

"That makes sense—you can't pay them until you have the money. So they've been overpaid for four months and not five, right?"

"Yes."

"Are all the adjustments in the computer system?" Holly asked, twirling her mug around on the table.

Gwynn nodded. "All done—Cisco interest owners have either been paid in electronic fund transfers or a check. Simple letters are going out saying they didn't get paid for all the oil sales. Won't they be surprised when they check their bank accounts, if they do it before they receive the letter."

"I hope Patrick doesn't do any snooping into Prudell's computer today." Holly stood. "I'm going to set up a notification if he does."

Gwynn ate her sandwich and drank coffee as she gazed out at the woods, pondering if she'd be with Ruben on her next assignment. Then she sighed, thinking she was lucky to have another assignment, given her screw-ups on this one.

"Patrick hasn't been in the system yet," Holly said, standing in the doorway. "We'll hear a beeping sound from my computer if he enters their site. I wish I could prevent it, but I'd need to either adjust his computer or have software added to Prudell's system."

"It's too bad Paul isn't going with you," Gwynn said and saw the corners of Holly's mouth slightly curve up for a second, then Holly pressed her lips together. Gwynn assumed that meant Paul would be joining Holly on her next assignment. Ruben didn't like his people to mention were they were going or with whom while they're still working on an investigation. Also, they were never allowed to discuss ongoing investigations with other employees who weren't part of that team.

"I'm hoping Carlsen calls it an early night so Paul won't be out too late."

"Do you want me to help you pack?" Gwynn asked.

"No. I've got everything under control. Go lie down."

"If I completely zonk out, I don't want to sleep past six. Can you wake me?"

"Will do."

At 7 p.m., Ruben's image appeared on the monitor.

"Hi, boss," Holly said.

"You there, Paul?" Ruben asked.

"Yes. Just sitting by Carlsen's place."

"I don't have much time," Ruben said. "Gwynn, why did Hayes want you to come in?"

"To fix all the accounting on Cisco and Lander units—adjusting the volumes, revenues and paying the Cisco interest owners."

"Back to when the problem started?"

"Yes. Most were paid electronically, but one check will go out tomorrow."

"The flow lines are fixed?"

Gwynn's head bobbed up and down. "Yes."

"And how about the Lander interest owners?"

Gwynn briefed him on how they would be treated.

"So they won't immediately know." Ruben rubbed his chin with his knuckles. "Let's see if we can't inform Whitehead while Paul and Gwynn are still there. Holly and Paul proceed as discussed earlier: getting documents from Whitehead's place, erasing any Prudell documents on Patrick's computer. Holly, while you're on Patrick's computer use it to send Whitehead an email if Young's body hasn't been discovered."

"I'll call Gwynn," Holly said. "They'll be buzzing around the office when that happens."

"In the email say something like, 'The man heard the problem at Prudell's had ended, so I won't be giving you any more documents.'"

"Won't he wonder why 'the man' didn't contact him about that?" Holly asked.

"Then add, 'the man would have contacted you but he's having problems with his computer.' If Whitehead is half-smart, he'll figure that means someone is tapping into Young's computer."

A beeping sound came from Holly's computer.

"What's that?" Ruben asked.

Holly pushed a key on her computer, stopping the noise. "The kid just got into Prudell's system. The adjustments Gwynn made today are in it. I couldn't prevent him from getting in, so I put a notification on my computer. Patrick might be looking at the various places on the system where employees have gone and not the revenue. I can check when he gets out."

"Also look at his email and find out if he sent one to Whitehead or Young after he got into the system."

"When I checked Patrick's emails earlier, he hadn't sent or received one from Young during the past three months. They must communicate by cell phone or in person."

"He'll probably try to contact Young first." Ruben's head bent like he was looking at something below his computer screen. "Paul, if Whitehead should come looking for Carlsen, warn Carlsen and let him take care of Whitehead. We can't handle that problem. If the police aren't able to locate a shooter, it is going to be difficult for Gwynn to leave."

"How about a warning shot if I can't contact Carlsen?"

"Yes, but no bullet penetration unless he comes after you or Gwynn and remember Gwynn is your main responsibility. Since the flow lines are repaired, we're only tracking Carlsen now because Whitehead will probably go after him before he goes after Gwynn."

"Understood."

"Paul, when you and Holly are through retrieving docs and dealing with Patrick's computer, place an anonymous call about Williams' truck. Tuesday morning, make one about Young's cruiser."

"Got it, boss," Paul said.

"Gwynn, tomorrow, give your notice and make it for only one week. Find some excuse why it can't be longer. I want you and Paul on a plane Friday evening. You'll both get the details later this week. I need to get going." He disconnected.

"Gwynn, get your computer," Holly said. "I'm going to put a little program on it so you can monitor Patrick's emails after I'm gone." Within fifteen minutes after Gwynn handed over her computer, Holly had installed and set up the program so all Gwynn needed to do was click on an icon. While she was working on it, she noticed Patrick hadn't sent or received any emails after they heard the alert.

Holly's cell phone rang. "Hey," she answered. "That's right… okay." She hung up. "Paul thinks Turk is in for the evening. He's going to wait there until ten and then put a little disk on his exterior door handles."

"What do they do?"

"Make an obnoxious loud squealing sound if someone touches the knob. It will definitely wake up Turk and scare off the potential visitor. Paul will be here after he's taken care of that."

"What if Turk leaves?"

"Paul will be monitoring him. Hopefully, he can get back to retrieve the disk before Turk returns; otherwise, loud noise, no harm done. Paul's going to drive by the abandoned house on his way here to make sure the truck is still there."

Holly discovered Patrick had been in both the production and revenue files for the Lander unit and knew he had seen the adjustments. Every half an hour she checked Patrick's emails. No new ones were sent to Whitehead.

CHAPTER 41

Before Gwynn left for work on Monday, Holly verified Patrick hadn't sent Whitehead any emails after 11 p.m., the last time she looked the night before.

"I'm going to miss you," Gwynn said, hugging Holly.

"I like it when I'm the first to leave," Holly said, referring to investigations. "Waiting for the end of an employment notice can get pretty boring. Everything is normally over, but your last week here could be interesting."

"I've had enough action during this case. I hope I'm just an observer."

After Paul retrieved the disks off Carlsen's door, he drove back to the house and followed Gwynn to work. Then he returned and picked up Holly. They drove to Whitehead's place and entered the building with the key card Holly had made the day before. When they reached Whitehead's condo, Paul pulled an instrument out of his backpack, a mike that could pick up the faintest sound and pressed it against the door. "There's movement inside," he whispered, lowering it.

"You've got to be kidding," Holly whispered. "Why isn't he at work?"

Paul shrugged, took Holly's arm and led her away from that end of the hallway. "He drives a blue, heavy-duty Ford truck. Let's wait in the car and see if it leaves."

"Only for half an hour," Holly said. "If he hasn't left by then, we'll go to Robinson's and then return."

Paul and Holly watched and waited, but no truck left. Paul started the engine and pulled away from the curb. "Could be he got the day off since he worked over the weekend," he said, driving back to Bloomfield. "You have his office number?"

"No, but I can look it up." Holly lifted her cell phone from her purse and zoomed through several screens. "Got it. Should I call and ask for him or do you want too?"

"I'll do it." He pulled over to the side of the road and took his phone out of his breast pocket. "Number." After Holly gave it to him, he punched in the numbers. "Can I speak to Kevin Whitehead," he said, in a scratchy voice, three octaves lower than his. "Thank you." He clicked off. "He's expected in at one." Paul steered back onto the highway.

"Oh, great!" Shaking her head, her mouth thinned into a flat line. "After Patrick's, we'll pick up my car and both of us will drive back here. Otherwise, I won't get to the airport on time."

"Flying out of Albuquerque or Farmington?"

"Farmington. My plane isn't until 3:20 p.m., but I need to send my stuff and drop off the car."

"If we have time before one, you can mail your stuff and then you'll only have to deal with the car." Paul laid his hand on her thigh. "You have plenty of time."

"Maybe I could also drop off the car."

"Yeah, I can take you to the airport. Gwynn will still be at work."

They parked across the street from Robinson's place. The house appeared as if no one was at home. Paul pulled out his mike again, pointed it toward the house and walked around. "All I hear is the humming of the fridge," he said. "I'll keep watch outside."

"Let me call Gwynn to make sure Young hasn't been discovered."

"Hi, Holly," Gwynn answered.

"Any news about Young?"

"No. It's been pretty quiet here."

"Good." Holly disconnected and put on a pair of gloves. She picked the lock, entered and disconnected the alarm. Going into Patrick's room, she saw a stack of papers on his bed. She thumbed through them and discovered he had printed all of the revenue revisions for the Lander unit. Holly stuffed them in her backpack and searched his room for other Prudell documents, but didn't find any more. She situated herself in front of Patrick's computer and went to work deleting files, making sure there was no way he could retrieve them. She also made an adjustment to his operating system so he wouldn't be able to tap into Prudell's system again. When that was taken care of, she clicked on his email and found one he had sent to

Whitehead an hour earlier. It said: "Been trying to contact 'the man.' Do you know where he is?"

Holly took a deep breath—nothing to worry about, no mention of the revenue. Then she composed an email to Whitehead: "The problem at Prudell has ended so I won't be giving you any more docs. 'The man' would've contacted you, but he's having problems with his computer."

She didn't want Whitehead to get the message until after the documents had been retrieved from his place. Holly set it up so it wouldn't be delivered until 2:30 p.m. and hit send. Next, she deleted the message from Patrick's "Sent" folder and then from his "Trash" folder.

After closing and locking his door, she headed downstairs, reconnected the alarm and hurried to the car.

"How did it go?" Paul asked, easing the car back onto the street.

"The kid had printed off all the revenue adjustments and had sent Whitehead a message, looking for 'the man.'"

"Mention the revenue?"

"No. I sent Whitehead the message Ruben talked about last night, but it won't be delivered until 2:30 p.m. I didn't want to take a chance that Whitehead could hide the documents. It'd be okay if he destroyed them, but we'd have no way of knowing."

"Better safe than sorry."

"I want to shred what I got at Patrick's, before we take off again."

An hour later, Paul and Holly drove their cars out of the driveway and headed to Farmington. Paul parked behind her when she stopped to send boxes. Then she went to the car rental agency, moved her suitcase to Paul's car and delivered her car keys to the front desk.

"It feels so good to have that out of the way," Holly said. "But now I'm no longer armed."

"I am," Paul said. "And there's a pistol under the seat if we run into a problem."

"Whitehead will be at work, so we should be fine."

At 1 p.m., Paul and Holly entered Whitehead's condo. The documents were still in the television stand. Paul pushed them into his backpack.

"I'm going to hide his rifles," Holly said, walking toward his bedroom. "I think one was used at the storage tanks. He might try to get rid of it when he discovers his Cisco/Lander scheme has been unveiled." She opened his closet and picked them up. "I want the police to find them in here. Got any good hiding places?"

"Whitehead will think someone has stolen them, not concealed them." Paul went into the other bedroom and opened the closet. "Given their lengths, they won't fit everywhere. How about the top of this closet? There's boxes and bulky clothing on the shelf—sweaters, sweatshirts, a pair of ski pants."

"Let's stick them behind that," Holly said, handing them to Paul. "I'm getting his pistol. Don't want to make it too easy for revenge." She opened Whitehead's nightstand drawer and rummaged through it. "It's not here."

"Look in the other drawers."

They went through all the bedroom and kitchen drawers and then searched through the cabinets. "He's taken it with him," Paul said. "Did you see any ammo when you were here before?"

"Yes. In the nightstand."

Paul looked in it. No ammunition. "He's armed."

"And he'll be dangerous when he reads Patrick's email," Holly commented. "It's after two; I need to get going."

Paul reconnected the alarm system and they left Whitehead's condo. He dropped Holly off at the airport, went to a public telephone booth and placed the anonymous call to the county police department about Williams' truck.

It was 4 p.m. when Paul drove by Prudell's office and saw a patrol car parked out front.

CHAPTER 42

Shortly after Gwynn arrived at work, she gave her notice to Hayes. She told him it was because her fiancé had received a large raise and he didn't want to leave the company so she had decided to move back to New York.

"Will it be okay if my last day is this Friday? Ross, my fiancé, wants me to go with him on a business trip to Europe."

"Of course," Hayes said with a smile. "You must be pretty anxious to see him since he hasn't been able to visit since you've been here."

Gwynn returned his smile. "I am."

"When you talk to Susan, give her my best about her father."

"I will. Is there anything special you'd like me to take care of this week?"

"Just the payroll and invoices. I'll try to get a temp so you can work with that person for at least a couple of days before you leave."

"That would be good," Gwynn said and went into the lobby.

"Did you hear about Officer Young?" Marilyn asked with eyes wide open.

Gwynn gripped the counter. "No."

"He's missing."

"Missing?"

"Yes. My neighbor just called. She heard it from her friend that works at the police station."

"Are you sure that's accurate? I haven't heard anything on the news."

"That's exactly what I said to her, but her friend told her they didn't want to release that information until they had exhausted their local search since he wasn't scheduled to work over the weekend."

"How do they know he's missing?"

"A girlfriend called."

"He might not be missing at all. Maybe he just went away for the weekend."

Marilyn squinted. "With his patrol car?"

"That's missing, too?"

Marilyn nodded.

"That is strange. It isn't easy hiding a patrol car." *I know that first hand.*

Around 2:45 p.m., Detective Marsden entered the building along with a uniformed policeman and requested to see Ashton. Marilyn contacted him and a minute later, Ashton came into the lobby and escorted them to his office.

Gwynn had a hard time concentrating on her work as she wondered what it was about. Finally, she gave up and walked over to the counter. "Do you have any idea why Detective Marsden is here?"

"Earlier I asked Mr. Prudell if there was anything new on the cases. He said that Detective Marsden had called him over the weekend. The police had discovered some new evidence that the Detective wanted to talk to him about, but he never set up a time."

"Then what was the point of the call?"

"Mr. Prudell thought it was because he had been calling them every day to get an update on the shooting investigation. He doesn't appear to be too concerned about the break-in, but that's probably because no one was hurt there."

Gwynn rested her hands on the counter. "I haven't even asked today—how is Karl Lee doing?"

"Good. Real good. They think he'll make a complete recovery. Poor kid." Marilyn shook her head. "I'm still having a hard time believing Brad could have done that."

"It's amazing how Brad has vanished. You'd think he would have mentioned where he was going to at least one friend."

"They'll find him. It's just a matter of time."

Detective Marsden and the uniformed policeman rushed into the lobby and out the door. "What was that all about?" Gwynn said.

Ashton stepped into the lobby. "Marsden received a call in my office and leapt out of his chair. He told Engel, the uniformed policeman, they had a lead on the truck. They grabbed their plastic bag and hurried out."

"Was evidence in the plastic bag?" Marilyn asked.

"Yes. It was some documents about the Cisco unit. Marsden wanted to verify that they were some of the documents taken at the downtown office."

"Where did they find them?" Marilyn asked.

"Brad Williams had them."

"They just searched his house?" Gwynn asked, wrinkling her nose.

"No. They did that on Wednesday. Brad had a locker at a gym. They found them there."

"At a gym?" Marilyn asked in a tone of disbelief.

"Strange," Ashton said, "but had he not taken off, no one would have thought to look there… among sweaty clothes."

"Why would Brad have taken them?" Gwynn asked.

Ashton shrugged and raised his brows.

"Will the Detective and the officer come back or call you and let you know if it was the company truck?" Marilyn inquired.

Ashton gazed toward the front of the building. "They left a patrol car here so they have to come back sometime, but they might not come in." He turned. "Did you get the letters out in the noon mail?" he asked Marilyn.

"Yes, they're gone. I also have the letters printed we'll be sending to the Lander unit owners. Do you want to sign them now or should I bring them in when we're ready to distribute?"

"I'll take them now," Ashton said. After Marilyn handed him the letters, he went to his office.

Marilyn propped her elbows on the counter and leaned her chin on her hands. "This is a bad thing to say, but I've never looked so much forward to coming to work as I have lately with all these investigations. This is a pretty exciting place to work."

"It is," Gwynn said and returned to her desk.

At 5 p.m., when Gwynn left the office, the patrol car was still parked out front.

Gwynn unlocked the door to her house, stepped over the threshold and saw how barren the front room looked, with all of Holly's stuff gone. The two tables had been folded and were leaning against the far wall. She heard a rap on the back door and let Paul in. "Didn't Holly give you her key?"

He shook his head. "It must have slipped her mind."

"I'll get another one made tomorrow."

Paul pulled a device, with earplugs dangling from it, out of his pocket and attached it to the monitor on the kitchen table. Jumbled voices came through the airwaves and he said, "Try to ignore that. I don't want to turn it down." He took documents out of his backpack. "What were the police doing at your office?"

Gwynn filled him in on what happened at work.

"The cop just left it parked there?"

"Yeah. Marsden and Engel, the other officer's name, must have driven separately to Prudell.

"When I called in the anonymous tip, the officer on the phone sounded like he didn't want to be bothered writing the information down. Surprised Marsden was notified. I had thought I might need to call again." Paul zipped up his bag. "Where's your paper shredder?"

"I'll get it," she said and went into the bedroom. "Did you get everything taken care of at Whitehead's and Robinson's?"

"Yeah. The kid had printed off all the revenue adjustments. Holly shredded them earlier. And Whitehead is packing. His pistol wasn't anywhere in his place."

Gwynn's brows furrowed. "Why now? He doesn't know about Young yet and Brad was already dead when Holly and I checked Whitehead's place."

"He could've carried it before and left it in his nightstand since he was flying."

"Good point."

"Holly also hid his rifles. She didn't want to take a chance he'd get rid of them or use them when he learns about Young."

"In his condo?"

Paul nodded. "The cops will find them if they search his place."

"Yeah, he won't look for them there. He'll think they were snatched." She tapped her bottom lip. "By whom?"

"Turk Carlsen or you. A complete stranger wouldn't know about the rifles. If he notices they're gone before he finds out about Young, he might think Young took them." Paul quickly moved to the monitor and turned up the volume.

Turk's voice blared through the speaker. "… wasn't me."

"Where's Young!" Whitehead snapped.

"Haven't got the slightest idea. Let go of me," Turk growled.

Then came the unmistakable sound of a slap, followed by a thud.

Gwynn and Paul looked at each other.

"Get out of here!" Turk ordered.

A door slammed shut.

Gwynn bit her upper lip. "Do you think Whitehead will do anything before he discovers Young's fate?"

"That's a tough call. If Patrick tells Whitehead what he found, he might not wait to hear from 'the man.'"

"I'm going to check Patrick's emails. Holly set it up on my laptop." Gwynn put her computer down on the coffee table and Paul sat next to her on the couch. She clicked on the new icon. "Patrick received three from Whitehead." She went to the first one.

It said: "When did you hear from the man?"

Patrick responded: "I haven't heard from him since Friday."

Whitehead's next email said: "But you sent me an email that the man told you not to give me any more docs."

The reply said: "That wasn't from me. In my last email to you I said I was trying to contact 'the man' and I wanted to know if you knew where he was. That was it! But something's wrong with my computer, maybe a virus, didn't you get that email?"

Whitehead's said: "I got it."

"Mmm. Patrick didn't mention the docs Holly took, the revenue adjustments," Paul said, rubbing his chin.

"Maybe he thinks 'the man' came in and picked them up. Do you think Young would have a key to Robinson's house?"

"Possibly. The kid could've given him one since Young was an outstanding member of the police force... a trustworthy guy."

"Yeah. A real outstanding citizen," Gwynn said, turning off her computer. "I'm not planning on going anywhere tonight if you want to keep track of Turk."

"No. I'll stay here unless something comes over the monitor that needs my immediate attention. Early in the morning, I'm calling in the anonymous tip about Young. Whitehead will probably know before the day ends."

CHAPTER 43

When Gwynn arrived at work, Marilyn, Debra and Hayes were busy chitchatting at the counter about the discovery of Brad's truck.

"That house where it was found belongs to Turk Carlsen," Marilyn said.

"Really?" Debra said.

Gwynn joined in the conversation. "Did they catch Brad?"

"No, but there was a blood stain on the floor," Debra said.

The phone rang and the group dispersed as Marilyn picked up the receiver. "Prudell Energy Company. May I help you?" After a pause, she continued, "Let me get him." She pushed a button on her phone. "Mr. Prudell, Detective Marsden's on the line. He wants to talk to you … okay." Marilyn hung up.

A short while later Ashton stepped into the lobby. "Marilyn, I'm going to Marsden's office. I should be back within a couple of hours."

"Anything new?" she asked in an anxious tone.

"I'll let you know when I return."

Since Turk worked out of the downtown office, Gwynn decided to give Dave a call to find out what he knew.

"Hi, Gwynn," Dave said.

"Hi. I just heard Brad's truck was found at Turk's house."

"Turk owns the place, but that isn't where he lives. Turk hasn't even been there for months. He has a guy come and mow down the weeds every couple of weeks. Turk thinks the guy reported the truck, but he can't figure out why he didn't call him first."

"How would the guy know it was Brad's truck?" she asked.

"Since Brad shot Karl Lee, his picture has been all over the news along with the truck."

"But the company trucks all look the same."

"No," Dave said. "I took better care of mine than Brad and he has one of those unnecessary foot rails."

"Unnecessary? Does he have a Bose sound system?"

He replied, "His necessities and mine aren't the same."

"Debra said there was a blood stain on the floor."

"Yeah. They don't have a sample of Brad's, so they can't do a match."

"Do you think Brad was injured and someone picked him up?" she asked.

"Naw. Turk and I are probably his best pals. He also hangs out with Kevin, Janice's boyfriend, sometimes, but that guy wouldn't lift a finger to help anyone."

"That's not very nice to say," Gwynn said, hoping Dave would give more information.

"He's not a nice guy." Then Dave changed the subject. "Are you feeling bad you're leavin'?"

"In some ways, but like I told you at the restaurant, Ross is part of my life. I want to be with him."

"How about letting me take you to lunch on your last day?"

"Sounds good," she said. "You've got a date."

An hour later, Hayes had her come to his office so he could drill her about the case, thinking she might know more, since Brad was a suspect in the shooting at the well. Gwynn couldn't provide him with more information than Marilyn had already given him.

"Brad Williams seemed like such a pleasant person," Hayes said. "I just can't figure it out. He shot Karl Lee and it appears he was the one who shot Dave. Has the Detective come up with any kind of motive?"

"No. At least not that I know of."

"Since he was one of the Lander unit interest owners who were significantly overpaid, I could almost understand him going a little berserk after he realized he wasn't going to be paid those amounts anymore, but he didn't know that." Hayes tapped his fingertips on his desk.

Gwynn heard Ashton's voice in the lobby, but couldn't make out what was being said. "Mr. Prudell is back," she said. "I want to know if he found out anything."

"So do I." Hayes went with her to the lobby. "Have they figured out whose blood it was?" he asked Ashton.

Debra walked over to the counter to listen.

"No," Ashton said with drooping eyes. "Sam's been found dead, shot in the stomach."

"Sam?" Hayes said, as his brows tilted.

"Yes. In the trunk of his patrol car."

"But why?" Hayes asked.

Ashton shrugged.

"Do they think it was Brad?" Marilyn asked.

"They're going over his car and gathering fingerprints, but Sam drove around with a lot of different people. I suspect it's going to take some time to narrow it down. It could be someone he helped convict, some guy fresh out of prison, anything like that."

"He was working on the break-in and the shootings," Hayes said, "and Brad shot Karl Lee. Maybe he was trying to take him in."

"Could the blood in Turk's house be Officer Young's?" Debra asked.

"They're going to look into that," Ashton said.

Marilyn's features lined with concern. "Do you think Brad will come around here?"

"Until he's apprehended, I think we should all be extra cautious," Ashton said. "I don't want anyone working late in the building or parking behind it. Currently, the police have no motive, but it could be some kind of vendetta. His truck was traced to Dave's shooting. He shot Karl Lee." He scratched his chin. "And now if he's responsible for Sam's death, I just don't know where it's going to end."

At 3:20 p.m., Kevin Whitehead stormed into the Prudell's office building. Gwynn stood and saw his narrowed eyes and clenched jaw as he headed to the counter.

"May I help you?" Marilyn asked, scanning his face.

"I'm here to see Ashton Prudell," he said, sharply.

"Do you have an appointment?"

"No. Just tell him Kevin Whitehead wants to see him now!" Whitehead snapped.

"Let me check with Mr. Prudell." Marilyn picked up her phone and pushed a button. "Mr. Prudell there's a Mr. Whitehead here to see you. … I'll tell him."

"Mr. Whitehead, Mr. Prudell is too busy today. He asked me to set up an appointment for you." Marilyn flipped through Ashton's calendar.

"I don't need an appointment," Whitehead said and charged into the hallway. "Where are you Ash?" He turned right in the direction of Hayes' office.

Marilyn followed him. "Mr. Whitehead, you need an appointment."

Gwynn suspected Whitehead might be armed, so she hurried to the hallway and saw him pushing Marilyn, knocking her against a wall, as he went the opposite way.

"Kevin," Gwynn said from behind him, "you have to make an appointment. Mr. Prudell will see you, just not today."

Whitehead swung around and grabbed Gwynn's arm. "You're his spy, aren't you?"

Hayes and Ashton both stepped into the hallway.

"Let go of me," Gwynn said, jerking her arm and gripping his hand, as she attempted to free herself, without showing any of her skills.

Ashton raised his hand. "I'll see him. Kevin, this way." He gestured toward his office.

Whitehead released his hold on Gwynn, marched into Ashton's office and kicked the door shut.

"Everyone go back to work," Gwynn said as she ran out the front entrance. She rushed around the building the long way, so Whitehead wouldn't spot her through the floor-to-ceiling windows. One of the windows on the other side of Ashton's office was ajar. She pulled out her pistol, leaned against the exterior wall and listened.

"What's this all about Kevin?" Ashton asked.

"It's always about the same thing—Bridget," Whitehead said through gritted teeth.

Gwynn scrunched her face in confusion. *Huh. Bridget, Ashton's wife.*

Whitehead continued, "This time you've gone too far. You broke into my place! What did you expect to find? Something Bridget left?"

"Bridget has never been to your place!"

"While you were there, you stole some documents and my rifles!"

Ashton squinted. "I did what?"

"Or did you have Gwynn, your spy, do it?"

"Kevin I haven't got the foggiest idea what you're talking about, but I know Bridget doesn't want anything to do with you!"

A thud, smashing and clanging sounds rang out. Gwynn peeked around the window frame and saw the top of Ashton's desk had been swept clean and his books, paper, pens and pencils were scattered on the floor.

"What did you do that for?" Ashton asked.

"You ruined my life," Whitehead snapped. "You stole Bridget from me when you saw us together at her brother's company party. Then you couldn't even stand seeing her talking to me at Critten's annual parties, so you got me fired from a job I had for over seventeen years. What started it—that stupid fraternity problem? And now, somehow, you've sicced the police on me for Sam's death. You, the cheating husband, are you that desperate to keep me away from Bridget?"

"Kevin, you're wrong, I've never cheated on Bridget!"

"Tell that to Janice!"

"Whatever she's told you, it's not true. And you were let go at Critten Energy because you were stealing from the company. It had nothing to do with Bridget. As far as Sam's shooting, I didn't even know you were a suspect."

The throbbing sound of a siren came from off in the distance.

"You expect me to believe that? Don't play innocent with me about Sam. You found out! You know! And you want me punished!"

"Kevin, I don't know anything about Sam's death and I didn't get you fired from Critten. You did that to yourself. You should be lucky that you were just fired and not prosecuted. And you've been working for Brawny Oil for over three years and constantly calling Bridget since you arrived in Farmington. She's had to get her number changed five times! If I had all this power you seem to believe I possess, I'd get you fired from that job and out of our lives again!"

Whitehead's eyes bore into Ashton's, "If you're so smart, how did I steal from Critten?"

"You bought parcels of land under the name of a corporation when you knew Critten was planning to acquire them, because you were their landman on the deal. Then you negotiated with yourself for the sales price Critten would pay. Did you think you'd never get caught?"

"No!" Whitehead said. "It was you who caused me to lose that job! And it was you who sent the cops after me for Sam!"

"Kevin, I'm not after revenge for anything that's happened in the past and I haven't the slightest idea why anyone would think you were involved with Sam. I didn't even know you two knew each other."

"You got revenge. You married the only woman I've ever cared about. You got me fired from my job at Critten!" Whitehead drew his pistol from under his jacket. "You're a son-of-a-bitch. The rich boy! Given everything on a silver platter!"

Turk charged through the door, brandishing a gun. "Kevin, it's over. The cops will be here any second. Put down your weapon."

Whitehead lowered his pistol. "Turk, you don't get it! This bastard ruined my life!"

Turk's brow creased. "It wasn't the money?"

"No! It was to get even with this asshole!" He raised his weapon and aimed it at Ashton.

"Kevin, if you don't put down the gun, I'm going to shoot!" Turk cocked his pistol.

Whitehead swung his weapon toward Turk and pulled the trigger, striking him in the arm. Turk moaned, doubled over in pain and sank to the floor as his pistol discharged, shattering the window next to Gwynn.

Hunkering down below the broken window, Gwynn pointed her Beretta toward Whitehead and saw him move the barrel of his gun toward Ashton. She fired at the same time as she caught a glimpse of a weapon in Ashton's hand.

Whitehead's body plunged back, crashing into a bookcase and then dropped with a thump. He lay motionless, his chest covered with blood.

Gwynn holstered her weapon, crept away and stood up straight when she knew she couldn't be spotted from inside Ashton's office.

A policeman came around the building. "Miss," he said, quietly. "Get to the front of the building. It's dangerous out here."

"I just wanted to see what was going on," Gwynn said.

"That's how innocent bystanders are sometimes killed," the policeman informed her.

"Do you think Mr. Prudell's okay?"

"Just go to the front of the building. We'll let everyone know the status as soon as we've been able to make a determination."

Gwynn moved around the edge of the structure while the

policeman inched cautiously toward the window.

Marilyn, Hayes and Debra were huddled together in the front parking lot between two police cruisers. Marilyn was the first one to see Gwynn walking toward them from the side of the building. "What did you see?" she asked.

The sound of another blaring siren came from a few blocks away.

"With the shooting, that's probably an ambulance," Hayes said with downcast eyes.

Marilyn touched Gwynn's arm. "Go on, what did you see?"

"I didn't see anything. I was leaning against the wall and trying to listen."

"What did you hear?" Hayes asked in an anxious tone.

"Not a lot through a closed window, but it sounded like Whitehead was mad at Mr. Prudell over something and then I thought I heard Turk's voice just as a policeman pulled me away from the window. Just as well, because right after I left that spot, the window shattered."

Debra raised her hand and lifted a shard from Gwynn's hair. "You've got glass in your hair. You must have been close."

Gwynn lowered her head and scanned her body. "Am I cut anywhere?" she asked, trying to sound worried.

Hayes, Debra and Marilyn checked Gwynn's arms, neck and face.

"Bend over and see if you can't brush the rest of the glass out of your hair," Marilyn suggested.

Gwynn followed her instructions, as an ambulance stopped in the parking lot. Two paramedics stepped out of the cab, opened the back and pulled out a gurney. A policeman held the building door wide open while they rolled it through the entrance.

"God, I hope Mr. Prudell didn't get shot," Marilyn said, breathing rapidly and clutching her hands together.

"Was it Turk Carlsen's voice I heard in Mr. Prudell's office?" Gwynn asked, wondering how he happened to show up.

"Yes," Debra said. "He rushed through the lobby and asked where Whitehead was when Marilyn was on the phone talking to 9-1-1. I said he was in Mr. Prudell's office and he went into the hallway. I warned him not to go in there because there was a problem and Marilyn was calling the police, but he ignored me."

"Why were you calling 9-1-1?" Gwynn asked, knowing Mr. Prudell had dealt with other irate people and no one called the police.

"When Whitehead grabbed your arm," Hayes said. "I thought I saw the handle of a gun under his jacket. I could have been wrong, but I didn't want to take that chance, especially after the other shootings."

A police officer exited the building and went to one of the cruisers. Hayes walked over to him. "What's going on?"

"There are two victims. One will be transported to the hospital."

"And the other one?" Marilyn said, with moist eyes.

"He didn't survive his wound," the officer said, picking up his radio mike.

"Who?" Hayes asked.

"We can't release the name yet," he said and held his mike next to his mouth. "Now if you'll excuse me." He pushed a button and began talking into it.

Hayes put his arm around Marilyn's shoulders, trying to comfort her, while we all stared at the entrance, waiting for the gurney.

Fifteen minutes later, Turk was wheeled out of the building.

Marilyn ran up to him. "How is Mr. Prudell?"

"Fine. He wasn't injured."

Marilyn sighed and briefly closed her eyes. "Oh, thank God."

Gwynn stroked Turk's unbandaged arm. "You came to save Ashton."

His eyes meet hers. "I'm not a hero, quite the opposite. I'll probably be going to jail."

"What?" Gwynn said, squinting, while the paramedics raised Turk into the ambulance. Feeling bad that Turk was probably right, his mistake could land him behind bars, she watched the ambulance move onto the road. She wondered if Dave and Ashton would ever forgive him for what he had done.

"If Turk shot Mr. Whitehead, he won't go to jail for saving Mr. Prudell's life," Marilyn said.

"Did he shoot him?" Hayes asked.

"I don't know," Gwynn said. "Maybe Mr. Whitehead shot Turk."

"Then who would have shot Mr. Whitehead?" Hayes asked.

Gwynn's mind jumped to the bullet, her bullet lodged in Whitehead's body, and she wondered how the cops would handle that.

"Does Mr. Prudell have a gun in his office?" Debra asked.

"I've never seen one in there," Marilyn said.

Another ambulance entered the parking lot without any sirens throbbing. The paramedics pushed a gurney into the building. Within ten minutes, they rolled it out with a body bag lying on top.

Marilyn tilted her head toward the gurney. "Have any of you ever seen Mr. Whitehead before?"

"I have," Gwynn said. "He came into Marty's sometimes."

"Whitehead?" Hayes asked.

"Yeah. He knew some of Prudell's employees because those guys used to work at the same company as Whitehead."

"Which guys?" Hayes inquired.

"I only know Brad worked there."

A police officer came out of the office building and told them it was safe to go inside.

Gwynn went in, turned off her computer, picked up her purse and left while her fellow employees were leaning on the counter, waiting to hear details from the police of what had transpired in Prudell's office.

CHAPTER 44

Gwynn had just unlocked her door when the sound of a car engine and tires crunching up the gravel driveway caught her attention. She turned and saw Paul's car stopping next to the Mustang.

"You're not going to park on the street?" she asked.

"No," he said, closing his car door. "It no longer matters if anyone sees my car at your place."

They stepped into the house.

"You won't believe what I heard when I was listening by Ashton's window. Whitehead wanted revenge, but it was over Bridget, Ashton's wife. Not what we thought."

"Ashton's wife?" Paul said, narrowing his eyes.

"Yeah. Apparently, Whitehead had a thing for her that goes back to before she married Ashton."

"That was never on the radar."

"Did you see the shooting?" Gwynn asked, knowing Paul had powerful binoculars.

"Sure did and tonight we'll have to break into a morgue to snatch the bullet."

Opening the fridge door, Gwynn asked, "How will you know which one?"

"Yours is a 9mm and Prudell's wasn't."

She held up a beer. "Want one?"

Paul nodded.

Gwynn handed him a beer and got one for herself, and then they sat down at the kitchen table. "Won't the police try to get the bullets immediately?" she asked and took a sip.

"I doubt it since Prudell told them he shot Whitehead. They're not looking for another shooter, but it might create a problem when they pull two slugs out of the corpse."

"Do you know where they're taking him?"

"County morgue," he said between gulps.

"Do you know why Turk happened to show up when he did?"

"Yes. I called him."

Her eyes narrowed. "You called him?"

"On Williams' cell phone. I told him Whitehead was going after Ashton and he was at the Prudell building now."

"Did you try to imitate Brad's voice?"

"Must've done a good job. Carlsen called me Brad and asked where I was."

"Why did you call him?"

"I wanted a local on the scene who had a weapon. If Whitehead produced his pistol and Carlsen is a good guy, he'd defend Prudell. We might have helped—like you did, but the local person would get the credit. I didn't expect Prudell to be armed, but the way his hand shook I'm not sure if his bullet even hit Whitehead."

"How did you know Turk had a gun with him?"

"Shortly before Whitehead showed up at the Prudell building, he had an argument with Carlsen outside the downtown office. When Whitehead left there, Carlsen went to his truck and removed a pistol from the glove compartment and put it under the driver's seat."

"Since Whitehead shot Turk, how would we have handled it if Ashton hadn't been armed?"

Paul gave her a crooked smile. "Maybe we'd have to give Williams credit for it."

Gwynn smiled. "Yeah, the died guy could use a little credit. What do you think Whitehead did with Brad's body?"

"Probably buried him in a shallow grave. It might be years before it's discovered, if ever."

After dusk, Gwynn and Paul headed to the county morgue. Paul wore the Max Strait investigator outfit, the one he had on when he questioned Carlsen. Gwynn had on the blonde wig she had worn when she entered Whitehead's condo.

Two cars were parked in the lot next to the building. Paul drove around it, looking for windows and saw three in the back. He cut to the curb across the street from the structure and stopped.

"Stay in here," he said. "Call if another car pulls into the lot." He went to the back of the building and returned within ten minutes.

"Did you get it?" Gwynn asked.

"No. A guy's working in the morgue on Whitehead's body."

"They've probably already taken out the bullets."

"Possibly. In five minutes, go in the entrance and find some way to get the guy out of the morgue."

"But there are two cars in the lot."

"A man and a woman are cleaning. I didn't see anyone else inside." Paul went down the side of the building.

At the designated time, Gwynn walked through the building entrance. A bell stood on a desk in the foyer. She rang it and waited a moment, but no one appeared. She rang it again and a bald-headed man peered out from a door down the hallway.

"We're closed," the man said.

"This is really important. I need to talk to someone," Gwynn said in a stressful tone.

The man, wearing a pair of grey scrubs, came toward her. "What is it?" he said, sounding irritated.

"Is Kevin Whitehead's body here?"

"Yes."

"Oh, thank goodness. I've been calling all the morgues around here and I couldn't find him."

His eye lids pinched in the corners, "What was the emergency?"

"I went with him to lunch. He stuck my lipstick and cell phone in his pocket. I didn't have any pockets and I need my cell phone! I can't go without it! And I want my lipstick. It was brand new."

"Lady, you'll have to go to the police department tomorrow and try to retrieve your cell phone. I can't give it to you."

"So you found it!" she said, excitedly.

"He had one, but I don't know if that's yours. Even if it is, I can't release it to you."

"But I need it."

"Sorry."

Gwynn moved closer to him. "Oh, please," she said, giving him a flirty smile.

"Can't do."

"At least I know where it is. Do I need to talk to anyone special to get it?"

The man opened a desk drawer, pulled out a business card and handed it to her. "Call that number."

"Thanks." Gwynn turned and left the building.

Paul reached her before she crossed the street. "Meet you in the car. I'm going to wipe your prints off the doorknob."

Gwynn climbed into the car and Paul joined her a minute later. As he pushed on the accelerator, he said, "We've got a problem."

"What?"

"Only one slug was lying in the metal tray. A 9mm. Given the condition of the body, the mortician had finished working on it. It just needed to be put away."

"Prudell didn't hit him?"

"Fraid not. We're going to your office to look for the bullet before the police find it and suspect another shooter."

"Wouldn't they have already checked?"

"Prudell told them he only fired once and Carlsen's slug went out the window. There's a chance it might not have been discovered, so we'll search for it. If we find a hole in the wall and no slug, then we'll know we were too late."

Gwynn's cell phone buzzed. She plucked it out of her purse, glanced at the screen and saw Ruben's number.

"It's Ruben," she said and clicked the answer button. "Hello, Ross."

"I just called to hear your voice," he said. "I can't talk long because I have a meeting at ten."

Gwynn's eyes dropped to the clock on the dashboard. It read: 9:15 p.m.

"I'm out with a friend. I'll be home at eleven. Maybe you can call after your meeting."

"I'll try if it's not too late. Love you."

"Love you, too," she said and disconnected. "He wanted us to call him at ten, but I didn't think we'd be at the house that early."

"We won't be. So you set it up for eleven?"

"Yeah."

"When is Prudell installing surveillance cameras around the office?"

"Either Friday or Monday. It depends on how soon the security company can get to it." Gwynn smiled. "I guess with Williams still on the loose, the order won't be cancelled."

The exterior of the Prudell building was well lit. Paul parked a block away.

"Are we going in like this?" Gwynn asked, referring to her outfit.

"Yeah."

They moved stealthily toward the back of the structure. A board had been hammered over the broken window. Paul got a small flat strip of metal out of his backpack, expanded it and edged it in the next exposed window. He pushed a lever on the tool and the other side became wider and with that he unlatched the window. Paul collapsed the tool and dropped it into his backpack while Gwynn put on night goggles. A soft beeping sound came from inside as Paul slid the window open.

Gwynn climbed in, hurried to the alarm and punched in the code. "All clear," she said as the noise ended.

Wearing his night goggles, Paul entered through the window and they both began searching the wall behind where Whitehead had stood. After looking for ten minutes, they glanced at each other and shrugged.

"I'm going to check inside the bookcase," Paul said, eyeing the top shelf.

"I'll start on the side walls," Gwynn said, hunting for the slug.

Paul moved down to the next shelf and scrounged above the books. "I see it," he said, getting pliers out of his backpack. "Good spot. This place isn't obvious. I can fix it so it'll look like a crack in the wood.

At 10:50 p.m., Gwynn unlocked the door and entered the house with Paul. She got out her N-phone while Paul made a pot of coffee.

"I wish I knew how to hook up the N-phone to my computer like Holly does," Gwynn said.

"It's a program," Paul commented.

Gwynn placed the call and put it on speaker. She started to fill Ruben in when he interrupted and said, "I already know about Whitehead. What I don't know is whether or not Ashton Prudell deserved the credit he got for being the shooter."

"He wasn't the shooter," Paul said. "We've been spending the evening retrieving Gwynn's bullet and finding Prudell's slug in his office."

"I suspected it wasn't him, but it could've been either of you. All the clean-up is done?"

"Yes, boss," Gwynn said.

"Then Paul will be leaving tomorrow."

Gwynn frowned. She had hoped she wouldn't be left alone, but she knew Paul's job was done here.

"Gwynn, do you have anything else I should know about?"

"No."

"Then I'll talk to Paul. Take the phone off speaker."

Paul pushed the speaker button and walked out of the kitchen with the phone held against his ear.

CHAPTER 45

Paul was packed and ready to leave when Gwynn stepped out of the bathroom. "Are you going right now?" she asked.

"Yes," he said without giving any other details. He made two trips to the car, carrying out his duffle bags and one suitcase.

"I'm going to miss you," she said and gave him a hug. "Say 'Hi' to Holly, if you happen to see her."

"I will," Paul said, closing the door behind him.

Feeling deserted, Gwynn sat at the table and drank a cup of coffee while she listened to chirping birds through the open window.

Pulling into Prudell's parking lot, she saw a patrol car parked in front of the building. She walked through the entrance and asked, "Is Detective Marsden here?"

"Yes," Marilyn said. "Along with Officer Engel."

"Asking Mr. Prudell more questions?"

"I don't know," Marilyn said. "Mr. Prudell got here before I did and he was expecting them." She leaned on the counter. "You missed all the excitement."

"There was more after I left?"

"Yes." Marilyn cocked her head. "You didn't see the news on television."

Gwynn shook her head. "No."

"A reporter showed up with a crew and while they were setting up equipment Detective Marsden, Dave and Mrs. Prudell came. Mr. Prudell was interviewed along with Detective Marsden. I was on the news, too. They asked me a few questions about how Mr. Whitehead acted when he requested to see Mr. Prudell."

Gwynn surmised that was how Ruben knew about Whitehead. "Did they ask about the other cases?"

Marilyn nodded. "Yes. That's what the reporter talked to Detective Marsden about. Some of Mr. Whitehead's business cards were discovered in Officer Young's cruiser so the police had questioned him about that. Mr. Whitehead had denied ever being in the patrol car, but later they found his fingerprints were all over the inside of it. Detective Marsden planned on questioning him again."

"How did they know they were his fingerprints? Did he have a record?"

"He didn't have a record. The reporter never asked how the police got Mr. Whitehead's fingerprints."

"And the other cases?"

"The reporter asked the Detective about the blood stain on the floor of the abandoned house where Brad's truck was found. He wanted to know if it was Officer Young's blood."

"Was it?"

"No."

"Was he asked if it was Brad's?" Gwynn tucked a loose strand of hair behind her ear.

"Yes, but Detective Marsden wouldn't answer that question."

"I wonder if it was."

"If it was, Brad wasn't badly injured," Marilyn said, adjusting her elbows on the counter and clasping her hands together. "Mr. Prudell told me, this morning, before Detective Marsden showed up, that Brad had called Turk yesterday."

Gwynn tilted her brow. "How did he know that?"

"He saw Turk in the hospital last night."

"How's he doing?"

"The bullet severed a bone in his arm, but he'll be okay. I mentioned to Mr. Prudell that Turk thought he might be going to jail. Mr. Prudell didn't have any idea what that was about."

"Maybe Turk was concerned because he didn't have a license to carry a concealed weapon or something like that."

Marilyn nodded. "Yeah. You're probably right. Poor guy. Shot and worried about that."

Detective Marsden and Officer Engel walked through the lobby and out the main door.

"I better get to work," Gwynn said, heading to her desk.

Around 9 a.m., a short, twenty-four-year old average-looking woman with curly blonde hair entered the building. Gwynn wondered if she was the temp Hayes had mentioned the day before.

"I'm here to see Alex Hayes," the woman said to Marilyn.

"You must be Emma Parrish," Marilyn said.

"Yes."

"Mr. Hayes is expecting you. Let me take you to his office."

A half-an-hour later, Hayes walked over to Gwynn with the woman, introduced them and left Emma with Gwynn to train. Since some of Gwynn's tasks only occur once a month, there wasn't a point in teaching that to someone that only planned on being with Prudell for a couple of weeks. "Are you looking for a permanent position," she asked, "or do you only want a temporary job?"

"I'm hoping to be hired on full-time," Emma said.

Gwynn noticed Emma's low cut sweater that revealed a full bosom and guessed she wouldn't have any problem getting hired by Ashton Prudell.

Emma continued, "I've heard nothing but good things about Prudell. It's too bad about the problem that happened yesterday, but Mr. Hayes told me they were installing surveillance cameras and extra security equipment."

"This is a safe place to work," Gwynn said.

"Since that guy's dead, I'm not worried about it."

"Well then, let's get started training you on everything."

Emma pulled a notepad out of her bag. "Mr. Hayes mentioned all the things you do. I know a few days won't be enough time to learn it all. Probably two weeks wouldn't be enough, so I'm going to make a lot of notes."

Right after lunch, Gwynn went over to Marilyn. "Did Mr. Prudell tell you what the officers wanted this morning?" she asked quietly, so Emma couldn't hear.

"Yes." Marilyn rested her forearms on the counter. "It was about Mr. Whitehead and Officer Young. Mr. Prudell didn't even know they knew each other. He suspects the officers are looking for a motive for Officer Young's murder. He also thinks Brad played a role in it. That makes sense since Officer Young was looking for him."

"Yeah. I've been trying to figure out a connection between

Officer Young and Kevin, but I didn't know either of them very well. I never saw them talking to each other at Marty's."

"Officer Young went there?"

"I saw him a couple of times."

"Mr. Prudell is still pretty upset about his death. They were good friends."

Gwynn didn't comment as she thought *that friendship only went one way*.

Marilyn went on, "It's too bad you're leaving so soon, you might not know when they find Brad or how those cases get resolved, unless it's on the news. Send me your email address when you get settled."

"I will," Gwynn said, knowing that would never happen.

Gwynn and Emma had just returned from the file room when Dave came into the office and went to Gwynn's cubicle.

"Did you drive over?" Gwynn asked.

"Yes. The leg feels pretty good." Dave gazed at Emma. "This must be the new person."

Gwynn introduced them and wrote notes while Dave flirted with Emma. After spending time with him, she thought he cared for her and would miss her, but watching him hitting on Emma told her he had moved on, even before she left.

"Emma," Dave said. "I'm taking Gwynn to lunch tomorrow, her last day, why don't you come?"

Emma looked at Gwynn. "Will that be okay with you?"

"Sure. Dave, do you want us to go there or are you coming here?"

"The downtown office. It'll give Emma a chance to see it."

Friday at 12:30 p.m., Gwynn parked next to the downtown office and walked with Emma toward the entrance. She observed a man emerge from the building who reminded her of Ruben. Dave followed him outside and shook his hand. The man turned and she saw it was Ruben. He strode past Gwynn without giving any sign of recognition that he knew her. She maintained her pace and kept her eyes forward. That was when she realized Ruben's client wasn't Ashton; it was Dave.

As soon as Gwynn said her farewells at work, she went to the house and loaded her duffle bags, boxes and suitcases in the car. She drove to a destination in Albuquerque where Ruben had told her to drop off her Mustang and leave her belongings in the trunk, except for one suitcase with her Beretta and knife inside, along with clothing for a couple of days. Her vehicle would be delivered to her new destination. Ruben didn't fill her in on the new assignment details, but he told her she would be working with Gordon, one of Ruben's employees who Gwynn knew, and Gordon would pick her up at the airport when she landed.

Walking down the airport corridor toward her gate, Gwynn saw Ruben approaching from the opposite direction. She wanted to run to him, but restrained herself and kept her face from showing any emotion, in case he was working. He headed straight to her and smiled when he was a foot away. Without saying a word, he wrapped his arms around her. Gwynn's cheeks became flushed as she felt his warm, firm lips against hers.

She threw her arms around his neck. "Are you going with me?" she said, hoping.

"No."

Gwynn's hands dropped to her side and her shoulders slumped in disappointment.

Ruben embraced her again. "You're going with me."

Her eyes glowed as he took her hand and they continued down the corridor.

THE END

ABOUT THE AUTHOR

Inge-Lise Goss, *USA Today* bestselling, award-winning author, was born in Denmark, raised in Utah and graduated from the University of Utah. She is a certified public accountant and has audited oil and gas companies for over twenty years.

Goss now lives in the foothills of Red Rock Canyon with her husband and their dog, Ted. She spends most of her time in her den writing stories. There, with her muse by her side, her imagination has no boundaries, and her dreams come alive. When she's not pounding away on the keyboard, she can be found reading, rowing, or trying to perfect her golf game, which she fears is a lost cause.

Visit www.Inge-LiseGoss.com to learn more.